The Love Boat
and Other Stories

F. Scott Fitzgerald

ALMA CLASSICS

ALMA CLASSICS
an imprint of

ALMA BOOKS LTD
Thornton House
Thornton Road
Wimbledon Village
London SW19 4NG
United Kingdom
www.almaclassics.com

This collection first published by Alma Books Ltd in 2015
Repr. 2019, 2020

Extra Material © Richard Parker

Printed and bound by CPI Group (UK) Ltd, Croydon, CR0 4YY

ISBN: 978-1-84749-414-6

Contents

Other books by F. SCOTT FITZGERALD
published by Alma Classics

All the Sad Young Men

Babylon Revisited and Other Stories

Basil and Josephine

The Beautiful and Damned

Flappers and Philosophers

The Great Gatsby

Image on the Heart and Other Stories

The Intimate Strangers and Other Stories

The Last Tycoon

The Last of the Belles and Other Stories

The Pat Hobby Stories

Tales of the Jazz Age

Tender Is the Night

This Side of Paradise

F. Scott Fitzgerald (1896–1940)

Edward Fitzgerald,
Fitzgerald's father

Mary McQuillan Fitzgerald,
Fitzgerald's mother

Ginevra King

Zelda Fitzgerald

The Fitzgeralds' house in Montgomery, Alabama

The Fitzgeralds' grave in Rockville, Maryland, inscribed with the closing line from *The Great Gatsby*

THE SATURDAY EVENING POST

OCT. 8, 1927

5 cts.

Arthur Conan Doyle—F. Scott Fitzgerald—Horatio Winslow—Hal G. Evarts
Nunnally Johnson—Henry L. Stimson—Thomas Beer—Ben Ames Williams

The 8th October 1927 issue of the *Saturday Evening Post*,
which included Fitzgerald's story 'The Love Boat'

The Love Boat
and Other Stories

The Smilers

1

W E ALL HAVE THAT EXASPERATED MOMENT! There are times when you almost tell the harmless old lady next door what you really think of her face – that it ought to be on a night nurse in a house for the blind; when you'd like to ask the man you've been waiting ten minutes for if he isn't all overheated from racing the postman down the block; when you nearly say to the waiter that if they deducted a cent from the bill for every degree the soup was below tepid the hotel would owe you half a dollar; when – and this is the infallible earmark of true exasperation – a smile affects you as an oil baron's undershirt affects a cow's husband.

But the moment passes. Scars may remain on your dog or your collar or your telephone receiver, but your soul has slid gently back into its place between the lower edge of your heart and the upper edge of your stomach, and all is at peace.

But the imp who turns on the shower bath of exasperation apparently made it so hot one time in Sylvester Stockton's early youth that he never dared dash in and turn it off – in consequence no first old man in an amateur production of a Victorian comedy was ever more pricked and prodded by the daily phenomena of life than was Sylvester at thirty.

Accusing eyes behind spectacles – suggestion of a stiff neck – this will have to do for his description, since he is not the hero of this story. He is the plot. He is the factor that makes it one story instead of three stories. He makes remarks at the beginning and end.

The late-afternoon sun was loitering pleasantly along Fifth Avenue when Sylvester, who had just come out of that hideous public library where he had been consulting some ghastly book, told his impossible chauffeur (it is true that I am following his movements through his own spectacles) that he wouldn't need his stupid, incompetent services any longer. Swinging his cane (which he found too short) in his left hand (which he should have cut off long ago since it was constantly offending him), he began walking slowly down the avenue.

When Sylvester walked at night he frequently glanced behind and on both sides to see if anyone was sneaking up on him. This had become a constant mannerism. For this reason he was unable to pretend that he didn't see Betty Tearle sitting in her machine in front of Tiffany's.

Back in his early twenties he had been in love with Betty Tearle. But he had depressed her. He had misanthropically dissected every meal, motor trip and musical comedy that they attended together, and on the few occasions when she had tried to be especially nice to him – from a mother's point of view he had been rather desirable – he had suspected hidden motives and fallen into a deeper gloom than ever. Then one day she told him that she would go mad if he ever again parked his pessimism in her sun parlour.

And ever since then she had seemed to be smiling – uselessly, insultingly, charmingly smiling.

"Hello, Sylvo," she called.

"Why – how do, Betty." He wished she wouldn't call him Sylvo – it sounded like a – like a darn monkey or something.

"How goes it?" she asked cheerfully. "Not very well, I suppose."

"Oh, yes," he answered stiffly, "I manage."

"Taking in the happy crowd?"

"Heavens, yes." He looked around him. "Betty, why are they happy? What are they smiling at? What do they find to smile at?"

Betty flashed him a glance of radiant amusement.

"The women may smile because they have pretty teeth, Sylvo."

"You smile," continued Sylvester cynically, "because you're comfortably married and have two children. You imagine you're happy, so you suppose everyone else is."

Betty nodded.

"You may have hit it, Sylvo…" The chauffeur glanced around and she nodded at him. "Goodbye."

Sylvo watched with a pang of envy which turned suddenly to exasperation as he saw she had turned and smiled at him once more. Then her car was out of sight in the traffic, and with a voluminous sigh he galvanized his cane into life and continued his stroll.

At the next corner he stopped in at a cigar store and there he ran into Waldron Crosby. Back in the days when Sylvester had been a prize pigeon in the eyes of debutantes he had also been a game partridge from the point of view of promoters. Crosby, then a young bond salesman, had given him much safe and sane advice and saved him many dollars. Sylvester liked Crosby as much as he could like anyone. Most people did like Crosby.

"Hello, you old bag of nerves," cried Crosby genially, "come and have a big gloom-dispelling Corona."

Sylvester regarded the cases anxiously. He knew he wasn't going to like what he bought.

"Still out at Larchmont, Waldron?" he asked.

"Right-o."

"How's your wife?"

"Never better."

"Well," said Sylvester suspiciously, "you brokers always look as if you're smiling at something up your sleeve. It must be a hilarious profession."

Crosby considered.

"Well," he admitted, "it varies – like the moon and the price of soft drinks – but it has its moments."

"Waldron," said Sylvester earnestly, "you're a friend of mine – please do me the favour of not smiling when I leave you. It seems like a – like a mockery."

A broad grin suffused Crosby's countenance.

"Why, you crabbed old son-of-a-gun!"

But Sylvester with an irate grunt had turned on his heel and disappeared.

He strolled on. The sun finished its promenade and began calling in the few stray beams it had left among the westward streets. The avenue darkened with black bees from the department stores; the traffic swelled into an interlaced jam; the buses were packed four deep like platforms above the thick crowd; but Sylvester, to whom the daily shift and change of the city was a matter only of sordid monotony, walked on, taking only quick sideward glances through his frowning spectacles.

He reached his hotel and was elevated to his four-room suite on the twelfth floor.

"If I dine downstairs," he thought, "the orchestra will play either 'Smile, Smile, Smile' or 'The Smiles That You Gave to Me'.* But then if I go to the Club I'll meet all the cheerful people I know, and if I go somewhere else where there's no music, I won't get anything fit to eat."

He decided to have dinner in his rooms.

An hour later, after disparaging some broth, a squab and a salad, he tossed fifty cents to the room waiter, and then held up his hand warningly.

"Just oblige me by not smiling when you say thanks?"

He was too late. The waiter had grinned.

"Now, will you please tell me," asked Sylvester peevishly, "what on earth you have to smile about?"

The waiter considered. Not being a reader of the magazines he was not sure what was characteristic of waiters, yet he supposed something characteristic was expected of him.

"Well, mister," he answered, glancing at the ceiling with all the ingenuousness he could muster in his narrow, sallow countenance, "it's just something my face does when it sees four bits* comin'."

Sylvester waved him away.

"Waiters are happy because they've never had anything better," he thought. "They haven't enough imagination to want anything."

At nine o'clock from sheer boredom he sought his expressionless bed.

2

A S SYLVESTER LEFT THE CIGAR STORE, Waldron Crosby followed him out, and turning off Fifth Avenue down a cross street entered a brokerage office. A plump man with nervous hands rose and hailed him.

"Hello, Waldron."

"Hello, Potter – I just dropped in to hear the worst."

The plump man frowned.

"We've just got the news," he said.

"Well, what is it? Another drop?"

"Closed at seventy-eight. Sorry, old boy."

"Whew!"

"Hit pretty hard?"

"Cleaned out!"

The plump man shook his head, indicating that life was too much for him, and turned away.

Crosby sat there for a moment without moving. Then he rose, walked into Potter's private office and picked up the phone.

"Gi'me Larchmont 838."

In a moment he had his connection.

"Mrs Crosby there?"

A man's voice answered him.

"Yes; this you, Crosby? This is Dr Shipman."

"Dr Shipman?" Crosby's voice showed sudden anxiety.

"Yes – I've been trying to reach you all afternoon. The situation's changed and we expect the child tonight."

"Tonight?"

"Yes. Everything's OK. But you'd better come right out."

"I will. Goodbye."

He hung up the receiver and started out the door, but paused as an idea struck him. He returned, and this time called a Manhattan number.

"Hello, Donny, this is Crosby."

"Hello, there, old boy. You just caught me; I was going—"

"Say, Donny, I want a job right away, quick."

"For whom?"

"For me."

"Why, what's the—"

"Never mind. Tell you later. Got one for me?"

"Why, Waldron, there's not a blessed thing here except a clerkship. Perhaps next—"

"What salary goes with the clerkship?"

"Forty – say forty-five a week."

"I've got you. I start tomorrow."

"All right. But say, old man—"

"Sorry, Donny, but I've got to run."

Crosby hurried from the brokerage office with a wave and a smile at Potter. In the street he took out a handful of small change and after surveying it critically hailed a taxi.

"Grand Central – quick!" he told the driver.

3

AT SIX O'CLOCK BETTY TEARLE signed the letter, put it into an envelope and wrote her husband's name upon it. She went into his room and after a moment's hesitation set a black cushion on the bed and laid the white letter on it so that it could not fail to attract his attention when he came in. Then with a quick glance around the room she walked into the hall and upstairs to the nursery.

"Clare," she called softly.

"Oh, Mummy!" Clare left her doll's house and scurried to her mother.

"Where's Billy, Clare?"

Billy appeared eagerly from under the bed.

"Got anything for me?" he enquired politely.

His mother's laugh ended in a little catch and she caught both her children to her and kissed them passionately. She found that she was crying quietly and their flushed little faces seemed cool against the sudden fever racing though her blood.

"Take care of Clare – always – Billy darling…"

Billy was puzzled and rather awed.

"You're crying," he accused gravely.

"I know – I know I am…"

Clare gave a few tentative sniffles, hesitated, and then clung to her mother in a storm of weeping.

"I d-don't feel good, Mummy – I don't feel good."

Betty soothed her quietly.

"We won't cry any more, Clare dear – either of us."

But as she rose to leave the room her glance at Billy bore a mute appeal, too vain, she knew, to be registered on his childish consciousness.

Half an hour later as she carried her travelling bag to a taxicab at the door she raised her hand to her face in mute admission that a veil served no longer to hide her from the world.

"But I've chosen," she thought dully.

As the car turned the corner she wept again, resisting a temptation to give up and go back.

"Oh, my God!" she whispered. "What am I doing? What have I done? What have I done?"

4

WHEN JERRY, THE SALLOW, narrow-faced waiter, left Sylvester's rooms he reported to the head waiter, and then checked out for the day.

He took the subway south and alighting at Williams Street walked a few blocks and entered a billiard parlour.

An hour later he emerged with a cigarette drooping from his bloodless lips, and stood on the sidewalk as if hesitating before making a decision. He set off eastward.

As he reached a certain corner his gait suddenly increased and then quite as suddenly slackened. He seemed to want to pass by, yet some magnetic attraction was apparently exerted on him, for with a sudden face-about he turned in at the door of a cheap restaurant – half cabaret, half chop-suey parlour – where a miscellaneous assortment gathered nightly.

Jerry found his way to a table situated in the darkest and most obscure corner. Seating himself with a contempt for his surroundings that betokened familiarity rather than superiority he ordered a glass of claret.

The evening had begun. A fat woman at the piano was expelling the last jauntiness from a hackneyed foxtrot, and a lean, dispirited male was assisting her with lean, dispirited notes from a violin. The attention of the patrons was directed at a dancer wearing soiled stockings and done largely in peroxide and rouge who was about to step upon a small platform, meanwhile exchanging pleasantries with a fat, eager person at the table beside her who was trying to capture her hand.

Over in the corner Jerry watched the two by the platform and, as he gazed, the ceiling seemed to fade out, the walls growing into tall buildings and the platform becoming the top of a Fifth Avenue bus on a breezy spring night three years ago. The fat, eager person disappeared, the short skirt of the dancer rolled down and the rouge faded from her cheeks – and he was beside her again in an old delirious ride, with the lights blinking kindly at them from the tall buildings beside and the voices of the street merging into a pleasant somnolent murmur around them.

"Jerry," said the girl on top of the bus, "I've said that when you were gettin' seventy-five I'd take a chance with you. But, Jerry, I can't wait for ever."

Jerry watched several street numbers sail by before he answered.

"I don't know what's the matter," he said helplessly, "they won't raise me. If I can locate a new job—"

"You better hurry, Jerry," said the girl. "I'm gettin' sick of just livin' along. If I can't get married I got a couple of chances to work in a cabaret – get on the stage maybe."

"You keep out of that," said Jerry quickly. "There ain't no need, if you just wait about another month or two."

"I can't wait for ever, Jerry," repeated the girl. "I'm tired of stayin' poor alone."

"It won't be so long," said Jerry clenching his free hand, "I can make it somewhere, if you'll just wait."

But the bus was fading out and the ceiling was taking shape and the murmur of the April streets was fading into the rasping whine of the violin – for that was all three years before and now he was sitting here.

The girl glanced up on the platform and exchanged a metallic impersonal smile with the dispirited violinist, and Jerry shrank farther back in his corner watching her with burning intensity.

"Your hands belong to anybody that wants them now," he cried silently and bitterly. "I wasn't man enough to keep you out of that – not man enough, by God, by God!"

But the girl by the door still toyed with the fat man's clutching fingers as she waited for her time to dance.

SYLVESTER STOCKTON TOSSED restlessly upon his bed. The room, big as it was, smothered him, and a breeze drifting in and bearing with it a rift of moon seemed laden only with the cares of the world he would have to face next day.

"They don't understand," he thought. "They don't see, as I do, the underlying misery of the whole damn thing. They're hollow optimists. They smile because they think they're always going to be happy.

"Oh, well," he mused drowsily, "I'll run up to Rye tomorrow and endure more smiles and more heat. That's all life is – just smiles and heat, smiles and heat."

Myra Meets His Family

1

PROBABLY EVERY BOY WHO HAS ATTENDED an eastern college in the last ten years has met Myra half a dozen times, for the Myras live on the eastern colleges, as kittens live on warm milk. When Myra is young, seventeen or so, they call her a "wonderful kid"; in her prime – say, at nineteen – she is tendered the subtle compliment of being referred to by her name alone; and after that she is a "prom trotter" or "the famous coast-to-coast Myra".

You can see her practically any winter afternoon if you stroll through the Biltmore lobby.* She will be standing in a group of sophomores just in from Princeton or New Haven, trying to decide whether to dance away the mellow hours at the Club de Vingt or the Plaza Red Room. Afterwards one of the sophomores will take her to the theatre and ask her down to the February prom – and then dive for a taxi to catch the last train back to college.

Invariably she has a somnolent mother sharing a suite with her on one of the floors above.

When Myra is about twenty-four she thinks over all the nice boys she might have married at one time or other, sighs a little and does the best she can. But no remarks, please! She has given her youth to you; she has blown fragrantly through many ballrooms to the tender tribute of many eyes; she has roused strange surges of romance in a hundred pagan young breasts; and who shall say she hasn't counted?

The particular Myra whom this story concerns will have to have a paragraph of history. I will get it over with as swiftly as possible.

When she was sixteen she lived in a big house in Cleveland and attended Derby School in Connecticut, and it was while she was still there that she started going to prep-school dances and college proms. She decided to spend the war at Smith College, but in January of her freshman year, falling violently in love with a young infantry officer, she failed all her mid-year examinations and retired to Cleveland in disgrace. The young infantry officer arrived about a week later.

Just as she had about decided that she didn't love him after all he was ordered abroad, and in a great revival of sentiment she rushed down to the port of embarkation with her mother to bid him goodbye. She wrote him daily for two months, and then weekly for two months, and then once more. This last letter he never got, for a machine-gun bullet ripped through his head one rainy July morning. Perhaps this was just as well, for the letter informed him that it had all been a mistake, and that something told her they would never be happy together, and so on.

The "something" wore boots and silver wings and was tall and dark. Myra was quite sure that it was the real thing at last, but as an engine went through his chest at Kelly Field* in mid-August she never had a chance to find out.

Instead she came east again, a little slimmer, with a becoming pallor and new shadows under her eyes, and throughout armistice year she left the ends of cigarettes all over New York on little china trays marked "Midnight Frolic" and "Coconut Grove" and "Palais Royal". She was twenty-one now, and Cleveland people said that her mother ought to take her back home – that New York was spoiling her.

You will have to do your best with that. The story should have started long ago.

It was an afternoon in September when she broke a theatre date in order to have tea with young Mrs Arthur Elkins, once her room-mate at school.

"I wish," began Myra as they sat down exquisitely, "that I'd been a *señorita* or a *mademoiselle* or something. Good grief! What is there to do over here once you're out, except marry and retire!"

Lilah Elkins had seen this form of ennui before.

"Nothing," she replied coolly. "Do it."

"I can't seem to get interested, Lilah," said Myra, bending forward earnestly. "I've played round so much that even while I'm kissing the man I just wonder how soon I'll get tired of him. I never get carried away like I used to."

"How old are you, Myra?"

"Twenty-one last spring."

"Well," said Lilah complacently, "take it from me, don't get married unless you're absolutely through playing round. It means giving up an awful lot, you know."

"Through! I'm sick and tired of my whole pointless existence. Funny, Lilah, but I do feel ancient. Up at New Haven last spring men danced with me that seemed like little boys – and once I overheard a girl say in the dressing room, 'There's Myra Harper! She's been coming up here for eight years.' Of course she was about three years off, but it did give me the calendar blues."

"You and I went to our first prom when we were sixteen – five years ago."

"Heavens!" sighed Myra. "And now some men are afraid of me. Isn't that odd? Some of the nicest boys. One man dropped me like a hotcake after coming down from Morristown for three straight weekends. Some kind friend told him I was husband hunting this year and he was afraid of getting in too deep."

"Well, you are husband hunting, aren't you?"

"I suppose so – after a fashion." Myra paused and looked about her rather cautiously. "Have you ever met Knowleton Whitney? You know what a wiz he is on looks, and his father's worth a fortune, they say. Well, I noticed that the first time he met me he started when he heard my name and fought shy – and, Lilah darling, I'm not so ancient and homely as all that, am I?"

"You certainly are not!" laughed Lilah. "And here's my advice: pick out the best thing in sight – the man who has all the mental, physical, social and financial qualities you want, and then go after him hammer and tongs – the way we used to. After you've got him don't say to yourself, 'Well, he can't sing like Billy,' or 'I wish he played better golf.' You can't have everything. Shut your eyes and turn off your sense of humour, and then after you're married it'll be very different and you'll be mighty glad."

"Yes," said Myra absently, "I've had that advice before."

"Drifting into romance is easy when you're eighteen," continued Lilah emphatically, "but after five years of it your capacity for it simply burns out."

"I've had such nice times," sighed Myra, "and such sweet men. To tell you the truth I have decided to go after someone."

"Who?"

"Knowleton Whitney. Believe me, I may be a bit blasé, but I can still get any man I want."

"You really want him?"

"Yes – as much as I'll ever want anyone. He's smart as a whip, and shy – rather sweetly shy – and they say his family have the best-looking place in Westchester County."

Lilah sipped the last of her tea and glanced at her wristwatch.

"I've got to tear, dear."

They rose together and, sauntering out on Park Avenue, hailed taxicabs.

"I'm awfully glad, Myra; and I know you'll be glad too."

Myra skipped a little pool of water and, reaching her taxi, balanced on the running board like a ballet dancer.

"Bye, Lilah. See you soon."

"Goodbye, Myra. Good luck!"

And knowing Myra as she did, Lilah felt that her last remark was distinctly superfluous.

2

THAT WAS ESSENTIALLY THE REASON that one Friday night six weeks later Knowleton Whitney paid a taxi bill of seven dollars and ten cents and with a mixture of emotions paused beside Myra on the Biltmore steps.

The outer surface of his mind was deliriously happy, but just below that was a slowly hardening fright at what he had done. He, protected since his freshman year at Harvard from the snares of fascinating fortune hunters, dragged away from several sweet young things by the acquiescent nape of his neck, had taken advantage of his family's absence in the

West to become so enmeshed in the toils that it was hard to say which was toils and which was he.

The afternoon had been like a dream: November twilight along Fifth Avenue after the matinee, and he and Myra looking out at the swarming crowds from the romantic privacy of a hansom cab – quaint device – then tea at the Ritz and her white hand gleaming on the arm of a chair beside him; and suddenly quick broken words. After that had come the trip to the jeweller's and a mad dinner in some little Italian restaurant where he had written "Do you?" on the back of the bill of fare and pushed it over for her to add the ever-miraculous "You know I do!" And now at the day's end they paused on the Biltmore steps.

"Say it," breathed Myra close to his ear.

He said it. Ah, Myra, how many ghosts must have flitted across your memory then!

"You've made me so happy, dear," she said softly.

"No – you've made me happy. Don't you know – Myra—"

"I know."

"For good?"

"For good. I've got this, you see." And she raised the diamond solitaire to her lips. She knew how to do things, did Myra.

"Goodnight."

"Goodnight. Goodnight."

Like a gossamer fairy in shimmering rose she ran up the wide stairs and her cheeks were glowing wildly as she rang the elevator bell.

At the end of a fortnight she got a telegraph from him saying that his family had returned from the West and expected her up in Westchester County for a week's visit. Myra wired her train time, bought three new evening dresses and packed her trunk.

It was a cool November evening when she arrived, and stepping from the train in the late twilight she shivered slightly and looked eagerly round for Knowleton. The station platform swarmed for a moment with men returning from the city; there was a shouting medley of wives and chauffeurs, and a great snorting of automobiles as they backed and turned and slid away. Then before she realized it the platform was quite deserted and not a single one of the luxurious cars remained. Knowleton must have expected her on another train.

With an almost inaudible "Damn!" she started towards the Elizabethan station to telephone, when suddenly she was accosted by a very dirty, dilapidated man who touched his ancient cap to her and addressed her in a cracked, querulous voice.

"You Miss Harper?"

"Yes," she confessed, rather startled. Was this unmentionable person by any wild chance the chauffeur?

"The chauffeur's sick," he continued in a high whine. "I'm his son." Myra gasped.

"You mean Mr Whitney's chauffeur?"

"Yes; he only keeps just one since the war. Great on economizin' – regelar Hoover." He stamped his feet nervously and smacked enormous gauntlets together. "Well, no use waitin' here gabbin' in the cold. Le's have your grip."

Too amazed for words and not a little dismayed, Myra followed her guide to the edge of the platform, where she looked in vain for a car. But she was not left to wonder long, for the person led her steps to a battered old flivver,* wherein was deposited her grip.

"Big car's broke," he explained. "Have to use this or walk."

He opened the front door for her and nodded.

"Step in."

"I b'lieve I'll sit in the back if you don't mind."

"Surest thing you know," he cackled, opening the back door. "I thought the trunk bumpin' round back there might make you nervous."

"What trunk?"

"Yourn."

"Oh, didn't Mr Whitney – can't you make two trips?"

He shook his head obstinately.

"Wouldn't allow it. Not since the war. Up to rich people to set 'n example; that's what Mr Whitney says. Le's have your check, please."

As he disappeared Myra tried in vain to conjure up a picture of the chauffeur if this was his son. After a mysterious argument with the station agent he returned, gasping violently, with the trunk on his back. He deposited it in the rear seat and climbed up front beside her.

It was quite dark when they swerved out of the road and up a long dusky driveway to the Whitney place, whence lighted windows flung great blots of cheerful, yellow light over the gravel and grass and trees. Even now she could see that it was very beautiful, that its blurred outline was Georgian colonial and that great shadowy garden parks were flung out at both sides. The car plumped to a full stop before a square stone doorway and the chauffeur's son climbed out after her and pushed open the outer door.

"Just go right in," he cackled; and as she passed the threshold she heard him softly shut the door, closing out himself and the dark.

Myra looked round her. She was in a large sombre hall panelled in old English oak and lit by dim shaded lights clinging like luminous yellow turtles at intervals along the wall. Ahead of her was a broad staircase and on both sides there were several doors, but there was no sight or sound of life, and an intense stillness seemed to rise ceaselessly from the deep crimson carpet.

She must have waited there a full minute before she began to have that unmistakable sense of someone looking at her. She forced herself to turn casually round.

A sallow little man, bald and clean shaven, trimly dressed in a frock coat and white spats, was standing a few yards away regarding her quizzically. He must have been fifty at the least, but even before he moved she had noticed a curious alertness about him – something in his pose which promised that it had been instantaneously assumed and would be instantaneously changed in a moment. His tiny hands and feet and the odd twist to his eyebrows gave him a faintly elfish expression, and she had one of those vague transient convictions that she had seen him before, many years ago.

For a minute they stared at each other in silence and then she flushed slightly and discovered a desire to swallow.

"I suppose you're Mr Whitney." She smiled faintly and advanced a step towards him. "I'm Myra Harper."

For an instant longer he remained silent and motionless, and it flashed across Myra that he might be deaf; then suddenly he jerked into spirited life exactly like a mechanical toy started by pressure of a button.

"Why, of course – why, naturally. I know – ah!" he exclaimed excitedly in a high-pitched elfin voice. Then raising himself on his toes in a sort of attenuated ecstasy of enthusiasm and smiling a wizened smile, he minced towards her across the dark carpet.

She blushed appropriately.

"That's awfully nice of—"

"Ah!" he went on. "You must be tired; a rickety, cindery, ghastly trip, I know. Tired and hungry and thirsty, no doubt, no doubt!" He looked round him indignantly. "The servants are frightfully inefficient in this house!"

Myra did not know what to say to this, so she made no answer. After an instant's abstraction Mr Whitney crossed over with his furious energy and pressed a button; then almost as if he were dancing he was by her side again, making thin, disparaging gestures with his hands.

"A little minute," he assured her, "sixty seconds, scarcely more. Here!"

He rushed suddenly to the wall and with some effort lifted a great carved Louis XIV chair and set it down carefully in the geometrical centre of the carpet.

"Sit down – won't you? Sit down! I'll go get you something. Sixty seconds at the outside."

She demurred faintly, but he kept on repeating "Sit down!" in such an aggrieved yet hopeful tone that Myra sat down. Instantly her host disappeared.

She sat there for five minutes and a feeling of oppression fell over her. Of all the receptions she had ever received this was decidedly the oddest – for though she had read somewhere that Ludlow Whitney was considered one of the most eccentric figures in the financial world, to find a sallow, elfin little man who, when he walked, danced, was rather a blow to her sense of form. Had he gone to get Knowleton! She revolved her thumbs in interminable concentric circles.

Then she started nervously at a quick cough at her elbow. It was Mr Whitney again. In one hand he held a glass of milk and in the other a blue kitchen bowl full of those hard cubical crackers used in soup.

"Hungry from your trip!" he exclaimed compassionately. "Poor girl, poor little girl, starving!" He brought out this last word with such emphasis that some of the milk plopped gently over the side of the glass.

Myra took the refreshments submissively. She was not hungry, but it had taken him ten minutes to get them so it seemed ungracious to refuse. She sipped gingerly at the milk and ate a cracker, wondering vaguely what to say. Mr Whitney, however, solved the problem for her by disappearing again – this time by way of the wide stairs – four steps at a hop – the back of his bald head gleaming oddly for a moment in the half dark.

Minutes passed. Myra was torn between resentment and bewilderment that she should be sitting on a high comfortless chair in the middle of this big hall munching crackers. By what code was a visiting fiancée ever thus received!

Her heart gave a jump of relief as she heard a familiar whistle on the stairs. It was Knowleton at last, and when he came in sight he gasped with astonishment.

"Myra!"

She carefully placed the bowl and glass on the carpet and rose, smiling.

"Why," he exclaimed, "they didn't tell me you were here!"

"Your father – welcomed me."

"Lordy! He must have gone upstairs and forgotten all about it. Did he insist on your eating this stuff? Why didn't you just tell him you didn't want any?"

"Why – I don't know."

"You mustn't mind Father, dear. He's forgetful and a little unconventional in some ways, but you'll get used to him."

He pressed a button and a butler appeared.

"Show Miss Harper to her room and have her bag carried up – and her trunk if it isn't there already." He turned to Myra. "Dear, I'm awfully sorry I didn't know you were here. How long have you been waiting?"

"Oh, only a few minutes."

It had been twenty at least, but she saw no advantage in stressing it. Nevertheless it had given her an oddly uncomfortable feeling.

Half an hour later as she was hooking the last eye on her dinner dress there was a knock on the door.

"It's Knowleton, Myra; if you're about ready we'll go in and see Mother for a minute before dinner."

She threw a final approving glance at her reflection in the mirror and turning out the light joined him in the hall. He led her down a central passage which crossed to the other wing of the house, and stopping before a closed door he pushed it open and ushered Myra into the weirdest room upon which her young eyes had ever rested.

It was a large luxurious boudoir, panelled, like the lower hall, in dark English oak and bathed by several lamps in a mellow orange glow that blurred its every outline into a misty amber. In a great armchair piled high with cushions and draped with a curiously figured cloth of silk reclined a very sturdy old lady with bright white hair, heavy features and an air about her of having been there for many years. She lay somnolently against the cushions, her eyes half-closed, her great bust rising and falling under her black negligee.

But it was something else that made the room remarkable, and Myra's eyes scarcely rested on the woman, so engrossed was she in another feature of her surroundings. On the carpet, on the chairs and sofas, on the great canopied bed and on the soft angora rug in front of the fire sat and sprawled and slept a great army of white poodle dogs. There must have been almost two dozen of them, with curly hair twisting in front of their wistful eyes and wide yellow bows flaunting from their necks. As Myra and Knowleton entered, a stir went over the dogs; they raised one-and-twenty cold black noses in the air and from one-and-twenty little throats went up a great clatter of staccato barks until the room was filled with such an uproar that Myra stepped back in alarm.

But at the din the somnolent fat lady's eyes trembled open and in a low husky voice that was in itself oddly like a bark she snapped out: "Hush that racket!" and the clatter instantly ceased. The two or three poodles round the fire turned their silky eyes on each other reproachfully, and lying down with little sighs faded out on the white angora rug; the tousled ball on the lady's lap dug his nose into the crook of an elbow and went back to sleep, and except for the patches of white wool scattered about the room Myra would have thought it all a dream.

"Mother," said Knowleton after an instant's pause, "this is Myra."

From the lady's lips flooded one low husky word: "Myra?"

"She's visiting us, I told you."

Mrs Whitney raised a large arm and passed her hand across her forehead wearily.

"Child!" she said – and Myra started, for again the voice was like a low sort of growl – "you want to marry my son Knowleton?"

Myra felt that this was putting the tonneau* before the radiator, but she nodded. "Yes, Mrs Whitney."

"How old are you?" This very suddenly.

"I'm twenty-one, Mrs Whitney."

"Ah – and you're from Cleveland?" This was in what was surely a series of articulate barks.

"Yes, Mrs Whitney."

"Ah…"

Myra was not certain whether this last ejaculation was conversation or merely a groan, so she did not answer.

"You'll excuse me if I don't appear downstairs," continued Mrs Whitney, "but when we're in the East I seldom leave this room and my dear little doggies."

Myra nodded and a conventional health question was trembling on her lips when she caught Knowleton's warning glance and checked it.

"Well," said Mrs Whitney with an air of finality, "you seem like a very nice girl. Come in again."

"Goodnight, Mother," said Knowleton.

"Night!" barked Mrs Whitney drowsily, and her eyes sealed gradually up as her head receded back again into the cushions.

Knowleton held open the door and Myra, feeling a bit blank, left the room. As they walked down the corridor she heard a burst of furious sound behind them; the noise of the closing door had again roused the poodle dogs.

When they went downstairs they found Mr Whitney already seated at the dinner table.

"Utterly charming, completely delightful!" he exclaimed, beaming nervously. "One big family, and you the jewel of it, my dear."

Myra smiled, Knowleton frowned and Mr Whitney tittered.

"It's been lonely here," he continued, "desolate, with only us three. We expect you to bring sunlight and warmth, the peculiar radiance and efflorescence of youth. It will be quite delightful. Do you sing?"

"Why – I have. I mean, I do, some."

He clapped his hands enthusiastically.

"Splendid! Magnificent! What do you sing? Opera? Ballads? Popular music?"

"Well, mostly popular music."

"Good; personally I prefer popular music. By the way, there's a dance tonight."

"Father," demanded Knowleton sulkily, "did you go and invite a crowd here?"

"I had Monroe call up a few people – just some of the neighbours," he explained to Myra. "We're all very friendly hereabouts; give informal things continually. Oh, it's quite delightful."

Myra caught Knowleton's eye and gave him a sympathetic glance. It was obvious that he had wanted to be alone with her this first evening and was quite put out.

"I want them to meet Myra," continued his father. "I want them to know this delightful jewel we've added to our little household."

"Father," said Knowleton suddenly, "eventually of course Myra and I will want to live here with you and Mother, but for the first two or three years I think an apartment in New York would be more the thing for us."

Crash! Mr Whitney had raked across the tablecloth with his fingers and swept his silver to a jangling heap on the floor.

"Nonsense!" he cried furiously, pointing a tiny finger at his son. "Don't talk that utter nonsense! You'll live here, do you understand me? Here! What's a home without children?"

"But, Father—"

In his excitement Mr Whitney rose and a faint unnatural colour crept into his sallow face.

"Silence!" he shrieked. "If you expect one bit of help from me you can have it under my roof – nowhere else! Is that clear? As for you, my exquisite young lady," he continued, turning his wavering finger on Myra, "you'd better understand that the best thing you can do is to decide to settle down right here. This is my home, and I mean to keep it so!"

He stood then for a moment on his tiptoes, bending furiously indignant glances first on one, then on the other, and then suddenly he turned and skipped from the room.

"Well," gasped Myra, turning to Knowleton in amazement, "what do you know about that!"

3

SOME HOURS LATER SHE CREPT into bed in a great state of restless discontent. One thing she knew – she was not going to live in this house. Knowleton would have to make his father see reason to the extent of giving them an apartment in the city. The sallow little man made her nervous; she was sure Mrs Whitney's dogs would haunt her dreams; and there was a general casualness in the chauffeur, the butler, the maids and even the guests she had met that night, that did not in the least coincide with her ideas on the conduct of a big estate.

She had lain there an hour perhaps when she was startled from a slow reverie by a sharp cry which seemed to proceed from the adjoining room. She sat up in bed and listened, and in a minute it was repeated. It sounded exactly like the plaint of a weary child stopped summarily by the placing of a hand over its mouth. In the dark silence her bewilderment shaded gradually off into uneasiness. She waited for the cry to recur, but straining her ears she heard only the intense crowded stillness of three o'clock. She wondered where Knowleton slept, remembered that his bedroom was over in the other wing just beyond his mother's. She was alone over here – or was she?

With a little gasp she slid down into bed again and lay listening. Not since childhood had she been afraid of the dark, but the unforeseen presence of someone next door startled her and sent her imagination racing through a host of mystery stories that at one time or another had whiled away a long afternoon.

She heard the clock strike four and found she was very tired. A curtain drifted slowly down in front of her imagination, and changing her position she fell suddenly to sleep.

Next morning, walking with Knowleton under starry frosted bushes in one of the bare gardens, she grew quite light-hearted and wondered at her depression of the night before. Probably all families seemed odd when one visited them for the first time in such an intimate capacity. Yet her determination that she and Knowleton were going to live elsewhere than with the white dogs and the jumpy little man was not abated. And if the nearby Westchester County society was typified by the chilly crowd she had met at the dance...

"The family," said Knowleton, "must seem rather unusual. I've been brought up in an odd atmosphere, I suppose, but Mother is really quite normal outside of her penchant for poodles in great quantities, and Father in spite of his eccentricities seems to hold a secure position in Wall Street."

"Knowleton," she demanded suddenly, "who lives in the room next door to me?"

Did he start and flush slightly – or was that her imagination?

"Because," she went on deliberately, "I'm almost sure I heard someone crying in there during the night. It sounded like a child, Knowleton."

"There is no one in there," he said decidedly. "It was either your imagination or something you ate. Or possibly one of the maids was sick."

Seeming to dismiss the matter without effort he changed the subject.

The day passed quickly. At lunch Mr Whitney seemed to have forgotten his temper of the previous night; he was as nervously enthusiastic as ever; and watching him Myra again had that impression that she had seen him somewhere before. She and Knowleton paid another visit to Mrs Whitney – and again the poodles stirred uneasily and set up a barking, to be summarily silenced by the harsh throaty voice. The conversation was short and of inquisitional flavour. It was terminated as before by the lady's drowsy eyelids and a paean of farewell from the dogs.

THE LOVE BOAT AND OTHER STORIES

In the evening she found that Mr Whitney had insisted on organizing an informal neighbourhood vaudeville. A stage had been erected in the ballroom and Myra sat beside Knowleton in the front row and watched proceedings curiously. Two slim and haughty ladies sang, a man performed some ancient card tricks, a girl gave impersonations, and then to Myra's astonishment Mr Whitney appeared and did a rather effective buck-and-wing dance. There was something inexpressibly weird in the motion of the well-known financier flitting solemnly back and forth across the stage on his tiny feet. Yet he danced well, with an effortless grace and an unexpected suppleness, and he was rewarded with a storm of applause.

In the half dark the lady on her left suddenly spoke to her.

"Mr Whitney is passing the word along that he wants to see you behind the scenes."

Puzzled, Myra rose and ascended the side flight of stairs that led to the raised platform. Her host was waiting for her anxiously.

"Ah," he chuckled, "splendid!"

He held out his hand, and wonderingly she took it. Before she realized his intention he had half led, half drawn her out onto the stage. The spotlight's glare bathed them, and the ripple of conversation washing the audience ceased. The faces before her were pallid splotches on the gloom and she felt her ears burning as she waited for Mr Whitney to speak.

"Ladies and gentlemen," he began, "most of you know Miss Myra Harper. You had the honour of meeting her last night. She is a delicious girl, I assure you. I am in a position to know. She intends to become the wife of my son."

He paused and nodded and began clapping his hands. The audience immediately took up the clapping and Myra stood there in motionless horror, overcome by the most violent confusion of her life.

The piping voice went on: "Miss Harper is not only beautiful but talented. Last night she confided to me that she sang. I asked whether she preferred the opera, the ballad or the popular song, and she confessed that her taste ran to the latter. Miss Harper will now favour us with a popular song."

And then Myra was standing alone on the stage, rigid with embarrassment. She fancied that on the faces in front of her she saw critical expectation, boredom, ironic disapproval. Surely this was the height of bad form – to drop a guest unprepared into such a situation.

In the first hush she considered a word or two explaining that Mr Whitney had been under a misapprehension – then anger came to her assistance. She tossed her head and those in front saw her lips close together sharply.

Advancing to the platform's edge she said succinctly to the orchestra leader: "Have you got 'Wave That Wishbone'?"

"Lemme see. Yes, we got it."

"All right. Let's go!"

She hurriedly reviewed the words, which she had learnt quite by accident at a dull house party the previous summer. It was perhaps not the song she would have chosen for her first public appearance, but it would have to do. She smiled radiantly, nodded at the orchestra leader and began the verse in a light clear alto.

As she sang a spirit of ironic humour slowly took possession of her – a desire to give them all a run for their money. And she did. She injected an East Side snarl into every word of slang; she ragged; she shimmied; she did a tickle-toe step she had learnt once in an amateur musical comedy; and in a burst of inspiration finished up in an Al Jolson position, on her knees with her arms stretched out to her audience in syncopated appeal.

Then she rose, bowed and left the stage.

For an instant there was silence, the silence of a cold tomb; then perhaps half a dozen hands joined in a faint, perfunctory applause that in a second had died completely away.

"Heavens!" thought Myra. "Was it as bad as all that? Or did I shock 'em?"

Mr Whitney, however, seemed delighted. He was waiting for her in the wings and seizing her hand shook it enthusiastically.

"Quite wonderful!" he chuckled. "You are a delightful little actress – and you'll be a valuable addition to our little plays. Would you like to give an encore?"

"No!" said Myra shortly, and turned away.

In a shadowy corner she waited until the crowd had filed out, with an angry unwillingness to face them immediately after their rejection of her effort.

When the ballroom was quite empty she walked slowly up the stairs, and there she came upon Knowleton and Mr Whitney alone in the dark hall, evidently engaged in a heated argument.

They ceased when she appeared and looked towards her eagerly.

"Myra," said Mr Whitney, "Knowleton wants to talk to you."

"Father," said Knowleton intensely, "I ask you—"

"Silence!" cried his father, his voice ascending testily. "You'll do your duty – now."

Knowleton cast one more appealing glance at him, but Mr Whitney only shook his head excitedly and turning, disappeared phantom-like up the stairs.

Knowleton stood silent a moment and finally with a look of dogged determination took her hand and led her towards a room that opened off the hall at the back. The yellow light fell through the door after them and she found herself in a dark wide chamber where she could just distinguish on the walls great square shapes which she took to be frames. Knowleton pressed a button, and immediately forty portraits sprang into life – old gallants from colonial days, ladies with floppity Gainsborough hats, fat women with ruffs and placid clasped hands.

She turned to Knowleton enquiringly, but he led her forward to a row of pictures on the side.

"Myra," he said slowly and painfully, "there's something I have to tell you. These" – he indicated the pictures with his hand – "are family portraits."

There were seven of them, three men and three women, all of them of the period just before the Civil War. The one in the middle, however, was hidden by crimson-velvet curtains.

"Ironic as it may seem," continued Knowleton steadily, "that frame contains a picture of my great-grandmother."

Reaching out, he pulled a little silken cord and the curtains parted, to expose a portrait of a lady dressed as a European but with the unmistakable features of a Chinese.

"My great-grandfather, you see, was an Australian tea importer. He met his future wife in Hong Kong."

Myra's brain was whirling. She had a sudden vision of Mr Whitney's yellowish face, peculiar eyebrows and tiny hands and feet – she remembered ghastly tales she had heard of reversions to type – of Chinese babies – and then with a final surge of horror she thought of that sudden hushed cry in the night. She gasped, her knees seemed to crumple up and she sank slowly to the floor.

In a second Knowleton's arms were round her.

"Dearest, dearest!" he cried. "I shouldn't have told you! I shouldn't have told you!"

As he said this Myra knew definitely and unmistakably that she could never marry him, and when she realized it she cast at him a wild pitiful look, and for the first time in her life fainted dead away.

4

WHEN SHE NEXT RECOVERED full consciousness she was in bed. She imagined a maid had undressed her, for on turning up the reading lamp she saw that her clothes had been neatly put away. For a minute she lay there, listening idly while the hall clock struck two, and then her overwrought nerves jumped in terror as she heard again that child's cry from the room next door. The morning seemed suddenly infinitely far away. There was some shadowy secret near her – her feverish imagination pictured a Chinese child brought up there in the half dark.

In a quick panic she crept into a negligee and, throwing open the door, slipped down the corridor towards Knowleton's room. It was very dark in the other wing, but when she pushed open his door she could see by the faint hall light that his bed was empty and had not been slept in. Her terror increased. What could take him out at this hour of the night? She started for Mrs Whitney's room, but at the thought of the dogs and her bare ankles she gave a little discouraged cry and passed by the door.

Then she suddenly heard the sound of Knowleton's voice issuing from a faint crack of light far down the corridor, and with a glow of joy she fled towards it. When she was within a foot of the door she found she could see through the crack – and after one glance all thought of entering left her.

Before an open fire, his head bowed in an attitude of great dejection, stood Knowleton, and in a corner, feet perched on the table, sat Mr Whitney in his shirtsleeves, very quiet and calm, and pulling contentedly on a huge black pipe. Seated on the table was a part of Mrs Whitney – that is, Mrs Whitney without any hair. Out of the familiar great bust projected Mrs Whitney's head, but she was bald; on her cheeks was the faint stubble of a beard, and in her mouth was a large black cigar, which she was puffing with obvious enjoyment.

"A thousand," groaned Knowleton as if in answer to a question. "Say twenty-five hundred and you'll be nearer the truth. I got a bill from the Graham Kennels today for those poodle dogs. They're soaking me two hundred and saying that they've got to have 'em back tomorrow."

"Well," said Mrs Whitney in a low baritone voice, "send 'em back. We're through with 'em."

"That's a mere item," continued Knowleton glumly. "Including your salary, and Appleton's here, and that fellow who did the chauffeur, and seventy supes* for two nights, and an orchestra – that's nearly twelve hundred, and then there's the rent on the costumes and that darn Chinese portrait and the bribes to the servants. Lord! There'll probably be bills for one thing or another coming in for the next month."

"Well, then," said Appleton, "for pity's sake pull yourself together and carry it through to the end. Take my word for it, that girl will be out of the house by twelve noon."

Knowleton sank into a chair and covered his face with his hands.

"Oh—"

"Brace up! It's all over. I thought for a minute there in the hall that you were going to baulk at that Chinese business."

"It was the vaudeville that knocked the spots out of me," groaned Knowleton. "It was about the meanest trick ever pulled on any girl, and she was so darned game about it!"

"She had to be," said Mrs Whitney cynically.

"Oh, Kelly, if you could have seen the girl look at me tonight just before she fainted in front of that picture. Lord, I believe she loves me! Oh, if you could have seen her!"

Outside Myra flushed crimson: she leant closer to the door, biting her lip until she could taste the faintly bitter savour of blood.

"If there was anything I could do now," continued Knowleton – "anything in the world that would smooth it over I believe I'd do it."

Kelly crossed ponderously over, his bald shiny head ludicrous above his feminine negligee, and put his hand on Knowleton's shoulder.

"See here, my boy – your trouble is just nerves. Look at it this way: you undertook somep'n to get yourself out of an awful mess. It's a cinch the girl was after your money – now you've beat her at her own game an' saved yourself an unhappy marriage and your family a lot of suffering. Ain't that so, Appleton?"

"Absolutely!" said Appleton emphatically. "Go through with it."

"Well," said Knowleton with a dismal attempt to be righteous, "if she really loves me she wouldn't have let it all affect her this much. She's not marrying my family."

Appleton laughed.

"I thought we'd tried to make it pretty obvious that she is."

"Oh, shut up!" cried Knowleton miserably.

Myra saw Appleton wink at Kelly.

"'At's right," he said, "she's shown she was after your money. Well, now then, there's no reason for not going through with it. See here. On one side, you've proved she didn't love you and you're rid of her and free as air. She'll creep away and never say a word about it – and your family never the wiser. On the other side twenty-five hundred thrown to the bow-wows, miserable marriage, girl sure to hate you as soon as she finds out, and your family all broken up and probably disownin' you for marryin' her. One big mess, I'll tell the world."

"You're right," admitted Knowleton gloomily. "You're right, I suppose – but oh, the look in that girl's face! She's probably in there now lying awake, listening to the Chinese baby…"

Appleton rose and yawned.

"Well…" he began.

But Myra waited to hear no more. Pulling her silk kimono close about her she sped like lightning down the soft corridor, to dive headlong and breathless into her room.

"My heavens!" she cried, clenching her hands in the darkness. "My heavens!"

5

JUST BEFORE DAWN MYRA DROWSED into a jumbled dream that seemed to act on through interminable hours. She awoke about seven and lay listlessly with one blue-veined arm hanging over the side of the bed. She who had danced in the dawn at many proms was very tired.

A clock outside her door struck the hour, and with her nervous start something seemed to collapse within her – she turned over and began to weep furiously into her pillow, her tangled hair spreading like a dark aura round her head. To her, Myra Harper, had been done this cheap vulgar trick by a man she had thought shy and kind.

Lacking the courage to come to her and tell her the truth he had gone into the highways and hired men to frighten her.

Between her fevered broken sobs she tried in vain to comprehend the workings of a mind which could have conceived this in all its subtlety. Her pride refused to let her think of it as a deliberate plan of Knowleton's. It was probably an idea fostered by this little actor Appleton or by the fat Kelly with his horrible poodles. But it was all unspeakable – unthinkable. It gave her an intense sense of shame.

But when she emerged from her room at eight o'clock and, disdaining breakfast, walked into the garden she was a very self-possessed young beauty, with dry cool eyes only faintly shadowed. The ground was firm and frosty with the promise of winter, and she found grey sky and dull air vaguely comforting and one with her mood. It was a day for thinking and she needed to think.

And then turning a corner suddenly she saw Knowleton seated on a stone bench, his head in his hands, in an attitude of profound dejection. He wore his clothes of the night before and it was quite evident that he had not been to bed.

He did not hear her until she was quite close to him, and then as a dry twig snapped under her heel he looked up wearily. She saw that the night had played havoc with him – his face was deathly pale and his eyes were pink and puffed and tired. He jumped up with a look that was very like dread.

"Good morning," said Myra quietly.

"Sit down," he began nervously. "Sit down; I want to talk to you! I've got to talk to you."

Myra nodded and taking a seat beside him on the bench clasped her knees with her hands and half closed her eyes.

"Myra, for heaven's sake have pity on me!"

She turned wondering eyes on him.

"What do you mean?"

He groaned.

"Myra, I've done a ghastly thing – to you, to me, to us. I haven't a word to say in favour of myself – I've been just rotten. I think it was a sort of madness that came over me."

"You'll have to give me a clue to what you're talking about."

"Myra… Myra" – like all large bodies his confession seemed difficult to imbue with momentum – "Myra… Mr Whitney is not my father."

"You mean you were adopted?"

"No, I mean – Ludlow Whitney is my father, but this man you've met isn't Ludlow Whitney."

"I know," said Myra coolly. "He's Warren Appleton, the actor."

Knowleton leapt to his feet.

"Oh," lied Myra easily, "I recognized him the first night. I saw him five years ago in *The Swiss Grapefruit*."

At this Knowleton seemed to collapse utterly. He sank down limply onto the bench.

"You knew?"

"Of course! How could I help it? It simply made me wonder what it was all about."

With a great effort he tried to pull himself together.

"I'm going to tell you the whole story, Myra."

"I'm all ears."

"Well, it starts with my mother – my real one, not the woman with those idiotic dogs; she's an invalid and I'm her only child. Her one idea in life has always been for me to make a fitting match, and her idea of a fitting match centres on social position in England. Her greatest disappointment was that I wasn't a girl so I could marry a title; instead she wanted to drag me to England – marry me off to the sister of an earl or the daughter of a duke. Why, before she'd let me stay up here alone this fall she made me promise I wouldn't go to see any girl more than twice. And then I met you."

He paused for a second and continued earnestly: "You were the first girl in my life whom I ever thought of marrying. You intoxicated me, Myra. It was just as though you were making me love you by some invisible force."

"I was," murmured Myra.

"Well, that first intoxication lasted a week, and then one day a letter came from Mother saying she was bringing home some wonderful English girl, Lady Helena Something-or-Other. And the same day a man told me that he'd heard I'd been caught by the most famous husband hunter in New York. Well, between these two things I went half-crazy. I came into town to see you and call it off – got as far as the Biltmore entrance and didn't dare. I started wandering down Fifth Avenue like a wild man, and then I met Kelly. I told him the whole story – and within an hour we'd hatched up this ghastly plan. It was his plan – all the details. His histrionic instinct got the better of him and he had me thinking it was the kindest way out."

"Finish," commanded Myra crisply.

"Well, it went splendidly, we thought. Everything – the station meeting, the dinner scene, the scream in the night, the vaudeville – though I thought that was a little too much – until… until… Oh, Myra, when you fainted under that picture and I held you there in my arms, helpless as a baby, I knew I loved you. I was sorry then, Myra."

There was a long pause while she sat motionless, her hands still clasping her knees – then he burst out with a wild plea of passionate sincerity.

"Myra!" he cried. "If by any possible chance you can bring yourself to forgive and forget I'll marry you when you say, let my family go to the devil, and love you all my life."

For a long while she considered, and Knowleton rose and began pacing nervously up and down the aisle of bare bushes, his hands in his pockets, his tired eyes pathetic now, and full of dull appeal. And then she came to a decision.

"You're perfectly sure?" she asked calmly.

"Yes."

"Very well, I'll marry you today."

With her words the atmosphere cleared and his troubles seemed to fall from him like a ragged cloak. An Indian summer sun drifted out from behind the grey clouds and the dry bushes rustled gently in the breeze.

"It was a bad mistake," she continued, "but if you're sure you love me now, that's the main thing. We'll go to town this morning, get a licence, and I'll call up my cousin, who's a minister in the First Presbyterian Church. We can go west tonight."

"Myra!" he cried jubilantly. "You're a marvel and I'm not fit to tie your shoestrings. I'm going to make up to you for this, darling girl."

And taking her supple body in his arms he covered her face with kisses.

The next two hours passed in a whirl. Myra went to the telephone and called her cousin, and then rushed upstairs to pack. When she came down a shining roadster was waiting miraculously in the drive and by ten o'clock they were bowling happily towards the city.

They stopped for a few minutes at the City Hall and again at the jeweller's, and then they were in the house of the Reverend Walter Gregory on 69th Street, where a sanctimonious gentleman with twinkling eyes and a slight stutter received them cordially and urged them to a breakfast of bacon and eggs before the ceremony.

On the way to the station they stopped only long enough to wire Knowleton's father, and then they were sitting in their compartment on the Broadway Limited.

"Darn!" exclaimed Myra. "I forgot my bag. Left it at Cousin Walter's in the excitement."

"Never mind. We can get a whole new outfit in Chicago."

She glanced at her wristwatch.

"I've got time to telephone him to send it on."

She rose.

"Don't be long, dear."

She leant down and kissed his forehead.

"You know I couldn't. Two minutes, honey."

Outside Myra ran swiftly along the platform and up the steel stairs to the great waiting room, where a man met her – a twinkly-eyed man with a slight stutter.

"How d-did it go, M-myra?"

"Fine! Oh, Walter, you were splendid! I almost wish you'd join the ministry so you could officiate when I do get married."

"Well – I r-rehearsed for half an hour after I g-got your telephone call."

"Wish we'd had more time. I'd have had him lease an apartment and buy furniture."

"H'm," chuckled Walter. "Wonder how far he'll go on his honeymoon."

"Oh, he'll think I'm on the train till he gets to Elizabeth." She shook her little fist at the great contour of the marble dome. "Oh, he's getting off too easy – far too easy!"

"I haven't f-figured out what the f-fellow did to you, M-myra."

"You never will, I hope."

They had reached the side drive and he hailed her a taxicab.

"You're an angel!" beamed Myra. "And I can't thank you enough."

"Well, any time I can be of use t-to you… By the way, what are you going to do with all the rings?"

Myra looked laughingly at her hand.

"That's the question," she said. "I may send them to Lady Helena Something-or-Other – and – well, I've always had a strong penchant for souvenirs. Tell the driver 'Biltmore', Walter."

Two for a Cent

W HEN THE RAIN WAS OVER the sky became yellow in the west and the air was cool. Close to the street, which was of red dirt and lined with cheap bungalows dating from 1910, a little boy was riding a big bicycle along the sidewalk. His plan afforded a monotonous fascination. He rode each time for about a hundred yards, dismounted, turned the bicycle around so that it adjoined a stone step and getting on again, not without toil or heat, retraced his course. At one end this was bounded by a coloured girl of fourteen holding an anaemic baby, and at the other by a scarred, ill-nourished kitten, squatting dismally on the kerb. These four were the only souls in sight.

The little boy had accomplished an indefinite number of trips oblivious alike to the melancholy advances of the kitten at one end and the admiring vacuousness of the coloured girl at the other when he swerved dangerously to avoid a man who had turned the corner into the street and recovered his balance only after a moment of exaggerated panic.

But if the incident was a matter of gravity to the boy, it attracted scarcely an instant's notice from the newcomer, who turned suddenly from the sidewalk and stared with obvious and peculiar interest at the house before which he was standing. It was the oldest house in the street, built with clapboards and a shingled roof. It was a *house* – in the barest sense of the word: the sort of house that a child would draw on a blackboard. It was of a period, but of no design, and its exterior had obviously been made only as a decent cloak for what was within. It antedated the stucco bungalows by about thirty years and except for the bungalows, which were reproducing their species with prodigious avidity as though by some monstrous affiliation with the guinea pig, it was the most common type of house in the country. For thirty years such dwellings had satisfied the canons of the middle class; they had satisfied its financial canons by being cheap; they had satisfied its aesthetic canons by being hideous. It was a house built by a race whose more energetic complement hoped either to move up or move on, and it was the more remarkable that its instability had survived so many summers and retained its pristine hideousness and discomfort so obviously unimpaired.

The man was about as old as the house, that is to say, about forty-five. But unlike the house, he was neither hideous nor cheap. His clothes were too good to have been made outside of a metropolis – moreover, they were so good that it was impossible to tell in which metropolis they were made. His name was Abercrombie and the most important event of his life had taken place in the house before which he was standing. He had been born there.

It was one of the last places in the world where he should have been born. He had thought so within a very few years after the event and he thought so now – an ugly home in a third-rate Southern town where his father had owned a partnership in a grocery store. Since then Abercrombie had played golf with the President of the United States and sat between two duchesses at dinner. He had been bored with the President, he had been bored and not a little embarrassed with the duchesses – nevertheless, the two incidents had pleased him and still sat softly upon his naive vanity. It delighted him that he had gone far.

He looked fixedly at the house for several minutes before he perceived that no one lived there. Where the shutters were not closed it was because there were no shutters to be closed and in these vacancies, blind vacuous expanses of grey window looked unseeingly down at him. The grass had grown wantonly long in the yard and faint green moustaches were sprouting facetiously in the wide cracks of the walk. But it was evident that the property had been recently occupied for upon the porch lay half a dozen newspapers rolled into cylinders for quick delivery and as yet turned only to a faint resentful yellow.

They were not nearly so yellow as the sky when Abercrombie walked up on the porch and sat down upon an immemorial bench, for the sky was every shade of yellow, the colour of tan, the colour of gold, the colour of peaches. Across the street and beyond a vacant lot rose a rampart of vivid red-brick houses and it seemed to Abercrombie that the picture they rounded out was beautiful – the warm earthy brick and the sky fresh after the rain, changing and grey as a dream. All his life when he had wanted to rest his mind he had called up into it the image those two things had made for him when the air was clear just at this hour. So Abercrombie sat there thinking about his young days.

Ten minutes later another man turned the corner of the street, a different sort of man, both in the texture of his clothes and the texture of his soul. He was forty-six years old and he was a shabby drudge, married to a woman who, as a girl, had known better days. This latter fact, in the republic, may be set down in the red italics of misery.

His name was Hemmick – Henry W. or George D. or John F. – the stock that produced him had had little imagination left to waste either upon his name or his design. He was a clerk in a factory which made ice for the long Southern summer. He was responsible to the man who owned the patent for canning ice, who, in his turn was responsible only to God. Never in his life had Henry W. Hemmick discovered a new way to advertise canned ice nor had it transpired that by taking a diligent correspondence course in ice canning he had secretly been preparing himself for a partnership. Never had he rushed home to his wife, crying: "You can have that servant now, Nell, I have been made general superintendent." You will have to take him as you took Abercrombie, for what he is and will always be. This is a story of the dead years.

When the second man reached the house he turned in and began to mount the tipsy steps, noticed Abercrombie, the stranger, with a tired surprise, and nodded to him.

"Good evening," he said.

Abercrombie voiced his agreement with the sentiment.

"Cool" – The newcomer covered his forefinger with his handkerchief and sent the swatched digit on a complete circuit of his collar band. "Have you rented this?" he asked.

"No, indeed, I'm just – resting. Sorry if I've intruded – I saw the house was vacant—"

"Oh, you're not intruding!" said Hemmick hastily. "I don't reckon anybody *could* intrude in this old barn. I got out two months ago. They're not ever goin' to rent it any more. I got a little girl about this high" – he held his hand parallel to the ground and at an indeterminate distance – "and she's mighty fond of an old doll that got left here when we moved. Began hollerin' for me to come over and look it up."

"You used to live here?" enquired Abercrombie with interest.

"Lived here eighteen years. Came here'n I was married, raised four children in this house. Yes, *sir*. I know this old fellow." He struck the doorpost with the flat of his hand. "I know every leak in her roof and every loose board in her old floor."

Abercrombie had been good to look at for so many years that he knew if he kept a certain attentive expression on his face his companion would continue to talk – indefinitely.

"You from up north?" enquired Hemmick politely, choosing with habituated precision the one spot where the anaemic wooden railing would support his weight. "I thought so," he resumed at Abercrombie's nod. "Don't take long to tell a Yankee."

"I'm from New York."

"So?" The man shook his head with inappropriate gravity. "Never have got up there, myself. Started to go a couple of times, before I was married, but never did get to go."

He made a second excursion with his finger and handkerchief and then, as though having come suddenly to a cordial decision, he replaced the handkerchief in one of his bumpy pockets and extended the hand towards his companion.

"My name's Hemmick."

"Glad to know you." Abercrombie took the hand without rising. "Abercrombie's mine."

"I'm mighty glad to know you, Mr Abercrombie."

Then for a moment they both hesitated, their two faces assumed oddly similar expressions, their eyebrows drew together, their eyes looked far away. Each was straining to force into activity some minute cell long sealed and forgotten in his brain. Each made a little noise in his throat, looked away, looked back, laughed. Abercrombie spoke first.

"We've met."

"I know," agreed Hemmick, "but whereabouts? That's what's got me. You from New York, you say?"

"Yes, but I was born and raised in this town. Lived in this house till I left here when I was about seventeen. As a matter of fact, I remember you – you were a couple of years older."

"Well," he said vaguely, "I sort of remember, too. I *begin* to remember – I got your name all right and I guess maybe it was your daddy had this house before I rented it. But all I can recollect about you is, that there was a boy named Abercrombie and he went away."

In a few moments they were talking easily. It amused them both to have come from the same house – amused Abercrombie especially, for he was a vain man, rather absorbed, that evening, in his own early poverty. Though he was not given to immature impulses, he found it necessary somehow to make it clear in a few sentences that five years after he had gone away from the house and the town he had been able to send for his father and mother to join him in New York.

Hemmick listened with that exaggerated attention which men who have not prospered generally render to men who have. He would have continued to listen had Abercrombie become more expansive, for he was beginning faintly to associate him with an Abercrombie who had figured in the newspapers for several years at the head of shipping boards and financial committees. But Abercrombie, after a moment, made the conversation less personal.

"I didn't realize you had so much heat here, I guess I've forgotten a lot in twenty-five years."

"Why, this is a *cool* day," boasted Hemmick, "this is *cool*. I was just sort of overheated from walking when I came up."

"It's too hot," insisted Abercrombie with a restless movement; then he added abruptly, "I don't like it here. It means nothing to me – nothing – I've wondered if it did, you know, that's why I came down. And I've decided.

"You see," he continued hesitantly, "up to recently the North was still full of professional Southerns, some real, some by sentiment, but all given to flowery monologues on the beauty of their old family planta-tions and all jumping up and howling when the band played 'Dixie'.* You know what I mean" – he turned to Hemmick – "it got to be a sort of a national joke. Oh, I was in the game, too, I suppose, I used to stand

41

up and perspire and cheer, and I've given young men positions for no particular reason except that they claimed to come from South Carolina or Virginia…" – again he broke off and became suddenly abrupt – "but I'm through, I've been here six hours and I'm through!"

"Too hot for you?" enquired Hemmick, with mild surprise.

"Yes! I've felt the heat and I've seen the men – those two or three dozen loafers standing in front of the stores on Jackson Street – in thatched straw hats" – then he added, with a touch of humour, "They're what my son calls 'slash-pocket, belted-back boys'. Do you know the ones I mean?"

"Jelly beans," Hemmick nodded gravely, "we call 'em jelly beans.* No-account lot of boys all right. They got signs up in front of most of the stores asking 'em not to stand there."

"They ought to!" asserted Abercrombie, with a touch of irascibility. "That's my picture of the South now, you know – a skinny, dark-haired young man with a gun on his hip and a stomach full of corn liquor or Dope Dola, leaning up against a drugstore waiting for the next lynching."

Hemmick objected, though with apology in his voice.

"You got to remember, Mr Abercrombie, that we haven't had the money down here since the war—"

Abercrombie waved this impatiently aside.

"Oh, I've heard all that," he said, "and I'm tired of it. And I've heard the South lambasted till I'm tired of that, too. It's not taking France and Germany fifty years to get on their feet, and their war made your war look like a little fracas up an alley. And it's not your fault and it's not anybody's fault. It's just that this is too damn hot to be a white man's country and it always will be. I'd like to see 'em pack two or three of these states full of darkies and drop 'em out of the Union."

Hemmick nodded, thoughtfully, though without thought. He had never thought; for over twenty years he had seldom ever held opinions, save the opinions of the local press, or of some majority made articulate through passion. There was a certain luxury in thinking that he had never been able to afford. When cases were set before him he either accepted them outright if they were comprehensible to him or rejected them if they required a modicum of concentration. Yet he was not a stupid man.

He was poor and busy and tired and there were no ideas at large in his community, even had he been capable of grasping them. The idea that he did not think would have been equally incomprehensible to him. He was a closed book, half-full of badly printed, uncorrelated trash.

Just now, his reaction to Abercrombie's assertion was exceedingly simple. Since the remarks proceeded from a man who was a Southerner by birth, who was successful – moreover, who was confident and decisive and persuasive and suave – he was inclined to accept them without suspicion or resentment.

He took one of Abercrombie's cigars and pulling on it, still with a stern imitation of profundity upon his tired face, watched the colour glide out of the sky and the grey veils come down. The little boy and his bicycle, the baby, the nursemaid, the forlorn kitten, all had departed. In the stucco bungalows pianos gave out hot weary notes that inspired the crickets to competitive sound, and squeaky gramophones filled in the intervals with patches of whining ragtime until the impression was created that each living room in the street opened directly out into the darkness.

"What *I* want to find out," Abercrombie was saying with a frown, "is why I didn't have sense enough to *know* that this was a worthless town. It was entirely an accident that I left here, an utterly blind chance, and as it happened, the very train that took me away was full of luck for me. The man I sat beside gave me my start in life." His tone became resentful. "But I thought this was all right. I'd have stayed except that I'd gotten into a scrape down at the high school – I got expelled and my daddy told me he didn't want me at home any more. Why didn't I know the place wasn't any good? Why didn't I *see*?"

"Well, you'd probably never known anything better?" suggested Hemmick mildly.

"That wasn't any excuse," insisted Abercrombie. "If I'd been any good I'd have known. As a matter of fact – as – a – matter – of – fact," he repeated slowly, "I think that at heart I was the sort of boy who'd have lived and died here happily and never known there was anything better." He turned to Hemmick with a look almost of distress. "It worries me to think that my – that what's happened to me can be ascribed to chance.

But that's the sort of boy I think I was. I didn't start off with the Dick Whittington idea – I started off by accident."

After this confession, he stared out into the twilight with a dejected expression that Hemmick could not understand. It was impossible for the latter to share any sense of the importance of such a distinction – in fact from a man of Abercrombie's position it struck him as unnecessarily trivial. Still he felt that some manifestation of acquiescence was only polite.

"Well," he offered, "it's just that some boys get the bee to get up and go north and some boys don't. I happened to have the bee to go north. But I didn't. That's the difference between you and me."

Abercrombie turned to him intently.

"You did?" he asked, with unexpected interest. "You wanted to get out?"

"At one time." At Abercrombie's eagerness Hemmick began to attach a new importance to the subject. "At one time," he repeated, as though the singleness of the occasion was a thing he had often mused upon.

"How old were you?"

"Oh – 'bout twenty."

"What put it into your head?"

"Well let me see…" – Hemmick considered – "I don't know whether I remember sure enough but it seems to me that when I was down to the university – I was there two years – one of the professors told me that a smart boy ought to go north. He said, business wasn't going to amount to much down here for the next fifty years. And I guessed he was right. My father died about then, so I got a job as runner in the bank here, and I didn't have much interest in anything except saving up enough money to go north. I was bound to go."

"Why didn't you? Why didn't you?" insisted Abercrombie in an aggrieved tone.

"Well," Hemmick hesitated. "Well, I right near did but – things didn't work out and I didn't get to go. It was a funny sort of business. It all started about the smallest thing you can think of. It all started about a penny."

"A penny?"

"That's what did it – one little penny. That's why I didn't go 'way from here and all, like I intended."

44

"Tell me about it, man," exclaimed his companion. He looked at his watch impatiently. "I'd like to hear the story."

Hemmick sat for a moment, distorting his mouth around the cigar.

"Well, to begin with," he said at length, "I'm going to ask you if you remember a thing that happened here about twenty-five years ago. A fellow named Hoyt, the cashier of the Cotton National Bank, disappeared one night with about thirty thousand dollars, in cash. Say, man, they didn't talk about anything else down here at the time. The whole town was shaken up about it, and I reckin you can imagine the disturbance it caused down at all the banks and especially at the Cotton National."

"I remember."

"Well, they caught him, and they got most of the money back, and by and by the excitement died down, except in the bank where the thing had happened. Down there it seemed as if they'd never get used to it. Mr Deems, the first vice president, who'd always been pretty kind and decent, got to be a changed man. He was suspicious of the clerks, the tellers, the janitor, the watchman, most of the officers, and yes, by golly, I guess he got so he kept an eye on the president himself.

"I don't mean he was just watchful – he was downright hipped on the subject. He'd come up and ask you funny questions when you were going about your business. He'd walk into the teller's cage on tiptoe and watch him without saying anything. If there was any mistake of any kind in the bookkeeping, he'd not only fire a clerk or so, but he'd raise such a riot that he made you want to push him into a vault and slam the door on him.

"He was just about running the bank then, and he'd affected the other officers, and – oh, you can imagine the havoc a thing like that could work on any sort of an organization. Everybody was so nervous that they made mistakes whether they were careful or not. Clerks were staying downtown until eleven at night trying to account for a lost nickel. It was a thin year, anyhow, and everything financial was pretty rickety, so one thing worked on another until the crowd of us were as near craziness as anybody can be and carry on the banking business at all.

"I was a runner – and all through the heat of one godforsaken summer I ran. I ran and I got mighty little money for it, and that was the time I hated that bank and this town, and all I wanted was to get out and go north. I was getting ten dollars a week, and I'd decided that when I'd saved fifty out of it I was going down to the depot and buy me a ticket to Cincinnati. I had an uncle in the banking business there, and he said he'd give me an opportunity with him. But he never offered to pay my way, and I guess he thought if I was worth having I'd manage to get up there by myself. Well, maybe I wasn't worth having because, anyhow, I never did.

"One morning on the hottest day of the hottest July I ever knew – and you know what that means down here – I left the bank to call on a man named Harlan and collect some money that'd come due on a note. Harlan had the cash waiting for me all right, and when I counted it I found it amounted to three hundred dollars and eighty-six cents, the change being in brand-new coin that Harlan had drawn from another bank that morning. I put the three one-hundred-dollar bills in my wallet and the change in my vest pocket, signed a receipt and left. I was going straight back to the bank.

"Outside the heat was terrible. It was enough to make you dizzy, and I hadn't been feeling right for a couple of days, so, while I waited in the shade for a streetcar, I was congratulating myself that in a month or so I'd be out of this and up where it was some cooler. And then as I stood there it occurred to me all of a sudden that outside of the money which I'd just collected, which, of course, I couldn't touch, I didn't have a cent in my pocket. I'd have to walk back to the bank, and it was about fifteen blocks away. You see, on the night before, I'd found that my change came to just a dollar, and I'd traded it for a bill at the corner store and added it to the roll in the bottom of my trunk. So there was no help for it – I took off my coat and I stuck my handkerchief into my collar and struck off through the suffocating heat for the bank.

"Fifteen blocks – you can imagine what that was like, and I was sick when I started. From away up by Juniper Street – you remember where that is: the new Mieger Hospital's there now – all the way down to Jackson. After about six blocks I began to stop and rest whenever I found a patch of shade wide enough to hold me, and as I got pretty near I could just keep going by thinking of the big glass of iced tea my mother'd have waiting beside my plate at lunch. But after that I began getting too sick to even want the iced tea – I wanted to get rid of that money and then lie down and die.

"When I was still about two blocks away from the bank I put my hand into my watch pocket and pulled out that change; was sort of jingling it in my hand; making myself believe that I was so close that it was convenient to have it ready. I happened to glance into my hand, and all of a sudden I stopped up short and reached down quick into my watch pocket. The pocket was empty. There was a little hole in the bottom, and my hand held only a half-dollar, a quarter and a dime. I had lost one cent.

"Well, sir, I can't tell you, I can't express to you the feeling of discouragement that this gave me. One penny, mind you – but think: just the week before a runner had lost his job because he was a little bit shy twice. It was only carelessness; but there you were! They were all in a panic that they might get fired themselves, and the best thing to do was to fire someone else – first.

"So you can see that it was up to me to appear with that penny.

"Where I got the energy to care as much about it as I did is more than I can understand. I was sick and hot and weak as a kitten, but it never occurred to me that I could do anything except find or replace that penny, and immediately I began casting about for a way to do it. I looked into a couple of stores, hoping I'd see someone I knew, but while there were a few fellows loafing in front, just as you saw them today, there wasn't one that I felt like going up to and saying: 'Here! You got a penny?' I thought of a couple of offices where I could have gotten it without much trouble, but they were some distance off, and besides being pretty dizzy, I hated to go out of my route when I was carrying bank money, because it looked kind of strange.

"So what should I do but commence walking back along the street towards the Union Depot where I last remembered having the penny. It was a brand-new penny, and I thought maybe I'd see it shining where it dropped. So I kept walking, looking pretty carefully at the sidewalk and thinking what I'd better do. I laughed a little, because I felt sort of silly for worrying about a penny, but I didn't enjoy laughing, and it really didn't seem silly to me at all.

"Well, by and by I got back to the Union Depot without having either seen the old penny or having thought what was the best way to get another. I hated to go all the way home, 'cause we lived a long distance out; but what else was I to do? So I found a piece of shade close to the depot, and stood there considering, thinking first one thing and then another, and not getting anywhere at all. One little penny, just *one* – something almost any man in sight would have given me; something even the nigger baggage-smashers were jingling around in their pockets... I must have stood there about five minutes. I remember there was a line of about a dozen men in front of an army recruiting station they'd just opened, and a couple of them began to yell 'Join the army!' at me. That woke me up and I moved on back towards the bank, getting worried now, getting mixed up and sicker and sicker and knowing a million ways to find a penny and not one that seemed convenient or right. I was exaggerating the importance of losing it, and I was exaggerating the difficulty of finding another, but you just have to believe that it seemed about as important to me just then as though it were a hundred dollars.

"Then I saw a couple of men talking in front of Moody's soda place, and recognized one of them – Mr Burling – who'd been a friend of my father's. That was a relief, I can tell you. Before I knew it I was chattering to him so quick that he couldn't follow what I was getting at.

"'Now,' he said, 'you know I'm a little deaf and can't understand when you talk that fast! What is it you want, Harry? Tell me from the beginning.'

"'Have you got any change with you?' I asked him just as loud as I dared. 'I just want...' Then I stopped short; a man a few feet away had turned around and was looking at us. It was Mr Deems, the first vice president of the Cotton National Bank."

Hemmick paused, and it was still light enough for Abercrombie to see that he was shaking his head to and fro in a puzzled way. When he spoke his voice held a quality of pained surprise, a quality that it might have carried over twenty years.

"I never *could* understand what it was that came over me then. I must have been sort of crazy with the heat – that's all I can decide. Instead of just saying 'Howdy' to Mr Deems, in a natural way, and telling Mr

Burling I wanted to borrow a nickel for tobacco, because I'd left my purse at home, I turned away quick as a flash and began walking up the street at a great rate, feeling like a criminal who had come near being caught.

"Before I'd gone a block I was sorry. I could almost hear the conversation that must've been taking place between those two men:

"'What do you reckon's the matter with that young man?' Mr Burling would say without meaning any harm. 'Came up to me all excited and wanted to know if I had any money, and then he saw you and rushed away like he was crazy.'

"And I could almost see Mr Deems's big eyes getting narrow with suspicion and watch him twist up his trousers and come strolling along after me. I was in a real panic now, and no mistake. Suddenly I saw a one-horse surrey* going by, and recognized Bill Kennedy, a friend of mine, driving it. I yelled at him, but he didn't hear me. Then I yelled again, but he didn't pay any attention, so I started after him at a run, swaying from side to side, I guess, like I was drunk, and calling his name every few minutes. He looked around once, but he didn't see me; he kept right on going and turned out of sight at the next corner. I stopped then because I was too weak to go any farther. I was just about to sit down on the curb and rest when I looked around, and the first thing I saw was Mr Deems walking after me as fast as he could come. There wasn't any of my imagination about it this time – the look in his eyes showed he wanted to know what was the matter with *me*!

"Well, that's about all I remember clearly until about twenty minutes later, when I was at home trying to unlock my trunk with fingers that were trembling like a tuning fork. Before I could get it open, Mr Deems and a policeman came in. I began talking all at once about not being a thief and trying to tell them what had happened, but I guess I was sort of hysterical, and the more I said the worse matters were. When I managed to get the story out it seemed sort of crazy, even to me – and it was true – it was true, true as I've told you – every word! – that one penny that I lost somewhere down by the station…" Hemmick broke off and began laughing grotesquely – as though the excitement that had come over him as he finished his tale was a weakness of which he was ashamed. When he resumed it was with an affectation of nonchalance.

"I'm not going into the details of what happened because nothing much did – at least not on the scale you judge events by up north. It cost me my job, and I changed a good name for a bad one. Somebody tattled and somebody lied, and the impression got around that I'd lost a lot of the bank's money and had been tryin' to cover it up.

"I had an awful time getting a job after that. Finally I got a statement out of the bank that contradicted the wildest of the stories that had started, but the people who were still interested said it was just because the bank didn't want any fuss or scandal – and the rest had forgotten: that is they'd forgotten what had happened, but they remembered that somehow I just wasn't a young fellow to be trusted…"

Hemmick paused and laughed again, still without enjoyment, but bitterly, uncomprehendingly, and with a profound helplessness.

"So, you see, that's why I didn't go to Cincinnati," he said slowly. "My mother was alive then, and this was a pretty bad blow to her. She had an idea – one of those old-fashioned Southern ideas that stick in people's heads down here – that somehow I ought to stay here in town and prove myself honest. She had it on her mind, and she wouldn't hear of my going. She said that the day I went'd be the day she'd die. So I sort of had to stay till I'd got back my – my reputation."

"How long did that take?" asked Abercrombie quietly.

"About – ten years."

"Oh…"

"Ten years," repeated Hemmick, staring out into the gathering darkness. "This is a little town, you see: I say ten years because it was about ten years when the last reference to it came to my ears. But I was married long before that; had a kid. Cincinnati was out of my mind by that time."

"Of course," agreed Abercrombie.

They were both silent for a moment – then Hemmick added apologetically:

"That was sort of a long story, and I don't know if it could have interested you much. But you asked me…"

"It *did* interest me," answered Abercrombie politely. "It interested me tremendously. It interested me much more than I thought it would."

It occurred to Hemmick that he himself had never realized what a curious, rounded tale it was. He saw dimly now that what had seemed to him only a fragment, a grotesque interlude was really significant, complete. It was an interesting story; it was a story upon which turned the failure of his life. Abercrombie's voice broke in upon his thoughts.

"You see, it's so different from my story," Abercrombie was saying. "It was an accident that you stayed – and it was an accident that I went away. You deserve more actual – actual credit, if there is such a thing in the world, for your intention of getting out and getting on. You see, I'd more or less gone wrong at seventeen. I was – well, what you call a jelly bean. All I wanted was to take it easy through life – and one day I just happened to see a sign up above my head that had on it: 'Special rate to Atlanta, three dollars and forty-two cents'. So I took out my change and counted it—"

Hemmick nodded. Still absorbed in his own story, he had forgotten the importance, the comparative magnificence of Abercrombie. Then suddenly he found himself listening sharply:

"I had just three dollars and forty-one cents in my pocket. But, you see, I was standing in line with a lot of other young fellows down by the Union Depot about to enlist in the army for three years. And I saw that extra penny on the walk not three feet away. I saw it because it was brand new and shining in the sun like gold."

The Alabama night had settled over the street, and as the blue drew down upon the dust the outlines of the two men had become less distinct, so that it was not easy for anyone who passed along the walk to tell that one of these men was of the few and the other of no importance. All the detail was gone – Abercrombie's fine gold wristwatch, his collar, that he ordered by the dozen from London, the dignity that sat upon him in his chair – all faded and were engulfed with Hemmick's awkward suit and preposterous humped shoes into that pervasive depth of night that, like death, made nothing matter, nothing differentiate, nothing remain. And a little later on a passer-by saw only the two glowing discs about the size of a penny that marked the rise and fall of their cigars.

Dice, Brassknuckles and Guitar

PARTS OF NEW JERSEY, as you know, are under water, and other parts are under continual surveillance by the authorities. But here and there lie patches of garden country dotted with old-fashioned frame mansions, which have wide shady porches and a red swing on the lawn. And perhaps, on the widest and shadiest of the porches there is even a hammock left over from the hammock days, stirring gently in a mid-Victorian wind.

When tourists come to such last-century landmarks they stop their cars and gaze for a while and then mutter: "Well, thank God this age is joined on to *something*," or else they say: "Well, of course, that house is mostly halls and has a thousand rats and one bathroom, but there's an atmosphere about it…"

The tourist doesn't stay long. He drives on to his Elizabethan villa of pressed cardboard or his early-Norman meat market or his medieval Italian pigeon coop – because this is the twentieth century and Victorian houses are as unfashionable as the works of Mrs Humphry Ward.*

He can't see the hammock from the road – but sometimes there's a girl in the hammock. There was this afternoon. She was asleep in it and apparently unaware of the aesthetic horrors which surrounded her, the stone statue of Diana, for instance, which grinned idiotically under the sunlight on the lawn.

There was something enormously yellow about the whole scene – there was this sunlight, for instance, that was yellow, and the hammock was of the particularly hideous yellow peculiar to hammocks, and the girl's yellow hair was spread out upon the hammock in a sort of invidious comparison.

She slept with her lips closed and her hands clasped behind her head, as it is proper for young girls to sleep. Her breast rose and fell slightly with no more emphasis than the sway of the hammock's fringe.

Her name, Amanthis, was as old-fashioned as the house she lived in. I regret to say her mid-Victorian connections ceased abruptly at this point.

Now if this were a moving picture (as, of course, I hope it will someday be) I would take as many thousand feet of her as I was allowed – then I would move the camera up close and show the yellow down on the back of her neck where her hair stopped and the warm colour of her cheeks and arms, because I like to think of her sleeping there, as you yourself might have slept, back in your young days. Then I would hire a man named Israel Glucose to write some idiotic line of transition, and switch thereby to another scene that was taking place at no particular spot far down the road.

In a moving automobile sat a Southern gentleman accompanied by his body servant. He was on his way, after a fashion, to New York, but he was somewhat hampered by the fact that the upper and lower portions of his automobile were no longer in exact juxtaposition. In fact from time to time the two riders would dismount, shove the body onto the chassis, corner to corner, and then continue onward, vibrating slightly in involuntary unison with the motor.

Except that it had no door in back the car might have been built early in the mechanical age. It was covered with the mud of eight states and adorned in front by an enormous but defunct motometer* and behind by a mangy pennant bearing the legend "Tarleton, Ga."* In the dim past someone had begun to paint the hood yellow but unfortunately had been called away when but half through the task.

As the gentleman and his body servant were passing the house where Amanthis lay beautifully asleep in the hammock, something happened – the body fell off the car. My only apology for stating this so suddenly is that it happened very suddenly indeed. When the noise had died down and the dust had drifted away master and man arose and inspected the two halves.

"Look-a-there," said the gentleman in disgust, "the doggone thing got all separated that time."

"She bust in two," agreed the body servant.

"Hugo," said the gentleman, after some consideration, "we got to get a hammer an' nails an' *tack* it on."

They glanced up at the Victorian house. On all sides faintly irregular fields stretched away to a faintly irregular unpopulated horizon. There was no choice, so the black Hugo opened the gate and followed his master up a gravel walk, casting only the blasé glances of a confirmed traveller at the red swing and the stone statue of Diana which turned on them a storm-crazed stare.

At the exact moment when they reached the porch Amanthis awoke, sat up suddenly and looked them over.

The gentleman was young, perhaps twenty-four, and his name was Jim Powell. He was dressed in a tight and dusty ready-made suit which was evidently expected to take flight at a moment's notice, for it was secured to his body by a line of six preposterous buttons.

There were supernumerary buttons upon the coat sleeves also and Amanthis could not resist a glance to determine whether or not more buttons ran up the side of his trouser leg. But the trouser bottoms were distinguished only by their shape, which was that of a bell. His vest was cut low, barely restraining an amazing necktie from fluttering in the wind.

He bowed formally, dusting his knees with a thatched straw hat. Simultaneously he smiled, half shutting his faded blue eyes and displaying white and beautifully symmetrical teeth.

"Good evenin'," he said in abandoned Georgian. "My automobile has met with an accident out yonder by your gate. I wondered if it wouldn't be too much to ask you if I could have the use of a hammer and some tacks – nails, for a little while."

Amanthis laughed. For a moment she laughed uncontrollably. Mr Jim Powell laughed, politely and appreciatively, with her. His body servant, deep in the throes of coloured adolescence, alone preserved a dignified gravity.

"I better introduce who I am, maybe," said the visitor. "My name's Powell. I'm a resident of Tarleton, Georgia. This here nigger's my boy, Hugo."

"Your *son*!" The girl stared from one to the other in wild fascination.

"No, he's my body servant, I guess you'd call it. We call a nigger a boy down yonder."

At this reference to the finer customs of his native soil the boy Hugo put his hands behind his back and looked darkly and superciliously down the lawn.

"Yas'm," he muttered, "I'm a body servant."

"Where you going in your automobile?" demanded Amanthis.

"Goin' north for the summer."

"Where to?"

The tourist waved his hand with a careless gesture as if to indicate the Adirondacks, the Thousand Islands, Newport* – but he said:

"We're tryin' New York."

"Have you ever been there before?"

"Never have. But I been to Atlanta lots of times. An' we passed through all kinds of cities this trip. Man!"

He whistled to express the enormous spectacularity of his recent travels.

"Listen," said Amanthis intently, "you better have something to eat. Tell your – your body servant to go round in back and ask the cook to send us out some sandwiches and lemonade. Or maybe you don't drink lemonade – very few people do any more."

Mr Powell by a circular motion of his finger sped Hugo on the designated mission. Then he seated himself gingerly in a rocking chair and began revolving his thatched straw hat rapidly in his hands.

"You cer'nly are mighty kind," he told her. "An' if I wanted anything stronger than lemonade I got a bottle of good old corn out in the car. I brought it along because I thought maybe I wouldn't be able to drink the whiskey they got up here."

"Listen," she said, "my name's Powell too. Amanthis Powell."

"Say, is that right?" He laughed ecstatically. "Maybe we're kin to each other. I come from mighty good people," he went on. "Pore though. I got some money because my aunt she was using it to keep her in a sanitarium and she died." He paused, presumably out of respect to his late aunt. Then he concluded with brisk nonchalance, "I ain't touched the principal but I got a lot of the income all at once so I thought I'd come north for the summer."

At this point Hugo reappeared on the veranda steps and became audible.

"White lady back there she asked me don't I want eat some too. What I tell her?"

"You tell her yes ma'am if she be so kind," directed his master. And as Hugo retired he confided to Amanthis: "That boy's got no sense at all. He don't want to do nothing without I tell him he can. I brought him up," he added, not without pride.

When the sandwiches arrived Mr Powell stood up. He was unaccustomed to white servants and obviously expected an introduction.

"Are you a married lady?" he enquired of Amanthis, when the servant was gone.

"No," she answered, and added from the security of eighteen, "I'm an old maid."

Again he laughed politely.

"You mean you're a society girl."

She shook her head. Mr Powell noted with embarrassed enthusiasm the particular yellowness of her yellow hair.

"Does this old place look like it?" she said cheerfully. "No, you perceive in me a daughter of the countryside. Colour – one hundred per cent spontaneous – in the daytime anyhow. Suitors – promising young barbers from the neighbouring village with somebody's late hair still clinging to their coat sleeves."

"Your daddy oughtn't to let you go with a country barber," said the tourist disapprovingly. He considered – "You ought to be a New York society girl."

"No." Amanthis shook her head sadly. "I'm too good-looking. To be a New York society girl you have to have a long nose and projecting teeth and dress like the actresses did three years ago."

Jim began to tap his foot rhythmically on the porch and in a moment Amanthis discovered that she was unconsciously doing the same thing.

"Stop!" she commanded. "Don't make me do that."

He looked down at his foot.

"Excuse me," he said humbly. "I don't know – it's just something I do."

This intense discussion was now interrupted by Hugo who appeared on the steps bearing a hammer and a handful of nails.

Mr Powell arose unwillingly and looked at his watch.

"We got to go, daggone it," he said, frowning heavily. "See here. Wouldn't you *like* to be a New York society girl and go to those dances an' all, like you read about, where they throw gold pieces away?"

She looked at him with a curious expression.

"Don't your folks know some society people?" he went on.

"All I've got's my daddy – and, you see, he's a judge."

"That's too bad," he agreed.

She got herself by some means from the hammock and they went down towards the road, side by side.

"Well, I'll keep my eyes open for you and let you know," he persisted. "A pretty girl like you ought to go around in society. We may be kin to each other, you see, and us Powells ought to stick together."

"What are you going to do in New York?"

They were now almost at the gate and the tourist pointed to the two depressing sectors of his automobile.

"I'm goin' to drive a taxi. This one right here. Only it's got so it busts in two all the time."

"You're going to drive *that* in New York?"

Jim looked at her uncertainly. Such a pretty girl should certainly control the habit of shaking all over upon no provocation at all.

"Yes ma'am," he said with dignity.

Amanthis watched while they placed the upper half of the car upon the lower half and nailed it severely into place. Then Mr Powell took the wheel and his body servant climbed in beside him.

"I'm cer'nly very much obliged to you indeed for your hospitality. Convey my respects to your father."

"I will," she assured him. "Come back and see me, if you don't mind barbers in the room."

He dismissed this unpleasant thought with a gesture.

"Your company would always be charming." He put the car into gear as though to drown out the temerity of his parting speech. "You're the prettiest girl I've seen up north – by far."

Then with a groan and a rattle Mr Powell of southern Georgia with his own car and his own body servant and his own ambitions and his own private cloud of dust continued on north for the summer.

She thought she would never see him again. She lay in her hammock, slim and beautiful, opened her left eye slightly to see June come in and then closed it and retired contentedly back into her dreams.

But one day when the midsummer vines had climbed the precarious sides of the red swing on the lawn, Mr Jim Powell of Tarleton, Georgia, came vibrating back into her life. They sat on the wide porch as before.

"I've got a great scheme," he told her.

"Did you drive your taxi like you said?"

"Yes ma'am, but the business was right bad. I waited around in front of all those hotels and theatres an' nobody ever got in."

"Nobody?"

"Well, one night there was some drunk fellas, they got in, only just as I was gettin' started my automobile came apart. And another night it was rainin' and there wasn't no other taxis and a lady got in because she said she had to go a long ways. But before we got there she made me stop and she got out. She seemed kinda mad and she went walkin' off in the rain. Mighty proud lot of people they got up in New York."

"And so you're going home?" asked Amanthis sympathetically.

"No *ma'am*. I got an idea." His blue eyes grew narrow. "Has that barber been around here – with hair on his sleeves?"

"No. He's – he's gone away."

"Well, then, first thing is I want to leave this car of mine here with you, if that's all right. It ain't the right colour for a taxi. To pay for its keep I'd like to have you drive it as much as you want. Long as you got a hammer an' nails with you there ain't much bad that can happen—"

"I'll take care of it," interrupted Amanthis, "but where are *you* going?"

"Southampton. It's about the most aristocratic watering trough – watering place there is around here, so that's where I'm going."

She sat up in amazement.

"What are you going to do there?"

"Listen." He leant towards her confidentially. "Were you serious about wanting to be a New York society girl?"

"Deadly serious."

"That's all I wanted to know," he said inscrutably. "You just wait here on this porch a couple of weeks and – and sleep. And if any barbers come to see you with hair on their sleeves you tell 'em you're too sleepy to see 'em."

"What then?"

"Then you'll hear from me. Just tell your old daddy he can do all the judging he wants but you're goin' to do some *dancin'*. Ma'am," he continued decisively, "you talk about society! Before one month I'm goin' to have you in more society than you ever saw."

Further than this he would say nothing. His manner conveyed that she was going to be suspended over a perfect pool of gaiety and violently immersed, to an accompaniment of: "Is it gay enough for you, ma'am? Shall I let in a little more excitement, ma'am?"

"Well," answered Amanthis, lazily considering, "there are few things for which I'd forgo the luxury of sleeping through July and August – but if you'll write me a letter I'll – I'll run up to Southampton."

Jim snapped his fingers ecstatically.

"More society," he assured her with all the confidence at his command, "than anybody ever saw."

Three days later a young man wearing a straw hat that might have been cut from the thatched roof of an English cottage rang the doorbell of the enormous and astounding Madison Harlan house at Southampton. He asked the butler if there were any people in the house between the ages of sixteen and twenty. He was informed that Miss Genevieve Harlan and Mr Ronald Harlan answered that description and thereupon he handed in a most peculiar card and requested in fetching Georgian that it be brought to their attention.

As a result he was closeted for almost an hour with Mr Ronald Harlan (who was a student at the Hillkiss School) and Miss Genevieve Harlan (who was not uncelebrated at Southampton dances). When he left he bore a short note in Miss Harlan's handwriting which he presented together with his peculiar card at the next large estate. It happened to be that of the Clifton Garneaus. Here, as if by magic, the same audience was granted him.

He went on – it was a hot day, and men who could not afford to do so were carrying their coats on the public highway, but Jim, a native of southernmost Georgia, was as fresh and cool at the last house as at the first. He visited ten houses that day. Anyone following him in his course might have taken him to be some curiously gifted book agent with a much sought-after volume as his stock-in-trade.

There was something in his unexpected demand for the adolescent members of the family which made hardened butlers lose their critical acumen. As he left each house a close observer might have seen that fascinated eyes followed him to the door and excited voices whispered something which hinted at a future meeting.

The second day he visited twelve houses. Southampton has grown enormously – he might have kept on his round for a week and never seen the same butler twice – but it was only the palatial, the amazing houses which intrigued him.

On the third day he did a thing that many people have been told to do and few have done – he hired a hall. Perhaps the sixteen-to-twenty-year-old people in the enormous houses had told him to. The hall he hired had once been "Mr Snorkey's Private Gymnasium for Gentlemen". It was situated over a garage on the south edge of Southampton and in the days of its prosperity had been, I regret to say, a place where gentlemen could, under Mr Snorkey's direction, work off the effects of the night before. It was now abandoned – Mr Snorkey had given up and gone away and died.

We will now skip three weeks during which time we may assume that the project which had to do with hiring a hall and visiting the two dozen largest houses in Southampton got under way.

The day to which we will skip was the July day on which Mr James Powell sent a wire to Miss Amanthis Powell saying that if she still aspired to the gaiety of the highest society she should set out for Southampton by the earliest possible train. He himself would meet her at the station.

Jim was no longer a man of leisure, so when she failed to arrive at the time her wire had promised he grew restless. He supposed she was coming on a later train, turned to go back to his – his project – and met her entering the station from the street side.

"Why, how did you—"

"Well," said Amanthis, "I arrived this morning instead, and I didn't want to bother you so I found a respectable, not to say dull, boarding house on the Ocean Road."

She was quite different from the indolent Amanthis of the porch ham-mock, he thought. She wore a suit of robin's-egg blue and a rakish young hat with a curling feather – she was attired not unlike those young ladies between sixteen and twenty who of late were absorbing his attention. Yes, she would do very well.

He bowed her profoundly into a taxicab and got in beside her.

"Isn't it about time you told me your scheme?" she suggested.

"Well, it's about these society girls up here." He waved his hand airily. "I know 'em all."

"Where are they?"

"Right now they're with Hugo. You remember – that's my body servant."

"With Hugo!" Her eyes widened. "Why? What's it all about?"

"Well, I got – I got sort of a school, I guess you'd call it."

"A school?"

"It's a sort of academy. And I'm the head of it. I invented it."

He flipped a card from his case as though he were shaking down a thermometer.

"Look."

She took the card. In large lettering it bore the legend

JAMES POWELL, JM
Dice, Brassknuckles and Guitar

She stared in amazement.

"Dice, Brassknuckles and Guitar?" she repeated in awe.

"Yes ma'am."

"What does it mean? What – do you *sell* 'em?"

"No ma'am, I teach 'em. It's a profession."

"Dice, Brassknuckles and Guitar? What's the JM?"

"That stands for Jazz Master."

"But what *is* it? What's it about?"

"Well, you see, it's like this. One night when I was in New York I got talkin' to a young fella who was drunk. He was one of my fares. And he'd taken some society girl somewhere and lost her."

"*Lost* her?"

"Yes ma'am. He forgot her, I guess. And he was right worried. Well, I got to thinkin' that these girls nowadays – these society girls – they lead a sort of dangerous life and my course of study offers a means of protection against these dangers."

"You teach 'em to use brassknuckles?"

"Yes, ma'am, if necessary. Look here, you take a girl and she goes into some cafe where she's got no business to go. Well then, her escort he gets a little too much to drink an' he goes to sleep an' then some other fella comes up and says, 'Hello, sweet mamma,' or whatever one of those mashers says up here. What does she do? She can't scream, on account of no real lady'll scream nowadays – no – She just reaches down in her pocket and slips her fingers into a pair of Powell's defensive brassknuckles, debutante's size, executes what I call the Society Hook, and *Wham!* that big fella's on his way to the cellar."

"Well – what – what's the guitar for?" whispered the awed Amanthis. "Do they have to knock somebody over with the guitar?"

"No, *ma'am*!" exclaimed Jim in horror. "No, ma'am. In my course no lady would be taught to raise a guitar against anybody. I teach 'em to play. Shucks! You ought to hear 'em. Why, when I've given 'em two lessons you'd think some of 'em was coloured."

"And the dice?"

"Dice? I'm related to a dice. My grandfather was a dice. I teach 'em how to make those dice perform. I protect pocketbook as well as person."

"Did you… Have you got any pupils?"

"Ma'am, I got all the really nice, rich people in the place. What I told you ain't all. I teach lots of things. I teach 'em the jellyroll – and the Mississippi Sunrise. Why, there was one girl she came to me and said she wanted to learn to snap her fingers. I mean *really* snap 'em – like they do. She said she never could snap her fingers since she was little. I gave her two lessons and now *Wham!* Her daddy says he's goin' to leave home."

"When do you have it?" demanded the weak and shaken Amanthis.

"Three times a week. We're goin' there right now."

"And where do I fit in?"

"Well, you'll just be one of the pupils. I got it fixed up that you come from very high-tone people down in New Jersey. I didn't tell 'em your daddy was a judge – I told 'em he was the man that had the patent on lump sugar."

She gasped.

"So all you got to do," he went on, "is to pretend you never saw no barber."

They were now at the south end of the village and Amanthis saw a row of cars parked in front of a two-storey building. The cars were all low, long, rakish and of a brilliant hue. They were the sort of car that is manufactured to solve the millionaire's problem on his son's eighteenth birthday.

Then Amanthis was ascending a narrow stairs to the second storey. Here, painted on a door from which came the sounds of music and laughter were the words:

JAMES POWELL, JM
Dice, Brassknuckles and Guitar
Mon. – Wed. – Fri.
Hours 3–5 p.m.

"Now if you'll just step this way…" said the Principal, pushing open the door.

Amanthis found herself in a long, bright room, populated with girls and men of about her own age. The scene presented itself to her at first as a sort of animated afternoon tea but after a moment she began to see, here and there, a motive and a pattern to the proceedings.

The students were scattered into groups, sitting, kneeling, standing, but all rapaciously intent on the subjects which engrossed them. From six young ladies gathered in a ring around some indistinguishable objects came a medley of cries and exclamations – plaintive, pleading, supplicating, exhorting, imploring and lamenting – their voices serving as tenor to an undertone of mysterious clatters.

Next to this group, four young men were surrounding an adolescent black, who proved to be none other than Mr Powell's late body servant.

The young men were roaring at Hugo apparently unrelated phrases, expressing a wide gamut of emotion. Now their voices rose to a sort of clamour, now they spoke softly and gently, with mellow implication. Every little while Hugo would answer them with words of approbation, correction or disapproval.

"What are they doing?" whispered Amanthis to Jim.

"That there's a course in Southern accent. Lot of young men up here want to learn Southern accent – so we teach it – Georgia, Florida, Alabama, Eastern Shore, Ole Virginian. Some of 'em even want straight nigger – for song purposes."

They walked around among the groups. Some girls with metal knuckles were furiously insulting two punching bags on each of which was painted the leering, winking face of a "masher". A mixed group, led by a banjo tom-tom, were rolling harmonic syllables from their guitars. There were couples dancing flat-footed in the corner to a phonograph record made by Rastus Muldoon's Savannah Band; there were couples stalking a slow Chicago with a Memphis Side Swoop solemnly around the room.

"Are there any rules?" asked Amanthis.

Jim considered.

"Well," he answered finally, "they can't smoke unless they're over sixteen, and the boys have got to shoot square dice and I don't let 'em bring liquor into the academy."

"I see."

"And now, Miss Powell, if you're ready I'll ask you to take off your hat and go over and join Miss Genevieve Harlan at that punching bag in the corner." He raised his voice. "Hugo," he called, "there's a new student here. Equip her with a pair of Powell's Defensive Brassknuckles – debutante size."

I regret to say that I never saw Jim Powell's famous Jazz School in action nor followed his personally conducted tours into the mysteries of Dice, Brassknuckles and Guitar. So I can give you only such details as were later reported to me by one of his admiring pupils. During all the discussion of it afterwards no one ever denied that it was an enormous success, and no pupil ever regretted having received its degree – Bachelor of Jazz.

The parents innocently assumed that it was a sort of musical and dancing academy, but its real curriculum was transmitted from Santa Barbara to Biddeford Pool by that underground associated press which links up the so-called younger generation. Invitations to visit Southampton were at a premium – and Southampton generally is almost as dull for young people as Newport.

The academy branched out with a small but well-groomed Jazz Orchestra.

"If I could keep it dark," Jim confided to Amanthis, "I'd have up Rastus Muldoon's Band from Savannah. That's the band I've always wanted to lead."

He was making money. His charges were not exorbitant – as a rule his pupils were not particularly flush – but he moved from his boarding house to the Casino Hotel where he took a suite and had Hugo serve him his breakfast in bed.

The establishing of Amanthis as a member of Southampton's younger set was easier than he had expected. Within a week she was known to everyone in the school by her first name. Miss Genevieve Harlan took such a fancy to her that she was invited to a sub-deb dance* at the Harlan house – and evidently acquitted herself with tact, for thereafter she was invited to almost every such entertainment in Southampton.

Jim saw less of her than he would have liked. Not that her manner towards him changed – she walked with him often in the mornings, she was always willing to listen to his plans – but after she was taken up by the fashionable her evenings seemed to be monopolized. Several times Jim arrived at her boarding house to find her out of breath, as if she had just come in at a run, presumably from some festivity in which he had no share.

So as the summer waned he found that one thing was lacking to complete the triumph of his enterprise. Despite the hospitality shown to Amanthis, the doors of Southampton were closed to him. Polite to, or rather fascinated by him as his pupils were from three to five, after that hour they moved in another world.

His was the position of a golf professional who, though he may fraternize, and even command, on the links, loses his privileges with the sundown. He may look in the club window but he cannot dance. And, likewise, it was not given to Jim to see his teachings put into effect. He could hear the gossip of the morning after – that was all.

But while the golf professional, being English, holds himself proudly below his patrons, Jim Powell, who "came from a right good family down there – pore though", lay awake many nights in his hotel bed and heard the music drifting into his window from the Katzbys' house or the Beach Club, and turned over restlessly and wondered what was the matter. In the early days of his success he had bought himself a dress suit, thinking that he would soon have a chance to wear it – but it still lay untouched in the box in which it had come from the tailor's.

Perhaps, he thought, there was some real gap which separated him from the rest. It worried him. One boy in particular, Martin Van Vleck, son of Van Vleck the ashcan king, made him conscious of the gap. Van Vleck was twenty-one, a tutoring school product who still hoped to enter Yale. Several times Jim had heard him make remarks not intended for Jim's ears – once in regard to the suit with multiple buttons, again in reference to Jim's long, pointed shoes. Jim had passed these over.

He knew that Van Vleck was attending the school chiefly to monopolize the time of little Martha Katzby, who was just sixteen and too young to have attention of a boy of twenty-one – especially the attention of Van Vleck, who was so spiritually exhausted by his educational failures that he drew on the rather exhaustible innocence of sixteen.

It was late in September, two days before the Harlan dance which was to be the last and biggest of the season for this younger crowd. Jim, as usual, was not invited. He had hoped that he would be. The two young Harlans, Ronald and Genevieve, had been his first patrons when he arrived at Southampton – and it was Genevieve who had taken such a fancy to Amanthis. To have been at their dance – the most magnificent dance of all – would have crowned and justified the success of the waning summer.

His class, gathering for the afternoon, was loudly anticipating the next day's revel with no more thought of him than if he had been the family butler. Hugo, standing beside Jim, chuckled suddenly and remarked:

"Look yonder that man Van Vleck. He paralysed. He been havin' powerful lotta corn this evenin'."

Jim turned and stared at Van Vleck, who had linked arms with little Martha Katzby and was saying something to her in a low voice. Jim saw her try to draw away.

He put his whistle to his mouth and blew it.

"All right," he cried. " Le's go! Group one tossin' the drumstick, high an' zigzag, group two, test your mouth organs for the Riverfront Shuffle. Promise 'em sugar! Flatfoots this way! Orchestra – let's have the Florida Drag-out played as a dirge."

There was an unaccustomed sharpness in his voice and the exercises began with a mutter of facetious protest.

With his smouldering grievance directing itself towards Van Vleck, Jim was walking here and there among the groups when Hugo tapped him suddenly on the arm. He looked around. Two participants had withdrawn from the mouth-organ institute – one of them was Van Vleck and he was giving a drink out of his flask to fifteen-year-old Ronald Harlan.

Jim strode across the room. Van Vleck turned defiantly as he came up.

"All right," said Jim, trembling with anger, "you know the rules. You get out!"

The music died slowly away and there was a sudden drifting over in the direction of the trouble. Somebody snickered. An atmosphere of anticipation formed instantly. Despite the fact that they all liked Jim their sympathies were divided – Van Vleck was one of them.

"Get out!" repeated Jim, more quietly.

"Are you talking to me?" enquired Van Vleck coldly.

"Yes."

"Then you better say 'sir'."

"I wouldn't say 'sir' to anybody that'd give a little boy whiskey! You get out!"

"Look here!" said Van Vleck furiously. "You've butted in once too much. I've known Ronald since he was two years old. Ask *him* if he wants *you* to tell him what he can do!"

Ronald Harlan, his dignity offended, grew several years older and looked haughtily at Jim.

"Mind your own business!" he said defiantly, albeit a little guiltily.

"Hear that?" demanded Van Vleck. "My God, can't you see you're just a servant? Ronald here'd no more think of asking you to his party than he would his bootlegger."

"You better get out!" cried Jim incoherently.

Van Vleck did not move. Reaching out suddenly, Jim caught his wrist and jerking it behind his back forced his arm upward until Van Vleck bent forward in agony. Jim leant and picked the flask from the floor with his free hand. Then he signed Hugo to open the hall door, uttered an abrupt "You *step*!" and marched his helpless captive out into the hall where he literally *threw* him downstairs, head over heels bumping from wall to banister, and hurled his flask after him.

Then he re-entered his academy, closed the door behind him and stood with his back against it.

"It – it happens to be a rule that nobody drinks while in this academy." He paused, looking from face to face, finding there sympathy, awe, disapproval, conflicting emotions. They stirred uneasily. He caught Amanthis's eye, fancied he saw a faint nod of encouragement and, with almost an effort, went on:

"I just *had* to throw that fella out an' you-all know it." Then he concluded with a transparent affectation of dismissing an unimportant matter: "All right, let's go! Orchestra!…"

But no one felt exactly like going on. The spontaneity of the proceedings had been violently disturbed. Someone made a run or two on the sliding guitar and several of the girls began whamming at the leer on the punching bags, but Ronald Harlan, followed by two other boys, got their hats and went silently out the door.

Jim and Hugo moved among the groups as usual until a certain measure of routine activity was restored but the enthusiasm was unrecapturable and Jim, shaken and discouraged, considered discontinuing school for the day. But he dared not. If they went home in this mood they might not come back. The whole thing depended on a mood. He must recreate it, he thought frantically – now, at once!

But try as he might, there was little response. He himself was not happy – he could communicate no gaiety to them. They watched his efforts listlessly and, he thought, a little contemptuously.

Then the tension snapped when the door burst suddenly open, precipitating a brace of middle-aged and excited women into the room. No person over twenty-one had ever entered the academy before – but Van Vleck had gone direct to headquarters. The women were Mrs Clifton Garneau and Mrs Poindexter Katzby, two of the most fashionable and, at present, two of the most flurried women in Southampton. They were in search of their daughters as, in these days, so many women continually are.

The business was over in about three minutes.

"And as for you!" cried Mrs Clifton Garneau in an awful voice. "Your idea is to run a bar and – and *opium* den for children! You ghastly, horrible, unspeakable man! I can smell morphin fumes! Don't tell me I can't smell morphin fumes. I can smell morphin fumes!"

"And," bellowed Mrs Poindexter Katzby, "you have coloured men around! You have coloured girls hidden! I'm going to the police!"

Not content with herding their own daughters from the room, they insisted on the exodus of their friends' daughters. Jim was not a little touched when several of them – including even little Martha Katzby, before she was snatched fiercely away by her mother – came up and shook hands with him. But they were all going, haughtily, regretfully or with shamefaced mutters of apology.

"Goodbye," he told them wistfully. "In the morning I'll send you the money that's due you."

And, after all, they were not sorry to go. Outside, the sounds of their starting motors, the triumphant *put-put* of their cut-outs cutting the warm September air, was a jubilant sound – a sound of youth and hopes high as the sun. Down to the ocean, to roll in the waves and forget – forget him and their discomfort at his humiliation.

They were gone – he was alone with Hugo in the room. He sat down suddenly with his face in his hands.

"Hugo," he said huskily. "They don't want us up here."

"Don't you care," said a voice.

He looked up to see Amanthis standing beside him.

"You better go with them," he told her. "You better not be seen here with me."

"Why?"

"Because you're in society now and I'm no better to those people than a servant. You're in society – I fixed that up. You better go or they won't invite you to any of their dances."

"They won't anyhow, Jim," she said gently. "They didn't invite me to the one tomorrow night."

He looked up indignantly.

"They *did*n't?"

She shook her head.

"I'll *make* 'em!" he said wildly. "I'll tell 'em they got to. I'll – I'll…"

She came close to him with shining eyes.

"Don't you mind, Jim," she soothed him. "Don't you mind. They don't matter. We'll have a party of our own tomorrow – just you and I."

"I come from right good folks," he said defiantly. "Pore though."

She laid her hand softly on his shoulder.

"I understand. You're better than all of them put together, Jim."

He got up and went to the window and stared out mournfully into the late afternoon.

"I reckon I should have let you sleep in that hammock."

She laughed.

"I'm awfully glad you didn't."

He turned and faced the room, and his face was dark.

"Sweep up and lock up, Hugo," he said, his voice trembling. "The summer's over and we're going down home."

Autumn had come early. Jim Powell woke next morning to find his room cool, and the phenomenon of frosted breath in September absorbed him for a moment to the exclusion of the day before. Then the lines of his face drooped with unhappiness as he remembered the humiliation which had washed the cheery glitter from the summer. There was nothing left for him except to go back where he was known, where under no provocation were such things said to white people as had been said to him here.

After breakfast a measure of his customary light-heartedness returned. He was a child of the South – brooding was alien to his nature. He could conjure up an injury only a certain number of times before it faded into the great vacancy of the past.

But when, from force of habit, he strolled over to his defunct establishment, already as obsolete as Snorkey's late sanatorium, melancholy again dwelt in his heart. Hugo was there, a spectre of despair, deep in the lugubrious blues amidst his master's broken hopes.

Usually a few words from Jim were enough to raise him to an inarticulate ecstasy, but this morning there were no words to utter. For two months Hugo had lived on a pinnacle of which he had never dreamt. He had enjoyed his work simply and passionately, arriving before school hours and lingering long after Mr Powell's pupils had gone.

The day dragged towards a not-too-promising night. Amanthis did not appear and Jim wondered forlornly if she had not changed her mind about dining with him that night. Perhaps it would be better if she were not seen with them. But then, he reflected dismally, no one would see them anyhow – everybody was going to the big dance at the Harlans' house.

When twilight threw unbearable shadows into the school hall he locked it up for the last time, took down the sign "James Powell, JM, Dice, Brassknuckles and Guitar", and went back to his hotel. Looking over his scrawled accounts he saw that there was another month's rent to pay on his school and some bills for windows broken and new equipment that had hardly been used. Jim had lived in state, and he realized that financially he would have nothing to show for the summer after all.

When he had finished he took his new dress suit out of its box and inspected it, running his hand over the satin of the lapels and lining. This, at least, he owned and perhaps in Tarleton somebody would ask him to a party where he could wear it.

"Shucks!" he said scoffingly. "It was just a no-account old academy, anyhow. Some of those boys round the garage down home could of beat it all hollow."

Whistling 'Jeanne of Jelly-bean Town' to a not-dispirited rhythm Jim encased himself in his first dress suit and walked downtown.

"Orchids," he said to the clerk. He surveyed his purchase with some pride. He knew that no girl at the Harlan dance would wear anything lovelier than these exotic blossoms that leant languorously backwards against green ferns.

In a taxicab, carefully selected to look like a private car, he drove to Amanthis's boarding house. She came down wearing a rose-coloured evening dress into which the orchids melted like colours into a sunset.

"I reckon we'll go to the Casino Hotel," he suggested, "unless you got some other place…"

At their table, looking out over the dark ocean, his mood became a contented sadness. The windows were shut against the cool but the orchestra played 'Kalula' and 'South Sea Moon' and for a while, with her young loveliness opposite him, he felt himself to be a romantic participant in the life around him. They did not dance, and he was glad – it would have reminded him of that other brighter and more radiant dance to which they could not go.

After dinner they took a taxi and followed the sandy roads for an hour, glimpsing the now starry ocean through the casual trees.

"I want to thank you," she said, "for all you've done for me, Jim."

"That's all right – we Powells ought to stick together."

"What are you going to do?"

"I'm going to Tarleton tomorrow."

"I'm sorry," she said softly. "Are you going to drive down?"

"I got to. I got to get the car south because I couldn't get what she was worth by sellin' it. You don't suppose anybody's stole my car out of your barn?" he asked in sudden alarm.

She repressed a smile.

"No."

"I'm sorry about this – about you," he went on huskily, "and – and I would like to have gone to just one of their dances. You shouldn't of stayed with me yesterday. Maybe it kept 'em from asking you."

"Jim," she suggested eagerly, "let's go and stand outside and listen to their old music. We don't care."

"They'll be coming out," he objected.

"No, it's too cold. Besides there's nothing they could do to you any more than they *have* done."

She gave the chauffeur a direction and a few minutes later they stopped in front of the heavy Georgian beauty of the Madison Harlan house whence the windows cast their gaiety in bright patches on the lawn.

There was laughter inside and the plaintive wind of fashionable horns, and now and again the slow, mysterious shuffle of dancing feet.

"Let's go up close," whispered Amanthis in an ecstatic trance, "I want to hear."

They walked towards the house, keeping in the shadow of the great trees. Jim proceeded with awe – suddenly he stopped and seized Amanthis's arm.

"Man!" he cried in an excited whisper. "Do you know what that is?"

"A nightwatchman?" Amanthis cast a startled look around.

"It's Rastus Muldoon's Band from Savannah! I heard 'em once, and I *know*. It's Rastus Muldoon's Band!"

They moved closer till they could see first pompadours, then slicked male heads and high coiffures and finally even bobbed hair pressed under black ties. They could distinguish chatter below the ceaseless laughter. Two figures appeared on the porch, gulped something quickly from flasks and returned inside. But the music had bewitched Jim Powell. His eyes were fixed and he moved his feet like a blind man.

Pressed in close behind some dark bushes they listened. The number ended. A breeze from the ocean blew over them and Jim shivered slightly. Then, in a wistful whisper:

"I've always wanted to lead that band. Just once." His voice grew listless. "Come on. Let's go. I reckon I don't belong around here."

He held out his arm to her but instead of taking it she stepped suddenly out of the bushes and into a bright patch of light.

"Come on, Jim," she said startlingly. "Let's go inside."

"What?…"

She seized his arm and though he drew back in a sort of stupefied horror at her boldness she urged him persistently towards the great front door.

"Watch out!" he gasped. "Somebody's coming out of that house and see us."

"No, Jim," she said firmly. "Nobody's coming out of that house – but two people are going in."

"Why?" he demanded wildly, standing in full glare of the porte-cochère* lamps. "Why?"

"Why?" she mocked him. "Why, just because this dance happens to be given for me."

He thought she was mad.

The great doors swung open and a gentleman stepped out on the porch. In horror Jim recognized Mr Madison Harlan. He made a movement as though to break away and run. But the man walked down the steps holding out both hands to Amanthis.

"Hello at last," he cried. "Where on earth have you two been? Cousin Amanthis—" He kissed her, and turned cordially to Jim. "And for you, Mr Powell," he went on, "to make up for being late you've got to promise that for just one number you're going to lead that band."

New Jersey was warm, all except the part that was under water, and that mattered only to the fishes. All the tourists who rode through the long green miles stopped their cars in front of a spreading old-fashioned country house and looked at the red swing on the lawn and the wide shady porch, and sighed and drove on – swerving a little to avoid a jet-black body servant in the road. The body servant was applying a hammer and nails to a decayed flivver which flaunted from its rear the legend, "Tarleton, Ga."

A girl with yellow hair and a warm colour to her face was lying in the hammock looking as though she could fall asleep any moment. Near her sat a gentleman in an extraordinarily tight suit. They had come down together the day before from the fashionable resort at Southampton.

"When you first appeared," she was explaining, "I never thought I'd see you again so I made that up about the barber and all. As a matter of fact, I've been around quite a bit – with or without brassknuckles. I'm coming out this autumn."

"I reckon I had a lot to learn," said Jim.

"And you see," went on Amanthis, looking at him rather anxiously, "I'd been invited up to Southampton to visit my cousins – and when you said you were going, I wanted to see what you'd do. I always slept at the Harlans' but I kept a room at the boarding house so you wouldn't know. The reason I didn't get there on the right train was because I had to come early and warn a lot of people to pretend not to know me."

Jim got up, nodding his head in comprehension.

"I reckon I and Hugo had better be movin' along. We got to make Baltimore by night."

"That's a long way."

"I want to sleep south tonight," he said simply.

Together they walked down the path and past the idiotic statue of Diana on the lawn.

"You see," added Amanthis gently, "you don't have to be rich up here in order to – to go around, any more than you do in Georgia…" She broke off abruptly. "Won't you come back next year and start another academy?"

"No ma'am, not me. That Mr Harlan told me I could go on with the one I had but I told him no."

"Haven't you – didn't you make money?"

"No ma'am," he answered. "I got enough of my own income to just get me home. I didn't have my principal long. One time I was way ahead but I was livin' high and there was my rent an' apparatus and those musicians. Besides, there at the end I had to pay what they'd advanced me for their lessons."

"You shouldn't have done that!" cried Amanthis indignantly.

"They didn't want me to, but I told 'em they'd have to take it."

He didn't consider it necessary to mention that Mr Harlan had tried to present him with a cheque.

They reached the automobile just as Hugo drove in his last nail. Jim opened a pocket of the door and took from it an unlabelled bottle containing a whitish-yellow liquid.

"I intended to get you a present," he told her awkwardly, "but my money got away before I could, so I thought I'd send you something from Georgia. This here's just a personal remembrance. It won't do for you to drink but maybe after you come out into society you might want to show some of those young fellas what good old corn tastes like."

She took the bottle.

"Thank you, Jim."

"That's all right." He turned to Hugo. "I reckon we'll go along now. Give the lady the hammer."

"Oh, you can have the hammer," said Amanthis tearfully. "Oh, won't you promise to come back?"

"Someday – maybe."

He looked for a moment at her yellow hair and her blue eyes misty with sleep and tears. Then he got into his car and as his foot found the clutch his whole manner underwent a change.

"I'll say goodbye, ma'am," he announced with impressive dignity, "we're going south for the winter."

The gesture of his straw hat indicated Palm Beach, St Augustine, Miami. His body servant spun the crank, gained his seat and became part of the intense vibration into which the automobile was thrown.

"South for the winter," repeated Jim, and then he added softly, "You're the prettiest girl I ever knew. You go back up there and lie down in that hammock, and sleep – sle-eep…"

It was almost a lullaby, as he said it. He bowed to her, magnificently, profoundly, including the whole North in the splendour of his obeisance—

Then they were gone down the road in quite a preposterous cloud of dust. Just before they reached the first bend Amanthis saw them come to a full stop, dismount and shove the top part of the car onto the bottom part. They took their seats again without looking around. Then the bend – and they were out of sight, leaving only a faint brown mist to show that they had passed.

Diamond Dick and the
First Law of Woman

W HEN DIANA DICKEY came back from France in the spring of
1919, her parents considered that she had atoned for her nefari-
ous past. She had served a year in the Red Cross and she was presumably
engaged to a young American ace of position and charm. They could
ask no more; of Diana's former sins only her nickname survived:

Diamond Dick!* – she had selected it herself, of all the names in the
world, when she was a thin, black-eyed child of ten.

"Diamond Dick," she would insist, "that's my name. Anybody that
won't call me that's a double darn fool."

"But that's not a nice name for a little lady," objected her governess.
"If you want to have a boy's name why don't you call yourself George
Washington?"

"Be-cause my name's Diamond Dick," explained Diana patiently.
"Can't you understand? I got to be named that be-cause if I don't I'll
have a fit and upset the family, see?"

She ended by having the fit – a fine frenzy that brought a disgusted
nerve specialist out from New York – and the nickname too. And once
in possession she set about modelling her facial expression on that of
a butcher boy who delivered meats at Greenwich back doors. She stuck
out her lower jaw and parted her lips on one side, exposing sections of
her first teeth – and from this alarming aperture there issued the harsh
voice of one far gone in crime.

"Miss Caruthers," she would sneer crisply, "what's the idea of no
jam? Do you wanta whack the side of the head?"

"*Diana!* I'm going to call your mother *this minute!*"

"Look at here!" threatened Diana darkly. "If you call her you're liable
to get a bullet the side of the head."

Miss Caruthers raised her hand uneasily to her bangs. She was somewhat awed.

"Very well," she said uncertainly, "if you want to act like a little ragamuffin…"

Diana did want to. The evolutions which she practised daily on the sidewalk and which were thought by the neighbours to be some new form of hopscotch were in reality the preliminary work on an apache slouch.* When it was perfected, Diana lurched forth into the streets of Greenwich, her face violently distorted and half obliterated by her father's slouch hat, her body reeling from side to side, jerked hither and yon by the shoulders, until to look at her long was to feel a faint dizziness rising to the brain.

At first it was merely absurd, but when Diana's conversation commenced to glow with weird rococo phrases, which she imagined to be the dialect of the underworld, it became alarming. And a few years later she further complicated the problem by turning into a beauty – a dark little beauty with tragedy eyes and a rich voice stirring in her throat.

Then America entered the war and Diana on her eighteenth birthday sailed with a canteen unit to France.

The past was over; all was forgotten. Just before the armistice was signed, she was cited in orders for coolness under fire. And – this was the part that particularly pleased her mother – it was rumoured that she was engaged to be married to Mr Charley Abbot of Boston and Bar Harbor, "a young aviator of position and charm".

But Mrs Dickey was scarcely prepared for the changed Diana who landed in New York. Seated in the limousine bound for Greenwich, she turned to her daughter with astonishment in her eyes.

"Why, everybody's proud of you, Diana," she cried, "the house is simply bursting with flowers. Think of all you've seen and done, at *nineteen*!"

Diana's face, under an incomparable saffron hat, stared out into Fifth Avenue, gay with banners for the returning divisions.

"The war's over," she said in a curious voice, as if it had just occurred to her this minute.

"Yes," agreed her mother cheerfully, "and we won. I knew we would all the time."

She wondered how to best introduce the subject of Mr Abbot.

"You're quieter," she began tentatively. "You look as if you were more ready to settle down."

"I want to come out this fall."

"But I thought..." Mrs Dickey stopped and coughed – "Rumours had led me to believe..."

"Well, go on, Mother. What did you hear?"

"It came to my ears that you were engaged to that young Charles Abbot."

Diana did not answer and her mother licked nervously at her veil. The silence in the car became oppressive. Mrs Dickey had always stood somewhat in awe of Diana – and she began to wonder if she had gone too far.

"The Abbots are such nice people in Boston," she ventured uneasily. "I've met his mother several times – she told me how devoted—"

"Mother!" Diana's voice, cold as ice, broke in upon her loquacious dream. "I don't care what you heard or where you heard it, but I'm not engaged to Charley Abbot. And please don't ever mention the subject to me again."

In November, Diana made her debut in the ballroom of the Ritz. There was a touch of irony in this "introduction to life" – for at nineteen Diana had seen more of reality, of courage and terror and pain, than all the pompous dowagers who peopled the artificial world.

But she was young and the artificial world was redolent of orchids and pleasant, cheerful snobbery and orchestras which set the rhythm of the year, summing up the sadness and suggestiveness of life in new tunes. All night the saxophones wailed the hopeless comment of the 'Beale Street Blues',* while five hundred pairs of gold and silver slippers shuffled the shining dust. At the grey tea hour there were always rooms that throbbed incessantly with this low sweet fever, while fresh faces drifted here and there like rose petals blown by the sad horns around the floor.

In the centre of this twilight universe Diana moved with the season, keeping half a dozen dates a day with half a dozen men, drowsing asleep at dawn with the beads and chiffon of an evening dress tangled among dying orchids on the floor beside her bed.

The year melted into summer. The flapper craze startled New York, and skirts went absurdly high and the sad orchestras played new tunes.

For a while Diana's beauty seemed to embody this new fashion as once it had seemed to embody the higher excitement of the war; but it was noticeable that she encouraged no lovers, that for all her popularity her name never became identified with that of any one man. She had had a hundred "chances", but when she felt that an interest was becoming an infatuation she was at pains to end it once and for all.

A second year dissolved into long dancing nights and swimming trips to the warm South. The flapper movement scattered to the winds and was forgotten; skirts tumbled precipitously to the floor and there were fresh songs from the saxophones for a new crop of girls. Most of those with whom she had come out were married now – some of them had babies. But Diana, in a changing world, danced on to newer tunes.

With a third year it was hard to look at her fresh and lovely face and realize that she had once been in the war. To the young generation it was already a shadowy event that had absorbed their older brothers in the dim past – ages ago. And Diana felt that when its last echoes had finally died away her youth, too, would be over. It was only occasionally now that anyone called her "Diamond Dick". When it happened, as it did sometimes, a curious puzzled expression would come into her eyes as though she could never connect the two pieces of her life that were broken sharply asunder.

Then, when five years had passed, a brokerage house failed in Boston and Charley Abbot, the war hero, came back from Paris, wrecked and broken by drink and with scarcely a penny to his name.

Diana saw him first at the Restaurant Mont Mihiel, sitting at a side table with a plump, indiscriminate blonde from the half-world. She excused herself unceremoniously to her escort and made her way towards him. He looked up as she approached and she felt a sudden faintness, for he was worn to a shadow and his eyes, large and dark like her own, were burning in red rims of fire.

"Why, Charley…"

He got drunkenly to his feet and they shook hands in a dazed way. He murmured an introduction, but the girl at the table evinced her displeasure at the meeting by glaring at Diana with cold blue eyes.

"Why, Charley…" said Diana again, "you've come home, haven't you."

"I'm here for good."

"I want to see you, Charley. I – want to see you as soon as possible. Will you come out to the country tomorrow?"

"Tomorrow?" He glanced with an apologetic expression at the blonde girl. "I've got a date. Don't know about tomorrow. Maybe later in the week—"

"Break your date."

His companion had been drumming with her fingers on the cloth and looking restlessly around the room. At this remark she wheeled sharply back to the table.

"Charley," she ejaculated, with a significant frown.

"Yes, I know," he said to her cheerfully, and turned to Diana. "I can't make it tomorrow. I've got a date."

"It's absolutely necessary that I see you tomorrow," went on Diana ruthlessly. "Stop looking at me in that idiotic way and say you'll come out to Greenwich."

"What's the idea?" cried the other girl in a slightly raised voice. "Why don't you stay at your own table? You must be tight."

"Now Elaine!" said Charley, turning to her reprovingly.

"I'll meet the train that gets to Greenwich at six," Diana went on coolly. "If you can't get rid of this – this woman" – she indicated his companion with a careless wave of her hand – "send her to the movies."

With an exclamation the other girl got to her feet and for a moment a scene was imminent. But nodding to Charley, Diana turned from the table, beckoned to her escort across the room and left the cafe.

"I don't like her," cried Elaine querulously when Diana was out of hearing. "Who is she anyhow? Some old girl of yours?"

"That's right," he answered, frowning. "Old girl of mine. In fact, my only old girl."

"Oh, you've known her all your life."

"No." He shook his head. "When I first met her she was a canteen worker in the war."

"*She* was!" Elaine raised her brows in surprise. "Why she doesn't look—"

"Oh, she's not nineteen any more – she's nearly twenty-five." He laughed.

"I saw her sitting on a box at an ammunition dump near Soissons one day with enough lieutenants around her to officer a regiment. Three weeks after that we were engaged!"

"Then what?" demanded Elaine sharply.

"Usual thing," he answered with a touch of bitterness. "She broke it off. Only unusual part of it was that I never knew why. Said goodbye to her one day and left for my squadron. I must have said something or done something then that started the big fuss. I'll never know. In fact I don't remember anything about it very clearly because a few hours later I had a crash and what happened just before has always been damn dim in my head. As soon as I was well enough to care about anything I saw that the situation was changed. Thought at first that there must be another man."

"Did she break the engagement?"

"She cer'nly did. While I was getting better she used to sit by my bed for hours looking at me with the funniest expression in her eyes. Finally I asked for a mirror – I thought I must be all cut up or something. But I wasn't. Then one day she began to cry. She said she'd been thinking it over and perhaps it was a mistake and all that sort of thing. Seemed to be referring to some quarrel we'd had when we said goodbye just before I got hurt. But I was still a pretty sick man and the whole thing didn't seem to make any sense unless there was another man in it somewhere. She said that we both wanted our freedom, and then she looked at me as if she expected me to make some explanation or apology – and I couldn't think what I'd done. I remember leaning back in the bed and wishing I could die right then and there. Two months later I heard she'd sailed for home."

Elaine leant anxiously over the table.

"Don't go to the country with her, Charley," she said. "Please don't go. She wants you back – I can tell by looking at her."

He shook his head and laughed.

"Yes she does," insisted Elaine, "I can tell. I hate her. She had you once and now she wants you back. I can see it in her eyes. I wish you'd stay in New York with me."

"No," he said stubbornly. "Going out and look her over. Diamond Dick's an old girl of mine."

Diana was standing on the station platform in the late afternoon, drenched with golden light. In the face of her immaculate freshness Charley Abbot felt ragged and old. He was only twenty-nine, but four wild years had left many lines around his dark, handsome eyes. Even his walk was tired – it was no longer a demonstration of fitness and physical grace. It was a way of getting somewhere, failing other forms of locomotion; that was all.

"Charley," Diana cried, "where's your bag?"

"I only came to dinner – I can't possibly spend the night."

He was sober, she saw, but looked as if he needed a drink badly. She took his arm and guided him to a red-wheeled coupé parked in the street.

"Get in and sit down," she commanded. "You walk as if you were about to fall down anyhow."

"Never felt better in my life."

She laughed scornfully.

"Why do you have to get back tonight?" she demanded.

"I promised – you see I had an engagement—"

"Oh, let her wait!" exclaimed Diana impatiently. "She didn't look as if she had much else to do. Who is she anyhow?"

"I don't see how that could possibly interest you, Diamond Dick."

She flushed at the familiar name.

"Everything about you interests me. Who is that girl?"

"Elaine Russel. She's in the movies – sort of."

"She looked pulpy," said Diana thoughtfully. "I keep thinking of her. You look pulpy too. What are you doing with yourself – waiting for another war?"

They turned into the drive of a big rambling house on the Sound.* Canvas was being stretched for dancing on the lawn.

"Look!" She was pointing at a figure in knickerbockers on a side veranda. "That's my brother Breck. You've never met him. He's home from New Haven for the Easter holidays and he's having a dance tonight."

A handsome boy of eighteen came down the veranda steps towards them.

"He thinks you're the greatest man in the world," whispered Diana. "Pretend you're wonderful."

There was an embarrassed introduction.

"Done any flying lately?" asked Breck immediately.

"Not for some years," admitted Charley.

"I was too young for the war myself," said Breck regretfully, "but I'm going to try for a pilot's licence this summer. It's the only thing, isn't it – flying, I mean."

"Why, I suppose so," said Charley somewhat puzzled. "I hear you're having a dance tonight."

Breck waved his hand carelessly.

"Oh, just a lot of people from around here. I should think anything like that'd bore you to death – after all you've seen."

Charley turned helplessly to Diana.

"Come on," she said, laughing, "we'll go inside."

Mrs Dickey met them in the hall and subjected Charley to a polite but somewhat breathless scrutiny. The whole household seemed to treat him with unusual respect, and the subject had a tendency to drift immediately to the war.

"What are you doing now?" asked Mr Dickey. "Going into your father's business?"

"There isn't any business left," said Charley frankly. "I'm just about on my own."

Mr Dickey considered for a moment.

"If you haven't made any plans why don't you come down and see me at my office someday this week. I've got a little proposition that may interest you."

It annoyed Charley to think that Diana had probably arranged all this.

He needed no charity. He had not been crippled, and the war was over five years. People did not talk like this any more.

The whole first floor had been set with tables for the supper that would follow the dance, so Charley and Diana had dinner with Mr and Mrs Dickey in the library upstairs. It was an uncomfortable meal at which Mr Dickey did the talking and Diana covered up the gaps with nervous gaiety. He was glad when it was over and he was standing with Diana on the veranda in the gathering darkness.

"Charley..." She leant close to him and touched his arm gently. "Don't go to New York tonight. Spend a few days down here with me. I want to talk to you and I don't feel that I can talk tonight with this party going on."

"I'll come out again – later in the week," he said evasively.

"Why not stay tonight?"

"I promised I'd be back at eleven."

"At eleven?" She looked at him reproachfully. "Do you have to account to that girl for your evenings?"

"I like her," he said defiantly. "I'm not a child, Diamond Dick, and I rather resent your attitude. I thought you closed out your interest in my life five years ago."

"You won't stay?"

"No."

"All right – then we only have an hour. Let's walk out and sit on the wall by the Sound."

Side by side they started through the deep twilight where the air was heavy with salt and roses.

"Do you remember the last time we walked somewhere together?" she whispered.

"Why – no. I don't think I do. Where was it?"

"It doesn't matter – if you've forgotten."

When they reached the shore she swung herself up on the low wall that skirted the water.

"It's spring, Charley."

"Another spring."

"No – just spring. If you say 'another spring' it means you're getting old." She hesitated. "Charley..."

"Yes, Diamond Dick."

"I've been waiting to talk to you like this for five years."

Looking at him out of the corner of her eye she saw he was frowning and changed her tone.

"What kind of work are you going into, Charley?"

"I don't know. I've got a little money left and I won't have to do anything for a while. I don't seem to fit into business very well."

"You mean like you fitted into the war."

"Yes." He turned to her with a spark of interest. "I belonged to the war. It seems a funny thing to say but I think I'll always look back to those days as the happiest in my life."

"I know what you mean," she said slowly. "Nothing quite so intense or so dramatic will ever happen to our generation again."

They were silent for a moment. When he spoke again his voice was trembling a little.

"There are things lost in it – parts of me – that I can look for and never find. It was my war in a way, you see, and you can't quite hate what was your own." He turned to her suddenly. "Let's be frank, Diamond Dick – we loved each other once and it seems – seems rather silly to be stalling this way with you."

She caught her breath.

"Yes," she said faintly, "let's be frank."

"I know what you're up to and I know you're doing it to be kind. But life doesn't start all over again when a man talks to an old love on a spring night."

"I'm not doing it to be kind."

He looked at her closely.

"You lie, Diamond Dick. But – even if you loved me now it wouldn't matter. I'm not like I was five years ago – I'm a different person, can't you see? I'd rather have a drink this minute than all the moonlight in the world. I don't even think I could love a girl like you any more."

She nodded.

"I see."

"Why wouldn't you marry me five years ago, Diamond Dick?"

"I don't know," she said after a minute's hesitation, "I was wrong."

"Wrong!" he exclaimed bitterly. "You talk as if it had been guesswork, like betting on white or red."

"No, it wasn't guesswork."

There was a silence for a minute – then she turned to him with shining eyes.

"Won't you kiss me, Charley?" she asked simply.

He started.

"Would it be so hard to do?" she went on. "I've never asked a man to kiss me before."

With an exclamation he jumped off the wall.

"I'm going to the city," he said.

"Am I – such bad company as all that?"

"Diana." He came close to her and put his arms around her knees and looked into her eyes. "You know that if I kiss you I'll have to stay. I'm afraid of you – afraid of your kindness, afraid to remember anything about you at all. And I couldn't go from a kiss of yours to – another girl."

"Goodbye," she said suddenly.

He hesitated for a moment then he protested helplessly.

"You put me in a terrible position."

"Goodbye."

"Listen, Diana—"

"Please go away."

He turned and walked quickly towards the house.

Diana sat without moving while the night breeze made cool puffs and ruffles on her chiffon dress. The moon had risen higher now and floating in the Sound was a triangle of silver scales, trembling a little to the stiff, tinny drip of the banjos on the lawn.

Alone at last – she was alone at last. There was not even a ghost left now to drift with through the years. She might stretch out her arms as far as they could reach into the night without fear that they would brush friendly cloth. The thin silver had worn off from all the stars.

She sat there for almost an hour, her eyes fixed upon the points of light on the other shore. Then the wind ran cold fingers along her silk stockings so she jumped off the wall, landing softly among the bright pebbles of the sand.

"Diana!"

Breck was coming towards her, flushed with the excitement of his party. "Diana! I want you to meet a man in my class at New Haven. His brother took you to a prom three years ago."

She shook her head.

"I've got a headache; I'm going upstairs."

Coming closer Breck saw that her eyes were glittering with tears. "Diana, what's the matter?"

"Nothing."

"Something's the matter."

"Nothing, Breck. But oh, take care, take care! Be careful who you love."

"Are you in love with – Charley Abbot?"

She gave a strange, hard little laugh.

"Me? Oh, God, no, Breck! I don't love anybody. I wasn't made for anything like love, I don't even love myself any more. It was you I was talking about. That was advice, don't you understand?"

She ran suddenly towards the house, holding her skirts high out of the dew. Reaching her own room she kicked off her slippers and threw herself on the bed in the darkness.

"I should have been careful," she whispered to herself. "All my life I'll be punished for not being more careful. I wrapped all my love up like a box of candy and gave it away."

Her window was open and outside on the lawn the sad, dissonant horns were telling a melancholy story. A blackamoor was two-timing the lady to whom he had pledged faith. The lady warned him, in so many words, to stop fooling 'round Sweet Jelly Roll, even though Sweet Jelly Roll was the colour of pale cinnamon...*

The phone on the table by her bed rang imperatively. Diana took up the receiver.

"Yes."

"One minute please, New York calling."

It flashed through Diana's head that it was Charley – but that was impossible. He must still be on the train.

"Hello." A woman was speaking. "Is this the Dickey residence?"

"Yes."

"Well, is Mr Charles Abbot there?"

Diana's heart seemed to stop beating as she recognized the voice – it was the blonde girl of the cafe.

"What?" she asked dazedly.

"I would like to speak to Mr Abbot at once please."

"You – you can't speak to him. He's gone."

There was a pause. Then the girl's voice, suspiciously:

"He isn't gone."

Diana's hands tightened on the telephone.

"I know who's talking," went on the voice, rising to a hysterical note, "and I want to speak to Mr Abbot. If you're not telling the truth, and he finds out, there'll be trouble."

"Be quiet!"

"If he's gone, where did he go?"

"I don't know."

"If he isn't at my apartment in half an hour I'll know you're lying and I'll—"

Diana hung up the receiver and tumbled back on the bed – too weary of life to think or care. Out on the lawn the orchestra was singing and the words drifted in her window on the breeze.

Lis-sen while I – get you tole:
Stop foolin' 'roun' sweet – Jelly Roll…

She listened. The Negro voices were wild and loud – life was in that key, so harsh a key. How abominably helpless she was! Her appeal was ghostly, impotent, absurd, before the barbaric urgency of this other girl's desire.

Just treat me pretty, just treat me sweet
Cause I possess a fo'ty-fo' that don't repeat.

The music sank to a weird, threatening minor. It reminded her of something – some mood in her own childhood – and a new atmosphere seemed to open up around her. It was not so much a definite memory as it was a current, a tide setting through her whole body.

Diana jumped suddenly to her feet and groped for her slippers in the darkness. The song was beating in her head and her little teeth set together in a click. She could feel the tense golf muscles rippling and tightening along her arms.

Running into the hall she opened the door to her father's room, closed it cautiously behind her and went to the bureau. It was in the top drawer

– black and shining among the pale anaemic collars. Her hand closed around the grip and she drew out the bullet clip with steady fingers. There were five shots in it.

Back in her room she called the garage.

"I want my roadster at the side entrance right away!"

Wriggling hurriedly out of her evening dress to the sound of breaking snaps she let it drop in a soft pile on the floor, replacing it with a golf sweater, a checked sport skirt and an old blue and white blazer which she pinned at the collar with a diamond bar. Then she pulled a tam-o'-shanter over her dark hair and looked once in the mirror before turning out the light.

"Come on, Diamond Dick!" she whispered aloud.

With a short exclamation she plunged the automatic into her blazer pocket and hurried from the room.

Diamond Dick! The name had jumped out at her once from a lurid cover, symbolizing her childish revolt against the softness of life. Diamond Dick was a law unto himself, making his own judgements with his back against the wall. If justice was slow he vaulted into his saddle and was off for the foothills, for in the unvarying rightness of his instincts he was higher and harder than the law. She had seen in him a sort of deity, infinitely resourceful, infinitely just. And the commandment he laid down for himself in the cheap, ill-written pages was first and foremost to keep what was his own.

An hour and a half from the time when she had left Greenwich, Diana pulled up her roadster in front of the Restaurant Mont Mihiel. The theatres were already dumping their crowds into Broadway and half a dozen couples in evening dress looked at her curiously as she slouched through the door. A moment later she was talking to the head waiter.

"Do you know a girl named Elaine Russel?"

"Yes, Miss Dickey. She comes here quite often."

"I wonder if you can tell me where she lives."

The head waiter considered.

"Find out," she said sharply, "I'm in a hurry."

He bowed. Diana had come there many times with many men. She had never asked him a favour before.

His eyes roved hurriedly around the room.

"Sit down," he said.

"I'm all right. You hurry."

He crossed the room and whispered to a man at a table – in a minute he was back with the address, an apartment on 49th Street.

In her car again she looked at her wristwatch – it was almost midnight, the appropriate hour. A feeling of romance, of desperate and dangerous adventure thrilled her, seemed to flow out of the electric signs and the rushing cabs and the high stars. Perhaps she was only one out of a hundred people bound on such an adventure tonight – for her there had been nothing like this since the war.

Skidding the corner into East 49th Street she scanned the apartments on both sides. There it was – "The Elkson" – a wide mouth of forbidding yellow light. In the hall a Negro elevator boy asked her name.

"Tell her it's a girl with a package from the moving picture company."

He worked a plug noisily.

"Miss Russel? There's a lady here says she's got a package from the moving picture company."

A pause.

"That's what she says... All right." He turned to Diana. "She wasn't expecting no package but you can bring it up." He looked at her, frowned suddenly. "You ain't got no package."

Without answering she walked into the elevator and he followed, shoving the gate closed with maddening languor...

"First door to your right."

She waited until the elevator door had started down again. Then she knocked, her fingers tightening on the automatic in her blazer pocket.

Running footsteps, a laugh; the door swung open and Diana stepped quickly into the room.

It was a small apartment, bedroom, bath and kitchenette, furnished in pink and white and heavy with last week's smoke. Elaine Russel had opened the door herself. She was dressed to go out and a green evening cape was over her arm. Charley Abbot sipping at a highball was stretched out in the room's only easy chair.

"What is it?" cried Elaine quickly.

With a sharp movement Diana slammed the door behind her and Elaine stepped back, her mouth falling ajar.

"Good evening," said Diana coldly, and then a line from a forgotten nickel novel flashed into her head, "I hope I don't intrude."

"What do you want?" demanded Elaine. "You've got your nerve to come butting in here!"

Charley who had not said a word set down his glass heavily on the arm of the chair. The two girls looked at each other with unwavering eyes.

"Excuse me," said Diana slowly, "but I think you've got my man."

"I thought you were supposed to be a lady!" cried Elaine in rising anger. "What do you mean by forcing your way into this room?"

"I mean business. I've come for Charley Abbot."

Elaine gasped.

"Why, you must be crazy!"

"On the contrary, I've never been so sane in my life. I came here to get something that belongs to me."

Charley uttered an exclamation but with a simultaneous gesture the two women waved him silent.

"All right," cried Elaine, "we'll settle this right now."

"I'll settle it myself," said Diana sharply. "There's no question or argument about it. Under other circumstances I might feel a certain pity for you – in this case you happen to be in my way. What is there between you two? Has he promised to marry you?"

"That's none of your business!"

"You'd better answer," Diana warned her.

"I won't answer."

Diana took a sudden step forward, drew back her arm and with all the strength in her slim hard muscles, hit Elaine a smashing blow in the cheek with her open hand.

Elaine staggered up against the wall. Charley uttered an exclamation and sprang forward to find himself looking into the muzzle of a forty-four held in a small determined hand.

"Help!" cried Elaine wildly. "Oh, she's hurt me! She's hurt me!"

"Shut up!" Diana's voice was hard as steel. "You're not hurt. You're just pulpy and soft. But if you start to raise a row I'll pump you full of tin as sure as you're alive. Sit down! Both of you. Sit *down*!" Elaine sat down quickly, her face pale under her rouge. After an instant's hesitation Charley sank down again into his chair.

"Now," went on Diana, waving the gun in a constant arc that included them both. "I guess you know I'm in a serious mood. Understand this first of all. As far as I'm concerned neither of you have any rights whatsoever and I'd kill you both rather than leave this room without getting what I came for. I asked if he'd promised to marry you."

"Yes," said Elaine sullenly.

The gun moved towards Charley.

"Is that so?"

He licked his lips, nodded.

"My God!" said Diana in contempt. "And you admit it. Oh, it's funny, it's absurd – if I didn't care so much I'd laugh."

"Look here!" muttered Charley. "I'm not going to stand much of this, you know."

"Yes you are! You're soft enough to stand anything now." She turned to the girl, who was trembling. "Have you any letters of his?"

Elaine shook her head.

"You lie," said Diana. "Go and get them! I'll give you three. One…"

Elaine rose nervously and went into the other room. Diana edged along the table, keeping her constantly in sight.

"Hurry!"

Elaine returned with a small package in her hand which Diana took and slipped into her blazer pocket.

"Thanks. You had 'em all carefully preserved I see. Sit down again and we'll have a little talk."

Elaine sat down. Charley drained off his whiskey and soda and leant back stupidly in his chair.

"Now," said Diana, "I'm going to tell you a little story. It's about a girl who went to a war once and met a man who she thought was the finest and bravest man she had ever known. She fell in love with him and he with her and all the other men she had ever known became like pale shadows compared with this man that she loved. But one day he was shot down out of the air, and when he woke up into the world he'd changed. He didn't know it himself but he'd forgotten things and become a different man. The girl felt sad about this – she saw that she wasn't necessary to him any more, so there was nothing to do but say goodbye.

"So she went away and every night for a while she cried herself to sleep but he never came back to her and five years went by. Finally word came to her that this same injury that had come between them was ruining his life. He didn't remember anything important any more – how proud and fine he had once been, and what dreams he had once had. And then the girl knew that she had the right to try and save what was left of his life because she was the only one who knew all the things he'd forgotten. But it was too late. She couldn't approach him any more – she wasn't coarse enough and gross enough to reach him now – he'd forgotten so much.

"So she took a revolver, very much like this one here, and she came after this man to the apartment of a poor, weak, harmless rat of a girl who had him in tow. She was going to either bring him to himself – or go back to the dust with him where nothing would matter any more."

She paused. Elaine shifted uneasily in her chair. Charley was leaning forward with his face in his hands.

"Charley!"

The word, sharp and distinct, startled him. He dropped his hands and looked up at her.

"Charley!" she repeated in a thin clear voice. "Do you remember Fontenay in the late fall?"

A bewildered look passed over his face.

"Listen, Charley. Pay attention. Listen to every word I say. Do you remember the poplar trees at twilight, and a long column of French infantry going through the town? You had on your blue uniform, Charley, with the little numbers on the tabs and you were going to the front in an hour. Try and remember, Charley!"

He passed his hand over his eyes and gave a funny little sigh. Elaine sat bolt upright in her chair and gazed from one to the other of them with wide eyes.

94

"Do you remember the poplar trees?" went on Diana. "The sun was going down and the leaves were silver and there was a bell ringing. Do you remember, Charley? Do you remember?"

Again silence. Charley gave a curious little groan and lifted his head.

"I can't – understand," he muttered hoarsely. "There's something funny here."

"Can't you remember?" cried Diana. The tears were streaming from her eyes. "Oh God! Can't you remember? The brown road and the poplar trees and the yellow sky." She sprang suddenly to her feet. "Can't you remember?" she cried wildly. "Think, think – there's time. The bells are ringing – the bells are ringing, Charley! And there's just one hour!"

Then he too was on his feet, reeling and swaying.

"Oh-h-h-h!" he cried.

"Charley," sobbed Diana, "remember, remember, remember!"

"I see!" he said wildly. "I can see now – I remember, oh I remember!"

With a choking sob his whole body seemed to wilt under him and he pitched back senseless into his chair.

In a minute the two girls were beside him.

"He's fainted!" Diana cried. "Get some water quick."

"You devil!" screamed Elaine, her face distorted. "Look what's happened! What right have you to do this? What right? What right?"

"What right?" Diana turned to her with black, shining eyes. "Every right in the world. I've been married to Charley Abbot for five years."

Charley and Diana were married again in Greenwich early in June. After the wedding her oldest friends stopped calling her Diamond Dick – it had been a most inappropriate name for some years, they said, and it was thought that the effect on her children might be unsettling, if not distinctly pernicious.

Yet perhaps if the occasion should arise Diamond Dick would come to life again from the coloured cover and, with spurs shining and buckskin fringes fluttering in the breeze, ride into the lawless hills to protect her own. For under all her softness Diamond Dick was always hard as steel – so hard that the years knew it and stood still for her and the clouds rolled apart and a sick man, hearing those untiring hoofbeats in the night, rose up and shook off the dark burden of the war.

The Third Casket

1

WHEN YOU COME INTO CYRUS GIRARD'S office suite on the thirty-second floor you think at first that there has been a mistake, that the elevator instead of bringing you upstairs has brought you uptown, and that you are walking into an apartment on Fifth Avenue where you have no business at all. What you take to be the sound of a stock ticker is only a businesslike canary swinging in a silver cage overhead, and while the languid debutante at the mahogany table gets ready to ask you your name you can feast your eyes on etchings, tapestries, carved panels and fresh flowers.

Cyrus Girard does not, however, run an interior-decorating establishment, though he has, on occasion, run almost everything else. The lounging aspect of his anteroom is merely an elaborate camouflage for the wild clamour of affairs that goes on ceaselessly within. It is merely the padded glove over the mailed fist, the smile on the face of the prizefighter.

No one was more intensely aware of this than the three young men who were waiting there one April morning to see Mr Girard. Whenever the door marked Private trembled with the pressure of enormous affairs they started nervously in unconscious unison. All three of them were on the hopeful side of thirty, each of them had just got off the train, and they had never seen one another before. They had been waiting side by side on a Circassian leather lounge for the best part of an hour.

Once the young man with the pitch-black eyes and hair had pulled out a package of cigarettes and offered it hesitantly to the two others. But the others had refused in such a politely alarmed way that the dark young man, after a quick look around, had returned the package unsampled to his pocket. Following this disrespectful incident a long silence had fallen, broken only by the clatter of the canary as it ticked off the bond market in bird land.

When the Louis XIII clock stood at noon the door marked Private swung open in a tense, embarrassed way, and a frantic secretary demanded that the three callers step inside. They stood up as one man.

"Do you mean – all together?" asked the tallest one in some embarrassment.

"All together."

Falling unwillingly into a sort of lock step and glancing neither to left or right, they passed through a series of embattled rooms and marched into the private office of Cyrus Girard, who filled the position of Telamonian Ajax* among the Homeric characters of Wall Street.

He was a thin, quiet-mannered man of sixty, with a fine, restless face and the clear, fresh, trusting eyes of a child. When the procession of young men walked in he stood up behind his desk with an expectant smile.

"Parrish?" he said eagerly.

The tall young man said, "Yes, sir," and was shaken by the hand.

"Jones?"

This was the young man with the black eyes and hair. He smiled back at Cyrus Girard and announced in a slightly Southern accent that he was mighty glad to meet him.

"And so you must be Van Buren," said Girard, turning to the third. Van Buren acknowledged as much. He was obviously from a large city – unflustered and very spick-and-span.

"Sit down," said Girard, looking eagerly from one to the other. "I can't tell you the pleasure of this minute."

They all smiled nervously and sat down.

"Yes, sir," went on the older man, "if I'd had any boys of my own I don't know but what I'd have wanted them to look just like you three." He saw that they were all growing pink, and he broke off with a laugh. "All right, I won't embarrass you any more. Tell me about the health of your respective fathers and we'll get down to business."

Their fathers, it seemed, were very well; they had all sent congratulatory messages by their sons for Mr Girard's sixtieth birthday.

"Thanks. Thanks. Now that's over." He leant back suddenly in his chair. "Well, boys, here's what I have to say. I'm retiring from business next year. I've always intended to retire at sixty, and my wife's always counted on it, and the time's come. I can't put it off any longer. I haven't any sons and I haven't any nephews and I haven't any cousins and I have a brother who's fifty years old and in the same boat I am. He'll perhaps hang on for ten years more down here; after that it looks as if the house, Cyrus Girard Incorporated, would change its name.

"A month ago I wrote to the three best friends I had in college, the three best friends I ever had in my life, and asked them if they had any sons between twenty-five and thirty years old. I told them I had room for just one young man here in my business, but he had to be about the best in the market. And as all three of you arrived here this morning I guess your fathers think you are. There's nothing complicated about my proposition. It'll take me three months to find out what I want to know, and at the end of that time two of you'll be disappointed; the other one can have about everything they used to give away in the fairy tales, half my kingdom and, if she wants him, my daughter's hand." He raised his head slightly. "Correct me, Lola, if I've said anything wrong."

At these words the three young men started violently, looked behind them, and then jumped precipitately to their feet. Reclining lazily in an armchair not two yards away sat a gold-and-ivory little beauty with dark eyes and a moving, childish smile that was like all the lost youth in the world. When she saw the startled expressions on their faces she gave vent to a suppressed chuckle in which the victims after a moment joined.

"This is my daughter," said Cyrus Girard, smiling innocently. "Don't be so alarmed. She has many suitors come from near and far – and all that sort of thing. Stop making these young men feel silly, Lola, and ask them if they'll come to dinner with us tonight."

Lola got to her feet gravely and her grey eyes fell on them one after another.

"I only know part of your names," she said.

"Easily arranged," said Van Buren. "Mine's George."

The tall young man bowed.

"I respond to John Hardwick Parrish," he confessed, "or anything of that general sound."

She turned to the dark-haired Southerner, who had volunteered no information. "How about Mr Jones?"

"Oh, just – Jones," he answered uneasily.

She looked at him in surprise.

"Why, how partial!" she exclaimed, laughing. "How – I might even say how fragmentary."

Mr Jones looked around him in a frightened way.

"Well, I tell you," he said finally, "I don't guess my first name is much suited to this sort of thing."

"What is it?"

"It's Rip."

"Rip!"

Eight eyes turned reproachfully upon him.

"Young man," exclaimed Girard, "you don't mean that my old friend in his senses named his son that!"

Jones shifted defiantly on his feet.

"No, he didn't," he admitted. "He named me Oswald."

There was a ripple of sympathetic laughter.

"Now you four go along," said Girard, sitting down at his desk. "Tomorrow at nine o'clock sharp you report to my general manager, Mr Galt, and the tournament begins. Meanwhile if Lola has her coupé-sport-limousine-roadster-landaulet, or whatever she drives now, she'll probably take you to your respective hotels."

After they had gone Girard's face grew restless again and he stared at nothing for a long time before he pressed the button that started the long-delayed stream of traffic through his mind.

"One of them's sure to be all right," he muttered, "but suppose it turned out to be the dark one. Rip Jones Incorporated!"

2

A S THE THREE MONTHS DREW to an end it began to appear that not one, but all of the young men were going to turn out all right. They were all industrious, they were all possessed of that mysterious ease known as personality and, moreover, they all had brains. If Parrish, the tall young man from the West, was a little quicker in sizing up the market; if Jones, the Southerner, was a bit the most impressive in his relations with customers, then Van Buren made up for it by spending his nights in the study of investment securities. Cyrus Girard's mind was no sooner drawn to one of them by some exhibition of shrewdness or resourcefulness than a parallel talent appeared in one of the others. Instead of having to enforce upon himself a strict neutrality he found himself trying to concentrate upon the individual merits of first one and then another – but so far without success.

Every weekend they all came out to the Girard place at Tuxedo Park, where they fraternized a little self-consciously with the young and lovely Lola, and on Sunday mornings tactlessly defeated her father at golf. On the last tense weekend before the decision was to be made Cyrus Girard asked them to meet him in his study after dinner. On their respective merits as future partners in Cyrus Girard Inc. he had been unable to decide, but his despair had evoked another plan, on which he intended to base his decision.

"Gentlemen," he said, when they had convoked in his study at the appointed hour, "I have brought you here to tell you that you're all fired."

Immediately the three young men were on their feet, with shocked, reproachful expressions in their eyes.

"Temporarily," he added, smiling good-humouredly. "So spare a decrepit old man your violence and sit down."

They sat down, with short relieved smiles.

"I like you all," he went on, "and I don't know which one I like better than the others. In fact – this thing hasn't come out right at all. So I'm going to extend the competition for two more weeks – but in an entirely different way."

They all sat forward eagerly in their chairs.

"Now my generation," he went on, "have made a failure of our leisure hours. We grew up in the most hard-boiled commercial age any country ever knew, and when we retire we never know what to do with the rest of our lives. Here I am, getting out at sixty, and miserable about it. I haven't any resources – I've never been much of a reader, I can't stand golf except once a week, and I haven't got a hobby in the world. Now someday you're going to be sixty too. You'll see other men taking it easy and having a good time, and you'll want to do the same. I want to find out which one of you will be the best sort of man after his business days are over."

He looked from one to the other of them eagerly. Parrish and Van Buren nodded at him comprehendingly. Jones after a puzzled half-moment nodded too.

"I want you each to take two weeks and spend them as you think you'll spend your time when you're too old to work. I want you to solve my problem for me. And whichever one I think has got the most out of his leisure – he'll be the man to carry on my business. I'll know it won't swamp him like it's swamped me."

"You mean you want us to enjoy ourselves?" enquired Rip Jones politely. "Just go out and have a big time?"

Cyrus Girard nodded.

"Anything you want to do."

"I take it Mr Girard doesn't include dissipation," remarked Van Buren.

"Anything you want to do," repeated the older man, "I don't bar anything. When it's all done I'm going to judge of its merits."

"Two weeks of travel for me," said Parrish dreamily. "That's what I've always wanted to do. I'll—"

"Travel!" interrupted Van Buren contemptuously. "When there's so much to do here at home? Travel, perhaps, if you have a year; but for two weeks… I'm going to try and see how the retired businessman can be of some use in the world."

"I said travel," repeated Parrish sharply. "I believe we're all to employ our leisure in the best—"

"Wait a minute," interrupted Cyrus Girard. "Don't fight this out in talk. Meet me in the office at 10.30 on the morning of August first – that's two weeks from tomorrow – and then let's see what you've done." He turned to Rip Jones. "I suppose you've got a plan too."

"No, sir," admitted Rip Jones with a puzzled look. "I'll have to think this over."

But though he thought it over for the rest of the evening Rip Jones went to bed still uninspired. At midnight he got up, found a pencil and wrote out a list of all the good times he had ever had. But all his holidays now seemed unprofitable and stale, and when he fell asleep at five his mind still threshed disconsolately on the prospect of hollow useless hours.

Next morning as Lola Girard was backing her car out of the garage she saw him hurrying towards her over the lawn.

"Ride in town, Rip?" she asked cheerfully.

"I reckon so."

"Why do you only reckon so? Father and the others left on the nine-o'clock train."

He explained to her briefly that they had all temporarily lost their jobs and there was no necessity of getting to the office today.

"I'm kind of worried about it," he said gravely. "I sure hate to leave my work. I'm going to run in this afternoon and see if they'll let me finish up a few things I had started."

"But you better be thinking how you're going to amuse yourself."

He looked at her helplessly.

"All I can think of doing is maybe take to drink," he confessed. "I come from a little town, and when they say leisure they mean hanging round the corner store." He shook his head. "I don't want any leisure. This is the first chance I ever had, and I want to make good."

"Listen, Rip," said Lola on a sudden impulse. "After you finish up at the office this afternoon you meet me and we'll fix up something together."

He met her, as she suggested, at five o'clock, but the melancholy had deepened in his dark eyes.

"They wouldn't let me in," he said. "I met your father in there, and he told me I had to find some way to amuse myself or I'd be just a bored old man like him."

"Never mind. We'll go to a show," she said consolingly, "and after that we'll run up on some roof and dance."

It was the first of a week of evenings they spent together. Sometimes they went to the theatre, sometimes to a cabaret; once they spent most of an afternoon strolling in Central Park. But she saw that from having been the most light-hearted and gay of the three young men, he was now the most moody and depressed. Everything whispered to him of the work he was missing.

Even when they danced at teatime, the click of bracelets on a hundred women's arms only reminded him of the busy office sound on Monday morning. He seemed incapable of inaction.

"This is mighty sweet of you," he said to her one afternoon, "and if it was after business hours I can't tell you how I'd enjoy it. But my mind is on all the things I ought to be doing. I'm – I'm right sad."

He saw then that he had hurt her, that by his frankness he had rejected all she was trying to do for him. But he was incapable of feeling differently.

"Lola, I'm mighty sorry," he said softly, "and maybe someday it'll be after hours again, and I can come to you—"

"I won't be interested," she said coldly. "And I see I was foolish ever to be interested at all."

He was standing beside her car when this conversation took place, and before he could reply she had thrown it into gear and started away.

He stood there looking after her sadly, thinking that perhaps he would never see her any more and that she would remember him always as ungrateful and unkind. But there was nothing he could have said. Something dynamic in him was incapable of any except a well-earned rest.

"If it was only after hours," he muttered to himself as he walked slowly away. "If it was only after hours."

3

AT TEN O'CLOCK ON THE MORNING of 1st August a tall, bronzed young man presented himself at the office of Cyrus Girard Inc., and sent in his card to the president. Less than five minutes later another young man arrived, less blatantly healthy, perhaps, but with the light of triumphant achievement blazing in his eyes. Word came out through the palpitating inner door that they were both to wait.

"Well, Parrish," said Van Buren condescendingly, "how did you like Niagara Falls?"

"I couldn't tell you," answered Parrish haughtily. "You can determine that on your honeymoon."

"My honeymoon!" Van Buren started. "How – what made you think I was contemplating a honeymoon?"

"I merely meant that when you do contemplate it you will probably choose Niagara Falls."

They sat for a few minutes in stony silence.

"I suppose," remarked Parrish coolly, "that you've been making a serious study of the deserving poor."

"On the contrary, I have done nothing of the kind." Van Buren looked at his watch. "I'm afraid that our competitor with the rakish name is going to be late. The time set was 10.30; it now lacks three minutes of the half-hour."

The private door opened, and at a command from the frantic secretary they both arose eagerly and went inside. Cyrus Girard was standing behind his desk waiting for them, watch in hand.

"Hello!" he exclaimed in surprise. "Where's Jones?"

Parrish and Van Buren exchanged a smile. If Jones were snagged somewhere so much the better.

"I beg your pardon, sir," spoke up the secretary, who had been lingering near the door, "Mr Jones is in Chicago."

"What's he doing there?" demanded Cyrus Girard in astonishment.

"He went out to handle the matter of those silver shipments. There wasn't anyone else who knew much about it, and Mr Galt thought—"

"Never mind what Mr Galt thought," broke in Girard impatiently. "Mr Jones is no longer employed by this concern. When he gets back from Chicago pay him off and let him go." He nodded curtly. "That's all."

The secretary bowed and went out. Girard turned to Parrish and Van Buren with an angry light in his eyes.

"Well, that finishes him," he said determinedly. "Any young man who won't attempt to obey my orders doesn't deserve a good chance." He sat down and began drumming with his fingers on the arm of his chair.

"All right, Parrish, let's hear what you've been doing with your leisure hours."

Parrish smiled ingratiatingly.

"Mr Girard," he began, "I've had a bully time. I've been travelling."

"Travelling where? The Adirondack? Canada?"

"No, sir. I've been to Europe."

Cyrus Girard sat up.

"I spent five days going over and five days coming back. That left me two days in London and a run over to Paris by aeroplane to spend the night. I saw Westminster Abbey, the Tower of London and the Louvre, and spent an afternoon at Versailles. On the boat I kept in wonderful condition – swam, played deck tennis, walked five miles every day, met some interesting people and found time to read. I came back after the greatest two weeks of my life, feeling fine and knowing more about my own country since I had something to compare it with. That, sir, is how I spent my leisure time and that's how I intend to spend my leisure time after I'm retired."

Girard leant back thoughtfully in his chair.

"Well, Parrish, that isn't half-bad," he said. "I don't know but what the idea appeals to me – take a run over there for the sea voyage and a glimpse of the London Stock Ex… I mean the Tower of London. Yes, sir, you've put an idea in my head." He turned to the other young man, who during this recital had been shifting uneasily in his chair. "Now, Van Buren, let's hear how you took your ease."

"I thought over the travel idea," burst out Van Buren excitedly, "and I decided against it. A man of sixty doesn't want to spend his time running back and forth between the capitals of Europe. It might fill up a year or so, but that's all. No, sir, the main thing is to have some strong interest – and especially one that'll be for the public good, because when a man gets along in years he wants to feel that he's leaving the world better for having lived in it. So I worked out a plan – it's for a historical and archaeological endowment centre, a thing that'd change the whole face of public education, a thing that any man would be interested in giving his time and money to. I've spent my whole two weeks working out the plan in detail, and let me tell you it'd be nothing but play work – just suited to the last years of an active man's life. It's been fascinating, Mr Girard. I've learnt more from doing it than I ever knew before – and I don't think I ever had a happier two weeks in my life."

When he had finished, Cyrus Girard nodded his head up and down many times in an approving and yet somehow dissatisfied way.

"Found an institute, eh?" he muttered aloud. "Well, I've always thought that maybe I'd do that someday – but I never figured on running it myself. My talents aren't much in that line. Still, it's certainly worth thinking over."

He got restlessly to his feet and began walking up and down the carpet, the dissatisfied expression deepening on his face. Several times he took out his watch and looked at it as if hoping that perhaps Jones had not gone to Chicago after all, but would appear in a few moments with a plan nearer his heart.

"What's the matter with me?" he said to himself unhappily. "When I say a thing I'm used to going through with it. I must be getting old."

Try as he might, however, he found himself unable to decide. Several times he stopped in his walk and fixed his glance first on one and then on the other of the two young men, trying to pick out some attractive characteristic to which he could cling and make his choice. But after several of these glances their faces seemed to blur together and he couldn't tell one from the other. They were twins who had told him the same story – of carrying the stock exchange by aeroplane to London and making it into a moving-picture show.

"I'm sorry, boys," he said haltingly. "I promised I'd decide this morning, and I will, but it means a whole lot to me and you'll have to give me a little time."

They both nodded, fixing their glances on the carpet to avoid encountering his distraught eyes.

Suddenly he stopped by the table and picking up the telephone called the general manager's office.

"Say, Galt," he shouted into the mouthpiece, "you sure you sent Jones to Chicago?"

"Positive," said a voice on the other end. "He came in here couple of days ago and said he was half-crazy for something to do. I told him it was against orders, but he said he was out of the competition anyhow and we needed somebody who was competent to handle that silver. So I—"

"Well you shouldn't have done it, see? I wanted to talk to him about something, and you shouldn't have done it."

Clack! He hung up the receiver and resumed his endless pacing up and down the floor. Confound Jones, he thought. Most ungrateful thing he ever heard of after he'd gone to all this trouble for his father's sake.

Outrageous! His mind went off on a tangent and he began to wonder whether Jones would handle that business out in Chicago. It was a complicated situation – but then, Jones was a trustworthy fellow. They were all trustworthy fellows. That was the whole trouble.

Again he picked up the telephone. He would call Lola; he felt vaguely that if she wanted to she could help him. The personal element had eluded him here; her opinion would be better than his own.

"I have to ask your pardon, boys," he said unhappily. "I didn't mean there to be all this fuss and delay. But it almost breaks my heart when I think of handing this shop over to anybody at all, and when I try to decide, it all gets dark in my mind." He hesitated. "Have either one of you asked my daughter to marry him?"

"I did," said Parrish, "three weeks ago."

"So did I," confessed Van Buren, "and I still have hopes that she'll change her mind."

Girard wondered if Jones had asked her also. Probably not; he never did anything he was expected to do. He even had the wrong name.

The phone in his hand rang shrilly and with an automatic gesture he picked up the receiver.

"Chicago calling, Mr Girard."

"I don't want to talk to anybody."

"It's personal. It's Mr Jones."

"All right," he said, his eyes narrowing. "Put him on."

A series of clicks – then Jones's faintly Southern voice over the wire.

"Mr Girard?"

"Yeah."

"I've been trying to get you since ten o'clock in order to apologize."

"I should think you would!" exploded Girard. "Maybe you know you're fired."

"I knew I would be," said Jones gloomily. "I guess I must be pretty dumb, Mr Girard, but I'll tell you the truth – I can't have a good time when I quit work."

"Of course you can't!" snapped Girard. "Nobody can…" He corrected himself. "What I mean is, it isn't an easy matter."

There was a pause at the other end of the line.

"That's exactly the way I feel," came Jones's voice regretfully. "I guess we understand each other, and there's no use my saying any more."

"What do you mean – we understand each other?" shouted Girard. "That's an impertinent remark, young man. We don't understand each other at all."

"That's what I meant," amended Jones. "I don't understand you and you don't understand me. I don't want to quit working and you – you do."

"Me quit work!" cried Girard, his face reddening. "Say, what are you talking about? Did you say I wanted to quit work?" He shook the telephone up and down violently. "Don't talk back to me, young man! Don't tell me I want to quit! Why – why, I'm not going to quit work at all! Do you hear that? I'm not going to quit work at all!"

The transmitter slipped from his grasp and bounced from the table to the floor. In a minute he was on his knees, groping for it wildly.

"Hello!" he cried. "Hello – hello! Say get Chicago back! I wasn't through!"

The two young men were on their feet. He hung up the receiver and turned to them, his voice husky with emotion.

"I've been an idiot," he said brokenly. "Quit work at sixty! Why – I must have been an idiot! I'm still a young man – I've got twenty good years in front of me! I'd like to see anybody send me home to die!"

The phone rang again and he took up the receiver with fire blazing in his eyes.

"Is this Jones? No, I want Mr Jones; Rip Jones. He's – he's my partner." There was a pause. "No, Chicago, that must be another party. I don't know any Mrs Jones – I want Mr—"

He broke off and the expression on his face changed slowly. When he spoke again his husky voice had grown suddenly quiet.

"Why – why, Lola…"

The Unspeakable Egg

1

WHEN FIFI VISITED HER LONG ISLAND AUNTS the first time she was only ten years old, but after she went back to New York the man who worked around the place said that the sand dunes would never be the same again. She had spoilt them. When she left, everything on Montauk Point seemed sad and futile and broken and old. Even the gulls wheeled about less enthusiastically, as if they missed the brown, hardy little girl with big eyes who played barefoot in the sand.

The years bleached out Fifi's tan and turned her a pale-pink colour, but she still managed to spoil many places and plans for many hopeful men. So when at last it was announced in the best newspapers that she had concentrated on a gentleman named Van Tyne everyone was rather glad that all the sadness and longing that followed in her wake should become the responsibility of one self-sacrificing individual; not better for the individual, but for Fifi's little world very much better indeed.

The engagement was not announced on the sporting page, nor even in the help-wanted column, because Fifi's family belonged to the Society for the Preservation of Large Fortunes; and Mr Van Tyne was descended from the man who accidentally founded that society, back before the Civil War. It appeared on the page of great names and was illustrated by a picture of a cross-eyed young lady holding the hand of a savage gentleman with four rows of teeth. That was how their pictures came out, anyhow, and the public was pleased to know that they were ugly monsters for all their money, and everyone was satisfied all around. The society editor set up a column telling how Mrs Van Tyne started off in the *Aquitania* wearing a blue travelling dress of starched felt with a round square hat to match; and so far as human events can be prophesied, Fifi was as good as married; or, as not a few young men considered, as bad as married.

"An exceptionally brilliant match," remarked Aunt Cal on the eve of the wedding, as she sat in her house on Montauk Point and clipped the notice for the cousins in Scotland, and then she added abstractedly, "All is forgiven."

"Why, Cal!" cried Aunt Josephine. "What do you mean when you say all is forgiven? Fifi has never injured you in any way."

"In the past nine years she has not seen fit to visit us here at Montauk Point, though we have invited her over and over again."

"But I don't blame her," said Aunt Josephine, who was only thirty-one herself. "What would a young pretty girl do down here with all this sand?"

"We like the sand, Jo."

"But we're old maids, Cal, with no vices except cigarettes and double-dummy mah-jong. Now Fifi, being young, naturally likes exciting, vicious things – late hours, dice playing, all the diversions we read about in these books."

She waved her hand vaguely.

"I don't blame her for not coming down here. If I were in her place…"

What unnatural ambitions lurked in Aunt Jo's head were never disclosed, for the sentence remained unfinished. The front door of the house opened in an abrupt, startled way, and a young lady walked into the room in a dress marked "Paris, France".

"Good evening, dear ladies," she cried, smiling radiantly from one to the other. "I've come down here for an indefinite time in order to play in the sand."

"Fifi!"

"Fifi!"

"Aunts!"

"But, my dear child," cried Aunt Jo, "I thought this was the night of the bridal dinner."

"It is," admitted Fifi cheerfully. "But I didn't go. I'm not going to the wedding either. I sent in my regrets today."

It was all very vague; but it seemed, as far as her aunts could gather, that young Van Tyne was too perfect – whatever that meant. After much urging Fifi finally explained that he reminded her of an advertisement for a new car.

"A new car?" enquired Aunt Cal, wide eyed. "What new car?"

"Any new car."

"Do you mean…"

Aunt Cal blushed.

"I don't understand this new slang, but isn't there some part of a car that's called – the clutch?"

"Oh, I like him physically," remarked Fifi coolly. Her aunts started in unison. "But he was just… oh, too perfect, too new; as if they'd fooled over him at the factory for a long time and put special curtains on him…"

Aunt Jo had visions of a black-leather sheikh.

"…and balloon tyres and a permanent shave. He was too civilized for me, Aunt Cal." She sighed. "I must be one of the rougher girls, after all."

She was as immaculate and dainty sitting there as though she were the portrait of a young lady and about to be hung on the wall. But underneath her cheerfulness her aunts saw that she was in a state of hysterical excitement, and they persisted in suspecting that something more definite and shameful was the matter.

"But it isn't," insisted Fifi. "Our engagement was announced three months ago, and not a single chorus girl has sued George for breach of promise. Not one! He doesn't use alcohol in any form except as hair tonic. Why, we've never even quarrelled until today!"

"You've made a serious mistake," said Aunt Cal.

Fifi nodded.

"I'm afraid I've broken the heart of the nicest man I ever met in my life, but it can't be helped. Immaculate! Why, what's the use of being immaculate, when, no matter how hard you try, you can't be half so immaculate as your husband? And tactful? George could introduce Mr Trotsky to Mr Rockefeller and there wouldn't be a single blow.* But after a certain point, I want to have all the tact in my family, and I told him so. I've never left a man practically at the church door before, so I'm going to stay here until everyone has had a chance to forget."

And stay she did – rather to the surprise of her aunts, who expected that next morning she would rush wildly and remorsefully back to New York. She appeared at breakfast very calm and fresh and cool, and as though she had slept soundly all night, and spent the day reclining under a red parasol beside the sunny dunes, watching the Atlantic roll in from the east. Her aunts intercepted the evening paper and burned it unseen in the open fire, under the impression that Fifi's flight would be recorded in red headlines across the front page. They accepted the fact that Fifi was here, and except that Aunt Jo was inclined to go mah-jong without a pair when she speculated on the too-perfect man, their lives went along very much the same. But not quite the same.

"What's the matter with that niece of yourn?" demanded the yardman gloomily of Aunt Josephine. "What's a young pretty girl want to come and hide herself down here for?"

"My niece is resting," declared Aunt Josephine stiffly.

"Them dunes ain't good for wore-out people," objected the yardman, soothing his head with his fingers. "There's a monotoness about them. I seen her yesterday take her parasol and like to beat one down, she got so mad at it. Someday she's going to notice how many of them there are, and all of a sudden go loony." He sniffed. "And then what kind of a proposition we going to have on our hands?"

"That will do, Percy," snapped Aunt Jo. "Go about your business. I want ten pounds of broken-up shells rolled into the front walk."

"What'll I do with that parasol?" he demanded. "I picked up the pieces."

"It's not my parasol," said Aunt Jo tartly. "You can take the pieces and roll them into the front walk too."

And so the June of Fifi's abandoned honeymoon drifted away, and every morning her rubber shoes left wet footprints along a desolate shore at the end of nowhere. For a while she seemed to thrive on the isolation, and the sea wind blew her cheeks scarlet with health; but after a week had passed, her aunts saw that she was noticeably restless and less cheerful even than when she came.

"I'm afraid it's getting on your nerves, my dear," said Aunt Cal one particularly wild and windy afternoon. "We love to have you here, but we hate to see you looking so sad. Why don't you ask your mother to take you to Europe for the summer?"

"Europe's too dressed up," objected Fifi wearily. "I like it here where everything's rugged and harsh and rude, like the end of the world. If you don't mind, I'd like to stay longer."

She stayed longer, and seemed to grow more and more melancholy as the days slipped by to the raucous calls of the gulls and the flashing tumult of the waves along the shore. Then one afternoon she returned at twilight from the longest of her long walks with a strange derelict of a man. And after one look at him her aunts thought that the gardener's prophecy had come true and that solitude had driven Fifi mad at last.

2

H E WAS A VERY RAGGED WRECK of a man as he stood in the doorway on that summer evening, blinking into Aunt Cal's eyes; rather like a beachcomber who had wandered accidentally out of a movie of the South Seas. In his hands he carried a knotted stick of a brutal, treacherous shape. It was a murderous-looking stick, and the sight of it caused Aunt Cal to shrink back a little into the room.

Fifi shut the door behind them and turned to her aunts as if this were the most natural occasion in the world.

"This is Mr Hopkins," she announced, and then turned to her companion for corroboration. "Or is it Hopwood?"

"Hopkins," said the man hoarsely. "Hopkins."

Fifi nodded cheerfully.

"I've asked Mr Hopkins to dinner," she said.

There was some dignity which Aunt Cal and Aunt Josephine had acquired, living here beside the proud sea, that would not let them show surprise. The man was a guest now; that was enough. But in their hearts all was turmoil and confusion. They would have been no more surprised had Fifi brought in a many-headed monster out of the Atlantic.

"Won't you – won't you sit down, Mr Hopkins?" said Aunt Cal nervously.

Mr Hopkins looked at her blankly for a moment, and then made a loud clicking sound in the back of his mouth. He took a step towards a chair and sank down on its gilt frailty as though he meant to annihilate it immediately. Aunt Cal and Aunt Josephine collapsed rather weakly on the sofa.

"Mr Hopkins and I struck up an acquaintance on the beach," explained Fifi. "He's been spending the summer down here for his health."

Mr Hopkins fixed his eyes glassily on the two aunts.

"I come down for my health," he said.

Aunt Cal made some small sound; but recovering herself quickly, joined Aunt Jo in nodding eagerly at the visitor, as if they deeply sympathized.

"Yeah," he repeated cheerfully.

"He thought the sea air would make him well and strong again," said Fifi eagerly. "That's why he came down here. Isn't that it, Mr Hopkins?"

"You said it, sister," agreed Mr Hopkins, nodding.

"So you see, Aunt Cal," smiled Fifi, "you and Aunt Jo aren't the only two people who believe in the medicinal quality of this location."

"No," agreed Aunt Cal faintly. "There are – there are three of us now."

Dinner was announced.

"Would you – would you" – Aunt Cal braced herself and looked Mr Hopkins in the eye – "would you like to wash your hands before dinner?"

"Don't mention it." Mr Hopkins waved his fingers at her carelessly.

They went in to dinner, and after some furtive backing and bumping due to the two aunts trying to keep as far as possible from Mr Hopkins, sat down at table.

"Mr Hopkins lives in the woods," said Fifi. "He has a little house all by himself, where he cooks his own meals and does his own washing week in and week out."

"How fascinating!" said Aunt Jo, looking searchingly at their guest for some signs of the scholarly recluse. "Have you been living near here for some time?"

"Not so long," he answered with a leer. "But I'm stuck on it, see? I'll maybe stay here till I rot."

"Are you – do you live far away?" Aunt Cal was wondering what price she could get for the house at a forced sale, and how she and her sister could ever bear to move.

"Just a mile down the line… This is a pretty gal you got here," he added, indicating their niece with his spoon.

"Why – yes." The two ladies glanced uneasily at Fifi.

"Someday I'm going to pick her up and run away with her," he added pleasantly.

Aunt Cal, with a heroic effort, switched the subject away from their niece. They discussed Mr Hopkins's shack in the woods. Mr Hopkins liked it well enough, he confessed, except for the presence of minute animal life, a small fault in an otherwise excellent habitat.

After dinner Fifi and Mr Hopkins went out to the porch, while her aunts sat side by side on the sofa turning over the pages of magazines and from time to time glancing at each other with stricken eyes. That a savage had a few minutes since been sitting at their dinner table, that he was now alone with their niece on the dark veranda – no such terrible adventure had ever been allotted to their prim, quiet lives before.

Aunt Cal determined that at nine, whatever the consequences, she would call Fifi inside; but she was saved this necessity, for after half an hour the young lady strolled in calmly and announced that Mr Hopkins had gone home. They looked at her, speechless.

"Fifi!" groaned Aunt Cal. "My poor child! Sorrow and loneliness have driven you insane!"

"We understand, my dear," said Aunt Jo, touching her handkerchief to her eyes. "It's our fault for letting you stay. A few weeks in one of those rest-cure places, or perhaps even a good cabaret, will—"

"What do you mean?" Fifi looked from one to the other in surprise. "Do you mean you object to my bringing Mr Hopkins here?"

Aunt Cal flushed a dull red and her lips shut tight together.

"'Object' is not the word. You find some horrible, brutal roustabout along the beach…"

She broke off and gave a little cry. The door had swung open suddenly and a hairy face was peering into the room.

"I left my stick."

Mr Hopkins discovered the unpleasant weapon leaning in the corner and withdrew as unceremoniously as he had come, banging the door shut behind him. Fifi's aunt sat motionless until his footsteps left the porch. Then Aunt Cal went swiftly to the door and pulled down the latch.

"I don't suppose he'll try to rob us tonight," she said grimly, "because he must know we'll be prepared. But I'll warn Percy to go around the yard several times during the night."

"Rob you!" cried Fifi incredulously.

"Don't excite yourself, Fifi," commanded Aunt Cal. "Just rest quietly in that chair while I call up your mother."

"I don't want you to call up my mother."

"Sit calmly and close your eyes and try to – try to count sheep jumping over a fence."

"Am I never to see another man unless he has a cutaway coat on?" exclaimed Fifi with flashing eyes. "Is this the Dark Ages, or the century of... of illumination? Mr Hopkins is one of the most attractive eggs I've ever met in my life."

"Mr Hopkins is a savage!" said Aunt Cal succinctly.

"Mr Hopkins is a very attractive egg."

"A very attractive what?"

"A very attractive egg."

"Mr Hopkins is a – a – an unspeakable egg," proclaimed Aunt Cal, adopting Fifi's locution.

"Just because he's natural," cried Fifi impatiently. "All right, I don't care; he's good enough for me."

The situation, it seemed, was even worse than they thought. This was no temporary aberration; evidently Fifi, in the reaction from her recent fiancé, was interested in this outrageous man. She had met him several days ago, she confessed, and she intended to see him tomorrow. They had a date to go walking.

The worst of it was that after Fifi had gone scornfully to bed, Aunt Cal called up her mother – and found that her mother was not at home; her mother had gone to White Sulphur Springs and wouldn't be home for a week. It left the situation definitely in the hands of Aunt Cal and Aunt Jo, and the situation came to a head the next afternoon at teatime, when Percy rushed in upon them excitedly through the kitchen door.

"Miss Marsden," he exclaimed in a shocked, offended voice, "I want to give up my position!"

"Why, Percy!"

"I can't help it. I lived here on the Point for more'n forty-five years, and I never seen such a sight as I seen just now."

"What's the matter?" cried the two ladies, springing up in wild alarm.

"Go to the window and look for yourself. Miss Fifi is kissing a tramp in broad daylight, down on the beach!"

3

FIVE MINUTES LATER two maiden ladies were making their way across the sand towards a couple who stood close together on the shore, sharply outlined against the bright afternoon sky. As they came closer Fifi and Mr Hopkins, absorbed in the contemplation of each other, perceived them and drew lingeringly apart. Aunt Cal began to speak when they were still thirty yards away.

"Go into the house, Fifi!" she cried.

Fifi looked at Mr Hopkins, who touched her hand reassuringly and nodded. As if under the influence of a charm, Fifi turned away from him, and with her head lowered walked with slender grace towards the house.

"Now, my man," said Aunt Cal, folding her arms, "what are your intentions?"

Mr Hopkins returned her glare rudely. Then he gave a low hoarse laugh.

"What's that to you?" he demanded.

"It's everything to us. Miss Marsden is our niece, and your attentions are unwelcome – not to say obnoxious."

Mr Hopkins turned half away.

"Aw, go on and blab your mouth out!" he advised her.

Aunt Cal tried a new approach.

"What if I were to tell you that Miss Marsden were mentally deranged?"

"What's that?"

"She's – she's a little crazy."

He smiled contemptuously.

"What's the idea? Crazy 'cause she likes me?"

"That merely indicates it," answered Aunt Cal bravely. "She's had an unfortunate love affair and it's affected her mind. Look here!" She opened the purse that swung at her waist. "If I give you fifty – a hundred dollars right now in cash, will you promise to move yourself ten miles up the beach?"

"Ah-h-h-h!" he exclaimed, so venomously that the two ladies swayed together.

"Two hundred!" cried Aunt Cal, with a catch in her voice.

He shook his finger at them.

"You can't buy me!" he growled. "I'm as good as anybody. There's chauffeurs and such that marry millionaires' daughters every day in the week. This is Umerica, a free country, see?"

"You won't give her up?" Aunt Cal swallowed hard on the words. "You won't stop bothering her and go away?"

He bent over suddenly and scooped up a large double handful of sand, which he threw in a high parabola so that it scattered down upon the horrified ladies, enveloping them for a moment in a thick mist. Then laughing once again in his hoarse, boorish way, he turned and set off at a loping run along the sand.

In a daze the two women brushed the casual sand from their shoulders and walked stiffly towards the house.

"I'm younger than you are," said Aunt Jo firmly when they reached the living room. "I want a chance now to see what I can do."

She went to the telephone and called a New York number.

"Dr Roswell Gallup's office? Is Dr Gallup there?" Aunt Cal sat down on the sofa and gazed tragically at the ceiling. "Dr Gallup? This is Miss Josephine Marsden, of Montauk Point… Dr Gallup, a very curious state of affairs has arisen concerning my niece. She has become entangled with a – a – an unspeakable egg." She gasped as she said this, and went on to explain in a few words the uncanny nature of the situation.

"And I think that perhaps psychoanalysis might clear up what my sister and I have been unable to handle."

Dr Gallup was interested. It appeared to be exactly his sort of a case.

"There's a train in half an hour that will get you here at nine o'clock," said Aunt Jo. "We can give you dinner and accommodate you overnight."

She hung up the receiver.

"There! Except for our change from bridge to mah-jong, this will be the first really modern step we've ever taken in our lives."

The hours passed slowly. At seven Fifi came down to dinner, as unperturbed as though nothing had happened; and her aunts played up bravely to her calmness, determined to say nothing until the doctor had actually arrived. After dinner Aunt Jo suggested mah-jong, but Fifi declared that she would rather read, and settled on the sofa with a volume of the encyclopaedia. Looking over her shoulder, Aunt Cal noted with alarm that she had turned to the article on the Australian bush.

It was very quiet in the room. Several times Fifi raised her head as if listening, and once she got up and went to the door and stared out for a long time into the night. Her aunts were both poised in their chairs to rush after her if she showed signs of bolting, but after a moment she closed the door with a sigh and returned to her chair. It was with relief that a little after nine they heard the sound of automobile wheels on the shell drive and knew that Dr Gallup had arrived at last.

He was a short, stoutish man, with alert black eyes and an intense manner. He came in, glancing eagerly about him, and his eye brightened as it fell on Fifi like the eye of a hungry man when he sees prospective food. Fifi returned his gaze curiously, evidently unaware that his arrival had anything to do with herself.

"Is this the lady?" he cried, dismissing her aunts with a perfunctory handshake and approaching Fifi at a lively hop.

"This gentleman is Dr Gallup, dear," beamed Aunt Jo, expectant and reassured. "He's an old friend of mine who's going to help you."

"Of course I am!" insisted Dr Gallup, jumping around her cordially. "I'm going to fix her up just fine."

"He understands everything about the human mind," said Aunt Jo.

"Not everything," admitted Dr Gallup, smiling modestly. "But we often make the regular doctors wonder." He turned roguishly to Fifi. "Yes, young lady, we often make the regular doctors wonder."

Clapping his hands together decisively, he drew up a chair in front of Fifi.

"Come," he cried, "let us see what can be the matter. We'll start by having you tell me the whole story in your own way. Begin."

"The story," remarked Fifi, with a slight yawn, "happens to be none of your business."

"None of my business!" he exclaimed incredulously. "Why, my girl, I'm trying to help you! Come now, tell old Dr Gallup the whole story."

"Let my aunts tell you," said Fifi coldly. "They seem to know more about it than I do."

Dr Gallup frowned.

"They've already outlined the situation. Perhaps I'd better begin by asking you questions."

"You'll answer the doctor's questions, won't you, dear?" coaxed Aunt Jo. "Dr Gallup is one of the most modern doctors in New York."

"I'm an old-fashioned girl," objected Fifi maliciously. "And I think it's immoral to pry into people's affairs. But go ahead and I'll try to think up a comeback for everything you say."

Dr Gallup overlooked the unnecessary rudeness of this remark and mustered a professional smile.

"Now, Miss Marsden, I understand that about a month ago you came out here for a rest."

Fifi shook her head.

"No, I came out to hide my face."

"You were ashamed because you had broken your engagement?"

"Terribly. If you desert a man at the altar you brand him for the rest of his life."

"Why?" he demanded sharply.

"Why not?"

"You're not asking me. I'm asking you… However, let that pass. Now, when you arrived here, how did you pass your time?"

"I walked mostly – walked along the beach."

"It was on one of these walks that you met the – ah – person your aunt told me of over the telephone?"

Fifi pinkened slightly.

"Yes."

"What was he doing when you first saw him?"

"He was looking down at me out of a tree."

There was a general exclamation from her aunts, in which the word "monkey" figured.

"Did he attract you immediately?" demanded Dr Gallup.

"Why, not especially. At first I only laughed."

"I see. Now, as I understand, this man was very – ah – very originally clad."

"Yes," agreed Fifi.

"He was unshaven?"

"Yes."

"Ah!" Dr Gallup seemed to go through a sort of convolution like a medium coming out of a trance. "Miss Fifi," he cried out triumphantly, "did you ever read *The Sheik*?"*

"Never heard of it."

"Did you ever read any book in which a girl was wooed by a so-called sheikh or caveman?"

"Not that I remember."

"What, then, was your favourite book when you were a girl?"

"*Little Lord Fauntleroy*."*

Dr Gallup was considerably disappointed. He decided to approach the case from a new angle.

"Miss Fifi, won't you admit that there's nothing behind this but some fancy in your head?"

"On the contrary," said Fifi startlingly, "there's a great deal more behind it than any of you suspect. He's changed my entire attitude on life."

"What do you mean?"

She seemed on the point of making some declaration, but after a moment her lovely eyes narrowed obstinately and she remained silent.

"Miss Fifi" – Dr Gallup raised his voice sharply – "the daughter of C. T. J. Calhoun, the biscuit man, ran away with a taxi driver. Do you know what she's doing now?"

"No."

"She's working in a laundry on the East Side, trying to keep her child's body and soul together."

He looked at her keenly; there were signs of agitation in her face.

"Estelle Holliday ran away in 1920 with her father's second man!" he cried. "Shall I tell you where I heard of her last? She stumbled into a charity hospital, bruised from head to foot, because her drunken husband had beaten her to within an inch of her life!"

Fifi was breathing hard. Her aunts leant forward. Dr Gallup sprang suddenly to his feet.

"But they were playing safe compared to you!" he shouted. "They didn't woo an ex-convict with blood on his hands."

And now Fifi was on her feet, too, her eyes flashing fire.

"Be careful!" she cried. "Don't go too far!"

"I can't go too far!" He reached in his pocket, plucked out a folded evening paper and slapped it down on the table.

"Read that, Miss Fifi!" he shouted. "It'll tell you how four man-killers entered a bank in West Crampton three weeks ago. It'll tell you how they shot down the cashier in cold blood, and how one of them, the most brutal, the most ferocious, the most inhuman, got away. And it will tell you that that human gorilla is now supposed to be hiding in the neighbourhood of Montauk Point!"

There was a short stifled sound as Aunt Jo and Aunt Cal, who had always done everything in complete unison, fainted away together. At the same moment there was loud, violent knocking, like the knocking of a heavy club, upon the barred front door.

4

"WHO'S THERE?" cried Dr Gallup, starting. "Who's there – or I'll shoot!"

His eyes roved quickly about the room, looking for a possible weapon.

"Who are you?" shouted a voice from the porch. "You better open up or I'll blow a hole through the door."

"What'll we do?" exclaimed Dr Gallup, perspiring freely.

Fifi, who had been sprinkling water impartially upon her aunts, turned around with a scornful smile.

"It's just Percy, the yardman," she explained. "He probably thinks that you're a burglar."

She went to the door and lifted the latch. Percy, gun in hand, peered cautiously into the room.

"It's all right, Percy. This is just an insane specialist from New York."

"Everything's a little insane tonight," announced Percy in a frightened voice. "For the last hour I've been hearing the sound of oars."

The eyes of Aunt Jo and Aunt Cal fluttered open simultaneously.

"There's a fog all over the Point," went on Percy dazedly, "and it's got voices in it. I couldn't see a foot before my face, but I could swear there was boats offshore, and I heard a dozen people talkin' and callin' to each other, just as if a lot of ghosts was havin' a picnic supper on the beach."

"What was that noise?" cried Aunt Jo, sitting upright.

"The door was locked," explained Percy, "so I knocked on it with my gun."

"No, I mean now!"

They listened. Through the open door came a low, groaning sound, issuing out of the dark mist which covered shore and sea alike.

"We'll go right down and find out!" cried Dr Gallup, who had recovered his shattered equilibrium; and, as the moaning sound drifted in again, like the last agony of some monster from the deep, he added, "I think you needed more than a psychoanalyst here tonight. Is there another gun in the house?"

Aunt Cal got up and took a small pearl-mounted revolver from the desk drawer.

"You can't leave us in this house alone," she declared emphatically. "Wherever you go we're going too!"

Keeping close together, the four of them, for Fifi had suddenly disappeared, made their way outdoors and down the porch steps, where they hesitated a moment, peering into the impenetrable haze, more mysterious than darkness upon their eyes.

"It's out there," whispered Percy, facing the sea.

"Forward we go!" muttered Dr Gallup tensely. "I'm inclined to think this is all a question of nerves."

They moved slowly and silently along the sand, until suddenly Percy caught hold of the doctor's arm.

"Listen!" he whispered sharply.

They all became motionless. Out of the neighbouring darkness a dim, indistinguishable figure had materialized, walking with unnatural rigidity along the shore. Pressed against his body he carried some long, dark drape that hung almost to the sand. Immediately he disappeared into the mist, to be succeeded by another phantom walking at the same military gait, this one with something white and faintly terrible dangling from his arm. A moment later, not ten yards away from them, in the direction in which the figure had gone, a faint dull glow sprang to life, proceeding apparently from behind the largest of the dunes.

Huddled together, they advanced towards the dune, hesitated, and then, following Dr Gallup's example, dropped to their knees and began to crawl cautiously up its shoreward side. The glow became stronger as they reached the top, and at the same moment their heads popped up over the crest. This is what they saw:

In the light of four strong pocket flashlights, borne by four sailors in spotless white, a gentleman was shaving himself, standing clad only in athletic underwear upon the sand. Before his eyes an irreproachable valet held a silver mirror which gave back the soapy reflection of his face. To right and left stood two additional menservants, one with a dinner coat and trousers hanging from his arm and the other bearing a white stiff shirt whose studs glistened in the glow of the electric lamps. There was not a sound except the dull scrape of the razor along its wielder's face and the intermittent groaning sound that blew in out of the sea.

But it was not the bizarre nature of the ceremony, with its dim, weird surroundings under the unsteady light, that drew from the two women a short involuntary sigh. It was the fact that the face in the mirror, the unshaven half of it, was terribly familiar, and in a moment they knew to whom that half-face belonged – it was the countenance of their niece's savage wooer who had lately prowled half-naked along the beach.

Even as they looked he completed one side of his face, whereupon a valet stepped forward and with a scissors sheared off the exterior growth more on the other, disclosing, in its entirety now, the symmetrical visage of a young, somewhat haggard but not unhandsome man. He lathered the bearded side, pulled the razor quickly over it and then applied a lotion to the whole surface, and inspected himself with considerable interest in the mirror. The sight seemed to please him, for he smiled. At a word one of the valets held forth the trousers in which he now encased his likely legs. Diving into his open shirt, he procured the collar, flipped a proper black bow with a practised hand and slipped into the waiting dinner coat. After a transformation which had taken place before their very eyes, Aunt Cal and Aunt Jo found themselves gazing upon as immaculate and impeccable a young man as they had ever seen.

"Walters!" he said suddenly, in a clear, cultured voice.

One of the white-clad sailors stepped forward and saluted.

"You can take the boats back to the yacht. You ought to be able to find it all right by the foghorn."

"Yes, sir."

"When the fog lifts you'd better stand out to sea. Meanwhile, wireless New York to send down my car. It's to call for me at the Marsden house on Montauk Point."

As the sailor turned away, his torch flashed upward, accidentally wavering upon the four amazed faces which were peering down at the curious scene.

"Look there, sir!" he exclaimed.

The four torches picked out the eavesdropping party at the top of the hill.

"Hands up, there!" cried Percy, pointing his rifle down into the glare of light.

"Miss Marsden!" called the young man eagerly. "I was just coming to call."

"Don't move!" shouted Percy; and then to the doctor, "Had I better fire?"

"Certainly not!" cried Dr Gallup. "Young man, does your name happen to be what I think it is?"

The young man bowed politely.

"My name is George Van Tyne."

A few minutes later the immaculate young man and two completely bewildered ladies were shaking hands. "I owe you more apologies than I can ever make," he confessed, "for having sacrificed you to the strange whim of a young girl."

"What whim?" demanded Aunt Cal.

"Why" – he hesitated – "you see, all my life I have devoted much attention to the so-called niceties of conduct: niceties of dress, of manner, of behaviour..."

He broke off apologetically.

"Go on," commanded Aunt Cal.

"And your niece has too. She always considered herself rather a model of – of civilized behaviour" – he flushed – "until she met me."

"I see," Dr Gallup nodded. "She couldn't bear to marry anyone who was more of a – shall we say, a dandy? – than herself."

"Exactly," said George Van Tyne, with a perfect eighteenth-century bow. "It was necessary to show her what a – what an..."

"...unspeakable egg," supplied Aunt Josephine.

"...what an unspeakable egg I could be. It was difficult, but not impossible. If you know what's correct, you must necessarily know what's incorrect; and my aim was to be as ferociously incorrect as possible. My one hope is that someday you'll be able to forgive me for throwing the sand – I'm afraid that my impersonation ran away with me."

A moment later they were all walking towards the house.

"But I still can't believe that a gentleman could be so – so unspeakable," gasped Aunt Jo. "And what will Fifi say?"

"Nothing," answered Van Tyne cheerfully. "You see, Fifi knew about it all along. She even recognized me in the tree that first day. She begged me to – to desist until this afternoon; but I refused until she had kissed me tenderly, beard and all."

Aunt Cal stopped suddenly.

"This is all very well, young man," she said sternly, "but since you have so many sides to you, how do we know that in one of your off moments you aren't the murderer who's hiding out on the Point?"

"The murderer?" asked Van Tyne blankly. "What murderer?"

"Ah, I can explain that, Miss Marsden." Dr Gallup smiled apologetically. "As a matter of fact, there wasn't any murderer."

"No murderer?" Aunt Cal looked at him sharply.

"No, I invented the bank robbery and the escaped murderer and all. I was merely applying a form of strong medicine to your niece."

Aunt Cal looked at him scornfully and turned to her sister. "All your modern ideas are not so successful as mah-jong," she remarked significantly.

The fog had blown back to sea, and as they came in sight of the house the lamps were glowing out into the darkness. On the porch waited an immaculate girl in a gleaming white dress, strung with beads which glistened in the new moonlight.

"The perfect man," murmured Aunt Jo, flushing, "is, of course, he who will make any sacrifice."

Van Tyne did not answer; he was engaged in removing some imperceptible flaw, less visible than a hair, from his elbow, and when he had finished he smiled. There was now not the faintest imperfection anywhere about him, except where the strong beating of his heart disturbed faintly the satin facing of his coat.

John Jackson's Arcady

1

THE FIRST LETTER, CRUMPLED into an emotional ball, lay at his elbow, and it did not matter faintly now what this second letter contained. For a long time after he had stripped off the envelope, he still gazed up at the oil painting of slain grouse over the sideboard, just as though he had not faced it every morning at breakfast for the past twelve years. Finally he lowered his eyes and began to read:

> *Dear Mr Jackson: This is just a reminder that you have consented to speak at our annual meeting Thursday. We don't want to dictate your choice of a topic, but it has occurred to me that it would be interesting to hear from you on What Have I Got Out of Life. Coming from you this should be an inspiration to everyone.*
>
> *We are delighted to have you anyhow, and we appreciate the honour that you confer on us by coming at all.*
>
>

Most cordially yours,

ANTHONY ROREBACK,

Sec. Civic Welfare League
>

"What have I got out of life?" repeated John Jackson aloud, raising up his head.

He wanted no more breakfast, so he picked up both letters and went out on his wide front porch to smoke a cigar and lie about for a lazy half-hour before he went downtown. He had done this each morning for ten years – ever since his wife ran off one windy night and gave him back the custody of his leisure hours. He loved to rest on this porch in the fresh warm mornings and through a porthole in the green vines watch the automobiles pass along the street, the widest, shadiest, pleasantest street in town.

"What have I got out of life?" he said again, sitting down on a creaking wicker chair; and then, after a long pause, he whispered, "Nothing."

The word frightened him. In all his forty-five years he had never said such a thing before. His greatest tragedies had not embittered him, only made him sad. But here beside the warm friendly rain that tumbled from his eaves onto the familiar lawn, he knew at last that life had stripped him clean of all happiness and all illusion.

He knew this because of the crumpled ball which closed out his hope in his only son. It told him what a hundred hints and indication had told him before: that his son was weak and vicious, and the language in which it was conveyed was no less emphatic for being polite. The letter was from the dean of the college in New Haven, a gentleman who said exactly what he meant in every word:

Dear Mr Jackson: It is with much regret that I write to tell you that your son, Ellery Hamil Jackson, has been requested to withdraw from the university. Last year largely, I am afraid, out of personal feeling towards you, I yielded to your request that he be allowed another chance. I see now that this was a mistake, and I should be failing in my duty if I did not tell you that he is not the sort of boy we want here. His conduct at the sophomore dance was such that several under-graduates took it upon themselves to administer violent correction.

It grieves me to write you this, but I see no advantage in presenting the case otherwise than as it is. I have requested that he leave New Haven by the day after tomorrow. I am, sir,

Yours very sincerely,
AUSTIN SCHEMMERHORN,
Dean of the College

What particularly disgraceful thing his son had done John Jackson did not care to imagine. He knew without any question that what the dean said was true. Why, there were houses already in this town where his son, John Jackson's son, was no longer welcome! For a while Ellery had been forgiven because of his father, and he had been more than forgiven at home, because John Jackson was one of those rare men who can forgive even their own families. But he would never be forgiven any more. Sitting on his porch this morning beside the gentle April rain, something had happened in his father's heart.

"What have I had out of life?" John Jackson shook his head from side to side with quiet, tired despair. "Nothing!"

He picked up the second letter, the civic-welfare letter, and read it over; and then helpless, dazed laughter shook him physically until he trembled in his chair. On Wednesday, at the hour when his delinquent boy would arrive at the motherless home, John Jackson would be standing on a platform downtown, delivering one hundred resounding platitudes of inspiration and cheer. "Members of the association" – their faces, eager, optimistic, impressed, would look up at him like hollow moons – "I have been requested to try to tell you in a few words what I have had from life…" Many people would be there to hear, for the clever young secretary had hit upon a topic with the personal note – what John Jackson, successful, able and popular, had found for himself in the tumultuous grab bag. They would listen with wistful attention, hoping that he would disclose some secret formula that would make their lives as popular and successful and happy as his own. They believed in rules; all the young men in the city believed in hard-and-fast rules, and many of them clipped coupons and sent away for little booklets that promised them the riches and good fortune they desired.

"Members of the association, to begin with, let me say that there is so much in life that if we don't find it, it is not the fault of life, but of ourselves."

The ring of the stale, dull words mingled with the patter of the rain went on and on endlessly, but John Jackson knew that he would never make that speech, or any speeches ever again. He had dreamt his last dream too long, but he was awake at last.

"I shall not go on flattering a world that I have found unkind," he whispered to the rain. "Instead, I shall go out of this house and out of this town and somewhere find again the happiness that I possessed when I was young."

Nodding his head, he tore both letters into small fragments and dropped them on the table beside him. For half an hour longer he sat there, rocking a little and smoking his cigar slowly and blowing the blue smoke out into the rain.

2

D OWN AT HIS OFFICE, his chief clerk, Mr Fowler, approached him with his morning smile.

"Looking fine, Mr Jackson. Nice day if it hadn't rained."

"Yeah," agreed John Jackson cheerfully. "Clear up in an hour. Anybody outside?"

"A lady named Mrs Ralston."

Mr Fowler raised his grizzled eyebrows in facetious mournfulness.

"Tell her I can't see her," said John Jackson, rather to his clerk's surprise.

"And let me have a pencil memorandum of the money I've given away through her these twenty years."

"Why – yes, sir."

Mr Fowler had always urged John Jackson to look more closely into his promiscuous charities; but now, after these two decades, it rather alarmed him.

When the list arrived – its preparation took an hour of burrowing through old ledgers and cheque stubs – John Jackson studied it for a long time in silence.

"That woman's got more money than you have," grumbled Fowler at his elbow. "Every time she comes in she's wearing a new hat. I bet she never hands out a cent herself – just goes around asking other people."

John Jackson did not answer. He was thinking that Mrs Ralston had been one of the first women in town to bar Ellery Jackson from her house. She did quite right, of course; and yet perhaps back there when Ellery was sixteen, if he had cared for some nice girl...

"Thomas J. MacDowell's outside. Do you want to see him? I said I didn't think you were in, because on second thoughts, Mr Jackson, you look tired this morning—"

"I'll see him," interrupted John Jackson.

He watched Fowler's retreating figure with an unfamiliar expression in his eyes. All that cordial diffuseness of Fowler's – he wondered what it covered in the man's heart. Several times, without Fowler's knowledge, Jackson had seen him giving imitations of the boss for the benefit of the other employees; imitations with a touch of malice in them that John Jackson had smiled at then, but that now crept insinuatingly into his mind.

"Doubtless he considers me a good deal of a fool," murmured John Jackson thoughtfully, "because I've kept him long after his usefulness was over. It's a way men have, I suppose, to despise anyone they can impose on."

Thomas J. MacDowell, a big barn door of a man with huge white hands, came boisterously into the office. If John Jackson had gone in for enemies he must have started with Tom MacDowell. For twenty years they had fought over every question of municipal affairs, and back in 1908 they had once stood facing each other with clenched hands on a public platform, because Jackson had said in print what everyone knew – that MacDowell was the worst political influence that the town had ever known. That was forgotten now; all that was remembered of it went into a peculiar flash of the eye that passed between them when they met.

"Hello, Mr Jackson," said MacDowell with full, elaborate cordiality. "We need your help and we need your money."

"How so?"

"Tomorrow morning, in the *Eagle*, you'll see the plan for the new Union Station. The only thing that'll stand in the way is the question of location. We want your land."

"My land?"

"The railroad wants to build on the twenty acres just this side of the river, where your warehouse stands. If you'll let them have it cheap we get our station; if not, we can just whistle into the air."

Jackson nodded.

"I see."

"What price?" asked MacDowell mildly.

"No price."

His visitor's mouth dropped open in surprise.

"That from you?" he demanded.

John Jackson got to his feet.

"I've decided not to be the local goat any more," he announced steadily. "You threw out the only fair, decent plan because it interfered with some private reservations of your own. And now that there's a snag, you'd like the punishment to fall on me. I tear down my warehouse and hand over some of the best property in the city for a song because you made a little 'mistake' last year!"

"But last year's over now," protested MacDowell. "Whatever happened then doesn't change the situation now. The city needs the station, and so" – there was a faint touch of irony in his voice – "and so naturally I come to its leading citizen, counting on his well-known public spirit."

"Go out of my office, MacDowell," said John Jackson suddenly. "I'm tired."

MacDowell scrutinized him severely.

"What's come over you today?"

Jackson closed his eyes.

"I don't want to argue," he said after a while.

MacDowell slapped his fat upper leg and got to his feet.

"This is a funny attitude from you," he remarked. "You better think it over."

"Goodbye."

Perceiving, to his astonishment, that John Jackson meant what he said, MacDowell took his monstrous body to the door.

"Well, well," he said, turning and shaking his finger at Jackson as if he were a bad boy, "who'd have thought it from you after all?"

When he had gone Jackson rang again for his clerk.

"I'm going away," he remarked casually. "I may be gone for some time – perhaps a week, perhaps longer. I want you to cancel every engagement I have and pay off my servants at home and close up my house."

Mr Fowler could hardly believe his ears.

"Close up your house?"

Jackson nodded.

"But why – why is it?" demanded Fowler in amazement.

Jackson looked out the high window upon the grey little city drenched now by slanting, slapping rain – his city, he had felt sometimes, in those rare moments when life had lent him time to be happy. That flash of green trees running up the main boulevard – he had made that possible, and Children's Park, and the white dripping buildings around Courthouse Square over the way.

"I don't know," he answered, "but I think I ought to get a breath of spring."

When Fowler had gone he put on his hat and raincoat and, to avoid anyone who might be waiting, went through an unused filing room that gave access to the elevator. The filing room was actively inhabited this morning, however; and, rather to his surprise, by a young boy about nine years old, who was laboriously writing his initials in chalk on the steel files.

"Hello!" exclaimed John Jackson.

He was accustomed to speak to children in a tone of interested equality. "I didn't know this office was occupied this morning."

The little boy looked at him steadily.

"My name's John Jackson Fowler," he announced.

"What?"

"My name's John Jackson Fowler."

"Oh, I see. You're – you're Mr Fowler's son?"

"Yeah, he's my father."

"I see." John Jackson's eyes narrowed a little. "Well, I bid you good morning."

He passed on out the door, wondering cynically what particular axe Fowler hoped to grind by this unwarranted compliment. John Jackson Fowler! It was one of his few sources of relief that his own son did not bear his name.

A few minutes later he was writing on a yellow blank in the telegraph office below:

ELLERY JACKSON, CHAPEL STREET, NEW HAVEN, CONNECTICUT. THERE IS NOT THE SLIGHTEST REASON FOR COMING HOME, BECAUSE YOU HAVE NO HOME TO COME TO ANY MORE. THE

MAMMOTH TRUST COMPANY OF NEW YORK WILL PAY YOU FIFTY DOLLARS A MONTH FOR THE REST OF YOUR LIFE, OR FOR AS LONG AS YOU CAN KEEP YOURSELF OUT OF JAIL. JOHN JACKSON.

"That's – that's a long message, sir," gasped the dispatcher, startled. "Do you want it to go straight?"

"Straight," said John Jackson, nodding.

3

HE RODE SEVENTY MILES that afternoon, while the rain dried up into rills of dust on the windows of the train and the country became green with vivid spring. When the sun was growing definitely crimson in the west he disembarked at a little lost town named Florence, just over the border of the next state. John Jackson had been born in this town; he had not been back here for twenty years.

The taxi driver, whom he recognized, silently, as a certain George Stirling, playmate of his youth, drove him to a battered hotel, where, to the surprise of the delighted landlord, he engaged a room. Leaving his raincoat on the sagging bed, he strolled out through a deserted lobby into the street.

It was a bright, warm afternoon, and the silver sliver of a moon riding already in the east promised a clear, brilliant night. John Jackson walked along a somnolent Main Street, where every shop and hitching post and horse fountain made some strange thing happen inside him, because he had known these things for more than inanimate objects as a little boy. At one shop, catching a glimpse of a familiar face through the glass, he hesitated; but changing his mind, continued along the street, turning off at a wide road at the corner. The road was lined sparsely by a row of battered houses, some of them repainted a pale unhealthy blue and all of them set far back in large plots of shaggy and unkempt land.

He walked along the road for a sunny half-mile – a half-mile shrunk up now into a short green aisle crowded with memories. Here, for example, a careless mule had stamped permanently on his thigh the mark of an iron shoe. In that cottage had lived two gentle old maids, who gave brown raisin cakes every Thursday to John Jackson and his little brother – the brother who had died as a child.

As he neared the end of his pilgrimage his breath came faster and the house where he was born seemed to run up to him on living feet. It was a collapsed house, a retired house, set far back from the road and sunned and washed to the dull colour of old wood.

One glance told him it was no longer a dwelling. The shutters that remained were closed tight, and from the tangled vines arose, as a single chord, a rich shrill sound of a hundred birds. John Jackson left the road and stalked across the yard knee-deep in abandoned grass. When he came near, something choked up his throat. He paused and sat down on a stone in a patch of welcome shade.

This was his own house, as no other house would ever be; within these plain walls he had been incomparably happy. Here he had known and learnt that kindness which he had carried into life. Here he had found the secret of those few simple decencies, so often invoked, so inimitable and so rare, which in the turmoil of competitive industry had made him to coarser men a source of half-scoffing, half-admiring surprise. This was his house, because his honour had been born and nourished here; he had known every hardship of the country poor, but no preventable regret.

And yet another memory, a memory more haunting than any other, and grown strong at this crisis in his life, had really drawn him back. In this yard, on this battered porch, in the very tree over his head, he seemed still to catch the glint of yellow hair and the glow of bright childish eyes that had belonged to his first love, the girl who had lived in the long-vanished house across the way. It was her ghost who was most alive here, after all.

He got up suddenly, stumbling through the shrubbery, and followed an almost obliterated path to the house, starting at the whirring sound of a blackbird which rose out of the grass close by. The front porch sagged dangerously at his step as he pushed open the door. There was no sound inside, except the steady slow throb of silence; but as he stepped in a word came to him, involuntary as his breath, and he uttered it aloud, as if he were calling to someone in the empty house.

"Alice," he cried; and then louder, "Alice!"

From a room at the left came a short, small, frightened cry. Startled, John Jackson paused in the door, convinced that his own imagination had evoked the reality of the cry.

"Alice!" he called doubtfully.

"Who's there?"

There was no mistake this time. The voice, frightened, strange, and yet familiar, came from what had once been the parlour, and as he listened John Jackson was aware of a nervous step within. Trembling a little, he pushed open the parlour door.

A woman with alarmed bright eyes and reddish-gold hair was standing in the centre of the bare room. She was of that age that trembles between the enduring youth of a fine, unworried life and the imperative call of forty years, and there was that indefinable loveliness in her face that youth gives sometimes just before it leaves a dwelling it has possessed for long. Her figure, just outside of slenderness, leant with dignified grace against the old mantel on which her white hand rested, and through a rift in the shutter a shaft of late sunshine fell through upon her gleaming hair.

When John Jackson came in the doorway her large grey eyes closed and then opened again, and she gave another little cry. Then a curious thing happened; they stared at each other for a moment without a word, her hand dropped from the mantel and she took a swaying step towards him. And, as if it were the most natural thing in the world, John Jackson came forward, too, and took her into his arms and kissed her as if she were a little child.

"Alice!" he said huskily.

She drew a long breath and pushed herself away from him.

"I've come back here," he muttered unsteadily, "and find you waiting in this room where we used to sit, just as if I'd never been away."

"I only dropped in for a minute," she said, as if that was the most important thing in the world. "And now, naturally, I'm going to cry."

"Don't cry."

"I've got to cry. You don't think" – she smiled through wet eyes – "you don't think that things like this hap – happen to a person every day."

John Jackson walked in wild excitement to the window and threw it open to the afternoon.

"What were you doing here?" he cried, turning around. "Did you just come by accident today?"

"I come every week. I bring the children sometimes, but usually I come alone."

"The children!" he exclaimed. "Have you got children?"

She nodded.

"I've been married for years and years."

They stood there looking at each other for a moment; then they both laughed and glanced away.

"I kissed you," she said.

"Are you sorry?"

She shook her head.

"And the last time I kissed you was down by that gate ten thousand years ago."

He took her hand, and they went out and sat side by side on the broken stoop. The sun was painting the west with sweeping bands of peach bloom and pigeon blood and golden yellow.

"You're married," she said. "I saw in the paper – years ago."

He nodded.

"Yes, I've been married," he answered gravely. "My wife went away with someone she cared for many years ago."

"Ah, I'm sorry." And after another long silence: "It's a gorgeous evening, John Jackson."

"It's a long time since I've been so happy."

There was so much to say and to tell that neither of them tried to talk, but only sat there holding hands, like two children who had wandered for a long time through a wood and now came upon each other with unimaginable happiness in an accidental glade. Her husband was poor, she said; he knew that from the worn, unfashionable dress which she wore with such an air. He was George Harland – he kept a garage in the village.

"George Harland – a red-headed boy?" he asked wonderingly.

She nodded.

"We were engaged for years. Sometimes I thought we'd never marry. Twice I postponed it, but it was getting late to be just a girl – I was twenty-five, and so finally we did. After that I was in love with him for over a year."

When the sunset fell together in a jumbled heap of colour in the bottom of the sky, they strolled back along the quiet road, still hand in hand.

"Will you come to dinner? I want you to see the children. My oldest boy is just fifteen."

She lived in a plain frame house two doors from the garage, where two little girls were playing around a battered and ancient but occupied baby carriage in the yard.

"Mother! Oh, Mother!" they cried.

Small brown arms swirled around her neck as she knelt beside them on the walk.

"Sister says Anna didn't come, so we can't have any dinner."

"Mother'll cook dinner. What's the matter with Anna?"

"Anna's father's sick. She couldn't come."

A tall, tired man of fifty, who was reading a paper on the porch, rose and slipped a coat over his suspenders as they mounted the steps.

"Anna didn't come," he said in a noncommittal voice.

"I know. I'm going to cook dinner. Who do you suppose this is here?"

The two men shook hands in a friendly way, and with a certain deference to John Jackson's clothes and his prosperous manner, Harland went inside for another chair.

"We've heard about you a great deal, Mr Jackson," he said as Alice disappeared into the kitchen. "We heard about a lot of ways you made them sit up and take notice over yonder."

John nodded politely, but at the mention of the city he had just left a wave of distaste went over him.

"I'm sorry I ever left here," he answered frankly. "And I'm not just saying that either. Tell me what the years have done for you, Harland, I hear you've got a garage."

"Yeah – down the road a ways. I'm doing right well, matter of fact. Nothing you'd call well in the city," he added in hasty depredation.

"You know, Harland," said John Jackson, after a moment, "I'm very much in love with your wife."

"Yeah?" Harland laughed. "Well, she's a pretty nice lady, I find."

"I think I always have been in love with her, all these years."

"Yeah?" Harland laughed again. That someone should be in love with his wife seemed the most casual pleasantry. "You better tell her about it. She don't get so many nice compliments as she used to in her young days."

Six of them sat down at table, including an awkward boy of fifteen, who looked like his father, and two little girls whose faces shone from a hasty toilet. Many things had happened in the town, John discovered; the factitious prosperity which had promised to descend upon it in the late Nineties had vanished when two factories had closed up and moved away, and the population was smaller now by a few hundred than it had been a quarter of a century ago.

After a plentiful plain dinner they all went to the porch, where the children silhouetted themselves in silent balance on the railing and unrecognizable people called greetings as they passed along the dark, dusty street. After a while the younger children went to bed, and the boy and his father arose and put on their coats.

"I guess I'll run up to the garage," said Harland. "I always go up about this time every night. You two just sit here and talk about old times."

As father and son moved out of sight along the dim street John Jackson turned to Alice and slipped his arm about her shoulder and looked into her eyes.

"I love you, Alice."

"I love you."

Never since his marriage had he said that to any woman except his wife. But this was a new world tonight, with spring all about him in the air, and he felt as if he were holding his own lost youth in his arms.

"I've always loved you," she murmured. "Just before I go to sleep every night, I've always been able to see your face. Why didn't you come back?"

Tenderly he smoothed her hair. He had never known such happiness before. He felt that he had established dominance over time itself, so that it rolled away for him, yielding up one vanished springtime after another to the mastery of his overwhelming emotion.

"We're still young, we two people," he said exultantly. "We made a silly mistake a long, long time ago, but we found out in time."

"Tell me about it," she whispered.

"This morning, in the rain, I heard your voice."

"What did my voice say?"

"It said, 'Come home.'"

"And here you are, my dear."

"Here I am."

Suddenly he got to his feet.

"You and I are going away," he said. "Do you understand that?"

"I always knew that when you came for me I'd go."

Later, when the moon had risen, she walked with him to the gate.

"Tomorrow!" he whispered.

"Tomorrow!"

His heart was going like mad, and he stood carefully away from her to let footsteps across the way approach, pass and fade out down the dim street. With a sort of wild innocence he kissed her once more and held her close to his heart under the April moon.

4

WHEN HE AWOKE IT WAS ELEVEN O'CLOCK, and he drew himself a cool bath, splashing around in it with much of the exultation of the night before.

"I have thought too much these twenty years," he said to himself. "It's thinking that makes people old."

It was hotter than it had been the day before, and as he looked out the window the dust in the street seemed more tangible than on the night before. He breakfasted alone downstairs, wondering with the incessant wonder of the city man why fresh cream is almost unobtainable in the country. Word had spread already that he was home, and several men rose to greet him as he came into the lobby. Asked if he had a wife and children, he said no, in a careless way, and after he had said it he had a vague feeling of discomfort.

"I'm all alone," he went on, with forced jocularity. "I wanted to come back and see the old town again."

"Stay long?" They looked at him curiously.

"Just a day or so."

He wondered what they would think tomorrow. There would be excited little groups of them here and there along the street with the startling and audacious news.

"See here," he wanted to say, "you think I've had a wonderful life over there in the city, but I haven't. I came down here because life had beaten me, and if there's any brightness in my eyes this morning it's because last night I found a part of my lost youth tucked away in this little town."

At noon, as he walked towards Alice's house, the heat increased and several times he stopped to wipe the sweat from his forehead. When he turned in at the gate he saw her waiting on the porch, wearing what was apparently a Sunday dress and moving herself gently back and forth in a rocking chair in a way that he remembered her doing as a girl.

"Alice!" he exclaimed happily.

Her finger rose swiftly and touched her lips.

"Look out!" she said in a low voice.

He sat down beside her and took her hand, but she replaced it on the arm of her chair and resumed her gentle rocking.

"Be careful. The children are inside."

"But I can't be careful. Now that life's begun all over again, I've forgotten all the caution that I learnt in the other life, the one that's past!"

"Sh-h-h!"

Somewhat irritated, he glanced at her closely. Her face, unmoved and unresponsive, seemed vaguely older than it had yesterday; she was white and tired. But he dismissed the impression with a low, exultant laugh.

"Alice, I haven't slept as I slept last night since I was a little boy, except that several times I woke up just for the joy of seeing the same moon we once knew together. I'd got it back."

"I didn't sleep at all."

"I'm sorry."

"I realized about two o'clock or three o'clock that I could never go away from my children – even with you."

He was struck dumb. He looked at her blankly for a moment, and then he laughed – a short, incredulous laugh.

"Never, never!" she went on, shaking her head passionately. "Never, never, never! When I thought of it I began to tremble all over, right in my bed." She hesitated. "I don't know what came over me yesterday evening, John. When I'm with you, you can always make me do or feel or think exactly what you like. But this is too late, I guess. It doesn't seem real at all; it just seems sort of crazy to me, as if I'd dreamt it, that's all."

John Jackson laughed again, not incredulously this time, but on a menacing note.

"What do you mean?" he demanded.

She began to cry and hid her eyes behind her hand because some people were passing along the road.

"You've got to tell me more than that," cried John Jackson, his voice rising a little. "I can't just take that and go away."

"Please don't talk so loud," she implored him. "It's so hot and I'm so confused. I guess I'm just a small-town woman, after all. It seems somehow awful to be talking here with you, when my husband's working all day in the dust and heat."

"Awful to be talking here?" he repeated.

"Don't look that way!" she cried miserably. "I can't bear to hurt you so. You have children, too, to think of – you said you had a son."

"A son." The fact seemed so far away that he looked at her, startled. "Oh, yes, I have a son."

A sort of craziness, a wild illogic in the situation had communicated itself to him; and yet he fought blindly against it as he felt his own mood of ecstasy slipping away. For twenty hours he had recaptured the power of seeing things through a mist of hope – hope in some vague, happy destiny that lay just over the hill – and now with every word she uttered the mist was passing, the hope, the town, the memory, the very face of this woman before his eyes.

"Never again in this world," he cried with a last despairing effort, "will you and I have a chance at happiness!"

But he knew, even as he said this, that it had never been a chance; simply a wild, desperate sortie from two long-beleaguered fortresses by night.

He looked up to see that George Harland had turned in at the gate.

"Lunch is ready," called Alice, raising her head with an expression of relief. "John's going to be with us too."

"I can't," said John Jackson quickly. "You're both very kind."

"Better stay." Harland, in oily overalls, sank wearily on the steps and with a large handkerchief polished the hot space beneath his thin grey hair. "We can give you some iced tea." He looked up at John. "I don't know whether these hot days make you feel your age like I feel mine."

"I guess – it affects all of us alike," said John Jackson with an effort. "The awful part of it is that I've got to go back to the city this afternoon."

"Really?" Harland nodded with polite regret.

"Why, yes. The fact is I promised to make a speech."

"Is that so? Speak on some city problem, I suppose."

"No; the fact is" – the words, forming in his mind to a senseless rhythm pushed themselves out – "I'm going to speak on What Have I Got Out of Life."

Then he became conscious of the heat indeed; and still wearing that smile he knew so well how to muster, he felt himself sway dizzily against the porch rail. After a minute they were walking with him towards the gate.

"I'm sorry you're leaving," said Alice, with frightened eyes. "Come back and visit your old town again."

"I will."

Blind with unhappiness, he set off up the street at what he felt must be a stumble; but some dim necessity made him turn after he had gone a little way and smile back at them and wave his hand. They were still standing there, and they waved at him and he saw them turn and walk together into their house.

"I must go back and make my speech," he said to himself as he walked on, swaying slightly, down the street. "I shall get up and ask aloud 'What have I got out of life?' And there before them all I shall answer, 'Nothing.' I shall tell them the truth; that life has beaten me at every turning and used me for its own obscure purposes over and over; that everything I have loved has turned to ashes, and that every time I have stooped to pat a dog I have felt his teeth in my hand. And so at last they will learn the truth about one man's heart."

5

T HE MEETING WAS AT FOUR, but it was nearly five when he dismounted from the sweltering train and walked towards the Civic
Club hall. Numerous cars were parked along the surrounding streets,
promising an unusually large crowd. He was surprised to find that even
the rear of the hall was thronged with standing people, and that there
were recurrent outbursts of applause at some speech which was being
delivered upon the platform.

"Can you find me a seat near the rear?" he whispered to an attendant.
"I'm going to speak later, but I don't – don't want to go upon the platform just now."

"Certainly, Mr Jackson."

The only vacant chair was half behind a pillar in a far corner of the
hall but he welcomed its privacy with relief; and settling himself, looked
curiously around him. Yes, the gathering was large, and apparently
enthusiastic. Catching a glimpse of a face here and there, he saw that
he knew most of them, even by name; faces of men he had lived beside
and worked with for over twenty years. All the better. These were the
ones he must reach now, as soon as that figure on the platform there
ceased mouthing his hollow cheer.

His eyes swung back to the platform, and as there was another ripple
of applause he leant his face around the corner to see. Then he uttered
a low exclamation – the speaker was Thomas MacDowell. They had
not been asked to speak together in several years.

"I've had many enemies in my life," boomed the loud voice over the
hall, "and don't think I've had a change of heart, now that I'm fifty and
a little grey. I'll go on making enemies to the end. This is just a little lull
when I want to take off my armour and pay tribute to an enemy – because
that enemy happens to be the finest man I ever knew."

John Jackson wondered what candidate or protégé of MacDowell's
was in question. It was typical of the man to seize any opportunity to
make his own hay.

"Perhaps I wouldn't have said what I've said," went on the booming
voice, "were he here today. But if all the young men in this city came up
to me and asked me, 'What is being honourable?' I'd answer them, 'Go

up to that man and look into his eyes.' They're not happy eyes. I've often sat and looked at him and wondered what went on back of them that made those eyes so sad. Perhaps the fine, simple hearts that spend their hours smoothing other people's troubles never find time for happiness of their own. It's like the man at the soda fountain who never makes an ice-cream soda for himself."

There was a faint ripple of laughter here, but John Jackson saw wonderingly that a woman he knew just across the aisle was dabbing with a handkerchief at her eyes.

His curiosity increased.

"He's gone away now," said the man on the platform, bending his head and staring down for a minute at the floor, "gone away suddenly, I understand. He seemed a little strange when I saw him yesterday; perhaps he gave in at last under the strain of trying to do many things for many men. Perhaps this meeting we're holding here comes a little too late now. But we'll all feel better for having said our say about him.

"I'm almost through. A lot of you will think it's funny that I feel this way about a man who, in fairness to him, I must call an enemy. But I'm going to say one thing more" – his voice rose defiantly – "and it's a stranger thing still. Here, at fifty, there's one honour I'd like to have more than any honour this city ever gave me, or ever had in its power to give. I'd like to be able to stand up here before you and call John Jackson my friend."

He turned away and a storm of applause rose like thunder through the hall. John Jackson half rose to his feet, and then sank back again in a stupefied way, shrinking behind the pillar. The applause continued until a young man arose on the platform and waved them silent.

"Mrs Ralston," he called, and sat down.

A woman rose from the line of chairs and came forward to the edge of the stage and began to speak in a quiet voice. She told a story about a man whom – so it seemed to John Jackson – he had known once, but whose actions, repeated here, seemed utterly unreal, like something that had happened in a dream. It appeared that every year many hundreds of babies in the city owed their lives to something this man had done five years before: he had put a mortgage upon his own house to assure the children's hospital on the edge of town. It told how this had been kept secret at the man's own request, because he wanted the city to take pride in the hospital as a community affair, when but for the man's effort, made after the community attempt had failed, the hospital would never have existed at all.

Then Mrs Ralston began to talk about the parks; how the town had baked for many years under the midland heat; and how this man, not a very rich man, had given up land and time and money for many months that a green line of shade might skirt the boulevards, and that the poor children could leave the streets and play in fresh grass in the centre of town.

That was only the beginning, she said; and she went on to tell how, when any such plan tottered, or the public interest lagged, word was brought to John Jackson, and somehow he made it go and seemed to give it life out of his own body, until there was scarcely anything in this city that didn't have a little of John Jackson's heart in it, just as there were few people in this city that didn't have a little of their hearts for John Jackson.

Mrs Ralston's speech stopped abruptly at this point. She had been crying a little for several moments, but there must have been many people there in the audience who understood what she meant – a mother or a child here and there who had been the recipients of some of that kindness – because the applause seemed to fill the whole room like an ocean, and echoed back and forth from wall to wall.

Only a few people recognized the short grizzled man who now got up from his chair in the rear of the platform, but when he began to speak silence settled gradually over the house.

"You didn't hear my name," he said in a voice which trembled a little, "and when they first planned this surprise meeting I wasn't expected to speak at all. I'm John Jackson's head clerk. Fowler's my name, and when they decided they were going to hold the meeting, anyhow, even though John Jackson had gone away, I thought perhaps I'd like to say a few words" – those who were closest saw his hands clench tighter – "say a few words that I couldn't say if John Jackson was here.

"I've been with him twenty years. That's a long time. Neither of us had grey hair when I walked into his office one day just fired from somewhere and asked him for a job. Since then I can't tell you, gentlemen, I can't tell you what his – his presence on this earth has meant to me. When he told me yesterday, suddenly, that he was going away, I thought to myself that if he never came back I didn't – I didn't want to go on living. That man makes everything in the world seem all right. If you knew how we felt around the office…" He paused and shook his head wordlessly. "Why, there's three of us there – the janitor and one of the other clerks and me – that have sons named after John Jackson. Yes, sir. Because none of us could think of anything better than for a boy to have that name or that example before him through life. But would we tell him? Not a chance. He wouldn't even know what it was all about. Why" – he sank his voice to a hushed whisper – "he'd just look at you in a puzzled way and say, 'What did you wish that on the poor kid for?'"

He broke off, for there was a sudden and growing interruption. An epidemic of head turning had broken out and was spreading rapidly from one corner of the hall until it affected the whole assemblage. Someone had discovered John Jackson behind the post in the corner, and first an exclamation and then a growing mumble that mounted to a cheer swept over the auditorium.

Suddenly two men had taken him by the arms and set him on his feet, and then he was pushed and pulled and carried towards the platform, arriving somehow in a standing position after having been lifted over many heads.

They were all standing now, arms waving wildly, voices filling the hall with tumultuous clamour. Some in the back of the hall began to sing "For he's a jolly good fellow", and five hundred voices took up the air and sang it with such feeling, with such swelling emotion, that all eyes were wet and the song assumed a significance far beyond the spoken words.

This was John Jackson's chance now to say to these people that he had got so little out of life. He stretched out his arms in a sudden gesture and they were quiet, listening, every man and woman and child.

"I have been asked…" His voice faltered. "My dear friends, I have been asked to – to tell you what I have got out of life…"

Five hundred faces, touched and smiling, every one of them full of encouragement and love and faith, turned up to him.

"What have I got out of life?"

He stretched out his arms wide, as if to include them all, as if to take to his breast all the men and women and children of this city. His voice rang in the hushed silence.

"Everything!"

At six o'clock, when he walked up his street alone, the air was already cool with evening. Approaching his house, he raised his head and saw that someone was sitting on the outer doorstep, resting his face in his hands. When John Jackson came up the walk, the caller – he was a young man with dark, frightened eyes – saw him and sprang to his feet.

"Father," he said quickly, "I got your telegram, but I – I came home."

John Jackson looked at him and nodded.

"The house was locked," said the young man in an uneasy way.

"I've got the key."

John Jackson unlocked the front door and preceded his son inside.

"Father," cried Ellery Jackson quickly, "I haven't any excuse to make – anything to say. I'll tell you all about it if you're still interested – if you can stand to hear…"

John Jackson rested his hand on the young man's shoulder.

"Don't feel too badly," he said in his kind voice. "I guess I can always stand anything my son does."

This was an understatement. For John Jackson could stand anything now for ever – anything that came, anything at all.

The Pusher-in-the-Face

THE LAST PRISONER WAS A MAN – his masculinity was not much in evidence, it is true; he would perhaps better be described as a "person", but he undoubtedly came under that general heading and was so classified in the court record. He was a small, somewhat shrivelled, somewhat wrinkled American who had been living along for probably thirty-five years.

His body looked as if it had been left by accident in his suit the last time it went to the tailor's and pressed out with hot, heavy irons to its present sharpness. His face was merely a face. It was the kind of face that makes up crowds, grey in colour with ears that shrank back against the head as if fearing the clamour of the city, and with the tired, tired eyes of one whose forebears have been underdogs for five thousand years.

Brought into the dock between two towering Celts in executive blue he seemed like the representative of a long-extinct race, a very fagged-out and shrivelled elf who had been caught poaching on a buttercup in Central Park.

"What's your name?"

"Stuart."

"Stuart what?"

"Charles David Stuart."

The clerk recorded it without comment in the book of little crimes and great mistakes.

"Age?"

"Thirty."

"Occupation?"

"Night cashier."

The clerk paused and looked at the judge. The judge yawned.

"Wha's charge?" he asked.

"The charge is" – the clerk looked down at the notation in his hand – "the charge is that he pushed a lady in the face."

"Pleads guilty?"

"Yes."

The preliminaries were now disposed of. Charles David Stuart, looking very harmless and uneasy, was on trial for assault and battery.

The evidence disclosed, rather to the judge's surprise, that the lady whose face had been pushed was not the defendant's wife.

On the contrary the victim was an absolute stranger – the prisoner had never seen her before in his life. His reasons for the assault had been two: first, that she talked during a theatrical performance; and second, that she kept joggling the back of his chair with her knees. When this had gone on for some time he had turned around and without any warning pushed her severely in the face.

"Call the plaintiff," said the judge, sitting up a little in his chair. "Let's hear what she has to say."

The courtroom, sparsely crowded and unusually languid in the hot afternoon, had become suddenly alert. Several men in the back of the room moved into benches near the desk and a young reporter leant over the clerk's shoulder and copied the defendant's name on the back of an envelope.

The plaintiff arose. She was a woman just this side of fifty with a determined, rather overbearing face under yellowish-white hair. Her dress was a dignified black and she gave the impression of wearing glasses; indeed the young reporter, who believed in observation, had so described her in his mind before he realized that no such adornment sat upon her thin, beaked nose.

It developed that she was Mrs George D. Robinson of 1219 Riverside Drive. She had always been fond of the theatre and sometimes she went to the matinee. There had been two ladies with her yesterday, her cousin, who lived with her, and a Miss Ingles – both ladies were in court.

This is what had occurred:

As the curtain went up for the first act a woman sitting behind had asked her to remove her hat. Mrs Robinson had been about to do so anyhow, and so she was a little annoyed at the request and had remarked as much to Miss Ingles and her cousin. At this point she had first noticed the defendant who was sitting directly in front, for he had turned around and looked at her quickly in a most insolent way. Then she had forgotten his existence until just before the end of the act when she made some remark to Miss Ingles – when suddenly he had stood up, turned around and pushed her in the face.

"Was it a hard blow?" asked the judge at this point.

"A hard blow!" said Mrs Robinson indignantly. "I should say it was. I had hot and cold applications on my nose all night."

"…on her nose all night."

This echo came from the witness bench where two faded ladies were leaning forward eagerly and nodding their heads in corroboration.

"Were the lights on?" asked the judge.

No, but everyone around had seen the incident and some people had taken hold of the man right then and there.

This concluded the case for the plaintiff. Her two companions gave similar evidence and in the minds of everyone in the courtroom the incident defined itself as one of unprovoked and inexcusable brutality.

The one element which did not fit in with this interpretation was the physiognomy of the prisoner himself. Of any one of a number of minor offences he might have appeared guilty – pickpockets were notoriously mild-mannered, for example – but of this particular assault in a crowded theatre he seemed physically incapable. He did not have the kind of voice or the kind of clothes or the kind of moustache that went with such an attack.

"Charles David Stuart," said the judge, "you've heard the evidence against you?"

"Yes."

"And you plead guilty?"

"Yes."

"Have you anything to say before I sentence you?"

"No." The prisoner shook his head hopelessly. His small hands were trembling.

"Not one word in extenuation of this unwarranted assault?"

The prisoner appeared to hesitate.

"Go on," said the judge. "Speak up – it's your last chance."

"Well," said Stuart with an effort, "she began talking about the plumber's stomach."

There was a stir in the courtroom. The judge leant forward.

"What do you mean?"

"Why, at first she was only talking about her own stomach to – to those two ladies there" – he indicated the cousin and Miss Ingles – "and that wasn't so bad. But when she began talking about the plumber's stomach it got different."

"How do you mean – different?"

Charles Stuart looked around helplessly.

"I can't explain," he said, his moustache wavering a little, "but when she began talking about the plumber's stomach you – you had to listen."

A snicker ran about the courtroom. Mrs Robinson and her attendant ladies on the bench were visibly horrified. The guard took a step nearer as if at a nod from the judge he would whisk off this criminal to the dingiest dungeon in Manhattan.

But much to his surprise the judge settled himself comfortably in his chair.

"Tell us about it, Stuart," he said not unkindly. "Tell us the whole story from the beginning."

This request was a shock to the prisoner and for a moment he looked as though he would have preferred the order of condemnation. Then after one nervous look around the room he put his hands on the edge of the desk, like the paws of a fox terrier just being trained to sit up, and began to speak in a quavering voice.

"Well, I'm a night cashier, your honour, in T. Cushmael's restaurant on Third Avenue. I'm not married" – he smiled a little, as if he knew they had all guessed *that* – "and so on Wednesday and Saturday afternoons I usually go to the matinee. It helps to pass the time till dinner. There's a drugstore, maybe you know, where you can get tickets for a dollar sixty-five to some of the shows and I usually go there and pick out something. They got awful prices at the box office now." He gave out a long silent whistle and looked feelingly at the judge. "Four or five dollars for one seat…"

The judge nodded his head.

"Well," continued Charles Stuart, "when I pay even a dollar sixty-five I expect to see my money's worth. About two weeks ago I went to one of these here mystery plays where they have one fella that did the crime and nobody knows who it was. Well, the fun at a thing like that is to guess who did it. And there was a lady behind me that'd been there before and she gave it all away to the fella with her. Gee" – his face fell and he shook his head from side to side – "I like to died right there. When I got home to my room I was so mad that they had to come and ask me to stop walking up and down. Dollar sixty-five of my money gone for nothing.

"Well, Wednesday came around again, and this show was one show I wanted to see. I'd been wanting to see it for months, and every time I went into the drugstore I asked them if they had any tickets. But they never did." He hesitated. "So Tuesday I took a chance and went over to the box office and got a seat. Two seventy-five it cost me." He nodded impressively. "Two seventy-five. Like throwing money away. But I wanted to see that show."

Mrs Robinson in the front row rose suddenly to her feet.

"I don't see what all this story has to do with it," she broke out a little shrilly. "I'm sure I don't care—"

The judge brought his gavel sharply down on the desk.

"Sit down, please," he said. "This is a court of law, not a matinee."

Mrs Robinson sat down, drawing herself up into a thin line and sniffing a little as if to say she'd see about this after a while. The judge pulled out his watch.

"Go on," he said to Stuart. "Take all the time you want."

"I got there first," continued Stuart in a flustered voice. "There wasn't anybody in there but me and the fella that was cleaning up. After a while the audience came in, and it got dark and the play started, but just as I was all settled in my seat and ready to have a good time I heard an awful row directly behind me. Somebody had asked this lady" – he pointed directly to Mrs Robinson – "to remove her hat like she should of done anyhow and she was sore about it. She kept telling the two ladies that was with her how she'd been at the theatre before and knew enough to take off her hat. She kept that up for a long time, five minutes maybe, and then every once in a while she'd think of something new and say it in a loud voice. So finally I turned around and looked at her because I wanted to see what a lady looked like that could be so inconsiderate as that. Soon as I turned back she began on me. She said I was insolent and then she said *Tchk! Tchk! Tchk!* a lot with her tongue and the two ladies that was with her said *Tchk! Tchk! Tchk!* until you could hardly hear yourself think, much less listen to the play. You'd have thought I'd done something terrible.

"By and by, after they calmed down and I began to catch up with what was doing on the stage, I felt my seat sort of creak forward and then creak back again and I knew the lady had her feet on it and I was in for a good rock. Gosh!" He wiped his pale, narrow brow on which the sweat had gathered thinly. "It was awful. I hope to tell you I wished I'd never come at all. Once I got excited at a show and rocked a man's chair without knowing it and I was glad when he asked me to stop. But I knew this lady wouldn't be glad if I asked her. She'd of just rocked harder than ever."

Some time before, the population of the courtroom had begun stealing glances at the middle-aged lady with yellowish-white hair. She was of a deep, lifelike lobster colour with rage.

"It got to be near the end of the act," went on the little pale man, "and I was enjoying it as well as I could, seeing that sometimes she'd push me towards the stage and sometimes she'd let go, and the seat and me would fall back into place. Then all of a sudden she began to talk. She said she had an operation or something – I remember she said she told the doctor that she guessed she knew more about her own stomach than he did. The play was getting good just then – the people next to me had their handkerchiefs out and was weeping – and I was feeling sort of that way myself. And all of a sudden this lady began to tell her friends what she told the plumber about his indigestion. Gosh!" Again he shook his head from side to side; his pale eyes fell involuntarily on Mrs Robinson – then looked quickly away. "You couldn't help but hear some and I begun missing things and then missing more things and then everybody began laughing and I didn't know what they were laughing at and, as soon as they'd leave off, her voice would begin again. Then there was a great big laugh that lasted for a long time and everybody bent over double and kept laughing and laughing, and I hadn't heard a word. First thing I knew the curtain came down and then I don't know what happened. I must have been a little crazy or something because I got up and closed my seat, and reached back and pushed the lady in the face."

As he concluded there was a long sigh in the courtroom as though everyone had been holding his breath waiting for the climax. Even the judge gasped a little and the three ladies on the witness bench burst into a shrill chatter and grew louder and louder and shriller and shriller until the judge's gavel rang out again upon his desk.

"Charles Stuart," said the judge in a slightly raised voice, "is this the only extenuation you can make for raising your hand against a woman of the plaintiff's age?"

Charles Stuart's head sank a little between his shoulders, seeming to withdraw as far as it was able into the poor shelter of his body.

"Yes, sir," he said faintly.

Mrs Robinson sprang to her feet.

"Yes, judge," she cried shrilly, "and there's more than that. He's a liar too, a dirty little liar. He's just proclaimed himself a dirty little—"

"Silence!" cried the judge in a terrible voice. "I'm running this court, and I'm capable of making my own decisions!" He paused. "I will now pronounce sentence upon Charles Stuart," he referred to the register, "upon Charles David Stuart of 212½ West 22nd Street."

The courtroom was silent. The reporter drew nearer – he hoped the sentence would be light – just a few days on the Island* in lieu of a fine.

The judge leant back in his chair and hid his thumbs somewhere under his black robe.

"Assault justified," he said. "Case dismissed."

The little man, Charles Stuart, came blinking out into the sunshine, pausing for a moment at the door of the court and looking furtively behind him as if he half expected that it was a judicial error. Then sniffling once or twice, not because he had a cold but for those dim psychological reasons that make people sniff, he moved slowly south with an eye out for a subway station.

He stopped at a news-stand to buy a morning paper; then entering the subway was borne south to 18th Street where he disembarked and walked east to Third Avenue. Here he was employed in an all-night restaurant built of glass and plaster white tile. Here he sat at a desk from curfew until dawn, taking in money and balancing the books of T. Cushmael, the proprietor. And here, through the interminable nights, his eyes, by turning a little to right or left, could rest upon the starched linen uniform of Miss Edna Schaeffer.

Miss Edna Schaeffer was twenty-three, with a sweet mild face and hair that was a living example of how henna should not be applied. She was unaware of this latter fact, because all the girls she knew used henna just this way, so perhaps the odd vermilion tint of her coiffure did not matter.

Charles Stuart had forgotten about the colour of her hair long ago – if he had ever noticed its strangeness at all. He was much more interested in her eyes, and in her white hands which, as they moved deftly among piles of plates and cups, always looked as if they should be playing the piano. He had almost asked her to go to a matinee with him once, but when she had faced him, her lips half-parted in a weary, cheerful smile, she had seemed so beautiful that he had lost courage and mumbled something else instead.

It was not to see Edna Schaeffer, however, that he had come to the restaurant so early in the afternoon. It was to consult with T. Cushmael, his employer, and discover if he had lost his job during his night in jail. T. Cushmael was standing in the front of the restaurant looking gloomily out the plate-glass window, and Charles Stuart approached him with ominous forebodings.

"Where've you been?" demanded T. Cushmael.

"Nowhere," answered Charles Stuart discreetly.

"Well, you're fired."

Stuart winced.

"Right now?"

Cushmael waved his hands apathetically.

"Stay two or three days if you want to, till I find somebody. Then" – he made a gesture of expulsion – "outside for you."

Charles Stuart assented with a weary little nod. He assented to everything. At nine o'clock, after a depressed interval during which he brooded upon the penalty of spending a night among the police, he reported for work.

"Hello, Mr Stuart," said Edna Schaeffer, sauntering curiously towards him as he took his place behind the desk. "What became of you last night? Get pinched?"

She laughed, cheerfully, huskily, charmingly he thought, at her joke.

"Yes," he answered on a sudden impulse, "I was in the 35th Street jail."

"Yes, you were," she scoffed.

"That's the truth," he insisted, "I was arrested."

Her face grew serious at once.

"Go *on*. What did you do?"

He hesitated.

"I pushed somebody in the face."

Suddenly she began to laugh, at first with amusement and then immoderately.

"It's a fact," mumbled Stuart. "I almost got sent to prison account of it."

Setting her hand firmly over her mouth Edna turned away from him and retired to the refuge of the kitchen. A little later, when he was pretending to be busy at the accounts, he saw her retailing the story to the two other girls.

The night wore on. The little man in the greyish suit with the greyish face attracted no more attention from the customers than the whirring electric fan over his head. They gave him their money and his hand slid their change into a little hollow in the marble counter. But to Charles Stuart the hours of this night, this last night, began to assume a quality of romance. The slow routine of a hundred other nights unrolled with a new enchantment before his eyes. Midnight was always a sort of a dividing point – after that the intimate part of the evening began. Fewer people came in, and the ones that did seemed depressed and tired: a casual ragged man for coffee, the beggar from the street corner who ate a heavy meal of cakes and a beefsteak, a few nightbound street women and a watchman with a red face who exchanged warning phrases with him about his health.

Midnight seemed to come early tonight and business was brisk until after one. When Edna began to fold napkins at a nearby table he was tempted to ask her if she too had not found the night unusually short. Vainly he wished that he might impress himself on her in some way, make some remark to her, some sign of his devotion that she would remember for ever.

She finished folding the vast pile of napkins, loaded it onto the stand and bore it away, humming to herself. A few minutes later the door opened and two customers came in. He recognized them immediately, and as he did so a flush of jealousy went over him. One of them, a young man in a handsome brown suit, cut away rakishly from his abdomen, had been a frequent visitor for the last ten days. He came in always at about this hour, sat down at one of Edna's tables, and drank two cups of coffee with lingering ease. On his last two visits he had been accompanied by his present companion, a swarthy Greek with sour eyes who ordered in a loud voice and gave vent to noisy sarcasm when anything was not to his taste.

It was chiefly the young man, though, who annoyed Charles Stuart. The young man's eyes followed Edna wherever she went and on his last two visits he had made unnecessary requests in order to bring her more often to his table.

"Good evening, girlie," Stuart heard him say tonight. "How's tricks?"

"OK," answered Edna formally. "What'll it be?"

"What have you?" smiled the young man. "Everything, eh? Well, what'd you recommend?"

Edna did not answer. Her eyes were staring straight over his head into some invisible distance.

He ordered finally at the urging of his companion. Edna withdrew and Stuart saw the young man turn and whisper to his friend, indicating Edna with his head.

Stuart shifted uncomfortably in his seat. He hated that young man and wished passionately that he would go away. It seemed as if his last night here, his last chance to watch Edna, and perhaps even in some blessed moment to talk to her a little, was marred by every moment this man stayed.

Half a dozen more people had drifted into the restaurant – two or three workmen, the news dealer from over the way – and Edna was too busy for a few minutes to be bothered with attentions. Suddenly Charles Stuart became aware that the sour-eyed Greek had raised his hand and was beckoning him. Somewhat puzzled he left his desk and approached the table.

"Say, fella," said the Greek, "what time does the boss come in?"

"Why – two o'clock. Just a few minutes now."

"All right. That's all. I just wanted to speak to him about something." Stuart realized that Edna was standing beside the table; both men turned towards her.

"Say, girlie," said the young man, "I want to talk to you. Sit down."

"I can't."

"Sure you can. The boss don't mind." He turned menacingly to Stuart. "She can sit down, can't she?"

Stuart did not answer.

"I say she can sit down, can't she?" said the young man more intently, and added, "Speak up, you little dummy."

Still Stuart did not answer. Strange blood currents were flowing all over his body. He was frightened; anything said determinedly had a way of frightening him. But he could not move.

"Sh!" said the Greek to his companion.

But the younger man was angered.

"Say," he broke out, "sometime somebody's going to take a paste at you when you don't answer what they say. Go on back to your desk!"

Still Stuart did not move.

"Go on away!" repeated the young man in a dangerous voice. "Hurry up! *Run!*"

Then Stuart ran. He ran as hard as he was able. But instead of running away from the young man he ran *towards* him, stretching out his hands as he came near in a sort of straight arm that brought his two palms, with all the force of his hundred and thirty pounds, against his victim's face. With a crash of china the young man went over backwards in his chair and, his head striking the edge of the next table, lay motionless on the floor.

The restaurant was in a small uproar. There was a terrified scream from Edna, an indignant protest from the Greek, and the customers arose with exclamations from their tables. Just at this moment the door opened and Mr Cushmael came in.

"Why you little fool!" cried Edna wrathfully. "What are you trying to do? Lose me my job?"

"What's this?" demanded Mr Cushmael, hurrying over. "What's the idea?"

"Mr Stuart pushed a customer in the face!" cried a waitress, taking Edna's cue. "For no reason at all!"

The population of the restaurant had now gathered around the prostrate victim. He was doused thoroughly with water and a folded tablecloth was placed under his head.

"Oh, he did, did he?" shouted Mr Cushmael in a terrible voice, seizing Stuart by the lapels of his coat.

"He's raving crazy!" sobbed Edna. "He was in jail last night for pushing a lady in the face. He told me so himself!"

A large labourer reached over and grasped Stuart's small trembling arm. Stuart gazed around dumbly. His mouth was quivering.

"Look what you done!" shouted Mr Cushmael. "You like to kill a man."

Stuart shivered violently. His mouth opened and he fought the air for a moment. Then he uttered a half-articulate sentence:

"Only meant to push him in the face."

"Push him in the face?" ejaculated Cushmael in a frenzy. "So you got to be a pusher-in-the-face, eh? Well, we'll push your face right into jail!"

"I – I couldn't help it," gasped Stuart. "Sometimes I can't help it." His voice rose unevenly. "I guess I'm a dangerous man and you better take me and lock me up!" He turned wildly to Cushmael. "I'd push you in the face if he'd let go of my arm. Yes, I would! I'd push you – right-in-the-*face*!"

For a moment an astonished silence fell, broken by the voice of one of the waitresses who had been groping under the table.

"Some stuff dropped out of this fella's back pocket when he tipped over," she explained, getting to her feet. "It's – why, it's a revolver and…"

She had been about to say handkerchief, but as she looked at what she was holding her mouth fell open and she dropped the thing quickly on the table. It was a small black mask about the size of her hand.

Simultaneously the Greek, who had been shifting uneasily upon his feet ever since the accident, seemed to remember an important engagement that had slipped his mind. He dashed suddenly around the table and made for the front door, but it opened just at that moment to admit several customers who, at the cry of "Stop him!" obligingly spread out their arms. Barred in that direction, he jumped an overturned chair, vaulted over the delicatessen counter, and set out for the kitchen, collapsing precipitately in the firm grasp of the chef in the doorway.

"Hold him! Hold him!" screamed Mr Cushmael, realizing the turn of the situation. "They're after my cash drawer!"

Willing hands assisted the Greek over the counter, where he stood panting and gasping under two dozen excited eyes.

"After my money, hey?" shouted the proprietor, shaking his fist under the captive's nose.

The stout man nodded, panting.

"We'd of got it too," he gasped, "if it hadn't been for that little pusher-in-the-face!"

Two dozen eyes looked around eagerly. The little pusher-in-the-face had disappeared.

The beggar on the corner had just decided to tip the policeman and shut up shop for the night when he suddenly felt a small, somewhat excited hand fall on his shoulder.

"Help a poor man to get a place to sleep..." he was beginning automatically when he recognized the little cashier from the restaurant. "Hello, brother," he added, leering up at him and changing his tone.

"You know what?" cried the little cashier in a strangely ominous tone. "I'm going to push you in the face!"

"What do you mean?" snarled the beggar. "Why, you Ga..."

He got no farther. The little man seemed to run at him suddenly, holding out his hands, and there was a sharp, smacking sound as the beggar came in contact with the sidewalk.

"You're a faker!" shouted Charles Stuart wildly. "I gave you a dollar when I first came here, before I found out you had ten times as much as I had. And you never gave it back!"

A stout, faintly intoxicated gentleman who was strutting expansively along the other sidewalk had seen the incident and came running benevolently across the street.

"What does this mean!" he exclaimed in a hearty, shocked voice. "Why poor fellow…" He turned indignant eyes on Charles Stuart and knelt unsteadily to raise the beggar.

The beggar stopped cursing and assumed a piteous whine.

"I'm a poor man, Cap'n…"

"This is – this is *horrible*!" cried the Samaritan, with tears in his eyes. "It's a disgrace! Police! *Pol!*…"

He got no farther. His hands, which he was raising for a megaphone, never reached his face – other hands reached his face, however, hands held stiffly out from a one-hundred-and-thirty-pound body! He sank down suddenly upon the beggar's abdomen, forcing out a sharp curse which faded into a groan.

"This beggar'll take you home in his car!" shouted the little man who stood over him. "He's got it parked around the corner."

Turning his face towards the hot strip of sky which lowered over the city the little man began to laugh, with amusement at first, then loudly and triumphantly until his high laughter ran out in the quiet street with a weird, elfish sound, echoing up the sides of the tall buildings, growing shriller and shriller until people blocks away heard its eerie cadence on the air and stopped to listen.

Still laughing the little man divested himself of his coat and then of his vest and hurriedly freed his neck of tie and collar. Then he spat upon his hands and with a wild, shrill, exultant cry began to run down the dark street.

He was going to clean up New York, and his first objective was the disagreeable policeman on the corner!

They caught him at two o'clock, and the crowd which had joined in the chase were flabbergasted when they found that the ruffian was only a weeping little man in his shirtsleeves. Someone at the station house was wise enough to give him an opiate instead of a padded cell, and in the morning he felt much better.

Mr Cushmael, accompanied by an anxious young lady with crimson hair, called at the jail before noon.

"I'll get you out," cried Mr Cushmael, shaking hands excitedly through the bars. "One policeman, he'll explain it all to the other."

"And there's a surprise for you too," added Edna softly, taking his other hand. "Mr Cushmael's got a big heart and he's going to make you his day man now."

"All right," agreed Charles Stuart calmly. "But I can't start till tomorrow."

"Why not?"

"Because this afternoon I got to go to a matinee – with a friend."

He relinquished his employer's hand but kept Edna's white fingers twined firmly in his.

"One more thing," he went on in a strong, confident voice that was new to him, "if you want to get me off don't have the case come up in the 35th Street court."

"Why not?"

"Because," he answered with a touch of swagger in his voice, "that's the judge I had when I was arrested last time."

"Charles," whispered Edna suddenly, "what would you do if I refused to go with you this afternoon?"

He bristled. Colour came into his cheeks and he rose defiantly from his bench.

"Why, I'd – I'd…"

"Never mind," she said, flushing slightly. "You'd do nothing of the kind."

One of My Oldest Friends

A LL AFTERNOON MARION had been happy. She wandered from room to room of their little apartment, strolling into the nursery to help the nurse girl feed the children from dripping spoons, and then reading for a while on their new sofa, the most extravagant thing they had bought in their five years of marriage.

When she heard Michael's step in the hall she turned her head and listened; she liked to hear him walk, carefully always as if there were children sleeping close by.

"Michael."

"Oh – hello." He came into the room, a tall, broad, thin man of thirty with a high forehead and kind black eyes.

"I've got some news for you," he said immediately. "Charley Hart's getting married."

"No!"

He nodded.

"Who's he marrying?"

"One of the little Lawrence girls from home." He hesitated. "She's arriving in New York tomorrow and I think we ought to do something for them while she's here. Charley's about my oldest friend."

"Let's have them up for dinner—"

"I'd like to do something more than that," he interrupted. "Maybe a theatre party. You see—" Again he hesitated. "It'd be a nice courtesy to Charley."

"All right," agreed Marion, "but we mustn't spend much – and I don't think we're under any obligation."

He looked at her in surprise.

"I mean," went on Marion, "we – we hardly see Charley any more. We hardly ever see him at all."

"Well, you know how it is in New York," explained Michael apologetically. "He's just as busy as I am. He has made a big name for himself and I suppose he's pretty much in demand all the time."

They always spoke of Charley Hart as their oldest friend. Five years before, when Michael and Marion were first married, the three of them had come to New York from the same western city. For over a year they had seen Charley nearly every day and no domestic adventure, no uprush of their hopes and dreams, was too insignificant for his ear. His arrival in times of difficulty never failed to give a pleasant, humorous cast to the situation.

Of course Marion's babies had made a difference, and it was several years now since they had called up Charley at midnight to say that the pipes had broken or the ceiling was falling in on their heads; but so gradually had they drifted apart that Michael still spoke of Charley rather proudly as if he saw him every day. For a while Charley dined with them once a month and all three found a great deal to say; but the meetings never broke up any more with "I'll give you a ring tomorrow". Instead it was "You'll have to come to dinner more often," or even, after three or four years, "We'll see you soon."

"Oh, I'm perfectly willing to give a little party," said Marion now, looking speculatively about her. "Did you suggest a definite date?"

"Week from Saturday." His dark eyes roamed the floor vaguely. "We can take up the rugs or something."

"No." She shook her head. "We'll have a dinner, eight people, very formal and everything, and afterwards we'll play cards."

She was already speculating on whom to invite. Charley of course, being an artist, probably saw interesting people every day.

"We could have the Willoughbys," she suggested doubtfully. "She's on the stage or something – and he writes movies."

"No – that's not it," objected Michael. "He probably meets that crowd at lunch and dinner every day until he's sick of them. Besides, except for the Willoughbys, who else like that do we know? I've got a better idea. Let's collect a few people who've drifted down here from home. They've all followed Charley's career and they'd probably enjoy seeing him again. I'd like them to find out how natural and unspoilt he is after all."

After some discussion they agreed on this plan and within an hour Marion had her first guest on the telephone:

"It's to meet Charley Hart's fiancée," she explained. "Charley Hart, the artist. You see, he's one of our oldest friends."

As she began her preparations her enthusiasm grew. She rented a serving maid to assure an impeccable service and persuaded the neighbourhood florist to come in person and arrange the flowers. All the "people from home" had accepted eagerly and the number of guests had swollen to ten.

"What'll we talk about, Michael?" she demanded nervously on the eve of the party. "Suppose everything goes wrong and everybody gets mad and goes home?"

He laughed.

"Nothing will. You see, these people all know each other—"

The phone on the table asserted itself and Michael picked up the receiver.

"Hello... why, hello, Charley."

Marion sat up alertly in her chair.

"Is that so? Well, I'm very sorry. I'm very, very sorry... I hope it's nothing serious."

"Can't he come?" broke out Marion.

"Sh!" Then into the phone, "Well, it certainly is too bad, Charley. No, it's no trouble for us at all. We're just sorry you're ill."

With a dismal gesture Michael replaced the receiver.

"The Lawrence girl had to go home last night and Charley's sick in bed with grip."

"Do you mean he can't come?"

"He can't come."

Marion's face contracted suddenly and her eyes filled with tears.

"He says he's had the doctor all day," explained Michael dejectedly. "He's got fever and they didn't even want him to go to the telephone."

"I don't care," sobbed Marion. "I think it's terrible. After we've invited all these people to meet him."

"People can't help being sick."

"Yes they *can*," she wailed illogically, "they can help it some way. And if the Lawrence girl was going to leave last night why didn't he let us know *then*?"

"He said she left unexpectedly. Up to yesterday afternoon they both intended to come."

"I don't think he c-cares a bit. I'll bet he's glad he's sick. If he'd cared he'd have brought her to see us long ago."

She stood up suddenly.

"I'll tell you one thing," she assured him vehemently, "I'm just going to telephone everybody and call the whole thing off."

"Why, Marion—"

But in spite of his half-hearted protests she picked up the phone book and began looking for the first number.

They bought theatre tickets next day hoping to fill the hollowness which would invest the evening. Marion had wept when the unintercepted florist arrived at five with boxes of flowers and she felt that she must get out of the house to avoid the ghosts who would presently people it. In silence they ate an elaborate dinner composed of all the things that she had bought for the party.

"It's only eight," said Michael afterwards. "I think it'd be sort of nice if we dropped in on Charley for a minute, don't you?"

"Why, no," Marion answered, startled, "I wouldn't think of it."

"Why not? If he's seriously sick I'd like to see how well he's being taken care of."

She saw that he had made up his mind, so she fought down her instinct against the idea and they taxied to a tall pile of studio apartments on Madison Avenue.

"You go on in," urged Marion nervously, "I'd rather wait out here."

"Please come in."

"Why? He'll be in bed and he doesn't want any women around."

"But he'd like to see you – it'd cheer him up. And he'd know that we understood about tonight. He sounded awfully depressed over the phone."

He urged her from the cab.

"Let's only stay a minute," she whispered tensely as they went up in the elevator. "The show starts at half-past eight."

"Apartment on the right," said the elevator man.

They rang the bell and waited. The door opened and they walked directly into Charley Hart's great studio room.

It was crowded with people; from end to end ran a long lamplit dinner table strewn with ferns and young roses, from which a gay murmur of laughter and conversation arose into the faintly smoky air. Twenty women in evening dress sat on one side in a row chatting across the flowers at twenty men, with an elation born of the sparkling Burgundy which dripped from many bottles into thin chilled glass. Up on the high narrow balcony which encircled the room a string quartet was playing something by Stravinsky in a key that was pitched just below the women's voices and filled the air like an audible wine.

The door had been opened by one of the waiters, who stepped back deferentially from what he thought were two belated guests – and immediately a handsome man at the head of the table started to his feet, napkin in hand, and stood motionless, staring towards the new-comers. The conversation faded into half silence and all eyes followed Charley Hart's to the couple at the door. Then, as if the spell was broken, conversation resumed, gathering momentum word by word – the moment was over.

"Let's get out!" Marion's low, terrified whisper came to Michael out of a void and for a minute he thought he was possessed by an illusion, that there was no one but Charley in the room after all. Then his eyes cleared and he saw that there were many people here – he had never seen so many! The music swelled suddenly into the tumult of a great brass band and a wind from the loud horns seemed to blow against them; without turning he and Marion each made one blind step backwards into the hall, pulling the door to after them.

"Marion!…"

She had run towards the elevator, stood with one finger pressed hard against the bell which rang through the hall like a last high note from the music inside. The door of the apartment opened suddenly and Charley Hart came out into the hall.

"Michael!" he cried. "Michael and Marion, I want to explain! Come inside. I want to *explain*, I tell you."

He talked excitedly – his face was flushed and his mouth formed a word or two that did not materialize into sound.

"Hurry up, Michael," came Marion's voice tensely from the elevator.

"Let me explain," cried Charley frantically. "I want…"

Michael moved away from him – the elevator came and the gate clanged open.

"You act as if I committed some crime." Charley was following Michael along the hall. "Can't you understand that this is all an accidental situation?"

"It's all right," Michael muttered, "I understand."

"No, you don't." Charley's voice rose with exasperation. He was working up anger against them so as to justify his own intolerable position. "You're going away mad and I asked you to come in and join the party. Why did you come up here if you won't come in? Did you?…"

Michael walked into the elevator.

"Down, please!" cried Marion. "Oh, I want to go down, *please*!"

The gates clanged shut.

They told the taxi man to take them directly home – neither of them could have endured the theatre. Driving uptown to their apartment, Michael buried his face in his hands and tried to realize that the friendship which had meant so much to him was over. He saw now that it had been over for some time, that not once during the past year had Charley sought their company and the shock of the discovery far outweighed the affront he had received.

When they reached home, Marion, who had not said a word in the taxi, led the way into the living room and motioned for her husband to sit down.

"I'm going to tell you something that you ought to know," she said. "If it hadn't been for what happened tonight I'd probably never have told you – but now I think you ought to hear the whole story."

She hesitated. "In the first place, Charley Hart wasn't a friend of yours at all."

"What?" He looked up at her dully.

"He wasn't your friend," she repeated. "He hasn't been for years. He was a friend of mine."

"Why, Charley Hart was—"

"I know what you're going to say – that Charley was a friend to both of us. But it isn't true. I don't know how he considered you at first but he stopped being your friend three or four years ago."

"Why…" Michael's eyes glowed with astonishment. "If that's true, why was he with us all the time?"

"On account of me," said Marion steadily. "He was in love with me."

"What?" Michael laughed incredulously. "You're imagining things. I know how he used to pretend in a kidding way—"

"It wasn't kidding," she interrupted, "not underneath. It began that way – and it ended by his asking me to run away with him."

Michael frowned.

"Go on," he said quietly, "I suppose this is true or you wouldn't be telling me about it – but it simply doesn't seem real. Did he just suddenly begin to – to…"

He closed his mouth suddenly, unable to say the words.

"It began one night when we three were out dancing." Marion hesitated. "And at first I thoroughly enjoyed it. He had a faculty for noticing things – noticing dresses and hats and the new ways I'd do my hair. He was good company. He could always make me feel important, somehow, and attractive. Don't get the idea that I preferred his company to yours – I didn't. I knew how completely selfish he was, and what a will-o'-the-wisp. But I encouraged him, I suppose – I thought it was fine. It was a new angle on Charley, and he was amusing at it just as he was at everything he did."

"Yes…" agreed Michael with an effort, "I suppose it was – hilariously amusing."

"At first he liked you just the same. It didn't occur to him that he was doing anything treacherous to you. He was just following a natural impulse – that was all. But after a few weeks he began to find you in the way. He wanted to take me to dinner without you along – and it couldn't be done. Well, that sort of thing went on for over a year."

"What happened then?"

"Nothing happened. That's why he stopped coming to see us any more."

Michael rose slowly to his feet.

"Do you mean—"

"Wait a minute. If you'll think a little you'll see it was bound to turn out that way. When he saw that I was trying to let him down easily so that he'd be simply one of our oldest friends again, he broke away. He didn't want to be one of our oldest friends – that time was over."

"I see."

"Well…" Marion stood up and began biting nervously at her lip, "that's all. I thought this thing tonight would hurt you less if you understood the whole affair."

"Yes," Michael answered in a dull voice, "I suppose that's true."

Michael's business took a prosperous turn, and when summer came they went to the country, renting a little old farmhouse where the children played all day on a tangled half-acre of grass and trees. The subject of Charley was never mentioned between them and as the months passed he receded to a shadowy background in their minds. Sometimes, just before dropping off to sleep, Michael found himself thinking of the happy times the three of them had had together five years before – then the reality would intrude upon the illusion and he would be repelled from the subject with almost physical distaste.

One warm evening in July he lay dozing on the porch in the twilight. He had had a hard day at his office and it was welcome to rest here while the summer light faded from the land.

At the sound of an automobile he raised his head lazily. At the end of the path a local taxicab had stopped and a young man was getting out. With an exclamation Michael sat up. Even in the dusk he recognized those shoulders, that impatient walk…

"Well, I'm damned," he said softly.

As Charley Hart came up the gravel path Michael noticed in a glance that he was unusually dishevelled. His handsome face was drawn and tired, his clothes were out of press and he had the unmistakable look of needing a good night's sleep.

He came up on the porch, saw Michael and smiled in a wan, embarrassed way.

"Hello, Michael."

Neither of them made any move to shake hands but after a moment Charley collapsed abruptly into a chair.

"I'd like a glass of water," he said huskily, "it's hot as hell."

"Without a word Michael went into the house – returned with a glass of water which Charley drank in great noisy gulps.

"Thanks," he said, gasping, "I thought I was going to pass away."

He looked about him with eyes that only pretended to take in his surroundings.

"Nice little place you've got here," he remarked; his eyes returned to Michael. "Do you want me to get out?"

"Why – no. Sit and rest if you want to. You look all-in."

"I am. Do you want to hear about it?"

"Not in the least."

"Well, I'm going to tell you anyhow," said Charley defiantly. "That's what I came out here for. I'm in trouble, Michael, and I haven't got anybody to go to except you."

"Have you tried your friends?" asked Michael coolly.

"I've tried about everybody – everybody I've had time to go to. God!" He wiped his forehead with his hand. "I never realized how hard it was to raise a simple two thousand dollars."

"Have you come to me for two thousand dollars?"

"Wait a minute, Michael. Wait till you hear. It just shows you what a mess a man can get into without meaning any harm. You see, I'm the treasurer of a society called the Independent Artists' Benefit – a thing to help struggling students. There was a fund, thirty-five hundred dollars, and it's been lying in my bank for over a year. Well, as you know, I live pretty high – make a lot and spend a lot – and about a month ago I began speculating a little through a friend of mine—"

"I don't know why you're telling me all this," interrupted Michael impatiently, "I—"

"Wait a minute, won't you – I'm almost through." He looked at Michael with frightened eyes. "I used that money sometimes without even realizing that it wasn't mine. I've always had plenty of my own, you see. Till this week." He hesitated. "This week there was a meeting of this society and they asked me to turn over the money. Well, I went to a couple of men to try and borrow it and as soon as my back was turned one of them blabbed. There was a terrible blow-up last night. They told me unless I handed over the two thousand this morning they'd send me to jail…" His voice rose and he looked around wildly. "There's a warrant out for me now – and if I can't get the money I'll kill myself, Michael; I swear to God I will; I won't go to prison. I'm an artist – not a businessman. I…"

He made an effort to control his voice.

"Michael," he whispered, "you're my oldest friend. I haven't got anyone in the world but you to turn to."

"You're a little late," said Michael uncomfortably, "you didn't think of me four years ago when you asked my wife to run away with you."

A look of sincere surprise passed over Charley's face.

"Are you mad at me about that?" he asked in a puzzled way. "I thought you were mad because I didn't come to your party."

Michael did not answer.

"I supposed she'd told you about that long ago," went on Charley. "I couldn't help it about Marion, I was lonesome and you two had each other. Every time I went to your house you'd tell me what a wonderful girl Marion was and finally I – I began to agree with you. How could I help falling in love with her, when for a year and a half she was the only decent girl I knew?" He looked defiantly at Michael. "Well, you've got her, haven't you? I didn't take her away. I never so much as kissed her – do you have to rub it in?"

"Look here," said Michael sharply, "just why should I lend you this money?"

"Well…" Charley hesitated, laughed uneasily. "I don't know any exact reason. I just thought you would."

"Why should I?"

"No reason at all, I suppose, from your way of looking at it."

"That's the trouble. If I gave it to you it would just be because I was slushy and soft. I'd be doing something that I don't want to do."

"All right," Charley smiled unpleasantly, "that's logical. Now that I think, there's no reason why you should lend it to me. Well…" He shoved his hands into his coat pocket and throwing his head back slightly seemed to shake the subject off like a cap. "I won't go to prison – and maybe you'll feel differently about it tomorrow."

"Don't count on that."

"Oh, I don't mean I'll ask you again. I mean something – quite different."

He nodded his head, turned quickly and walking down the gravel path was swallowed up in the darkness. Where the path met the road Michael heard his footsteps cease as if he were hesitating. Then they turned down the road towards the station a mile away.

Michael sank into his chair, burying his face in his hands. He heard Marion come out the door.

"I listened," she whispered, "I couldn't help it. I'm glad you didn't lend him anything."

She came close to him and would have sat down in his lap but an almost physical repulsion came over him and he got up quickly from his chair.

"I was afraid he'd work on your sentiment and make a fool of you," went on Marion. She hesitated. "He hated you, you know. He used to wish you'd die. I told him that if he ever said so to me again I'd never see him any more."

Michael looked up at her darkly.

"In fact, you were very noble."

"Why, Michael—"

"You let him say things like that to you – and then when he comes here, down and out, without a friend in the world to turn to, you say you're glad I sent him away."

"It's because I love you, dear—"

"No, it isn't!" He interrupted savagely. "It's because hate's cheap in this world. Everybody's got it for sale. My God! What do you suppose I think of myself now?"

"He's not worth feeling that way about."

"Please go away!" cried Michael passionately. "I want to be alone."

Obediently she left him and he sat down again in the darkness of the porch, a sort of terror creeping over him. Several times he made a motion to get up but each time he frowned and remained motionless. Then after another long while he jumped suddenly to his feet, cold sweat starting from his forehead. The last hour, the months just passed, were washed away and he was swept years back in time. Why, they were after Charley Hart, his old friend. Charley Hart who had come to him because he had no other place to go. Michael began to run hastily about the porch in a daze, hunting for his hat and coat.

"Why Charley!" he cried aloud.

He found his coat finally and, struggling into it, ran wildly down the steps. It seemed to him that Charley had gone only a few minutes before.

"Charley!" he called when he reached the road. "Charley, come back here. There's been a mistake!"

He paused, listening. There was no answer. Panting a little he began to run doggedly along the road through the hot night.

It was only half-past eight o'clock but the country was very quiet and the frogs were loud in the strip of wet marsh that ran along beside the road. The sky was salted thinly with stars and after a while there would be a moon, but the road ran among dark trees and Michael could scarcely see ten feet in front of him. After a while he slowed down to a walk, glancing at the phosphorous dial of his wristwatch – the New York train was not due for an hour. There was plenty of time.

In spite of this he broke into an uneasy run and covered the mile between his house and the station in fifteen minutes. It was a little station, crouched humbly beside the shining rails in the darkness. Beside it Michael saw the lights of a single taxi waiting for the next train.

The platform was deserted and Michael opened the door and peered into the dim waiting room. It was empty.

"That's funny," he muttered.

Rousing a sleepy taxi driver, he asked if there had been anyone waiting for the train. The taxi driver considered – yes, there had been a young man waiting, about twenty minutes ago. He had walked up and down for a while, smoking a cigarette, and then gone away into the darkness.

"That's funny," repeated Michael. He made a megaphone of his hands and facing towards the wood across the track shouted aloud.

"Charley!"

There was no answer. He tried again. Then he turned back to the driver.

"Have you any idea what direction he went?"

The man pointed vaguely down the New York road which ran along beside the railroad track.

"Down there somewhere."

With increasing uneasiness Michael thanked him and started swiftly along the road which was white now under the risen moon. He knew now as surely as he knew anything that Charley had gone off by himself to die. He remembered the expression on his face as he had turned away and the hand tucked down close in his coat pocket as if it clutched some menacing thing.

"Charley!" he called in a terrible voice.

The dark trees gave back no sound. He walked on past a dozen fields bright as silver under the moon, pausing every few minutes to shout and then waiting tensely for an answer.

It occurred to him that it was foolish to continue in this direction – Charley was probably back by the station in the woods somewhere. Perhaps it was all imagination, perhaps even now Charley was pacing the station platform waiting for the train from the city. But some impulse beyond logic made him continue. More than that – several times he had the sense that someone was in front of him, someone who just eluded him at every turning, out of sight and earshot, yet leaving always behind him a dim, tragic aura of having passed that way. Once he thought he heard steps among the leaves on the side of the road but it was only a piece of vagrant newspaper blown by the faint hot wind.

It was a stifling night – the moon seemed to be beating hot rays down upon the sweltering earth. Michael took off his coat and threw it over his arm as he walked. A little way ahead of him now was a stone bridge over the tracks and beyond that an interminable line of telephone poles which stretched in diminishing perspective towards an endless horizon. Well, he would walk to the bridge and then give up. He would have given up before except for this sense he had that someone was walking very lightly and swiftly just ahead.

Reaching the stone bridge he sat down on a rock, his heart beating in loud exhausted thumps under his dripping shirt. Well, it was hopeless – Charley was gone, perhaps out of range of his help for ever. Far away beyond the station he heard the approaching siren of the nine-thirty train.

Michael found himself wondering suddenly why he was here. He despised himself for being here. On what weak chord in his nature had Charley played in those few minutes, forcing him into this senseless, frightened run through the night? They had discussed it all and Charley had been unable to give a reason why he should be helped.

He got to his feet with the idea of retracing his steps but before turning he stood for a minute in the moonlight looking down the road. Across the track stretched the line of telephone poles and, as his eyes followed them as far as he could see, he heard again, louder now and not far away, the siren of the New York train which rose and fell with musical sharpness on the still night. Suddenly his eyes, which had been travelling down the tracks, stopped and were focused suddenly upon one spot in the line of poles, perhaps a quarter of a mile away. It was a pole just like the others and yet it was different – there was something about it that was indescribably different.

And watching it as one might concentrate on some figure in the pattern of a carpet, something curious happened in his mind and instantly he saw everything in a completely different light. Something had come to him in a whisper of the breeze, something that changed the whole complexion of the situation. It was this: he remembered having read somewhere that at some point back in the Dark Ages a man named Gerbert had all by himself summed up the whole of European civilization.* It became suddenly plain to Michael that he himself had just now been in a position like that. For one minute, one spot in time, all the mercy in the world had been vested in him.

He realized all this in the space of a second with a sense of shock and instantly he understood the reason why he should have helped Charley Hart. It was because it would be intolerable to exist in a world where there was no help – where any human being could be as alone as Charley had been alone this afternoon.

Why, that was it, of course – he had been trusted with that chance. Someone had come to him who had no other place to go – and he had failed.

All this time, this moment, he had been standing utterly motionless staring at the telephone pole down the track, the one that his eye had picked out as being different from the others. The moon was so bright now that near the top he could see a white bar set crosswise on the pole and as he looked the pole and the bar seemed to have become isolated as if the other poles had shrunk back and away.

Suddenly a mile down the track he heard the click and clamour of the electric train when it left the station, and as if the sound had startled him into life he gave a short cry and set off at a swaying run down the road, in the direction of the pole with the crossed bar.

The train whistled again. *Click – click – click* – it was nearer now, six hundred, five hundred yards away and as it came under the bridge he was running in the bright beam of its searchlight. There was no emotion in his mind but terror – he knew only that he must reach that pole before the train and it was fifty yards away, struck out sharp as a star against the sky.

There was no path on the other side of the tracks under the poles but the train was so close now that he dared wait no longer or he would be unable to cross at all. He darted from the road, cleared the tracks in two strides and with the sound of the engine at his heels raced along the rough earth. Twenty feet, thirty feet – as the sound of the electric train swelled to a roar in his ears he reached the pole and threw himself bodily on a man who stood close to the tracks, carrying him heavily to the ground with the impact of his body.

There was the thunder of steel in his ear, the heavy clump of the wheels on the rails, a swift roaring of air, and the nine-thirty train had gone past.

"Charley," he gasped incoherently, "Charley."

A white face looked up at him in a daze. Michael rolled over on his back and lay panting. The hot night was quiet now – there was no sound but the far-away murmur of the receding train.

"Oh, God!"

Michael opened his eyes to see that Charley was sitting up, his face in his hands.

"S'all right," gasped Michael, "s'all right, Charley. You can have the money. I don't know what I was thinking about. Why – why, you're one of my oldest friends."

Charley shook his head.

"I don't understand," he said brokenly. "Where did you come from – how did you get here?"

"I've been following you. I was just behind."

"I've been here for half an hour."

"Well, it's good you chose this pole to – to wait under. I've been looking at it from down by the bridge. I picked it out on account of the crossbar."

Charley had risen unsteadily to his feet and now he walked a few steps and looked up the pole in the full moonlight.

"What did you say?" he asked after a minute, in a puzzled voice. "Did you say this pole had a crossbar?"

"Why, yes. I was looking at it a long time. That's how…"

Charley looked up again and hesitated curiously before he spoke.

"There isn't any crossbar," he said.

Not in the Guidebook

THIS STORY BEGAN THREE DAYS before it got into the papers. Like many other news-hungry Americans in Paris this spring, I opened the *Franco-American Star* one morning, and having skimmed the hackneyed headlines (largely devoted to reporting the sempiternal "Lafayette-love-Washington"* bombast of French and American orators) I came upon something of genuine interest.

"Look at that!" I exclaimed, passing it over to the twin bed. But the occupant of the twin bed immediately found an article about Leonora Hughes, the dancer, in another column, and began to read it. So of course I demanded the paper back.

"You don't realize—" I began.

"I wonder," interrupted the occupant of the twin bed, "if she's a real blonde."

However, when I issued from the domestic suite a little later I found other men in various cafes saying, "Look at that!" as they pointed to the Item of Interest. And about noon I found another writer (whom I have since bribed with champagne to hold his peace) and together we went down into Franco-American officialdom to see.

It began on a boat, and with a young woman who, though she wasn't even faintly uneasy, was leaning over the rail. She was watching the parallels of longitude as they swam beneath the keel, and trying to read the numbers on them, but of course the SS *Olympic* travels too fast for that, and all that the young woman could see was the agate-green, foliage-like spray, changing and complaining around the stern. Though there was little to look at except the spray and a dismal Scandinavian tramp in the distance and the admiring millionaire who was trying to catch her eye from the first-class deck above, Milly Cooley was perfectly happy. For she was beginning life over.

Hope is a usual cargo between Naples and Ellis Island, but on ships bound east for Cherbourg it is noticeably rare. The first-class passengers specialize in sophistication and the steerage passengers go in for disillusion (which is much the same thing) but the young woman by the rail was going in for hope raised to the ultimate power. It was not her own life she was beginning over, but someone else's, and this is a much more dangerous thing to do.

Milly was a frail, dark, appealing girl with the spiritual, haunted eyes that so frequently accompany south-European beauty. By birth her mother and father had been respectively Czech and Romanian, but Milly had missed the overshort upper lip and the pendulous, pointed nose that disfigure the type; her features were regular and her skin was young and olive-white and clear.

The good-looking, pimply young man with eyes of a bright marbly blue who was asleep on a dunnage bag a few feet away was her husband – it was his life that Milly was beginning over. Through the six months of their marriage he had shown himself to be shiftless and dissipated, but now they were getting off to a new start. Jim Cooley deserved a new start, for he had been a hero in the war. There was a thing called "shell shock" which justified anything unpleasant in a war hero's behaviour – Jim Cooley had explained that to her on the second day of their honeymoon when he had got abominably drunk and knocked her down with his open hand.

"I get crazy," he said emphatically next morning, and his marbly eyes rolled back and forth realistically in his head. "I get started thinkin' I'm fightin' the war, an' I take a poke at whatever's in front of me, see?"

He was a Brooklyn boy, and he had joined the marines. And on a June twilight he had crawled fifty yards out of his lines to search the body of a Bavarian captain that lay out in plain sight. He found a copy of German regimental orders, and in consequence his own brigade attacked much sooner than would otherwise have been possible, and perhaps the war was shortened by so much as a quarter of an hour. The fact was appreciated by the French and American races in the form of engraved slugs of precious metal which Jim showed around for four years before it occurred to him how nice it would be to have a permanent audience.

Milly's mother was impressed with his martial achievement, and a marriage was arranged. Milly didn't realize her mistake until twenty-four hours after it was too late.

At the end of several months Milly's mother died and left her daughter two hundred and fifty dollars. The event had a marked effect on Jim. He sobered up and one night came home from work with a plan for turning over a new leaf, for beginning life over. By the aid of his war record he had obtained a job with a bureau that took care of American soldier graves in France. The pay was small but then, as everyone knew, living was dirt cheap over there. Hadn't the forty a month that he drew in the war looked good to the girls and the wine-sellers of Paris? Especially when you figured it in French money.

Milly listened to his tales of the land where grapes were full of champagne and then thought it all over carefully. Perhaps the best use for her money would be in giving Jim his chance, the chance that he had never had since the war. In a little cottage in the outskirts of Paris they could forget this last six months and find peace and happiness and perhaps even love as well.

"Are you going to try?" she asked simply.

"Of course I'm going to try, Milly."

"You're going to make me think I didn't make a mistake?"

"Sure I am, Milly; it'll make a different person out of me. Don't you believe it?"

She looked at him. His eyes were bright with enthusiasm, with determination. A warm glow had spread over him at the prospect – he had never really had his chance before.

"All right," she said finally. "We'll go."

They were there. The Cherbourg breakwater, a white stone snake, glittered along the sea at dawn: behind it red roofs and steeples and then small neat hills traced with a warm, orderly pattern of toy farms. "Do you like this French arrangement?" it seemed to say. "It's considered very charming, but if you don't agree just shift it about – set this road here, this steeple there. It's been done before, and it always comes out lovely in the end!"

It was Sunday morning, and Cherbourg was in flaring collars and high lace hats. Donkey carts and diminutive automobiles moved to the sound of incessant bells. Jim and Milly went ashore on a tugboat and were inspected by customs officials and immigration authorities. Then they were free with an hour before the Paris train, and they moved out into the bright thrilling world of French blue. At a point of vantage, a pleasant square that continually throbbed with soldiers and innumerable dogs and the clack of wooden shoes, they sat down at a cafe.

"Du vaah," said Jim to the waiter. He was a little disappointed when the answer came in English. After the man went for the wine he took out his two war medals and pinned them to his coat. The waiter returned with the wine, seemed not to notice the medals, made no remark. Milly wished Jim hadn't put them on – she felt vaguely ashamed.

After another glass of wine it was time for the train. They got into the strange little third-class carriage, an engine that was out of some boy's playroom began to puff and, in a pleasant, informal way, jogged them leisurely south through the friendly lived-over land.

"What are we going to do first when we get there?" asked Milly.

"First?" Jim looked at her abstractly and frowned. "Why, first I got to see about the job, see?" The exhilaration of the wine had passed and left him surly. "What do you want to ask so many questions for? Buy yourself a guidebook, why don't you?"

Milly felt a slight sinking of the heart; he hadn't grumbled at her like this since the trip was first proposed.

"It didn't cost as much as we thought, anyhow," she said cheerfully. "We must have over a hundred dollars left anyway."

He grunted. Outside the window Milly's eyes were caught by the sight of a dog drawing a legless man.

"Look!" she exclaimed. "How funny!"

"Aw, dry up. I've seen it all before."

An encouraging idea occurred to her: it was in France that Jim's nerves had gone to pieces, it was natural that he should be cross and uneasy for a few hours.

Westward through Caen, Lisieux and the rich green plains of Calvados. When they reached the third stop Jim got up and stretched himself.

"Going out on the platform," he said gloomily. "I need to get a breath of air; hot in here."

It was hot, but Milly didn't mind. Her eyes were excited with all she saw – a pair of little boys in black smocks began to stare at her curiously through the windows of the carriage.

"American?" cried one of them suddenly.

"Hello," said Milly, "what place is this?"

"Pardon?"

They came closer.

Suddenly the two boys poked each other in the stomach and went off into roars of laughter. Milly didn't see that she had said anything funny.

There was an abrupt jerk as the train started. Milly jumped up in alarm and put her head out the carriage window.

"Jim!" she called.

She looked up and down the platform. He wasn't there. The boys, seeing her distraught face, ran along beside the train as it moved from the station. He must have jumped for one of the rear cars. But...

"Jim!" she cried wildly. The station slid past. "Jim!"

Trying desperately to control her fright, she sank back into her seat and tried to think. Her first supposition was that he had gone to a cafe for a drink and missed the train – in that case she should have got off too while there was still time, for otherwise there was no telling what would happen to him. If this were one of his spells he might just go on drinking, until he had spent every cent of their money. It was unbelievably awful to imagine – but it was possible.

She waited, gave him ten, fifteen minutes to work his way up to this car – then she admitted to herself that he wasn't on the train. A dull panic began. The sudden change in her relations to the world was so startling that she thought neither of his delinquency nor of what must be done, but only of the immediate fact that she was alone. Erratic as his protection had been, it was something. Now – why, she might sit in this strange train until it carried her to China and there was no one to care!

After a long while it occurred to her that he might have left part of the money in one of the suitcases. She took them down from the rack and went feverishly through all the clothes. In the bottom of an old pair of pants that Jim had worn on the boat she found two bright American dimes. The sight of them was somehow comforting and she clasped them tight in her hand. The bags yielded up nothing more.

An hour later, when it was dark outside, the train slid in under the yellow misty glow of the Gare du Nord. Strange, incomprehensible station cries fell on her ears, and her heart was beating loudly as she wrenched at the handle of the door. She took her own bag with one hand and picked up Jim's suitcase in the other, but it was heavy and she couldn't get out the door with both, so in a rush of anger she left the suitcase in the carriage.

On the platform she looked left and right with the forlorn hope that he might appear, but she saw no one except a Swedish brother and sister from the boat whose tall bodies, straight and strong under the huge bundles they both carried, were hurrying out of sight. She took a quick step after them and then stopped, unable to tell them of the shameful thing that had happened to her. They had worries of their own.

With the two dimes in one hand and her suitcase in the other, Milly walked slowly along the platform. People hurried by her, baggage-smashers under forests of golf sticks, excited American girls full of the irrepressible thrill of arriving in Paris, obsequious porters from the big hotels. They were all walking and talking very fast, but Milly walked slowly because ahead of her she saw only the yellow arc of the waiting room and the door that led out of it and after that she did not know where she would go.

By 10 p.m. Mr Bill Driscoll was usually weary, for by that time he had a full twelve-hour day behind him. After that he only went out with the most celebrated people. If someone had tipped off a multimillionaire or a moving-picture director – at that time American directors were swarming over Europe looking for new locations – about Bill Driscoll, he would fortify himself with two cups of coffee, adorn his person with his new dinner coat and show them the most dangerous dives of Montmartre in the very safest way.

Bill Driscoll looked well in his new dinner coat, with his reddish-brown hair soaked in water and slicked back from his attractive forehead. Often he regarded himself admiringly in the mirror, for it was the first dinner coat he had ever owned. He had earned it himself, with his wits, as he had earned the swelling packet of American bonds which awaited him in a New York bank. If you had been in Paris during the past two years you must have seen his large white autobus with the provoking legend on the side:

WILLIAM DRISCOLL
HE SHOWS YOU THINGS NOT IN THE GUIDEBOOK

When he found Milly Cooley it was after three o'clock and he had just left Director and Mrs Claude Peebles at their hotel after escorting them to those celebrated apache dens, Zelli's and Le Rat Mort (which are about as dangerous, all things considered, as the Biltmore Hotel at noon), and he was walking homeward towards his *pension* on the Left Bank. His eye was caught by two disreputable-looking parties under the lamp post who were giving aid to what was apparently a drunken girl. Bill Driscoll decided to cross the street – he was aware of the tender affection which the French police bore towards embattled Americans, and he made a point of keeping out of trouble. Just at that moment Milly's subconscious self came to her aid and she called out "Let me go!" in an agonized moan.

The moan had a Brooklyn accent. It was a Brooklyn moan.

Driscoll altered his course uneasily and, approaching the group, asked politely what was the matter; whereat one of the disreputable parties desisted in his attempt to open Milly's tightly clasped left hand.

The man answered quickly that she had fainted. He and his friend were assisting her to the gendarmerie. They loosened their hold on her and she collapsed gently to the ground.

Bill came closer and bent over her, being careful to choose a position where neither man was behind him. He saw a young, frightened face that was drained now of the colour it possessed by day.

"Where did you find her?" he enquired in French.

"Here. Just now. She looked to be so tired…"

Billy put his hand in his pocket and when he spoke he tried very hard to suggest by his voice that he had a revolver there.

"She is American," he said. "You leave her to me."

The man made a gesture of acquiescence and took a step backwards, his hand going with a natural movement to his coat as if he intended buttoning it. He was watching Bill's right hand, the one in his coat pocket, and Bill happened to be left-handed. There is nothing much faster than an untelegraphed left-hand blow – this one travelled less than eighteen inches and the recipient staggered back against a lamp post, embraced it transiently and regretfully and settled to the ground. Nevertheless Bill Driscoll's successful career might have ended there, ended with the strong shout of *"Voleurs!"** which he raised into the Paris night, had the other man had a gun. The other man indicated that he had no gun by retreating ten yards down the street. His prostrate companion moved slightly on the sidewalk and, taking a step towards him, Billy drew back his foot and kicked him full in the head as a football player kicks a goal from placement. It was not a pretty gesture, but he had remembered that he was wearing his new dinner coat and he didn't want to wrestle on the ground for the piece of poisonous hardware.

In a moment two gendarmes in a great hurry came running down the moonlit street.

Two days after this it came out in the papers – "War hero deserts wife en route to Paris", I think, or "American bride arrives penniless, husbandless at Gare du Nord". The police were informed, of course, and word was sent out to the provincial departments to seek an American named James Cooley who was without *carte d'identité*. The newspapers learnt the story at the American Aid Society, and made a neat, pathetic job of it because Milly was young and pretty and curiously loyal to her husband. Almost her first words were to explain that it was all because his nerves had been shattered in the war.

Young Driscoll was somewhat disappointed to find that she was married. Not that he had fallen in love at first sight – on the contrary, he was unusually level-headed – but after the moonlight rescue, which rather pleased him, it didn't seem appropriate that she should have a heroic husband wandering over France. He had carried her to his own *pension* that night and his landlady, an American widow named Mrs Horton, had taken a fancy to Milly and wanted to look after her, but before eleven o'clock on the day the paper appeared, the office of the

American Aid Society was literally jammed with Samaritans. They were mostly rich old ladies from America who were tired of the Louvre and the Tuileries,* and anxious for something to do. Several eager but sheepish Frenchmen, inspired by a mysterious and unfathomable gallantry, hung about outside the door.

The most insistent of the ladies was a Mrs Coots, who considered that Providence had sent her Milly as a companion. If she had heard Milly's story in the street she wouldn't have listened to a word, but print makes things respectable. After it got into the *Franco-American Star*, Mrs Coots was sure Milly wouldn't make off with her jewels.

"I'll pay you well, my dear," she insisted shrilly. "Twenty-five a week. How's that?"

Milly cast an anxious glance at Mrs Horton's faded, pleasant face.

"I don't know…" she said hesitantly.

"I can't pay you anything." Mrs Horton was confused by Mrs Coots's affluent, positive manner. "You do as you like. I'd love to have you."

"You've certainly been kind," said Milly, "but I don't want to impose—"

Driscoll, who had been walking up and down with his hands in his pockets, stopped and turned towards her quickly.

"I'll take care of that," he said quickly. "You don't have to worry about that."

Mrs Coots's eyes flashed at him indignantly.

"She's better with me," she insisted. "Much better." She turned to the secretary and remarked in a pained, disapproving stage whisper, "Who is this forward young man?"

Again Milly looked appealingly at Mrs Horton.

"If it's not too much trouble I'd rather stay with you," she said. "I'll help you all I can…"

It took another half an hour to get rid of Mrs Coots, but finally it was arranged that Milly was to stay at Mrs Horton's *pension*, until some trace of her husband was found. Later the same day they ascertained that the American Bureau of Military Graves had never heard of Jim Cooley – he had no job promised him in France.

However distressing her situation, Milly was young and she was in Paris in mid-June. She decided to enjoy herself. At Mr Bill Driscoll's invitation

she went on an excursion to Versailles next day in his rubberneck wagon.*
She had never been on such a trip before. She sat among garment buyers
from Sioux City and schoolteachers from California and honeymoon
couples from Japan, and was whirled through fifteen centuries of Paris,
while their guide stood up in front with the megaphone pressed to his
voluble and original mouth.

"Building on your left is the Louvre, ladies and gentlemen. Excursion
number twenty-three leaving tomorrow at ten sharp takes you inside.
Sufficient to remark now that it contains fifteen thousand works of art
of every description. The oil used in its oil paintings would lubricate all
the cars in the state of Oregon over a period of two years. The frames
alone if placed end to end..."

Milly watching him, believed every word. It was hard to remember
that he had come to her rescue that night. Heroes weren't like that –
she knew; she had lived with one. They brooded constantly on their
achievements and retailed them to strangers at least once a day. When
she thanked this young man he told her gravely that Mr Carnegie* had
been trying to get him on the Ouija board all that day.

After a dramatic stop before the house in which Landru, the Bluebeard
of France, had murdered his fourteen wives,* the expedition proceeded
to Versailles. There, in the great hall of mirrors, Bill Driscoll delved
into the forgotten scandal of the eighteenth century as he described the
meeting between "Louie's girl and Louie's wife".*

"Du Barry skipped in, wearing a creation of mauve georgette, held
out by bronze hoops over a *tablier* of champagne lace. The gown had
a ruched collarette of Swedish fox, lined with yellow satin *fulgurante*
which matched the hansom that brought her to the party. She was nervous, ladies. She didn't know how the Queen was going to take it. After a
while the Queen walked in, wearing an oxidized silver gown with collar,
cuffs and flounces of Russian ermine and strappings of dentist's gold.
The bodice was cut with a very long waistline and the skirt arranged
full in front and falling in picot-edged points tipped with the crown
jewels. When du Barry saw her she leant over to King Louie and whispered: 'Royal Honey-boy, who's that lady with all the laundry on that
just came in the door?'

"'That isn't a lady,' said Louie, 'that's my wife.'"

That was the first of many trips that Milly took in the rubberneck wagon – to Malmaison, to Passy, to St Cloud. The weeks passed, three of them, and still there was no word from Jim Cooley, who seemed to have stepped off the face of the earth when he vanished from the train.

In spite of a sort of dull worry that possessed her when she thought of her situation, Milly was happier than she had ever been. It was a relief to be rid of the incessant depression of living with a morbid and broken man. Moreover, it was thrilling to be in Paris when it seemed that all the world was there, when each arriving boat dumped a new thousand into the pleasure ground, when the streets were so clogged with sightseers that Billy Driscoll's buses were reserved for days ahead. And it was pleasantest of all to stroll down to the corner and watch the blood-red sun sink like a slow penny into the Seine while she sipped coffee with Bill Driscoll at a cafe.

"How would you like to go to Château-Thierry with me tomorrow?" he asked her one evening.

The name struck a chord in Milly. It was at Château-Thierry that Jim Cooley, at the risk of his life, had made his daring expedition between the lines.

"My husband was there," she said proudly.

"So was I," he remarked. "And I didn't have any fun at all."

He thought for a moment.

"How old are you?" he asked suddenly.

"Eighteen."

"Why don't you get a divorce?"

The suggestion shocked Milly.

"I think you'd better," he continued, looking down. "It's easier here than anywhere else. Then you'd be free."

"I couldn't," she said, frightened. "It wouldn't be fair. You see he doesn't—"

"I know," he interrupted. "But I'm beginning to think that you're spoiling your life with this man. Is there anything except his war record to his credit?"

"Isn't that enough?" answered Milly gravely.

"Milly…" He raised his eyes. "Won't you think it over carefully?"

She got up uneasily. He looked very honest and safe and cool sitting there, and for a moment she was tempted to do what he said, to put the whole thing in his hands. But looking at him she saw now what she hadn't seen before, that the advice was not disinterested – there was more than an impersonal care for her future in his eyes. She turned away with a mixture of emotions.

Side by side and in silence they walked back towards the *pension*. From a high window the plaintive wail of a violin drifted down into the street, mingling with practice chords from an invisible piano and a shrill incomprehensible quarrel of French children over the way. The twilight was fast dissolving into a starry blue Parisian evening, but it was still light enough for them to make out the figure of Mrs Horton standing in front of the *pension*. She came towards them swiftly, talking as she came.

"I've got some news for you," she said. "The secretary of the American Aid Society just telephoned. They've located your husband, and he'll be in Paris the day after tomorrow."

When Jim Cooley, the war hero, left the train at the small town of Évreux, he walked very fast until he was several hundred yards from the station. Then, standing behind a tree, he watched until the train pulled out and the last puff of smoke burst up behind a little hill. He stood for several minutes, laughing and looking after the train, until abruptly his face resumed his normal injured expression and he turned to examine the place in which he had chosen to be free.

It was a sleepy provincial village with two high lines of silver sycamores along its principal street, at the end of which a fine fountain purred crystal water from a cat's mouth of cold stone. Around the fountain was a square and on the sidewalks of the square several groups of small iron tables indicated open-air cafes. A farm wagon drawn by a single white ox was toiling towards the fountain and several cheap French cars, together with an ancient American one, were parked along the street.

"It's a hick town," he said to himself with some disgust. "Reg'lar hick town."

But it was peaceful and green, and he caught sight of two stockingless ladies entering the door of a shop; and the little tables by the fountain were inviting. He walked up the street and at the first cafe sat down and ordered a lager beer.

"I'm free," he said to himself. "Free, by God!"

His decision to desert Milly had been taken suddenly – in Cherbourg, as they got on the train. Just at that moment he had seen a little French girl who was the real thing and he realized that he didn't want Milly "hanging on him" any more. Even on the boat he had played with the idea, but until Cherbourg he had never quite made up his mind. He was rather sorry now that he hadn't thought to leave Milly a little money, enough for one night – but then somebody would be sure to help her when she got to Paris. Besides, what he didn't know didn't worry him, and he wasn't going ever to hear about her again.

"Cognac this time," he said to the waiter.

He needed something strong. He wanted to forget. Not to forget Milly, that was easy, she was already behind him; but to forget himself. He felt that he had been abused. He felt that it was Milly who had deserted him, or at least that her cold mistrust was responsible for driving him away. What good would it have done if he had gone on to Paris anyways? There wasn't enough money left to keep two people for very long, and he had invented the job on the strength of a vague rumour that the American Bureau of Military Graves gave jobs to veterans who were broke in France. He shouldn't have brought Milly, wouldn't have if he had had the money to get over. But, though he was not aware of it, there was another reason why he had brought Milly. Jim Cooley hated to be alone.

"Cognac," he said to the waiter. "A big one. *Très grand*."

He put his hand in his pocket and fingered the blue notes that had been given him in Cherbourg in exchange for his American money. He took them out and counted them. Crazy-looking kale.* It was funny you could buy things with it just like you could do with the real mazuma.

He beckoned to the waiter.

"Hey!" he remarked conversationally. "This is funny money you got here, ain't it?"

But the waiter spoke no English, and was unable to satisfy Jim Cooley's craving for companionship. Never mind. His nerves were at rest now – body was glowing triumphantly from top to toe.

"This is the life," he muttered to himself. "Only live once. Might as well enjoy it." And then aloud to the waiter, "'Nother one of those big cognacs. Two of them. I'm set to go."

He went – for several hours. He awoke at dawn in a bedroom of a small inn, with red streaks in his eyes and fever pounding his head. He was afraid to look in his pockets until he had ordered and swallowed another cognac, and then he found that his worst fears were justified. Of the ninety-odd dollars with which he had got off the train only six were left.

"I must have been crazy," he whispered.

There remained his watch. His watch was large and methodical, and on the outer case two hearts were picked out in diamonds from the dark solid gold. It had been part of the booty of Jim Cooley's heroism, for when he had located the paper in the German officer's pocket he had found it clasped tight in the dead hand. One of the diamond hearts probably stood for some human grief back in Friedland or Berlin, but when Jim married he told Milly that the diamond hearts stood for their hearts and would be a token of their everlasting love. Before Milly fully appreciated this sentimental suggestion their enduring love had been tarnished beyond repair and the watch went back into Jim's pocket where it confined itself to marking time instead of emotion.

But Jim Cooley had loved to show the watch, and he found that parting with it would be much more painful than parting with Milly – so painful, in fact, that he got drunk in anticipation of the sorrow. Late that afternoon, already a reeling figure at which the town boys jeered along the streets, he found his way into the shop of a *bijoutier*,* and when he issued forth into the street he was in possession of a ticket of redemption and a note for two thousand francs which, he figured dimly, was about one hundred and twenty dollars. Muttering to himself, he stumbled back to the square.

"One American can lick three Frenchmen!" he remarked to three small stout bourgeois drinking their beer at a table.

They paid no attention. He repeated his jeer.

"One American…" tapping his chest, "can beat up three dirty frogs, see?"

Still they didn't move. It infuriated him. Lurching forward, he seized the back of an unoccupied chair and pulled at it. In what seemed less than a minute there was a small crowd around him and the three Frenchmen were all talking at once in excited voices.

"Aw, go on, I meant what I said!" he cried savagely. "One American can wipe up the ground with three Frenchmen!"

And now there were two men in uniform before him – two men with revolver holsters on their hips, dressed in red and blue.

"You heard what I said," he shouted, "I'm a hero – I'm not afraid of the whole damn French army!"

A hand fell on his arm, but with blind passion he wrenched it free and struck at the black-moustached face before him. Then there was a rushing, crashing noise in his ears as fists and then feet struck at him, and the world seemed to close like water over his head.

When they located him and, after a personal expedition by one of the American vice consuls, got him out of jail Milly realized how much these weeks had meant to her. The holiday was over. But even though Jim would be in Paris tomorrow, even though the dreary round of her life with him was due to recommence, Milly decided to take the trip to Château-Thierry just the same. She wanted a last few hours of happiness that she could always remember. She supposed they would return to New York – what chance Jim might have had of obtaining a position had vanished now that he was marked by a fortnight in a French prison.

The bus, as usual, was crowded. As they approached the little village of Château-Thierry, Bill Driscoll stood up in front with his megaphone and began to tell his clients how it had looked to him when his division went up to the line five years before.*

"It was nine o'clock at night," he said, "and we came out of a wood and there was the western front. I'd read about it for three years back in America, and here it was at last – it looked like the line of a forest fire at night except that fireworks were blazing up instead of grass. We relieved a French regiment in new trenches that weren't three feet deep. At that, most of us were too excited to be scared until the top sergeant was blown to pieces with shrapnel about two o'clock in the morning. That made us think. Two days later we went over and the only reason I didn't get hit was that I was shaking so much they couldn't aim at me."

The listeners laughed and Milly felt a faint thrill of pride. Jim hadn't been scared – she'd heard him say so, many times. All he'd thought about was doing a little more than his duty. When others were in the comparative safety of the trenches he had gone into no-man's-land alone.

After lunch in the village the party walked over the battlefield, changed now into a peaceful undulating valley of graves. Milly was glad she had come – the sense of rest after a struggle soothed her. Perhaps after the bleak future her life might be quiet as this peaceful land. Perhaps Jim would change someday. If he had risen once to such a height of courage there must be something deep inside him that was worthwhile, that would make him try once more.

Just before it was time to start home Driscoll, who had hardly spoken to her all day, suddenly beckoned her aside.

"I want to talk to you for the last time," he said.

The last time! Milly felt a flutter of unexpected pain. Was tomorrow so near?

"I'm going to say what's in my mind," he said, "and please don't be angry. I love you, and you know it; but what I'm going to say isn't because of that – it's because I want you to be happy."

Milly nodded. She was afraid she was going to cry.

"I don't think your husband's any good," he said.

She looked up.

"You don't know him," she exclaimed quickly. "You can't judge."

"I can judge from what he did to you. I think this shell-shock business is all a plain lie. And what does it matter what he did five years ago?"

"It matters to me," cried Milly. She felt herself growing a little angry. "You can't take that away from him. He acted brave."

Driscoll nodded.

"That's true. But other men were brave."

"You weren't," she said scornfully. "You just said you were scared to death – and when you said it all the people laughed. Well, nobody laughed at Jim – they gave him a medal because he wasn't afraid."

When Milly had said this she was sorry, but it was too late now. At his next words she leant forward in surprise.

"That was a lie too," said Bill Driscoll slowly. "I told it because I wanted them to laugh. I wasn't even in the attack."

He stared silently down the hill.

"Well, then," said Milly contemptuously, "how can you sit here and say things about my husband when – when you didn't even—"

"It was only a professional lie," he said impatiently. "I happened to be wounded the night before."

He stood up suddenly.

"There's no use," he said. "I seem to have made you hate me, and that's the end. There's no use saying any more."

He stared down the hill with haunted eyes.

"I shouldn't have talked to you here," he cried. "There's no luck here for me. Once before I lost something I wanted, not a hundred yards from this hill. And now I've lost you."

"What was it you lost?" demanded Milly bitterly. "Another girl?"

"There's never been any other girl but you."

"What was it then?"

He hesitated.

"I told you I was wounded," he said. "I was. For two months I didn't know I was alive. But the worst of it was that some dirty sneak thief had been through my pockets, and I guess he got the credit for a copy of German orders that I'd just brought in. He took a gold watch too. I'd pinched them both off the body of a German officer out between the lines."

Mr and Mrs William Driscoll were married the following spring and started off on their honeymoon in a car that was much larger than the king of England's. There were two dozen vacant places in it, so they gave many rides to tired pedestrians along the white poplar-lined roads of France. The wayfarers, however, always sat in the back seat as the conversation in front was not for profane ears. The tour progressed through Lyons, Avignon, Bordeaux, and smaller places not in the guidebook.

Presumption

1

S ITTING BY THE WINDOW and staring out into the early autumn dusk, San Juan Chandler remembered only that Noel was coming tomorrow; but when, with a romantic sound that was half gasp, half sigh, he turned from the window, snapped on the light and looked at himself in the mirror, his expression became more materially complicated. He leant closer. Delicacy baulked at the abominable word "pimple", but some such blemish had undoubtedly appeared on his cheek within the last hour, and now formed, with a pair from last week, a distressing constellation of three. Going into the bathroom adjoining his room – Juan had never possessed a bathroom to himself before – he opened a medicine closet, and, after peering about, carefully extracted a promising-looking jar of black ointment and covered each slight protuberance with a black gluey mound. Then, strangely dotted, he returned to the bedroom, put out the light and resumed his vigil over the shadowy garden.

He waited. That roof among the trees on the hill belonged to Noel Garneau's house. She was coming back to it tomorrow; he would see her there… A loud clock on the staircase inside struck seven. Juan went to the glass and removed the ointment with a handkerchief. To his chagrin, the spots were still there, even slightly irritated from the chemical sting of the remedy. That settled it – no more chocolate malted milks or eating between meals during his visit to Culpepper Bay. Taking the lid from the jar of talcum he had observed on the dressing table, he touched the laden puff to his cheek. Immediately his brows and lashes bloomed with snow and he coughed chokingly, observing that the triangle of humiliation was still observable upon his otherwise handsome face.

"Disgusting," he muttered to himself. "I never saw anything so disgusting." At twenty, such childish phenomena should be behind him.

Downstairs three gongs, melodious and metallic, hummed and sang. He listened for a moment, fascinated. Then he wiped the powder from his face, ran a comb through his yellow hair and went down to dinner.

Dinner at Cousin Cora's he had found embarrassing. She was so stiff and formal about things like that, and so familiar about Juan's private affairs. The first night of his visit he had tried politely to pull out her chair and bumped into the maid; the second night he remembered the experience – but so did the maid, and Cousin Cora seated herself unassisted. At home Juan was accustomed to behave as he liked; like all children of deferent and indulgent mothers, he lacked both confidence and good manners.

Tonight there were guests.

"This is San Juan Chandler, my cousin's son – Mrs Holyoke – and Mr Holyoke."

The phrase "my cousin's son" seemed to explain him away, seemed to account for his being in Miss Chandler's house: "You understand – we must have our poor relations with us occasionally." But a tone which implied that would be rude – and certainly Cousin Cora, with all her social position, couldn't be rude.

Mr and Mrs Holyoke acknowledged the introduction politely and coolly, and dinner was served. The conversation, dictated by Cousin Cora, bored Juan. It was about the garden and about her father, for whom she lived and who was dying slowly and unwillingly upstairs. Towards the salad Juan was wedged into the conversation by a question from Mr Holyoke and a quick look from his cousin.

"I'm just staying for a week," he answered politely, "then I've got to go home because college opens pretty soon."

"Where are you at college?"

Juan named his college, adding almost apologetically, "You see, my father went there."

He wished that he could have answered that he was at Yale or Princeton, where he wanted to go. He was prominent at Henderson and belonged to a good fraternity, but it annoyed him when people occasionally failed to recognize his alma mater's name.

"I suppose you've met all the young people here," supposed Mrs Holyoke, "…my daughter?"

"Oh, yes" – her daughter was the dumpy, ugly girl with the thick spectacles – "oh, yes." And he added, "I knew some people who lived here before I came."

"The little Garneau girl," explained Cousin Cora.

"Oh, yes. Noel Garneau," agreed Mrs Holyoke. "Her mother's a great beauty. How old is Noel now? She must be—"

"Seventeen," supplied Juan, "but she's old for her age."

"Juan met her on a ranch last summer. They were on a ranch together. What is it that they call those ranches, Juan?"

"Dude ranches."

"Dude ranches. Juan and another boy worked for their board." Juan saw no reason why Cousin Cora should have supplied this information; she continued on an even more annoying note: "Noel's mother sent her out there to keep her out of mischief, but Juan says the ranch was pretty gay itself."

Mr Holyoke supplied a welcome change of subject.

"Your name is…" he enquired, smiling and curious.

"San Juan Chandler. My father was wounded in the Battle of San Juan Hill* and so they called me after it – like Kenesaw Mountain Landis."*

He had explained this so many times that the sentences rolled off automatically – in school he had been called Santy, in college he was Don.

"You must come to dinner while you're here," said Mrs Holyoke vaguely.

The conversation slipped away from him as he realized freshly, strongly, that Noel would arrive tomorrow. And she was coming because he was here. She had cut short a visit in the Adirondacks on receipt of his letter. Would she like him now – in this place that was so different from Montana? There was a spaciousness, an air of money and pleasure about Culpepper Bay for which San Juan Chandler – a shy, handsome, spoilt, brilliant, penniless boy from a small Ohio city – was unprepared. At home, where his father was a retired clergyman, Juan went with the nice people. He didn't realize until this visit to a fashionable New England resort that where there are enough rich families to form a self-sufficient and exclusive group, such a group is invariably formed. On the dude ranch they had all dressed alike; here his ready-made Prince of Wales suit seemed exaggerated in style, his hat correct only in theory – an imitation hat – his very ties only projections of the ineffable Platonic ties which were worn here at Culpepper Bay. Yet all the differences were so small that he was unable quite to discern them.

But from the morning three days ago when he had stepped off the train into a group of young people who were waiting at the station for some friend of their own, he had been uneasy; and Cousin Cora's introductions, which seemed to foist him horribly upon whomever he was introduced to, did not lessen his discomfort. He thought mechanically that she was being kind, and considered himself lucky that her invitation had coincided with his wild desire to see Noel Garneau again. He did not realize that in three days he had come to hate Cousin Cora's cold and snobbish patronage.

Noel's fresh, adventurous voice on the telephone next morning made his own voice quiver with nervous happiness. She would call for him at two and they would spend the afternoon together. All morning he lay in the garden, trying unsuccessfully to renew his summer tan in the mild lemon light of the September sun, sitting up quickly whenever he heard the sound of Cousin Cora's garden shears at the end of a neighbouring border. He was back in his room, still meddling desperately with the white powder puff, when Noel's roadster stopped outside and she came up the front walk.

Noel's eyes were dark blue, almost violet, and her lips, Juan had often thought, were like very small, very soft, red cushions – only cushions sounded all wrong, for they were really the most delicate lips in the world. When she talked they parted to the shape of "Oo!" and her eyes opened wide as though she was torn between tears and laughter at the poignancy of what she was saying. Already, at seventeen, she knew that men hung on her words in a way that frightened her. To Juan her most indifferent remarks assumed a highly ponderable significance and begot an intensity in him – a fact which Noel had several times found somewhat of a strain.

He ran downstairs, down the gravel path towards her.

"Noel, my dear," he wanted so much to say, "you are the loveliest thing – the loveliest thing. My heart turns over when I see your beautiful face and smell that sweet fresh smell you have around you." That would have been the precious, the irreplaceable truth. Instead he faltered, "Why, hello, Noel! How are you?… Well, I certainly am glad. Well, is this your car? What kind is it? Well, you certainly look fine."

And he couldn't look at her, because when he did his face seemed to him to be working idiotically – like someone else's face. He got in, they drove off and he made a mighty effort to compose himself; but as her hand left the steering wheel to fall lightly on his, a perverse instinct made him jerk his hand away. Noel perceived the embarrassment and was puzzled and sorry.

They went to the tennis tournament at the Culpepper Club. He was so little aware of anything except Noel that later he told Cousin Cora they hadn't seen the tennis, and believed it himself.

Afterwards they loitered about the grounds, stopped by innumerable people who welcomed Noel home. Two men made him uneasy – one a small handsome youth of his own age with shining brown eyes that were bright as the glass eyes of a stuffed owl; the other a tall, languid dandy of twenty-five who was introduced to her, Juan rightly deduced, at his own request.

When they were in a group of girls he was more comfortable. He was able to talk, because being with Noel gave him confidence before these others, and his confidence before the others made him more confident with Noel. The situation improved.

There was one girl, a sharp, pretty blonde named Holly Morgan, with whom he had spent some facetiously sentimental hours the day before, and in order to show Noel that he had been able to take care of himself before her return he made a point of talking aside to Holly Morgan. Holly was not responsive. Juan was Noel's property, and though Holly liked him, she did not like him nearly well enough to annoy Noel.

"What time do you want me for dinner, Noel?" she asked.

"Eight o'clock," said Noel. "Billy Harper'll call for you."

Juan felt a twinge of disappointment. He had thought that he and Noel were to be alone for dinner; that afterwards they would have a long talk on the dark veranda and he would kiss her lips as he had upon that never-to-be-forgotten Montana night, and give her his DKE* pin to wear.

Perhaps the others would leave early – he had told Holly Morgan of his love for Noel; she should have sense enough to know.

At twilight Noel dropped him at Miss Chandler's gate, lingered for a moment with the engine cut off. The promise of the evening – the first lights in the houses along the bay, the sound of a remote piano, the little coolness in the wind – swung them both up suddenly into that paradise which Juan, drunk with ecstasy and terror, had been unable to evoke.

"Are you glad to see me?" she whispered.

"Am I glad?" The words trembled on his tongue. Miserably he struggled to bend his emotion into a phrase, a look, a gesture, but his mind chilled at the thought that nothing, nothing, nothing could express what he felt in his heart.

"You embarrass me," he said wretchedly. "I don't know what to say."

Noel waited, attuned to what she expected, sympathetic, but too young quite to see that behind the mask of egotism, of moody childishness, which the intensity of Juan's devotion compelled him to wear, there was a tremendous emotion.

"Don't be embarrassed," Noel said. She was listening to the music now, a tune they had danced to in the Adirondacks. The wings of a trance folded about her and the inscrutable someone who waited always in the middle distance loomed down over her with passionate words and dark romantic eyes. Almost mechanically, she started the engine and slipped the gear into first.

"At eight o'clock," she said, almost abstractedly. "Goodbye, Juan."

The car moved off down the road. At the corner she turned and waved her hand and Juan waved back, happier than he had ever been in his life, his soul dissolved to a sweet gas that buoyed up his body like a balloon. Then the roadster was out of sight and, all unaware, he had lost her.

2

COUSIN CORA'S CHAUFFEUR took him to Noel's door. The other male guest, Billy Harper, was, he discovered, the young man with the bright brown eyes whom he had met that afternoon. Juan was afraid of him; he was on such familiar, facetious terms with the two girls – towards Noel his attitude seemed almost irreverent – that Juan was slighted during the conversation at dinner. They talked of the Adirondacks and they all seemed to know the group who had been there. Noel and Holly spoke of boys at Cambridge and New Haven and of how wonderful it was that they were going to school in New York this winter. Juan meant to invite Noel to the autumn dance at his college, but he thought that he had better wait and do it in a letter, later on. He was glad when dinner was over.

The girls went upstairs. Juan and Billy Harper smoked.

"She certainly is attractive," broke out Juan suddenly, his repression bursting into words.

"Who? Noel?"

"Yes."

"She's a nice girl," agreed Harper gravely.

Juan fingered the DKE pin in his pocket.

"She's wonderful," he said. "I like Holly Morgan pretty well – I was handing her a sort of line yesterday afternoon – but Noel's really the most attractive girl I ever knew."

Harper looked at him curiously, but Juan, released from the enforced and artificial smile of dinner, continued enthusiastically: "Of course it's silly to fool with two girls. I mean, you've got to be careful not to get in too deep."

Billy Harper didn't answer. Noel and Holly came downstairs. Holly suggested bridge, but Juan didn't play bridge, so they sat talking by the fire. In some fashion Noel and Billy Harper became involved in a conversation about dates and friends, and Juan began boasting to Holly Morgan, who sat beside him on the sofa.

"You must come to a prom at college," he said suddenly. "Why don't you? It's a small college, but we have the best bunch in our house and the proms are fun."

"I'd love it."

"You'd only have to meet the people in our house."

"What's that?"

"DKE." He drew the pin from his pocket. "See?"

Holly examined it, laughed and handed it back.

"I wanted to go to Yale," he went on, "but my family always go to the same place."

"I love Yale," said Holly.

"Yes," he agreed vaguely, half hearing her, his mind moving between himself and Noel. "You must come up. I'll write you about it."

Time passed. Holly played the piano. Noel took a ukulele from the top of the piano, strummed it and hummed. Billy Harper turned the pages of the music. Juan listened, restless, unamused. Then they sauntered out into the dark garden, and finding himself beside Noel at last, Juan walked her quickly ahead until they were alone.

"Noel," he whispered, "here's my Deke pin. I want you to have it."

She looked at him expressionlessly.

"I saw you offering it to Holly Morgan," she said.

"Noel," he cried in alarm, "I wasn't offering it to her. I just showed it to her. Why, Noel, do you think—"

"You invited her to the prom."

"I didn't. I was just being nice to her."

The others were close behind. She took the Deke pin quickly and put her finger to his lips in a facile gesture of caress.

He did not realize that she had not been really angry about the pin or the prom, and that his unfortunate egotism was forfeiting her interest.

At eleven o'clock Holly said she must go, and Billy Harper drove his car to the front door.

"I'm going to stay a few minutes if you don't mind," said Juan, standing in the door with Noel. "I can walk home."

Holly and Billy Harper drove away. Noel and Juan strolled back into the drawing room, where she avoided the couch and sat down in a chair.

"Let's go out on the veranda," suggested Juan uncertainly.

"Why?"

"Please, Noel."

Unwillingly she obeyed. They sat side by side on a canvas settee and he put his arm around her.

"Kiss me," he whispered. She had never seemed so desirable to him before.

"No."

"Why not?"

"I don't want to. I don't kiss people any more."

"But – me?" he demanded incredulously.

"I've kissed too many people. I'll have nothing left if I keep on kissing people."

"But you'll kiss me, Noel?"

"Why?"

He could not even say, "Because I love you." But he could say it, he knew that he could say it, when she was in his arms.

"If I kiss you once, will you go home?"

"Why, do you want me to go home?"

"I'm tired. I was travelling last night and I can never sleep on a train. Can you? I can never…"

Her tendency to leave the subject willingly made him frantic.

"Then kiss me once," he insisted.

"You promise?"

"You kiss me first."

"No, Juan, you promise first."

"Don't you want to kiss me?"

"Oh-h-h!" she groaned.

With gathering anxiety Juan promised and took her in his arms. For one moment at the touch of her lips, the feeling of her, of Noel, close to him, he forgot the evening, forgot himself – rather became the inspired, romantic self that she had known. But it was too late. Her hands were on his shoulders, pushing him away.

"You promised."

"Noel…"

She got up. Confused and unsatisfied, he followed her to the door.

"Noel…"

"Goodnight, Juan."

As they stood on the doorstep her eyes rose over the line of dark trees towards the ripe harvest moon. Some glowing thing would happen to her soon, she thought, her mind far away. Something that would dominate her, snatch her up out of life, helpless, ecstatic, exalted.

"Goodnight, Noel. Noel, please—"

"Goodnight, Juan. Remember we're going swimming tomorrow. It's wonderful to see you again. Goodnight."

She closed the door.

3

TOWARDS MORNING HE AWOKE from a broken sleep, wondering if she had not kissed him because of the three spots on his cheek. He turned on the light and looked at them. Two were almost invisible. He went into the bathroom, doused all three with the black ointment and crept back into bed.

Cousin Cora greeted him stiffly at breakfast next morning.

"You kept your great-uncle awake last night," she said. "He heard you moving around in your room."

"I only moved twice," he said unhappily. "I'm terribly sorry."

"He has to have his sleep, you know. We all have to be more considerate when there's someone sick. Young people don't always think of that. And he was so unusually well when you came."

It was Sunday, and they were to go swimming at Holly Morgan's house, where a crowd always collected on the bright easy beach. Noel called for him, but they arrived before any of his half-humble remarks about the night before had managed to attract her attention. He spoke to those he knew and was introduced to others, made ill at ease again by their cheerful familiarity with one another, by the correct informality of their clothes. He was sure they noticed that he had worn only one suit during his visit to Culpepper Bay, varying it with white flannel trousers. Both pairs of trousers were out of press now, and after keeping his great-uncle awake, he had not felt like bothering Cousin Cora about it at breakfast.

Again he tried to talk to Holly, with the vague idea of making Noel jealous, but Holly was busy and she eluded him. It was ten minutes before he extricated himself from a conversation with the obnoxious Miss Holyoke. At the moment he managed this he perceived to his horror that Noel was gone.

When he last saw her she had been engaged in a light but somehow intent conversation with the tall well-dressed stranger she had met yesterday. Now she wasn't in sight. Miserable and horribly alone, he strolled up and down the beach, trying to look as if he were having a good time, seeming to watch the bathers, but keeping a sharp eye out for Noel. He felt that his self-conscious perambulations were attracting unbearable attention, and sat down unhappily on a sand dune beside Billy Harper. But Billy Harper was neither cordial nor communicative, and after a minute hailed a man across the beach and went to talk to him.

Juan was desperate. When, suddenly, he spied Noel coming down from the house with the tall man, he stood up with a jerk, convinced that his features were working wildly.

She waved at him.

"A buckle came off my shoe," she called. "I went to have it put on. I thought you'd gone in swimming."

He stood perfectly still, not trusting his voice to answer. He understood that she was through with him; there was someone else. Immediately he wanted above all things to be away. As they came nearer, the tall man glanced at him negligently and resumed his vivacious, intimate conversation with Noel. A group suddenly closed around them.

Keeping the group in the corner of his eye, Juan began to move carefully and steadily towards the gate that led to the road. He started when the casual voice of a man behind him said, "Going?" and he answered, "Got to," with what purported to be a reluctant nod. Once behind the shelter of the parked cars, he began to run, slowed down as several chauffeurs looked at him curiously. It was a mile and a half to the Chandler house and the day was broiling, but he walked fast lest Noel, leaving the party – "With that man," he thought bitterly – should overtake him trudging along the road. That would be more than he could bear.

There was the sound of a car behind him. Immediately Juan left the road and sought concealment behind a convenient hedge. It was no one from the party, but thereafter he kept an eye out for available cover, walking fast, or even running, over unpromising open spaces.

He was within sight of his cousin's house when it happened. Hot and dishevelled, he had scarcely flattened himself against the back of a tree when Noel's roadster, with the tall man at the wheel, flashed by down the road. Juan stepped out and looked after them. Then, blind with sweat and misery, he continued on towards home.

4

A T LUNCHEON, COUSIN CORA looked at him closely.
"What's the trouble?" she enquired. "Did something go wrong at the beach this morning?"

"Why, no," he exclaimed in simulated astonishment. "What made you think that?"

"You have such a funny look. I thought perhaps you'd had some trouble with the little Garneau girl."

He hated her.

"No, not at all."

"You don't want to get any idea in your head about her," said Cousin Cora.

"What do you mean?" He knew with a start what she meant.

"Any ideas about Noel Garneau. You've got your own way to make." Juan's face burned. He was unable to answer. "I say that in all kindness. You're not in any position to think anything serious about Noel Garneau."

Her implications cut deeper than her words. Oh, he had seen well enough that he was not essentially of Noel's sort, that being nice in Akron* wasn't enough at Culpepper Bay. He had that realization that comes to all boys in his position that for every advantage – that was what his mother called this visit to Cousin Cora's – he paid a harrowing price in self-esteem. But a world so hard as to admit such an intolerable state of affairs was beyond his comprehension. His mind rejected it all completely, as it had rejected the dictionary name for the three spots on his face. He wanted to let go, to vanish, to be home. He determined to go home tomorrow, but after this heart-rending conversation he decided to put off the announcement until tonight.

That afternoon he took a detective story from the library and retired upstairs to read on his bed. He finished the book by four o'clock and came down to change it for another. Cousin Cora was on the veranda arranging three tables for tea.

"I thought you were at the club," she exclaimed in surprise. "I thought you'd gone up to the club."

"I'm tired," he said. "I thought I'd read."

"Tired!" she exclaimed. "A boy your age! You ought to be out in the open air playing golf – that's why you have that spot on your cheek" – Juan winced; his experiments with the black salve had irritated it to a sharp redness – "instead of lying around reading on a day like this."

"I haven't any clubs," said Juan hurriedly.

"Mr Holyoke told you you could use his brother's clubs. He spoke to the caddie master. Run on now. You'll find lots of young people up there who want to play. I'll begin to think you're not having a good time."

In agony Juan saw himself dubbing about the course alone – seeing Noel coming under his eye. He never wanted to see Noel again except out in Montana – some bright day, when she would come saying, "Juan, I never knew – never understood what your love was."

Suddenly he remembered that Noel had gone into Boston for the afternoon. She would not be there. The horror of playing alone suddenly vanished.

The caddie master looked at him disapprovingly as he displayed his guest card, and Juan nervously bought a half-dozen balls at a dollar each in an effort to neutralize the imagined hostility. On the first tee he glanced around. It was after four and there was no one in sight except two old men practising drives from the top of a little hill. As he addressed his ball he heard someone come up on the tee behind him and he breathed easier at the sharp crack that sent his ball a hundred and fifty yards down the fairway.

"Playing alone?"

He looked around. A stout man of fifty, with a huge face, high forehead, long wide upper lip and great undershot jaw, was taking a driver from a bulging bag.

"Why – yes."

"Mind if I go round with you?"

"Not at all."

Juan greeted the suggestion with a certain gloomy relief. They were evenly matched, the older man's steady short shots keeping pace with

Juan's occasional brilliancy. Not until the seventh hole did the conversation rise above the fragmentary boasting and formalized praise which forms the small talk of golf.

"Haven't seen you around before."

"I'm just visiting here," Juan explained, "staying with my cousin, Miss Chandler."

"Oh yes – know Miss Chandler very well. Nice old snob."

"What?" enquired Juan.

"Nice old snob, I said. No offence… Your honour, I think."

Not for several holes did Juan venture to comment on his partner's remark.

"What do you mean when you say she's a nice old snob?" he enquired with interest.

"Oh, it's an old quarrel between Miss Chandler and me," answered the older man brusquely. "She's an old friend of my wife's. When we were married and came out to Culpepper Bay for the summer, she tried to freeze us out. Said my wife had no business marrying me. I was an outsider."

"What did you do?"

"We just let her alone. She came round, but naturally I never had much love for her. She even tried to put her oar in before we were married." He laughed. "Cora Chandler of Boston – how she used to boss the girls around in those days! At twenty-five she had the sharpest tongue in Back Bay. They were old people there, you know – Emerson and Whittier to dinner and all that. My wife belonged to that crowd too. I was from the Middle West… Oh, too bad. I should have stopped talking. That makes me two up again."

Suddenly Juan wanted to present his case to this man – not quite as it was, but adorned with a dignity and significance it did not so far possess. It began to round out in his mind as the sempiternal struggle of the poor young man against a snobbish, purse-proud world. This new aspect was comforting, and he put out of his mind the less pleasant realization that, superficially at least, money hadn't entered into it. He knew in his heart that it was his unfortunate egotism that had repelled Noel, his embarrassment, his absurd attempt to make her jealous with

Holly. Only indirectly was his poverty concerned; under different circumstances it might have given a touch of romance.

"I know exactly how you must have felt," he broke out suddenly as they walked towards the tenth tee. "I haven't any money and I'm in love with a girl who has – and it seems as if every busybody in the world is determined to keep us apart."

For a moment Juan believed this. His companion looked at him sharply.

"Does the girl care about you?" he enquired.

"Yes."

"Well, go after her, young man. All the money in this world hasn't been made by a long shot."

"I'm still in college," said Juan, suddenly taken aback.

"Won't she wait for you?"

"I don't know. You see, the pressure's pretty strong. Her family want her to marry a rich man" – his mind visualized the tall well-dressed stranger of this morning and invention soared – "an easterner that's visiting here, and I'm afraid they'll all sweep her off her feet. If it's not this man, it's the next."

His friend considered.

"You can't have everything, you know," he said presently. "I'm the last man to advise a young man to leave college, especially when I don't know anything about him or his abilities; but if it's going to break you up not to get her, you better think about getting to work."

"I've been considering that," said Juan frowning. The idea was ten seconds old in his mind.

"All girls are crazy now, anyhow," broke out the older man. "They begin to think of men at fifteen, and by the time they're seventeen they run off with the chauffeur next door."

"That's true," agreed Juan absently. He was absorbed in the previous suggestion. "The trouble is that I don't live in Boston. If I left college I'd want to be near her, because it might be a few months before I'd be able to support her. And I don't know how I'd go about getting a position in Boston."

"If you're Cora Chandler's cousin, that oughtn't to be difficult. She knows everybody in town. And the girl's family will probably help you out, once you've got her – some of them are fools enough for anything in these crazy days."

"I wouldn't like that."

"Rich girls can't live on air," said the older man grimly.

They played for a while in silence. Suddenly, as they approached a green, Juan's companion turned to him frowning.

"Look here, young man," he said, "I don't know whether you are really thinking of leaving college or whether I've just put the idea in your head. If I have, forget it. Go home and talk it over with your family. Do what they tell you to."

"My father's dead."

"Well, then ask your mother. She's got your best interest at heart."

His attitude had noticeably stiffened, as if he were sorry he had become even faintly involved in Juan's problem. He guessed that there was something solid in the boy, but he suspected his readiness to confide in strangers and his helplessness about getting a job. Something was lacking – not confidence, exactly – "It might be a few months before I was able to support her" – but something stronger, fiercer, more external. When they walked together into the caddie house he shook hands with him and was about to turn away, when impulse impelled him to add one word more.

"If you decide to try Boston come and see me," he said. He pressed a card into Juan's hand. "Goodbye. Good luck. Remember, a woman's like a streetcar—"

He walked into the locker room. After paying his caddie, Juan glanced down at the card which he still held in his hand.

"Harold Garneau," it read, "23–7 State Street."

A moment later Juan was walking nervously and hurriedly from the grounds of the Culpepper Club, casting no glance behind.

5

ONE MONTH LATER SAN JUAN CHANDLER arrived in Boston and took an inexpensive room in a small downtown hotel. In his pocket was two hundred dollars in cash and an envelope full of liberty bonds aggregating fifteen hundred dollars more – the whole being a fund which had been started by his father when he was born, to give him his chance in life. Not without argument had he come into possession of this – not without tears had his decision to abandon his last year at college been approved by his mother. He had not told her everything; simply that he had an advantageous offer of a position in Boston; the rest she guessed and was tactfully silent. As a matter of fact, he had neither a position nor a plan, but he was twenty-one now, with the blemishes of youth departed for ever. One thing Juan knew – he was going to marry Noel Garneau. The sting and hurt and shame of that Sunday morning ran through his dreams, stronger than any doubts he might have felt, stronger even than the romantic boyish love for her that had blossomed one dry, still Montana night. That was still there, but locked apart; what had happened later overlay it, muffled it. It was necessary now to his pride, his self-respect, his very existence, that he have her, in order to wipe out his memory of the day on which he had grown three years.

He hadn't seen her since. The following morning he had left Culpepper Bay and gone home.

Yes, he had a wonderful time. Yes, Cousin Cora had been very nice.

Nor had he written, though a week later a surprised but somehow flippant and terrible note had come from her, saying how pleasant it was to have seen him again and how bad it was to leave without saying goodbye.

"Holly Morgan sends her best," it concluded, with kind, simulated reproach. "Perhaps she ought to be writing instead of me. I always thought you were fickle, and now I know it."

The poor effort which she had made to hide her indifference made him shiver. He did not add the letter to a certain cherished package tied with blue ribbon, but burned it up in an ashtray – a tragic gesture which almost set his mother's house on fire.

So he began his life in Boston, and the story of his first year there is a fairy tale too immoral to be told. It is the story of one of those mad, illogical successes upon whose substantial foundations ninety-nine failures are later reared. Though he worked hard, he deserved no special credit for it – no credit, that is, commensurate with the reward he received. He ran into a man who had a scheme, a preposterous scheme, for the cold storage of seafood which he had been trying to finance for several years. Juan's inexperience allowed him to be responsive and he invested twelve hundred dollars. In his first year this appalling indiscretion paid him 400 per cent. His partner attempted to buy him out, but they reached a compromise and Juan kept his shares.

The inner sense of his own destiny which had never deserted him whispered that he was going to be a rich man. But at the end of that year an event took place which made him think that it didn't matter after all.

He had seen Noel Garneau twice – once entering a theatre and once riding through a Boston street in the back of her limousine, looking, he thought afterwards, bored and pale and tired. At the time he had thought nothing; an overwhelming emotion had seized his heart, held it helpless, suspended, as though it were in the grasp of material fingers. He had shrunk back hastily under the awning of a shop and waited trembling, horrified, ecstatic, until she went by. She did not know he was in Boston – he did not want her to know until he was ready. He followed her every move in the society columns of the papers. She was at school, at home for Christmas, at Hot Springs for Easter, coming out in the fall. Then she was a debutante, and every day he read of her at dinners and dances and assemblies and balls and charity functions and theatricals of the Junior League. A dozen blurred newspaper unlikenesses of her filled a drawer of his desk. And still he waited. Let Noel have her fling.

When he had been sixteen months in Boston, and when Noel's first season was dying away in the hum of the massed departure for Florida, Juan decided to wait no longer. So on a raw, damp February day, when children in rubber boots were building dams in the snow-filled gutters, a blond, handsome, well-dressed young man walked up the steps of the Garneaus' Boston house and handed his card to the maid. With his heart beating loud, he went into a drawing room and sat down.

A sound of a dress on the stairs, light feet in the hall, an exclamation – Noel!

"Why, Juan," she exclaimed, surprised, pleased, polite, "I didn't know you were in Boston. It's so good to see you. I thought you'd thrown me over for ever."

In a moment he found voice – it was easier now than it had been. Whether or not she was aware of the change, he was a nobody no longer. There was something solid behind him that would prevent him ever again from behaving like a self-centred child.

He explained that he might settle in Boston, and allowed her to guess that he had done extremely well; and, though it cost him a twinge of pain, he spoke humorously of their last meeting, implying that he had left the swimming party on an impulse of anger at her. He could not confess that the impulse had been one of shame. She laughed. Suddenly he grew curiously happy.

Half an hour passed. The fire glowed in the hearth. The day darkened outside and the room moved into that shadowy twilight, that weather of indoors, which is like a breathless starshine. He had been standing; now he sat down beside her on the couch.

"Noel…"

Footsteps sounded lightly through the hall as the maid went through to the front door. Noel reached up quickly and turned up the electric lamp on the table behind her head.

"I didn't realize how dark it was growing," she said rather quickly, he thought. Then the maid stood in the doorway.

"Mr Templeton," she announced.

"Oh, yes," agreed Noel.

Mr Templeton, with a Harvard-Oxford drawl, mature, very much at home, looked at him with just a flicker of surprise, nodded, mumbled a bare politeness and took an easy position in front of the fire. He exchanged several remarks with Noel which indicated a certain familiarity with her movements. Then a short silence fell. Juan rose.

"I want to see you soon," he said. "I'll phone, shall I, and you tell me when I can call?"

She walked with him to the door.

"So good to talk to you again," she told him cordially. "Remember, I want to see a lot of you, Juan."

When he left he was happier than he had been for two years. He ate dinner alone at a restaurant, almost singing to himself; and then, wild with elation, walked along the waterfront till midnight. He awoke thinking of her, wanting to tell people that what had been lost was found again. There had been more between them than the mere words said

– Noel's sitting with him in the half-darkness, her slight but perceptible nervousness as she came with him to the door.

Two days later he opened the *Transcript* to the society page and read down to the third item. There his eyes stopped, became like china eyes:

Mr and Mrs Harold Garneau announce the engagement of their daughter Noel to Mr Brooks Fish Templeton. Mr Templeton graduated from Harvard in the class of 1912 and is a partner in...

6

AT THREE O'CLOCK that afternoon Juan rang the Garneaus' doorbell and was shown into the hall. From somewhere upstairs he heard girls' voices, and another murmur came from the drawing room on the right, where he had talked to Noel only the week before.

"Can you show me into some room that isn't being used?" he demanded tensely of the maid. "I'm an old friend – it's very important – I've got to see Miss Noel alone."

He waited in a small den at the back of the hall. Ten minutes passed – ten minutes more; he began to be afraid she wasn't coming. At the end of half an hour the door bounced open and Noel came hurriedly in.

"Juan!" she cried happily. "This is wonderful! I might have known you'd be the first to come." Her expression changed as she saw his face, and she hesitated. "But why were you shown in here?" she went on quickly. "You must come and meet everyone. I'm rushing around today like a chicken without a head."

"Noel!" he said thickly.

"What?"

Her hand was on the doorknob. She turned, startled.

"Noel, I haven't come to congratulate you," Juan said, his face white and firm, his voice harsh with his effort at self-control. "I've come to tell you you're making an awful mistake."

"Why – Juan!"

"And you know it," he went on. "You know no one loves you as I love you, Noel. I want you to marry me."

She laughed nervously.

"Why, Juan, that's silly! I don't understand your talking like this. I'm engaged to another man."

"Noel, will you come here and sit down?"

"I can't, Juan – there're a dozen people outside. I've got to see them. It wouldn't be polite. Another time, Juan. *If* you come another time I'd love to talk to you."

"Now!" The word was stark, unyielding, almost savage. She hesitated.

"Ten minutes," he said.

"I've really got to go, Juan."

She sat down uncertainly, glancing at the door. Sitting beside her, Juan told her simply and directly everything that had happened to him since they had met, a year and a half before. He told her of his family, his Cousin Cora, of his inner humiliation at Culpepper Bay. Then he told her of his coming to Boston and of his success, and how at last, having something to bring her, he had come only to find he was too late. He kept back nothing. In his voice, as in his mind, there was no pretence now, no self-consciousness, but only a sincere and overmastering emotion. He had no defence for what he was doing, he said, save this – that he had somehow gained the right to present his case, to have her know how much his devotion had inspired him, to have her look once, if only in passing, upon the fact that for two years he had loved her faithfully and well.

When Juan finished, Noel was crying. It was terrible, she said, to tell her all this – just when she had decided about her life. It hadn't been easy, yet it was done now, and she was really going to marry this other man. But she had never heard anything like this before – it upset her. She was – oh, so terribly sorry, but there was no use. If he had cared so much he might have let her know before.

But how could he let her know? He had had nothing to offer her except the fact that one summer night out west they had been overwhelmingly drawn together.

"And you love me now," he said in a low voice. "You wouldn't cry, Noel, if you didn't love me. You wouldn't care."

"I'm – I'm sorry for you."

"It's more than that. You loved me the other day. You wanted me to sit beside you in the dark. Didn't I feel it – didn't I know? There's something between us, Noel – a sort of pull. Something you always do to me and I to you – except that one sad time. Oh, Noel, don't you know how it breaks my heart to see you sitting there two feet away from me, to want to put my arms around you and know you've made a senseless promise to another man?"

There was a knock outside the door.

"Noel!"

She raised her head, putting a handkerchief quickly to her eyes.

"Yes?"

"It's Brooks. May I come in?" Without waiting for an answer, Templeton opened the door and stood looking at them curiously. "Excuse me," he said. He nodded brusquely at Juan. "Noel, there are lots of people here—"

"In a minute," she said lifelessly.

"Aren't you well?"

"Yes."

He came into the room, frowning.

"What's been upsetting you, dear?" He glanced quickly at Juan, who stood up, his eyes blurred with tears. A menacing note crept into Templeton's voice. "I hope no one's been upsetting you."

For answer, Noel flopped down over a hill of pillows and sobbed aloud.

"Noel" – Templeton sat beside her, and put his arm on her shoulder – "Noel." He turned again to Juan, "I think it would be best if you left us alone, Mr…" the name escaped his memory. "Noel's a little tired."

"I won't go," said Juan.

"Please wait outside then. We'll see you later."

"I won't wait outside. I want to speak to Noel. It was you who interrupted."

"And I have a perfect right to interrupt." His face reddened angrily. "Just who the devil are you, anyhow?"

"My name is Chandler."

"Well, Mr Chandler, you're in the way here – is that plain? Your presence here is an intrusion and a presumption."

"We look at it in different ways."

They glared at each other angrily. After a moment Templeton raised Noel to a sitting posture.

"I'm going to take you upstairs, dear," he said. "This has been a strain today. If you lie down till dinnertime—"

He helped her to her feet. Not looking at Juan, and still dabbing her face with her handkerchief, Noel suffered herself to be persuaded into the hall. Templeton turned in the doorway.

"The maid will give you your hat and coat, Mr Chandler."

"I'll wait right here," said Juan.

7

H E WAS STILL THERE at half-past six, when, following a quick knock, a large broad bulk which Juan recognized as Mr Harold Garneau came into the room.

"Good evening, sir," said Mr Garneau, annoyed and peremptory. "Just what can I do for you?"

He came closer and a flicker of recognition passed over his face.

"Oh!" he muttered.

"Good evening, sir," said Juan.

"It's you, is it?" Mr Garneau appeared to hesitate. "Brooks Templeton said that you were – that you insisted on seeing Noel" – he coughed – "that you refused to go home."

"I want to see Noel, if you don't mind."

"What for?"

"That's between Noel and me, Mr Garneau."

"Mr Templeton and I are quite entitled to represent Noel in this case," said Mr Garneau patiently. "She has just made the statement before her mother and me that she doesn't want to see you again. Isn't that plain enough?"

"I don't believe it," said Juan stubbornly.

"I'm not in the habit of lying."

"I beg your pardon. I meant—"

"I don't want to discuss this unfortunate business with you," broke out Garneau contemptuously. "I just want you to leave right now – and not come back."

"Why do you call it an unfortunate business?" enquired Juan coolly.

"Goodnight, Mr Chandler."

"You call it an unfortunate business because Noel's broken her engagement."

"You are presumptuous, sir!" cried the older man. "Unbearably presumptuous."

"Mr Garneau, you yourself were once kind enough to tell me—"

"I don't give a damn what I told you!" cried Garneau. "You get out of here now!"

"Very well, I have no choice. I wish you to be good enough to tell Noel that I'll be back tomorrow afternoon."

Juan nodded, went into the hall and took his hat and coat from a chair. Upstairs, he heard running footsteps and a door opened and closed – not before he had caught the sound of impassioned voices and a short broken sob. He hesitated. Then he continued on along the hall towards the front door. Through a portière of the dining room he caught sight of a manservant laying the service for dinner.

He rang the bell the next afternoon at the same hour. This time the butler, evidently instructed, answered the door.

Miss Noel was not at home. Could he leave a note? It was no use; Miss Noel was not in the city. Incredulous but anxious, Juan took a taxicab to Harold Garneau's office.

"Mr Garneau can't see you. If you like, he will speak to you for a moment on the phone."

Juan nodded. The clerk touched a button on the waiting-room switchboard and handed an instrument to Juan.

"This is San Juan Chandler speaking. They told me at your residence that Noel had gone away. Is that true?"

"Yes." The monosyllable was short and cold. "She's gone away for a rest. Won't be back for several months. Anything else?"

"Did she leave any word for me?"

"No! She hates the sight of you."

"What's her address?"

"That doesn't happen to be your affair. Good morning."

Juan went back to his apartment and mused over the situation. Noel had been spirited out of town – that was the only expression he knew for it. And undoubtedly her engagement to Templeton was at least temporarily broken. He had toppled it over within an hour. He must see her again – that was the immediate necessity. But where? She was certainly with friends, and probably with relatives. That latter was the first clue to follow – he must find out the names of the relatives she had most frequently visited before.

He phoned Holly Morgan. She was in the South and not expected back in Boston till May.

Then he called the society editor of the *Boston Transcript*. After a short wait, a polite, attentive, feminine voice conversed with him on the wire.

"This is Mr San Juan Chandler," he said, trying to intimate by his voice that he was a distinguished leader of cotillions in the Back Bay.* "I want to get some information, if you please, about the family of Mr Harold Garneau."

"Why don't you apply directly to Mr Garneau?" advised the society editor, not without suspicion.

"I'm not on speaking terms with Mr Garneau."

A pause; then – "Well, really, we can't be responsible for giving out information in such a peculiar way."

"But there can't be any secret about who Mr and Mrs Garneau's relations are!" protested Juan in exasperation.

"But how can we be sure that you—"

He hung up the receiver. Two other papers gave no better results, a third was willing, but ignorant. It seemed absurd, almost like a conspiracy, that in a city where the Garneaus were so well known he could not obtain the desired names. It was as if everything had tightened up against his arrival on the scene. After a day of fruitless and embarrassing enquiries in stores, where his questions were looked upon with the suspicion that he might be compiling a sucker list, and of poring through back numbers of the *Social Register*, he saw that there was but one resource – that was Cousin Cora. Next morning he took the three-hour ride to Culpepper Bay.

It was the first time he had seen her for a year and a half, since the disastrous termination of his summer visit. She was offended – that he knew – especially since she had heard from his mother of the unexpected success. She greeted him coldly and reproachfully; but she told him what he wanted to know, because Juan asked his questions while she was still startled and surprised by his visit. He left Culpepper Bay with the information that Mrs Garneau had one sister, the famous Mrs Morton Poindexter, with whom Noel was on terms of great intimacy. Juan took the midnight train for New York.

The Morton Poindexters' telephone number was not in the New York phone book, and Information refused to divulge it; but Juan procured it by another reference to the *Social Register*. He called the house from his hotel.

"Miss Noel Garneau – is she in the city?" he enquired, according to his plan. If the name was not immediately familiar, the servant would reply that he had the wrong number.

"Who wants to speak to her, please?"

That was a relief; his heart sank comfortably back into place.

"Oh – a friend."

"No name?"

"No name."

"I'll see."

The servant returned in a moment.

No, Miss Garneau was not there, was not in the city, was not expected. The phone clicked off suddenly.

Late that afternoon a taxi dropped him in front of the Morton Poindexters' house. It was the most elaborate house that he had ever seen, rising to five storeys on a corner of Fifth Avenue and adorned even with that ghost of a garden which, however minute, is the proudest gesture of money in New York.

He handed no card to the butler, but it occurred to him that he must be expected, for he was shown immediately into the drawing room. When, after a short wait, Mrs Poindexter entered he experienced for the first time in five days a touch of uncertainty.

Mrs Poindexter was perhaps thirty-five, and of that immaculate fashion which the French describe as *bien soignée*.* The inexpressible loveliness of her face was salted with another quality which for want of a better word might be called dignity. But it was more than dignity, for it wore no rigidity, but instead a softness so adaptable, so elastic, that it would withdraw from any attack which life might bring against it, only to spring back at the proper moment, taut, victorious and complete. San Juan saw that even though his guess was correct as to Noel's being in the house, he was up against a force with which he had no contact before. This woman seemed to be not entirely of America, to possess resources which the American woman lacked or handled ineptly.

She received him with a graciousness which, though it was largely external, seemed to conceal no perturbation underneath. Indeed, her attitude appeared to be perfectly passive, just short of encouraging. It was with an effort that he resisted the inclination to lay his cards on the table.

"Good evening." She sat down on a stiff chair in the centre of the room and asked him to take an easy chair nearby. She sat looking at him silently until he spoke.

"Mrs Poindexter, I am very anxious to see Miss Garneau. I telephoned your house this morning and was told that she was not here." Mrs Poindexter nodded. "However, I know she is here," he continued evenly. "And I'm determined to see her. The idea that her father and mother can prevent me from seeing her, as though I had disgraced myself in some way – or that you, Mrs Poindexter, can prevent me from seeing her" – his voice rose a little – "is preposterous. This is not the year 1500 – nor even the year 1910."

He paused. Mrs Poindexter waited for a moment to see if he had finished. Then she said, quietly and unequivocally, "I quite agree with you."

Save for Noel, Juan thought he had never seen anyone so beautiful before.

"Mrs Poindexter," he began again, in a more friendly tone, "I'm sorry to seem rude. I've been called presumptuous in this matter, and perhaps to some extent I am. Perhaps all poor boys who are in love with wealthy girls are presumptuous. But it happens that I am no longer a poor boy, and I have good reason to believe that Noel cares for me."

"I see," said Mrs Poindexter attentively. "But of course I knew nothing about all that."

Juan hesitated, again disarmed by her complaisance. Then a surge of determination went over him.

"Will you let me see her?" he demanded. "Or will you insist on keeping up this farce a little longer?"

Mrs Poindexter looked at him as though considering.

"Why should I let you see her?"

"Simply because I ask you. Just as, when someone says 'Excuse me' you step aside for him in a doorway."

Mrs Poindexter frowned.

"But Noel is concerned in this matter as much as you. And I'm not like person in a crowd. I'm more like a bodyguard, with instructions to let no one pass, even if they say 'Excuse me' in a most appealing voice."

"You have instructions only from her father and mother," said Juan, with rising impatience. "She's the person concerned."

"I'm glad you begin to admit that."

"Of course I admit it," he broke out. "I want you to admit it."

"I do."

"Then what's the point of all this absurd discussion?" he demanded heatedly.

She stood up suddenly.

"I bid you good evening, sir."

Taken aback, Juan stood up too.

"Why, what's the matter?"

"I will not be spoken to like that," said Mrs Poindexter, still in a low cool voice. "Either you can conduct yourself quietly or you can leave this house at once."

Juan realized that he had taken the wrong tone. The words stung at him and for a moment he had nothing to say – as though he were a scolded boy at school.

"This is beside the question," he stammered finally. "I want to talk to Noel."

"Noel doesn't want to talk to you."

Suddenly Mrs Poindexter held out a sheet of notepaper to him. He opened it. It said:

Aunt Jo: As to what we talked about this afternoon: if that intolerable bore calls, as he will probably do, and begins his presumptuous whining, please speak to him frankly. Tell him I never loved him, that I never at any time claimed to love him and that his persistence is revolting to me. Say that I am old enough to know my own mind and that my greatest wish is never to see him again in this world.

Juan stood there aghast. His universe was suddenly about him. Noel did not care, she had never cared. It was all a preposterous joke on him, played by those to whom the business of life had been such jokes from the beginning. He realized now that fundamentally they were all akin – Cousin Cora, Noel, her father, this cold, lovely woman here – affirming the prerogative of the rich to marry always within their caste, to erect artificial barriers and standards against those who could presume upon a summer's philandering. The scales fell from his eyes and he saw his year and a half of struggle and effort not as progress towards a goal but only as a little race he had run by himself, outside, with no one to beat except himself – no one who cared.

Blindly he looked about for his hat, scarcely realizing it was in the hall. Blindly he stepped back when Mrs Poindexter's hand moved towards him half a foot through the mist and Mrs Poindexter's voice said softly, "I'm sorry." Then he was in the hall, the note still clutched in the hand that struggled through the sleeve of his overcoat, the words which he felt he must somehow say choking through his lips.

"I didn't understand. I regret very much that I've bothered you. It wasn't clear to me how matters stood – between Noel and me…"

His hand was on the doorknob.

"I'm sorry, too," said Mrs Poindexter. "I didn't realize from what Noel said that what I had to do would be so hard – Mr Templeton."

"Chandler," he corrected her dully. "My name's Chandler."

She stood dead still; suddenly her face went white.

"What?"

"My name – it's Chandler."

Like a flash she threw herself against the half-open door and it bumped shut. Then in a flash she was at the foot of the staircase.

"Noel!" she cried in a high, clear call. "Noel! Noel! Come down, Noel!" Her lovely voice floated up like a bell through the long high central hall. "Noel! Come down! It's Mr Chandler! It's Chandler!"

The Adolescent Marriage

1

C HAUNCEY GARNETT, THE ARCHITECT, once had a miniature city
constructed, composed of all the buildings he had ever designed.
It proved to be an expensive and somewhat depressing experiment; for
the toy did not result in a harmonious whole. Garnett found it depressing to be reminded that he himself had often gone in for monstrosities,
and even more depressing to realize that his architectural activities had
extended over half a century. In disgust, he distributed the tiny houses to
his friends and they ended up as the residences of undiscriminating dolls.

Garnett had never – at least not yet – been called a nice old man;
yet he was both old and nice. He gave six hours a day to his offices in
Philadelphia or to his branch in New York, and during the remaining
time demanded only a proper peace in which to brood quietly over his
crowded and colourful past. In several years no one had demanded a
favour that could not be granted with pen and cheque book, and it
seemed that he had reached an age safe from the intrusion of other
people's affairs. This calm, however, was premature, and it was violently
shattered one afternoon in the summer of 1925 by the shrill clamour
of a telephone bell.

George Wharton was speaking. Could Chauncey come to his house
at once on a matter of the greatest importance?

On the way to Chestnut Hill, Garnett dozed against the grey duvetyn
cushions of his limousine, his sixty-eight-year-old body warmed by
the June sunshine, his sixty-eight-year-old mind blank save for some
vivid, unsubstantial memory of a green branch overhanging green
water. Reaching his friend's house, he awoke placidly and without a
start. George Wharton, he thought, was probably troubled by some
unexpected surplus of money. He would want Garnett to plan one of

these modern churches, perhaps. He was of a younger generation than Garnett – a modern man.

Wharton and his wife were waiting in the gilt-and-morocco intimacy of the library.

"I couldn't come to your office," said Wharton immediately. "In a minute you'll understand why."

Garnett noticed that his friend's hands were slightly trembling.

"It's about Lucy," Wharton added.

It was a moment before Garnett placed Lucy as their daughter.

"What's happened to Lucy?"

"Lucy's married. She ran up to Connecticut about a month ago and got married." A moment's silence. "Lucy's only sixteen," continued Wharton. "The boy's twenty."

"That's very young," said Garnett considerately, "but then my grand-mother married at sixteen and no one thought much about it. Some girls develop much quicker than others."

"We know all that, Chauncey." Wharton waved it aside impatiently. "The point is, these young marriages don't work nowadays. They're not normal. They end in a mess."

Again Garnett hesitated.

"Aren't you a little premature in looking ahead for trouble? Why don't you give Lucy a chance? Why not wait and see if it's going to turn out a mess?"

"It's a mess already," cried Wharton passionately. "And Lucy's life's a mess. The one thing her mother and I cared about – her happiness – that's a mess, and we don't know what to do – what to do."

His voice trembled and he turned away to the window – came back again impulsively.

"Look at us, Chauncey. Do we look like the kind of parents who would drive a child into a thing like this? She and her mother have been like sisters – just like sisters. She and I used to go on parties together – football games and all that sort of thing – ever since she was a little kid. She's all we've got, and we always said we'd try to steer a middle course with her – give her enough liberty for her self-respect and yet keep an eye on where she went and who she went with, at least till she was eighteen. Why Chauncey, if you'd told me six weeks ago that this thing could happen…" He shook his head helplessly. Then he continued in a quieter voice. "When she came and told us what she'd done it just about broke our hearts, but we tried to make the best of it. Do you know how long the marriage – if you can call it that – lasted? Three weeks. It lasted three weeks. She came home with a big bruise on her shoulder where he'd hit her."

"Oh, dear!" said Mrs Wharton in a low tone. "Please…"

"We talked it over," continued her husband grimly, "and she decided to go back to this – this young…" again he bowed his head before the insufficiency of expletives – "and try to make a go of it. But last night she came home again, and now she says it's definitely over."

Garnett nodded. "Who's the man?" he enquired.

"Man!" cried Wharton. "It's a boy. His name's Llewellyn Clark."

"What's that?" exclaimed Garnett in surprise. "Llewellyn Clark? Jesse Clark's son? The young fellow in my office?"

"Yes."

"Why, he's a nice young fellow," Garnett declared. "I can't believe he'd—"

"Neither could I," interrupted Wharton quietly. "I thought he was a nice young fellow too. And what's more, I rather suspected that my daughter was a pretty decent young girl."

Garnett was astonished and annoyed. He had seen Llewellyn Clark not an hour before in the small drafting room he occupied in the Garnett & Linquist offices. He understood now why Clark wasn't going back to Boston Tech this fall. And in the light of this revelation he remembered that there had been a change in the boy during the past month – absences, late arrivals, a certain listlessness in his work.

Mrs Wharton's voice broke in upon the ordering of his mind.

"Please do something, Chauncey," she said. "Talk to him. Talk to them both. She's only sixteen and we can't bear to see her life ruined by a divorce. It isn't that we care what people will say; it's only Lucy we care about, Chauncey."

"Why don't you send her abroad for a year?"

Wharton shook his head.

"That doesn't solve the problem. If they have an ounce of character between them they'll make an attempt to live together."

"But if you think so badly of him—"

"Lucy's made her choice. He's got some money – enough. And there doesn't seem to be anything vicious in his record so far."

"What's his side of it?"

Wharton waved his hands helplessly.

"I'm damned if I know. Something about a hat. Some bunch of rubbish. Elsie and I have no idea why they ran away, and now we can't get a clear idea why they won't stick together. Unfortunately, his father and mother are dead." He paused. "Chauncey, if you could see your way clear…"

An unpleasant prospect began to take shape before Garnett's eyes. He was an old man with one foot, at least, in the chimney corner. From where he stood, this youngest generation was like something infinitely distant, and perceived through the large end of a telescope.

"Oh, of course," he heard himself saying vaguely. So hard to think back to that young time. Since his youth such a myriad of prejudices and conventions had passed through the fashion show and died away with clamour and acrimony and commotion. It would be difficult even to communicate with these children. How hollowly and fatuously his platitudes would echo on their ears. And how bored he would be with their selfishness and with their shallow confidence in opinions manufactured day before yesterday.

He sat up suddenly. Wharton and his wife were gone, and a slender, dark-haired girl whose body hovered delicately on the last edge of childhood had come quietly into the room. She regarded him for a moment with a shadow of alarm in her intent brown eyes; then sat down on a stiff chair near him.

"I'm Lucy," she said. "They told me you wanted to talk to me."

She waited. It occurred to Garnett that he must say something, but the form his speech should take eluded him.

"I haven't seen you since you were ten years old," he began uneasily.

"Yes," she agreed, with a small, polite smile.

There was another silence. He must say something to the point before her young attention slipped utterly away.

"I'm sorry you and Llewellyn have quarrelled," he broke out. "It's silly to quarrel like that. I'm very fond of Llewellyn, you know."

"Did he send you here?"

Garnett shook his head. "Are you – in love with him?" he enquired.

"Not any more."

"Is he in love with you?"

"He says so, but I don't think he is – any more."

"You're sorry you married him?"

"I'm never sorry for anything that's done."

"I see."

Again she waited.

"Your father tells me this is a permanent separation."

"Yes."

"May I ask why?"

"We just couldn't get along," she answered simply. "I thought he was terribly selfish and he thought the same about me. We fought all the time, from almost the first day."

"He hit you?"

"Oh, that!" She dismissed that as unimportant.

"How do you mean – selfish?"

"Just selfish," she answered childishly. "The most selfish thing I ever saw in my life. I never saw anything so selfish in my life."

"What did he do that was selfish?" persisted Garnett.

"Everything. He was so stingy – gosh!" Her eyes were serious and sad. "I can't stand anybody to be so stingy – about money," she explained contemptuously. "Then he'd lose his temper and swear at me and say he was going to leave me if I didn't do what he wanted me to." And she added, still very gravely, "Gosh!"

"How did he happen to hit you?"

"Oh, he didn't mean to hit me. I was trying to hit him on account of something he did, and he was trying to hold me and so I bumped into a still."

"A still!" exclaimed Garnett, startled.

"The woman had a still in our room because she had no other place to keep it – down on Beckton Street, where we lived."

"Why did Llewellyn take you to such a place?"

"Oh, it was a perfectly good place except that the woman had this still. We looked around two or three days and it was the only apartment we could afford." She paused reminiscently and then added, "It was very nice and quiet."

"H'm – you never really got along at all?"

"No." She hesitated. "He spoilt it all. He was always worrying about whether we'd done the right thing. He'd get out of bed at night and walk up and down worrying about it. I wasn't complaining. I was perfectly willing to be poor if we could get along and be happy. I wanted to go to cooking school, for instance, and he wouldn't let me. He wanted me to sit in the room all day and wait for him."

"Why?"

"He was afraid that I wanted to go home. For three weeks it was one long quarrel from morning till night. I couldn't stand it."

"It seems to me that a lot of this quarrelling was over nothing," ventured Garnett.

"I haven't explained it very well, I guess," she said with sudden weariness. "I knew a lot of it was silly and so did Llewellyn. Sometimes we'd apologize to each other, and be in love like we were before we were married. That's why I went back to him. But it wasn't any use." She stood up. "What's the good of talking about it any more? You wouldn't understand."

Garnett wondered if he could get back to his office before Llewellyn Clark went home. He could talk to Clark, while the girl only confused him as she teetered disconcertingly between adolescence and disillusion. But when Clark reported to him just as the five-o'clock bell rang, the same sensation of impotence stole over Garnett, and he stared at his apprentice blankly for a moment, as if he had never seen him before.

Llewellyn Clark looked older than his twenty years – a tall, almost thin, young man with dark-red hair of a fine, shiny texture, and auburn eyes. He was of a somewhat nervous type, talented and impatient, but Garnett could find little of the egotist in his reserved, attentive face.

"I hear you've been getting married," Garnet began abruptly.

Clark's cheeks deepened to the colour of his hair.

"Who told you that?" he demanded.

"Lucy Wharton. She told me the whole story."

"Then you know it, sir," said Clark almost rudely. "You know all there is to know."

"What do you intend to do?"

"I don't know." Clark stood up, breathing quickly. "I can't talk about it. It's my affair, you see. I—"

"Sit down, Llewellyn."

The young man sat down, his face working. Suddenly it crinkled uncontrollably and two great tears, stained faintly with the dust of the day's toil, gushed from his eyes.

"Oh, hell!" he said brokenly, wiping his eyes with the back of his hand.

"I've been wondering why you two can't make a go of it, after all." Garnett looked down at his desk. "I like you, Llewellyn, and I like Lucy. Why not fool everybody and—"

Llewellyn shook his head emphatically.

"Not me," he said. "I don't care a snap of my finger about her. She can go jump in the lake for all I care."

"Why did you take her away?"

"I don't know. We'd been in love for almost a year and marriage seemed a long way off. It came over us all of a sudden."

"Why couldn't you get along?"

"Didn't she tell you?"

"I want your version."

"Well, it started one afternoon when she took all our money and threw it away."

"Threw it away?"

"She took it and bought a new hat. It was only thirty-five dollars, but it was all we had. If I hadn't found forty-five cents in an old suit we wouldn't have had any dinner."

"I see," said Garnett dryly.

"Then – oh, one thing happened after another. She didn't trust me, she didn't think I could take care of her, she kept saying she was going home to her mother. And finally we began to hate each other. It was a great mistake, that's all, and I'll probably spend a good part of my life paying for it. Wait till it leaks out!" He laughed bitterly.

"Aren't you thinking about yourself a little too much?" suggested Garnett coldly.

Llewellyn looked at him in unfeigned surprise.

"About myself?" he repeated. "Mr Garnett, I'll give you my word of honour, this is the first time I've ever thought about that side of it. Right now I'd do anything in the world to save Lucy any pain – except live with her. She's got great things in her, Mr Garnett." His eyes filled again with tears. "She's just as brave and honest, and sweet sometimes. I'll never marry anybody else, you can bet your life on that, but – we were just poison to each other. I never want to see her any more."

After all, thought Garnett, it was only the old human attempt to get something for nothing – neither of them had brought to the marriage any trace of tolerance or moral experience. However trivial the reasons for their incompatibility, it was firmly established now in both their hearts, and perhaps they were wise in realizing that the wretched voyage, too hastily embarked upon, was over.

That night, Garnett had a long and somewhat painful talk with George Wharton, and on the following morning he went to New York, where he spent several days. When he returned to Philadelphia, it was with the information that the marriage of Lucy and Llewellyn Clark had been annulled by the state of Connecticut on the grounds of their minority. They were free.

2

ALMOST EVERYONE WHO KNEW Lucy Wharton liked her, and her friends rose rather valiantly to the occasion. There was a certain element, of course, who looked at her with averted eyes; there were slights, there were stares of the curious; but since it was wisely given out, upon Chauncey Garnett's recommendation, that the Whartons themselves had insisted upon the annulment, the burden of the affair fell less heavily upon Lucy than upon Llewellyn. He became not exactly a pariah – cities live too quickly to linger long over any single scandal

– but he was cut off entirely from the crowd in which he had grown up, and much bitter and unpleasant comment reached his ears.

He was a boy who felt things deeply, and in the first moment of depression he contemplated leaving Philadelphia. But gradually a mood of defiant indifference took possession of him; try as he might, he wasn't able to feel in his heart that he had done anything morally wrong. He hadn't thought of Lucy as being sixteen, but only as the girl whom he loved beyond understanding. What did age matter? Hadn't people married as children, almost one hundred – two hundred years ago? The day of his elopement with Lucy had been like an ecstatic dream; he the young knight, scorned by her father, the baron, as a mere youth, bearing her away, and all willing, on his charger, in the dead of the night.

And then the realization, almost before his eyes had opened from their romantic vision, that marriage meant the complicated adjustment of two lives to each other, and that love is a small part only of the long, long marriage day. Lucy was a devoted child whom he had contracted to amuse – an adorable and somewhat frightened child, that was all.

As suddenly as it had begun, it was over. Doggedly Llewellyn went his way, along with his mistake. And so quickly had his romance bloomed and turned to dust that after a month a merciful unreality began to clothe it as if it were something vaguely sad that had happened long ago.

One day in July he was summoned to Chauncey Garnett's private office. Few words had passed between them since their conversation the month before, but Llewellyn saw that there was no hostility in the older man's attitude.

He was glad of that, for now that he felt himself utterly alone, cut off from the world in which he had grown up, his work had come to be the most important thing in his life.

"What are you doing, Llewellyn?" asked Garnett, picking up a yellow pamphlet from the litter of his desk.

"Helping Mr Carson with the Municipal Country Club."

"Take a look at this." He handed the pamphlet to Llewellyn. "There isn't a gold mine in it, but there's a good deal of this gilt-edge hot air they call publicity. It's a syndicate of twenty papers, you see. The best plans for – what is it? – a neighbourhood store – you know, a small drugstore or grocery store that could fit into a nice street without being an eyesore. Or else for a suburban cottage – that'll be the regular thing. Or thirdly for a small factory recreation house."

Llewellyn read over the specifications.

"The last two aren't so interesting," he said. "Suburban cottage – that'll be the usual thing, as you say – recreation house, no. But I'd like to have a shot at the first, sir – the store."

Garnett nodded. "The best part is that the plan which wins each competition materializes as a building right away, and therein lies the prize. The building is yours. You design it, it's put up for you, then you sell it and the money goes into your pocket. Matter of six or seven thousand dollars – and there won't be more than six or seven hundred other young architects trying."

Llewellyn read it over again carefully.

"I like it," he said. "I'd like to try the store."

"Well, you've got one month. I wouldn't mind it a bit, Llewellyn, if that prize came into this office."

"I can't promise you that." Again Llewellyn ran his eyes over the conditions, while Garnett watched him with quiet interest.

"By the way," he asked suddenly, "what do you do with yourself all the time, Llewellyn?"

"How do you mean, sir?"

"At night – over the weekends. Do you ever go out?"

Llewellyn hesitated.

"Well, not so much – now."

"You mustn't let yourself brood over this business, you know."

"I'm not brooding."

Mr Garnett put his glasses carefully away in their case.

"Lucy isn't brooding," he said suddenly. "Her father told me that she's trying to live just as normal a life as possible."

Silence for a moment.

"I'm glad," said Llewellyn in an expressionless voice.

"You must remember that you're free as air now," said Garnett. "You don't want to let yourself dry up and get bitter. Lucy's father and mother are encouraging her to have callers and go to dances – behave just as she did before."

"Before Rudolf Rassendyll* came along," said Llewellyn grimly. He held up the pamphlet. "May I keep this, Mr Garnett?"

"Oh, yes." His employer's hand gave him permission to retire. "Tell Mr Carson that I've taken you off the country club for the present."

"I can finish that too," said Llewellyn promptly. "In fact…"

His lips shut. He had been about to remark that he was doing practically the whole thing himself anyhow.

"Well?"

"Nothing, sir. Thank you very much."

Llewellyn withdrew, excited by his opportunity and relieved by the news of Lucy. She was herself again, so Mr Garnett had implied; perhaps her life wasn't so irrevocably wrecked after all. If there were men to come and see her, to take her out to dances, then there were men to care for her. He found himself vaguely pitying them – if they knew what a handful she was, the absolute impossibility of dealing with her, even of talking to her. At the thought of those desolate weeks he shivered, as though recalling a nightmare.

Back in his room that night, he experimented with a few tentative sketches. He worked late, his imagination warming to the set task, but next day the result seemed "arty" and pretentious – like a design for a tea shop. He scrawled "Ye Olde-fashioned Butcher Shoppe – Veree Unsanitaree", across the face of it and tore it into pieces, which he tossed into the wastebasket.

During the first weeks in August he continued his work on the plans for the country club, trusting that for the more personal venture some burst of inspiration would come to him towards the end of the allotted time. And then one day occurred an incident which he had long dreaded in the secret corners of his mind – walking home along Chestnut Street he ran unexpectedly into Lucy.

It was about five o'clock, when the crowds were thickest. Suddenly they found themselves in an eddy facing each other, and then borne along side by side as if fate had pressed into service all these swarming hundreds to throw them together.

"Why, Lucy!" he exclaimed, raising his hat automatically. She stared at him with startled eyes. A woman laden with bundles collided with her and a purse slipped from Lucy's hand.

"Thank you very much," she said as he retrieved it. Her voice was tense, breathless. "That's all right. Give it to me. I have a car right here."

Their eyes joined for a moment, cool, impersonal, and he had a vivid memory of their last meeting – of how they had stood, like this, hating each other with a cold fury.

"Are you sure I can't help you?"

"Quite sure. Our car's at the kerb."

She nodded quickly. Llewellyn caught a glimpse of an unfamiliar limousine and a short smiling man of forty who helped her inside.

He walked home – for the first time in weeks he was angry, excited, confused. He must get away tomorrow. It was all too recent for any such casual encounter as this; the wounds she had left on him were raw and they opened easily.

"The little fool!" he said to himself bitterly. "The selfish little fool! She thought I wanted to walk along the street with her as if nothing had ever happened. She dares to imagine that I'm made of the same flimsy stuff as herself!"

He wanted passionately to spank her, to punish her in some way like an insolent child. Until dinnertime he paced up and down in his room, going over in his mind the forlorn and useless arguments, reproaches, imprecations, furies, that had made up their short married life. He rehearsed every quarrel from its trivial genesis down to the time when a merciful exhaustion intervened and brought them, almost hysterical, into each other's arms. A brief moment of peace – then again the senseless, miserable human battle.

"Lucy," he heard himself saying, "listen to me. It isn't that I want you to sit here waiting for me. It's your hands, Lucy. Suppose you went to cooking school and burned your pretty hands. I don't want your hands coarsened and roughened, and if you'll just have patience till next week when my money comes in… I won't stand it! Do you hear? I'm not going to have my wife doing that! No use of being stubborn."

Wearily, just as he had been made weary by those arguments in reality, he dropped into a chair and reached listlessly for his drawing materials. Laying them out, he began to sketch, crumpling each one into a ball before a dozen lines marred the paper. It was her fault, he whispered to himself, it was all her fault. "If I'd been fifty years old I couldn't have changed her." Yet he could not rid himself of her dark young face set sharp and cool against the August gloaming, against the hot hurrying crowds of that afternoon.

"Quite sure. Our car's at the kerb."

Llewellyn nodded to himself and tried to smile grimly.

"Well, I've got one thing to be thankful for," he told himself. "My responsibility will be over before long."

He had been sitting for a long while, looking at a blank sheet of drawing paper; but presently his pencil began to move in light strokes at the corner. He watched it idly, impersonally, as though it were a motion of his fingers imposed on him from outside. Finally he looked at the result with disapproval, scratched it out and then blocked it in again in exactly the same way.

Suddenly he chose a new pencil, picked up his ruler and made a measurement on the paper, and then another. An hour passed. The sketch took shape and outline, varied itself slightly, yielded in part to an eraser and appeared in an improved form. After two hours, he raised his head, and catching sight of his tense, absorbed face he started with surprise. There were a dozen half-smoked cigarettes in the tray beside him.

When he turned out his light at last it was half-past five. The milk wagons were rumbling through the twilit streets outside, and the first sunshine streaming pink over the roofs of the houses across the way fell upon the board which bore his night's work. It was the plan of a suburban bungalow.

3

As the August days passed, Llewellyn continued to think of Lucy with a certain anger and contempt. If she could accept so lightly what had happened just two months ago, he had wasted his emotion upon a girl who was essentially shallow. It cheapened his conception of her, of himself, of the whole affair. Again the idea came to him of leaving Philadelphia and making a new start farther west, but his interest in the outcome of the competition decided him to postpone his departure for a few weeks more.

The blueprints of his design were made and dispatched. Mr Garnett cautiously refused to make any prophecies, but Llewellyn knew that everyone in the office who had seen the drawing felt a vague excitement about it. Almost literally he had drawn a bungalow in the air – a bungalow that had never been lived in before. It was neither Italian, Elizabethan, New England or California Spanish, nor a mongrel form with features from each one. Someone dubbed it the tree house, and there was a certain happiness in the label; but its charm proceeded less from any bizarre quality than from the virtuosity of the conception as a whole – an unusual length here and there, an odd, tantalizing familiar slope of the roof, a door that was like the door to the secret places of a dream. Chauncey Garnett remarked that it was the first skyscraper he had ever seen built with one storey, but he recognized that Llewellyn's unquestionable talent had matured overnight. Except that the organizers of the competition were probably seeking something more adapted to standardization, it might have had a chance for the award.

Only Llewellyn was sure. When he was reminded that he was only twenty-one, he kept silent, knowing that, whatever his years, he would never again be twenty-one at heart. Life had betrayed him. He had squandered himself on a worthless girl and the world had punished him for it, as ruthlessly as though he had spent spiritual coin other than his own. Meeting Lucy on the street again, he passed her without a flicker of his eye – and returned to his room, his day spoilt by the sight of that young distant face, the insincere reproach of those dark haunting eyes.

A week or so later arrived a letter from New York informing him that from four hundred plans submitted the judges of the competition had chosen his for the prize. Llewellyn walked into Mr Garnett's office without excitement, but with a strong sense of elation, and laid the letter on his employer's desk.

"I'm especially glad," he said, "because before I go away I wanted to do something to justify your belief in me."

Mr Garnett's face assumed an expression of concern.

"It's this business of Lucy Wharton, isn't it?" he demanded. "It's still on your mind?"

"I can't stand meeting her," said Llewellyn. "It always makes me feel – like the devil."

"But you ought to stay till they put up your house for you."

"I'll come back for that, perhaps. I want to leave tonight."

Garnett looked at him thoughtfully.

"I don't like to see you go away," he said. "I'm going to tell you something I didn't intend to tell you. Lucy needn't worry you a bit any more – your responsibility is absolutely over."

"Why's that?" Llewellyn felt his heart quicken.

"She's going to marry another man."

"Going to marry another man!" repeated Llewellyn mechanically.

"She's going to marry George Hemmick, who represents her father's business in Chicago. They're going out there to live."

"I see."

"The Whartons are delighted," continued Garnett. "I think they've felt this thing pretty deeply – perhaps more deeply than it deserves. And I've been sorry all along that the brunt of it fell on you. But you'll find the girl you really want one of these days, Llewellyn, and meanwhile the sensible thing for everyone concerned is to forget that it happened at all."

"But I can't forget," said Llewellyn in a strained voice. "I don't understand what you mean by all that – you people – you and Lucy and her father and mother. First it was such a tragedy, and now it's something to forget! First I was this vicious young man and now I'm to go ahead and find the girl I want. Lucy's going to marry somebody and live in Chicago. Her father and mother feel fine because our elopement didn't get in the newspapers and hurt their social position. It came out 'all right'!"

Llewellyn stood there speechless, aghast and defeated by this manifestation of the world's indifference. It was all about nothing – his very self-reproaches had been pointless and in vain.

"So that's that," he said finally in a new and hard voice. "I realize now that from beginning to end I was the only one who had any conscience in this affair after all."

4

THE LITTLE HOUSE, FRAGILE yet arresting, all aglitter like a toy in its fresh coat of robin's-egg blue, stood out delicately against the clear sky. Set upon new-laid sod between two other bungalows, it swung the eye sharply towards itself, held your glance for a moment, then turned up the corners of your lips with the sort of smile reserved for children. Something went on in it, you imagined; something charming and not quite real. Perhaps the whole front opened up like the front of a doll's house; you were tempted to hunt for the catch because you felt an irresistible inclination to peer inside.

Long before the arrival of Llewellyn Clark and Mr Garnett a small crowd had gathered – the constant efforts of two policemen were required to keep people from breaking through the strong fence and trampling the tiny garden. When Llewellyn's eye first fell upon it, as their car rounded a corner, a lump rose in his throat. That was his own – something that had come alive out of his mind. Suddenly he realized that it was not for sale, that he wanted it more than anything in the world. It could mean to him what love might have meant, something always bright and warm where he could rest from whatever disappointments life might have in store. And unlike love, it would set no traps for him. His career opened up before him in a shining path and for the first time in months he was radiantly happy.

The speeches, the congratulations, passed in a daze. When he got up to make a stumbling but grateful acknowledgement, even the sight of Lucy standing close to another man on the edge of the crowd failed to send a pang through him, as it would have a month before. That was the past, and only the future counted. He hoped with all his heart, without reservations now, or bitterness, that she would be happy.

Afterwards, when the crowd melted away, he felt the necessity of being alone. Still in a sort of trance, he went inside the house again and wandered from room to room, touching the walls, the furniture, the window casements, with almost a caress. He pulled aside curtains and gazed out; he stood for a while in the kitchen and seemed to see the fresh bread and butter on the white boards of the table, and hear the kettle, murmurous on the stove. Then back through the dining room

– he remembered planning that the evening light should fall through the window just so – and into the bedroom, where he watched a breeze ruffle the edge of a curtain faintly, as if someone already lived here. He would sleep in this room tonight, he thought. He would buy things for a cold supper from a corner store. He was sorry for everyone who was not an architect, who could not make their own houses; he wished he could have set up every stick and stone with his own hands.

The September dusk fell. Returning from the store, he set out his purchases on the dining-room table – cold roast chicken, bread and jam, and a bottle of milk. He ate lingeringly, then he sat back in his chair and smoked a cigarette, his eyes wandering about the walls. This was home. Llewellyn, brought up by a series of aunts, scarcely remembered ever having had a home before – except, of course, where he had lived with Lucy. Those barren rooms in which they were so miserable together had been, nevertheless, a sort of home. Poor children – he looked back on them both, himself as well as her, from a great distance. Little wonder their love had made a faint, frail effort, a gesture, and then, unprepared for the oppression of those stifling walls, starved quickly to death.

Half an hour passed. Outside, the silence was heavy except for the complaint of some indignant dog far down the street. Llewellyn's mind, detached by the unfamiliar, almost mystical surroundings, drifted away from the immediate past; he was thinking of the day when he had first met Lucy, a year before. Little Lucy Wharton – how touched he had been by her trust in him, by her confidence that, at twenty, he was experienced in the ways of the world.

He got to his feet and began to walk slowly up and down the room – starting suddenly as the front doorbell pealed through the house for the first time. He opened the door and Mr Garnett stepped inside.

"Good evening, Llewellyn," he said. "I came back to see if the king was happy in his castle."

"Sit down," said Llewellyn tensely. "I've got to ask you something. Why is Lucy marrying this man? I want to know."

"Why, I think I told you that he's a good deal older," answered Garnett quietly. "She feels that he understands."

"I want to see her!" Llewellyn cried. He leant miserably against the mantelpiece. "I don't know what to do. Mr Garnett, we're in love with each other, don't you realize that? Can you stay in this house and not realize it? It's her house and mine. Why, every room in it is haunted with Lucy! She came in when I was at dinner and sat with me – just now I saw her in front of the mirror in the bedroom, brushing her hair—"

"She's out on the porch," interrupted Garnett quietly. "I think she wants to talk to you. In a few months she's going to have a child."

For a few minutes Chauncey Garnett moved about the empty room, looking at this feature or that, here and there, until the walls seemed to fade out and melt into the walls of the little house where he had brought his own wife more than forty years ago. It was long gone, that house – the gift of his father-in-law; it would have seemed an atrocity to this generation. Yet on many a forgotten late afternoon when he had turned in at its gate, and the gas had flamed out at him cheerfully from its windows, he had got from it a moment of utter peace that no other house had given him since.

Until this house. The same quiet secret thing was here. Was it that his old mind was confusing the two, or that love had built this out of the tragedy in Llewellyn's heart? Leaving the question unanswered he found his hat and walked out on the dark porch, scarcely glanced at the single shadow on the porch chair a few yards away.

"You see, I never bothered to get that annulment, after all," he said as if he were talking to himself. "I thought it over carefully and I saw that you two were good people. And I had an idea that eventually you'd do the right thing. Good people – so often do."

When he reached the kerb he looked back at the house. Again his mind – or his eyes – blurred and it seemed to him that it was that other house of forty years ago. Then, feeling vaguely ineffectual and a little guilty because he had meddled in other people's affairs, he turned and walked off hastily down the street.

Your Way and Mine

ONE SPRING AFTERNOON in the first year of the present century a young man was experimenting with a new typewriter in a brokerage office on lower Broadway. At his elbow lay an eight-line letter and he was endeavouring to make a copy on the machine but each attempt was marred by a monstrous capital rising unexpectedly in the middle of a word or by the disconcerting intrusion of some symbol such as $ or % into an alphabet whose membership was set at twenty-six many years ago. Whenever he detected a mistake he made a new beginning with a fresh sheet but after the fifteenth try he was aware of a ferocious instinct to cast the machine from the window.

The young man's short blunt fingers were too big for the keys. He was big all over; indeed his bulky body seemed to be in the very process of growth for it had ripped his coat at the back seam, while his trousers clung to thigh and calf like skin tights. His hair was yellow and tousled – you could see the paths of his broad fingers in it – and his eyes were of a hard brilliant blue but the lids drooping a little over them reinforced an impression of lethargy that the clumsy body conveyed. His age was twenty-one.

"What do you think the eraser's for, McComas?"

The young man looked around.

"What's that?" he demanded brusquely.

"The eraser," repeated the short alert human fox who had come in the outer door and paused behind him. "That there's a good copy except for one word. Use your head or you'll be sitting there until tomorrow."

The human fox moved on into his private office. The young man sat for a moment, motionless, sluggish. Suddenly he grunted, picked up the eraser referred to and flung it savagely out of the window.

Twenty minutes later he opened the door of his employer's office. In his hand was the letter, immaculately typed, and the addressed envelope.

"Here it is, sir," he said, frowning a little from his late concentration.

The human fox took it, glanced at it and then looked at McComas with a peculiar smile.

"You didn't use the eraser?"

"No, I didn't, Mr Woodley."

"You're one of those thorough young men, aren't you?" said the fox sarcastically.

"What?"

"I said 'thorough' but since you weren't listening I'll change it to 'pig-headed'. Whose time did you waste just to avoid a little erasure that the best typists aren't too proud to make? Did you waste your time or mine?"

"I wanted to make one good copy," answered McComas steadily. "You see, I never worked a typewriter before."

"Answer my question," snapped Mr Woodley. "When you sat there making two dozen copies of that letter were you wasting your time or mine?"

"It was mostly my lunchtime," McComas replied, his big face flushing to an angry pink. "I've got to do things my own way or not at all."

For answer Mr Woodley picked up the letter and envelope, folded them, tore them once and again and dropped the pieces into the wastepaper basket with a toothy little smile.

"That's my way," he announced. "What do you think of that?"

Young McComas had taken a step forward as if to snatch the fragments from the fox's hand.

"By golly," he cried. "By golly. Why, for two cents I'd spank you!"

With an angry snarl Mr Woodley sprang to his feet, fumbled in his pocket and threw a handful of change upon his desk.

Ten minutes later the outside man coming in to report perceived that neither young McComas nor his hat were in their usual places. But in the private office he found Mr Woodley, his face crimson and foam bubbling between his teeth, shouting frantically into the telephone. The outside man noticed to his surprise that Mr Woodley was in daring dishabille and that there were six suspender buttons scattered upon the office floor.

In 1902 Henry McComas weighed 196 pounds. In 1905 when he journeyed back to his home town, Elmira, to marry the love of his boyhood he tipped accurate beams at 210. His weight remained constant for two years but after the panic of 1907 it bounded to 220, about which comfortable figure it was apparently to hover for the rest of his life.

He looked mature beyond his years – under certain illuminations his yellow hair became a dignified white – and his bulk added to the impression of authority that he gave. During his first five years off the farm there was never a time when he wasn't scheming to get into business for himself.

For a temperament like Henry McComas's, which insisted on running at a pace of its own, independence was an utter necessity. He must make his own rules, willy-nilly, even though he join the ranks of those many abject failures who have also tried. Just one week after he had achieved his emancipation from other people's hierarchies he was moved to expound his point to Theodore Drinkwater, his partner – this because Drinkwater had wondered aloud if he intended never to come downtown before eleven.

"I doubt it," said McComas.

"What's the idea?" demanded Drinkwater indignantly. "What do you think the effect's going to be on our office force?"

"Does Miss Johnston show any sign of being demoralized?"

"I mean after we get more people. It isn't as if you were an old man, Mac, with your work behind you. You're only twenty-eight, not a day older than I. What'll you do at forty?"

"I'll be downtown at eleven o'clock," said McComas, "every working day of my life."

Later in the week one of their first clients invited them to lunch at a celebrated business club; the club's least member was a rajah of the swelling, expanding empire.

"Look around, Ted," whispered McComas as they left the dining room. "There's a man looks like a prizefighter, and there's one who looks like a ham actor. That's a plumber there behind you; there's a coal heaver and a couple of cowboys – do you see? There's a chronic invalid and a confidence man, a pawnbroker – that one on the right. By golly, where are all the big businessmen we came to see?"

The route back to their office took them by a small restaurant where the clerks of the district flocked to lunch.

"Take a look at them, Ted, and you'll find the men who know the rules – and think and act and look like just what they are."

"I suppose if they put on pink moustaches and came to work at five in the afternoon they'd get to be great men," scoffed Drinkwater.

"Posing is exactly what I don't mean. Just accept yourself. We're brought up on fairy stories about the new leaf, but who goes on believing them except those who have to believe and have to hope or else go crazy? I think America will be a happier country when the individual begins to look his personal limitations in the face. Anything that's in your character at twenty-one is usually there to stay."

In any case what was in Henry McComas's was there to stay. Henry McComas wouldn't dine with a client in a bad restaurant for a proposition of three figures, wouldn't hurry his luncheon for a proposition of four, wouldn't go without it for a proposition of five. And in spite of these peculiarities the exporting firm in which he owned 49 per cent of the stock began to pepper South America with locomotives, dynamos, barbwire, hydraulic engines, cranes, mining machinery and other appurtenances of civilization. In 1913 when Henry McComas was thirty-four he owned a house on 92nd Street and calculated that his income for the next year would come to thirty thousand dollars. And because of a sudden and unexpected demand from Europe which was not for pink lemonade, it came to twice that. The buying agent for the British government arrived, followed by the buying agents for the French, Belgian, Russian and Serbian governments, and a share of the commodities required was assembled under the stewardship of Drinkwater and McComas. There was a chance that they would be rich men. Then suddenly this eventually began to turn on the woman Henry McComas had married.

Stella McComas was the daughter of a small hay and grain dealer of upper New York. Her father was unlucky and always on the verge of failure, so she grew up in the shadow of worry. Later, while Henry McComas got his start in New York, she earned her living by teaching physical culture in the public schools of Utica. In consequence she brought to her marriage a belief in certain stringent rules for the care of the body and an exaggerated fear of adversity.

For the first years she was so impressed with her husband's rapid rise and so absorbed in her babies that she accepted Henry as something infallible and protective, outside the scope of her provincial wisdom. But as her little girl grew into short dresses and hair ribbons, and her little boy into the custody of an English nurse she had more time to look closely at her husband. His leisurely ways, his corpulency, his sometimes maddening deliberateness, ceased to be the privileged idiosyncrasies of success, and became only facts.

For a while he paid no great attention to her little suggestions as to his diet, her occasional crankiness as to his hours, her invidious comparisons between his habits and the fancied habits of other men. Then one morning a peculiar lack of taste in his coffee precipitated the matter into the light.

"I can't drink the stuff – it hasn't had any taste for a week," he complained. "And why is it brought in a cup from the kitchen? I like to put the cream and sugar in myself."

Stella avoided an answer but later he reverted to the matter.

"About my coffee. You'll remember – won't you? – to tell Rose."

Suddenly she smiled at him innocently.

"Don't you feel better, Henry?" she asked eagerly.

"What?"

"Less tired, less worried?"

"Who said I was tired and worried? I never felt better in my life."

"There you are." She looked at him triumphantly. "You laugh at my theories but this time you'll have to admit there's something in them. You feel better because you haven't had sugar in your coffee for over a week."

He looked at her incredulously.

"What have I had?"

"Saccharine."

He got up indignantly and threw his newspaper on the table.

"I might have known it," he broke out. "All that bringing it out from the kitchen. What the devil is saccharine?"

"It's a substitute, for people who have a tendency to run to fat."

For a moment he hovered on the edge of anger, then he sat down shaking with laughter.

"It's done you good," she said reproachfully.

"Well, it won't do me good any more," he said grimly. "I'm thirty-four years old and I haven't been sick a day in ten years. I've forgotten more about my constitution than you'll ever know."

"You don't live a healthy life, Henry. It's after forty that things begin to tell."

"Saccharine!" he exclaimed, again breaking into laughter. "Saccharine! I thought perhaps it was something to keep me from drink. You know they have these—"

Suddenly she grew angry.

"Well why not? You ought to be ashamed to be so fat at your age. You wouldn't be if you took a little exercise and didn't lie around in bed all morning."

Words utterly failed her.

"If I wanted to be a farmer," said her husband quietly, "I wouldn't have left home. This saccharine business is over today – do you see?"

Their financial situation rapidly improved. By the second year of the war they were keeping a limousine and chauffeur and began to talk vaguely of a nice summer house on Long Island Sound. Month by month a swelling stream of materials flowed through the ledgers of Drinkwater & McComas to be dumped on the insatiable bonfire across the ocean. Their staff of clerks tripled and the atmosphere of the office was so charged with energy and achievement that Stella herself often liked to wander in on some pretext during the afternoon.

One day early in 1916 she called to learn that Mr McComas was out and was on the point of leaving when she ran into Ted Drinkwater coming out of the elevator.

"Why, Stella," he exclaimed, "I was thinking about you only this morning."

The Drinkwaters and the McComases were close if not particularly spontaneous friends. Nothing but their husbands' intimate association would have thrown the two women together, yet they were "Henry, Ted, Mollie and Stella" to each other and in ten years scarcely a month had passed without their partaking in a superficially cordial family dinner. The dinner being over, each couple indulged in an unsparing post-mortem over the other without, however, any sense of disloyalty. They were used to each other – so Stella was somewhat surprised by Ted Drinkwater's personal eagerness at meeting her this afternoon.

"I want to see you," he said in his intent direct way. "Have you got a minute, Stella? Could you come into my office?"

"Why, yes."

As they walked between rows of typists towards the glassed privacy of Theodore Drinkwater, President, Stella could not help thinking that he made a more appropriate business figure than her husband. He was lean, terse, quick. His eye glanced keenly from right to left as if taking the exact measure of every clerk and stenographer in sight.

"Sit down, Stella."

She waited, a feeling of vague apprehension stealing over her.

Drinkwater frowned

"It's about Henry," he said.

"Is he sick?" she demanded quickly.

"No. Nothing like that." He hesitated. "Stella, I've always thought you were a woman with a lot of common sense."

She waited.

"This is a thing that's been on my mind for over a year," he continued. "He and I have battled it out so often that – that a certain coldness has grown up between us."

"Yes?" Stella's eyes blinked nervously.

"It's about the business," said Drinkwater abruptly. "A coldness with a business partner is a mighty unpleasant thing."

"What's the matter?"

"The old story, Stella. These are big years for us and he thinks business is going to wait while he carries on in the old country-store way. Down at eleven, hour and a half for lunch, won't be nice to a man he doesn't like for love or money. In the last six months he's lost us about three sizable orders by things like that."

Instinctively she sprang to her husband's defence.

"But hasn't he saved money too by going slow? On that thing about the copper, you wanted to sign right away and Henry—"

"Oh, that…" He waved it aside a little hurriedly. "I'm the last man to deny that Henry has a wonderful instinct in certain ways—"

"But it was a great big thing," she interrupted. "It would have practically ruined you if he hadn't put his foot down. He said…"

She pulled herself up short.

"Oh, I don't know," said Drinkwater with an expression of annoyance, "perhaps not so bad as that. Anyway, we all make mistakes and that's aside from the question. We have the opportunity right now of jumping into Class A. I mean it. Another two years of this kind of business and we can each put away our first million dollars. And, Stella, whatever happens, I am determined to put away mine. Even…" He considered his words for a moment. "Even if it comes to breaking with Henry."

"Oh!" Stella exclaimed. "I hope…"

"I hope not too. That's why I wanted to talk to you. Can't you do something, Stella? You're about the only person he'll listen to. He's so darn pig-headed he can't understand how he disorganizes the office. Get him up in the morning. No man ought to lie in bed till eleven."

"He gets up at half-past nine."

"He's down here at eleven. That's what counts. Stir him up. Tell him you want more money. Orders are more money and there are lots of orders around for anyone who goes after them."

"I'll see what I can do," she said anxiously. "But I don't know – Henry's difficult – very set in his ways."

"You'll think of something. You might…" He smiled grimly. "You might give him a few more bills to pay. Sometimes I think an extravagant wife's the best inspiration a man can have. We need more pep down here. I've got to be the pep for two. I mean it, Stella, I can't carry this thing alone."

Stella left the office with her mind in a panic. All the fears and uncertainties of her childhood had been brought suddenly to the surface. She saw Henry cast off by Ted Drinkwater and trying unsuccessfully to run a business of his own. With his easy-going ways! They would slide downhill, giving up the servants one by one, the car, the house. Before she reached home her imagination had envisaged poverty, her children at work – starvation. Hadn't Ted Drinkwater just told her that he himself was the life of the concern – that he kept things moving? What would Henry do alone?

For a week she brooded over the matter, guarding her secret but looking with a mixture of annoyance and compassion at Henry over the dinner table. Then she mustered up her resolution. She went to a real-estate agent and handed over her entire bank account of nine thousand dollars as the first payment on a house they had fearfully coveted on Long Island… That night she told Henry.

"Why, Stella, you must have gone crazy," he cried aghast. "You must have gone crazy. Why didn't you ask me?"

He wanted to take her by the shoulders and shake her.

"I was afraid, Henry," she answered truthfully.

He thrust his hands despairingly through his yellow hair.

"Just at this time, Stella. I've just taken out an insurance policy that's more than I can really afford – we haven't paid for the new car – we've had a new front put on this house – last week your sable coat. I was going to devote tonight to figuring just how close we were running on money."

"But can't you – can't you take something out of the business until things get better?" she demanded in alarm.

"That's just what I can't do. It's impossible. I can't explain because you don't understand the situation down there. You see Ted and I – can't agree on certain things…"

Suddenly a new light dawned on her and she felt her body flinch. Supposing that by bringing about this situation she had put her husband into his partner's hands. Yet wasn't that what she wanted – wasn't it necessary for the present that Henry should conform to Drinkwater's methods?

"Sixty thousand dollars," repeated Henry in a frightened voice that made her want to cry. "I don't know where I am going to get enough to buy it on mortgage." He sank into a chair. "I might go and see the people you dealt with tomorrow and make a compromise – let some of your nine thousand go."

"I don't think they would," she said, her face set. "They were awfully anxious to sell – the owner's going away."

She had acted on impulse, she said, thinking that in their increasing prosperity the money would be available. He had been so generous about the new car – she supposed that now at last they could afford what they wanted.

It was typical of McComas that after the first moment of surprise he wasted no energy in reproaches. But two days later he came home from work with such a heavy and dispirited look on his face that she could not help but guess that he and Ted Drinkwater had had it out – and that what she had wanted had come true. That night in shame and pity she cried herself to sleep.

A new routine was inaugurated in Henry McComas's life. Each morning Stella woke him at eight and he lay for fifteen minutes in an unwilling trance, as if his body were surprised at this departure from the custom of a decade. He reached the office at nine-thirty as promptly as he had once reached it at eleven – on the first morning his appearance caused a flutter of astonishment among the older employees – and he limited his lunchtime to a conscientious hour. No longer could he be found asleep on his office couch between two and three o'clock on summer afternoons – the couch itself vanished into that limbo which held his leisurely periods of digestion and his cherished surfeit of sleep. These were his concessions to Drinkwater in exchange for the withdrawal of sufficient money to cover his immediate needs.

Drinkwater of course could have bought him out, but for various reasons the senior partner did not consider this advisable. One of them, though he didn't admit it to himself, was his absolute reliance on McComas in all matters of initiative and decision. Another reason was the tumultuous condition of the market, for as 1916 boomed on with the tragic Battle of the Somme the Allied agents sailed once more to the city of plenty for the wherewithal of another year. Coincidentally Drinkwater & McComas moved into a suite that was like a floor in a country club and there they sat all day while anxious and gesticulating strangers explained what they must have, helplessly pledging their peoples to thirty years of economic depression. Drinkwater & McComas farmed out a dozen contracts a week and started the movement of countless tons towards Europe. Their names were known up and down the Street now – they had forgotten what it was to be kept waiting on a telephone.

But though profits increased and Stella, settled in the Long Island house, seemed for the first time in years perfectly satisfied, Henry McComas found himself growing irritable and nervous. What he missed most was the sleep for which his body hungered and which seemed to descend upon him at its richest just as he was shocked back into the living world each morning. And in spite of all material gains he was always aware that he was walking in his own paths no longer.

Their interests broadened and Drinkwater was frequently away on trips to the industrial towns of New England or the South. In consequence the detail of the office fell upon McComas – and he took it hard. A man capable of enormous concentration, he had previously harvested his power for hours of importance. Now he was inclined to fritter it away upon things that in perspective often proved to be inessentials. Sometimes he was engaged in office routine until six, then at home working until midnight when he tumbled, worn out but often still wide-eyed, into his beleaguered bed.

The firm's policy was to slight their smaller accounts in Cuba and the West Indies and concentrate upon the tempting business of the war, and all through the summer they were hurrying to clear the scenes for the arrival of a new purchasing commission in September. When it arrived it unexpectedly found Drinkwater in Pennsylvania, temporarily out of reach. Time was short and the orders were to be placed in bulk. After much anxious parley over the telephone McComas persuaded four members of the commission to meet him for an hour at his own house that night.

Thanks to his foresight everything was in order. If he hadn't been able to be specific over the phone the coup towards which he had been working would have ended in failure. When it was brought off he was due for a rest and he knew it acutely. He'd had sharp fierce headaches in the past few weeks – he had never known a headache before.

The commissioners had been indefinite as to what time he could expect them that night. They were engaged for dinner and would be free somewhere between nine and eleven. McComas reached home at six, rested for a half-hour in a steaming bath and then stretched himself gratefully on his bed. Tomorrow he would join Stella and the children in the country. His weekends had been too infrequent in this long summer of living alone in the 92nd Street house with a deaf housekeeper. Ted Drinkwater would have nothing to say now, for this deal, the most ambitious of all, was his own. He had originated and engineered it – it seemed as if fate had arranged Drinkwater's absence in order to give him the opportunity of concluding it himself.

He was hungry. He considered whether to take cold chicken and buttered toast at the hands of the housekeeper or to dress and go out to the little restaurant on the corner. Idly he reached his hand towards the bell, abandoned the attempt in the air, overcome by a pleasing languor which dispelled the headache that had bothered him all day.

That reminded him to take some aspirin and as he got up to go towards the bureau he was surprised at the weakened condition in which the hot bath had left him. After a step or two he turned about suddenly and plunged rather than fell back upon the bed. A faint feeling of worry passed over him and then an iron belt seemed to wind itself around his head and tighten, sending a spasm of pain through his body. He would ring for Mrs Corcoran, who would call a doctor to fix him up. In a minute – he wondered at his indecision – then he cried out sharply as he realized the cause of it. His will had already given his brain the order and his brain had signalled it to his hand. It was his hand that would not obey.

He looked at his hand. Rather white, relaxed, motionless, it lay upon the counterpane. Again he gave it a command, felt his neck cords tighten with the effort. It did not move.

"It's asleep," he thought, but with rising alarm. "It'll pass off in a minute."

Then he tried to reach his other hand across his body to massage away the numbness but the other hand remained with a sort of crazy indifference on its own side of the bed. He tried to lift his foot – his knees…

After a few seconds he gave a snort of nervous laughter. There was something ridiculous about not being able to move your own foot. It was like someone else's foot, a foot in a dream. For a moment he had the fantastic notion that he must be asleep. But no – the unmistakable sense of reality was in the room.

"This is the end," he thought, without fear, almost without emotion. "This thing, whatever it is, is creeping over me. In a minute I shall be dead."

But the minute passed and another minute, and nothing happened, nothing moved except the hand of the little leather clock on his dresser which crept slowly over the point of seven minutes to seven. He turned his head quickly from side to side, shaking it as a runner kicks his legs to warm up. But there was no answering response from the rest of his body, only a slight rise and fall between belly and chest as he breathed out and in and a faint tremble of his helpless limbs from the faint tremble of the bed.

"Help!" he called out. "Mrs Corcoran. Mrs Cor-cor-an, help! Mrs Corcor..."

There was no answer. She was in the kitchen probably. No way of calling her except by the bell, two feet over his head. Nothing to do but lie there until this passed off, or until he died, or until someone enquired for him at the front door.

The clock ticked past nine o'clock. In a house two blocks away the four members of the commission finished dinner, looked at their watches and issued forth into the September night with briefcases in their hands. Outside a private detective nodded and took his place beside the chauffeur in the waiting limousine. One of the men gave an address on 92nd Street.

Ten minutes later Henry McComas heard the doorbell ring through the house. If Mrs Corcoran was in the kitchen she would hear it too. On the contrary if she was in her room with the door shut she would hear nothing.

He waited, listening intently for the sound of footsteps. A minute passed. Two minutes. The doorbell rang again.

"Mrs Corcoran!" he cried desperately.

Sweat began to roll from his forehead and down the folds of his neck. Again he shook his head desperately from side to side, and his will made a last mighty effort to kick his limbs into life. Not a movement, not a sound, except a third peal of the bell, impatient and sustained this time and singing like a trumpet of doom in his ear.

Suddenly he began to swear at the top of his voice calling in turn upon Mrs Corcoran, upon the men in the street, asking them to break down the door, reassuring, imprecating, explaining. When he finished, the bell had stopped ringing; there was silence once more within the house.

A few minutes later the four men outside re-entered their limousine and drove south and west towards the docks. They were to sleep on board ship that night. They worked late for there were papers to go ashore but long after the last of them was asleep Henry McComas lay awake and felt the sweat rolling from his neck and forehead. Perhaps all his body was sweating. He couldn't tell.

For a year and a half Henry McComas lay silent in hushed and darkened rooms and fought his way back to life. Stella listened while a famous specialist explained that certain nervous systems were so constituted that only the individual could judge what was, or wasn't, a strain. The specialist realized that a host of hypochondriacs imposed upon this fact to nurse and pamper themselves through life when in reality they were as hardy and phlegmatic as the policeman on the corner, but it was nevertheless a fact. Henry McComas's large, lazy body had been the protection and insulation of a nervous intensity as fine and taut as a hair wire. With proper rest it functioned brilliantly for three or four hours a day – fatigued ever so slightly over the danger line it snapped like a straw.

Stella listened, her face wan and white. Then a few weeks later she went to Ted Drinkwater's office and told him what the specialist had said. Drinkwater frowned uncomfortably – he remarked that specialists were paid to invent consoling nonsense. He was sorry but business must go on, and he thought it best for everyone, including Henry, that the partnership be dissolved. He didn't blame Henry but he couldn't forget that just because his partner didn't see fit to keep in good condition they had missed the opportunity of a lifetime.

After a year Henry McComas found one day that he could move his arms down to the wrists; from that hour onward he grew rapidly well. In 1919 he went into business for himself with very little except his abilities and his good name and by the time this story ends, in 1926, his name alone was good for several million dollars.

What follows is another story. There are different people in it and it takes place when Henry McComas's personal problems are more or less satisfactorily solved; yet it belongs to what has gone before. It concerns Henry McComas's daughter.

Honoria was nineteen, with her father's yellow hair (and, in the current fashion, not much more of it), her mother's small pointed chin and eyes that she might have invented herself, deep-set yellow eyes with short stiff eyelashes that sprang from them like the emanations from a star in a picture. Her figure was slight and childish and when she smiled you were afraid that she might expose the loss of some baby teeth, but the teeth were there, a complete set, little and white. Many men had looked upon Honoria in flower. She expected to be married in the fall.

Whom to marry was another matter. There was a young man who travelled incessantly back and forth between London and Chicago playing in golf tournaments. If she married him she would at least be sure of seeing her husband every time he passed through New York. There was Max Van Camp who was unreliable, she thought, but good-looking in a brisk sketchy way. There was a dark man named Strangler who played polo and would probably beat her with a riding crop like the heroes of Ethel M. Dell.* And there was Russel Codman, her father's right-hand man, who had a future and whom she liked best of all.

He was not unlike her father in many ways – slow in thought, leisurely and inclined to stoutness – and perhaps these qualities had first brought him to Henry McComas's favour. He had a genial manner and a hearty confident smile, and he had made up his mind about Honoria when he first saw her stroll into her father's office one day three years before. But so far he hadn't asked her to marry him, and though this annoyed Honoria she liked him for it too – he wanted to be secure and successful before he asked her to share his life. Max Van Camp, on the other hand, had asked her a dozen times. He was a quick-witted "alive" young man of the new school, continually bubbling over with schemes that never got beyond McComas's wastepaper basket – one of those curious vagabonds of business who drift from position to position like strolling minstrels and yet manage to keep moving in an upward direction all their lives. He had appeared in McComas's office the year before bearing an introductory letter from a friend.

He got the position. For a long while neither he nor his employer, nor anyone in the office, was quite sure what the position was. McComas at that time was interested in exporting, in real-estate developments and, as a venture, in the possibilities of carrying the chain-store idea into new fields.

Van Camp wrote advertising, investigated properties and accomplished such vague duties as might come under the phrase, "We'll get Van Camp to do that." He gave the effect always of putting much more clamour and energy into a thing than it required and there were those who, because he was somewhat flashy and often wasted himself like an unemployed dynamo, called him a bluff and pronounced that he was usually wrong.

"What's the matter with you young fellows?" Henry McComas said to him one day. "You seem to think business is some sort of trick game, discovered about 1910, that nobody ever heard of before. You can't even look at a proposition unless you put it into this new language of your own. What do you mean you want to 'sell' me this proposition? Do you want to suggest it – or are you asking money for it?"

"Just a figure of speech, Mr McComas."

"Well, don't fool yourself that it's anything else. Business sense is just common sense with your personal resources behind it – nothing more."

"I've heard Mr Codman say that," agreed Max Van Camp meekly.

"He's probably right. See here..." he looked keenly at Van Camp; "how would you like a little competition with that same gentleman? I'll put up a bonus of five hundred dollars on who comes in ahead."

"I'd like nothing better, Mr McComas."

"All right. Now listen. We've got retail hardware stores in every city of over a thousand population in Ohio and Indiana. Some fellow named McTeague is homing in on the idea – he's taken the towns of twenty thousand and now he's got a chain as long as mine. I want to fight him in the towns of that size. Codman's gone to Ohio. Suppose you take Indiana. Stay six weeks. Go to every town of over twenty thousand in the state and buy up the best hardware stores in sight."

"Suppose I can only get the second-best?"

"Do what you can. There isn't any time to waste because McTeague's got a good start on us. Think you can leave tonight?"

He gave some further instructions while Van Camp fidgeted impatiently. His mind had grasped what was required of him and he wanted to get away. He wanted to ask Honoria McComas one more question, the same one, before it was time to go.

He received the same answer because Honoria knew she was going to marry Russel Codman, just as soon as he asked her to. Sometimes when she was alone with Codman she would shiver with excitement, feeling that now surely the time had come at last – in a moment the words would flow romantically from his lips. What the words would be she didn't know, couldn't imagine, but they would be thrilling and extraordinary, not like the spontaneous appeals of Max Van Camp which she knew by heart. She waited excitedly for Russel Codman's return from the West. This time, unless he spoke, she would speak herself. Perhaps he didn't want her after all, perhaps there was someone else. In that case she would marry Max Van Camp and make him miserable by letting him see that he was getting only the remnants of a blighted life.

Then before she knew it the six weeks were up and Russel Codman came back to New York. He reported to her father that he was going to see her that night. In her excitement Honoria found excuses for being near the front door. The bell rang finally and a maid stepped past her and admitted a visitor into the hall.

"Max," she cried.

He came towards her and she saw that his face was tired and white.

"Will you marry me?" he demanded without preliminaries.

She sighed.

"How many times, Max?"

"I've lost count," he said cheerfully. "But I haven't even begun. Do I understand that you refuse?"

"Yes, I'm sorry."

"Waiting for Codman?"

She grew annoyed.

"That's not your affair."

"Where's your father?"

She pointed, not deigning to reply.

Max entered the library where McComas rose to meet him.

"Well?" enquired the older man. "How did you make out?"

"How did Codman make out?" demanded Van Camp.

"Codman did well. He bought about eighteen stores – in several cases the very stores McTeague was after."

"I knew he would," said Van Camp.

"I hope you did the same."

"No," said Van Camp unhappily. "I failed."

"What happened?" McComas slouched his big body reflectively back in his chair and waited.

"I saw it was no use," said Van Camp after a moment. "I don't know what sort of places Codman picked up in Ohio but if it was anything like Indiana they weren't worth buying. These towns of twenty thousand haven't got three good hardware stores. They've got one man who won't sell out on account of the local wholesaler; then there's one man that McTeague's got, and after that only little places on the corner. Anything else you'll have to build up yourself. I saw right away that it wasn't worthwhile." He broke off. "How many places did Codman buy?"

"Eighteen or nineteen."

"I bought three."

McComas looked at him impatiently.

"How did you spend your time?" he asked. "Take you two weeks apiece to get them?"

"Took me two days," said Van Camp gloomily. "Then I had an idea."

"What was that?" McComas's voice was ironical.

"Well – McTeague had all the good stores."

"Yes."

"So I thought the best thing was to buy McTeague's company over his head."

"What?"

"Buy his company over his head," and Van Camp added with seeming irrelevance, "you see, I heard that he'd had a big quarrel with his uncle who owned 15 per cent of the stock."

"Yes." McComas was leaning forward now – the sarcasm gone from his face.

"McTeague only owned 25 per cent and the storekeepers themselves owned 40. So if I could bring round the uncle we'd have a majority. First I convinced the uncle that his money would be safer with McTeague as a branch manager in our organization—"

"Wait a minute – wait a minute," said McComas. "You go too fast for me. You say the uncle had 15 per cent – how'd you get the other 40?"

"From the owners. I told them the uncle had lost faith in McTeague and I offered them better terms. I had all their proxies on condition that they would be voted in a majority only."

"Yes," said McComas eagerly. Then he hesitated. "But it didn't work, you say. What was the matter with it? Not sound?"

"Oh, it was a sound scheme all right."

"Sound schemes always work."

"This one didn't."

"Why not?"

"The uncle died."

McComas laughed. Then he stopped suddenly and considered.

"So you tried to buy McTeague's company over his head?"

"Yes," said Max with a shamed look. "And I failed."

The door flew open suddenly and Honoria rushed into the room.

"Father," she cried. At the sight of Max she stopped, hesitated, and then carried away by her excitement continued:

"Father – did you ever tell Russel how you proposed to Mother?"

"Why, let me see – yes, I think I did."

Honoria groaned.

"Well, he tried to use it again on me."

"What do you mean?"

"All these months I've been waiting" – she was almost in tears – "waiting to hear what he'd say. And then – when it came – it sounded *familiar* – as if I'd heard it before."

"It's probably one of my proposals," suggested Van Camp. "I've used so many."

She turned on him quickly.

"Do you mean to say you've ever proposed to any other girl but me?"

"Honoria – would you mind?"

"Mind. Of course I wouldn't mind. I'd never speak to you again as long as I lived."

"You say Codman proposed to you in the words I used to your mother?" demanded McComas.

"Exactly," she wailed. "He knew them by heart."

"That's the trouble with him," said McComas thoughtfully. "He always was my man and not his own. You'd better marry Max, here."

"Why..." she looked from one to the other, "why – I never knew you liked Max, Father. You never showed it."

"Well, that's just the difference," said her father, "between your way and mine."

The Love Boat

1

THE BOAT FLOATED DOWN THE RIVER through the summer night like a Fourth of July balloon footloose in the heavens. The decks were brightly lit and restless with dancers, but bow and stern were in darkness; so the boat had no more outline than an accidental cluster of stars. Between the black banks it floated, softly parting the mild dark tide from the sea and leaving in its wake small excited gusts of music – 'Babes in the Woods' over and over, and 'Moonlight Bay'.* Past the scattered lights of Pokus Landing, where a poet in an attic window saw yellow hair gleam in the turn of a dance. Past Ulm, where the moon came up out of a boiler works, and West Esther, where it slid, unregretted, behind a cloud.

The radiance of the boat itself was enough for, among others, the three young Harvard graduates; they were weary and a little depressed and they gave themselves up promptly to its enchantment. Their own boat was casually drifting and a collision was highly possible, but no one made a movement to start the engine and get out of the way.

"It makes me very sad," one of them said. "It is so beautiful that it makes me want to cry."

"Go on and cry, Bill."

"Will you cry too?"

"We'll all cry."

His loud, facetious "Boo-hoo!" echoed across the night, reached the steamer and brought a small lively crowd to the rail.

"Look! It's a launch."

"Some guys in a launch."

Bill got to his feet. The two crafts were scarcely ten feet apart.

266

"Throw us a hempen rope," he pleaded eloquently. "Come on – be impulsive. Please do."

Once in a hundred years there would have been a rope at hand. It was there that night. With a thud the coil struck the wooden bottom and in an instant the motorboat was darting along behind the steamer, as if in the wake of a harpooned whale.

Fifty high-school couples left the dance and scrambled for a place around the suddenly interesting stern rail. Fifty girls gave forth immemorial small cries of excitement and sham fright. Fifty young men forgot the mild exhibitionism which had characterized their manner of the evening and looked grudgingly at the more effectual show-off of three others. Mae Purley, without the involuntary quiver of an eyelash, fitted the young man standing in the boat into her current dream, where he displaced Al Fitzpatrick with laughable ease. She put her hand on Al Fitzpatrick's arm and squeezed it a little because she had stopped thinking about him entirely and felt that he must be aware of it. Al, who had been standing with his eyes squinted up, watching the towed boat, looked tenderly at Mae and tried to put his arm about her shoulder. But Mae Purley and Bill Frothington, handsome and full of all the passionate promise in the world, had locked eyes across the intervening space.

They made love. For a moment they made love as no one ever dares to do after. Their glance was closer than an embrace, more urgent than a call. There were no words for it. Had there been, and had Mae heard them, she would have fled to the darkest corner of the ladies' washroom and hid her face in a paper towel.

"We want to come on board!" Bill called. "We're life-preserver salesmen! How about pulling us around to the side?"

Mr McVitty, the Principal, arrived on the scene too late to interfere. The three young Harvard graduates – Ellsworth Ames soaking wet, unconsciously Byronic with his dark curls plastered damply to his forehead, Hamilton Abbot and Bill Frothington surer-footed and dry – climbed and were hoisted over the side. The motorboat bobbed on behind.

With a sort of instinctive reverence for the moment, Mae Purley hung back in the shadow, not through lack of confidence but through excess

THE LOVE BOAT AND OTHER STORIES

of it. She knew that he would come straight to her. That was never the trouble and never had been – the trouble was in keeping up her own interest after she had satisfied the deep but casual curiosity of her lips. But tonight was going to be different. She knew this when she saw that he was in no hurry; he was leaning against the rail making a couple of high-school seniors – who suddenly seemed very embryonic to themselves – feel at ease.

He looked at her once.

"It's all right," his eyes said, without a movement of his face, "I understand as well as you. I'll be there in just a minute."

Life burned high in them both; the steamer and its people were at a distance and in darkness. It was one of those times.

"I'm a Harvard man," Mr McVitty was saying, "class of 1907." The three young men nodded with polite indifference. "I'm glad to know we won the race,"* continued the Principal, simulating a reborn enthusiasm which had never existed. "I haven't been to New London in fifteen years."

"Bill here rowed Number Two," said Ames. "That's a coaching launch we've got."

"Oh. You were on the crew?"

"Crew's over now," said Bill impatiently. "Everything's over."

"Well, let me congratulate you."

Shortly they froze him into silence. They were not his sort of Harvard man; they wouldn't have known his name in four years there together. But they would have been much more gracious and polite about it had it not been this particular night. They hadn't broken away from the hilarious mobs of classmates and relatives at New London to exchange discomfort with the master of a mill-town high school.

"Can we dance?" they demanded.

A few minutes later Bill and Mae Purley were walking down the deck side by side. Life had met over the body of Al Fitzpatrick, engulfing him. The two clear voices:

"Perhaps you'll dance with me," with the soft assurance of the moonlight itself, and: "I'd love to," were nothing that could be argued about, not by twice what Al Fitzpatrick pretended to be. The most consoling thought in Al's head was that they might be fought over.

268

What was it they said? Did you hear it? Can you remember? Later that night she remembered only his pale wavy hair and the long limbs that she followed around the dancing floor.

She was thin, a thin burning flame, colourless yet fresh. Her smile came first slowly, then with a rush, pouring out of her heart, shy and bold, as if all the life of that little body had gathered for a moment around her mouth and the rest of her was a wisp that the least wind would blow away. She was a changeling whose lips alone had escaped metamorphosis, whose lips were the only point of contact with reality.

"Then you live near?"

"Only about twenty-five miles from you," Bill said. "Isn't it funny?"

"Isn't it funny?"

They looked at each other, a trifle awed in the face of such manifest destiny. They stood between two lifeboats on the top deck. Mae's hand lay on his arm, playing with a loose ravel of his tweed coat. They had not kissed yet – that was coming in a minute. That was coming any time now, as soon as every cup of emotional moonlight had been drained of its possibilities and cast aside. She was seventeen.

"Are you glad I live near?"

She might have said "I'm delighted" or "Of course I am." But she whispered, "Yes; are you?"

"Mae – with an *e*," he said and laughed in a husky whisper. Already they had a joke together. "You look so darn beautiful."

She accepted the compliment in silence, meeting his eyes. He pressed her to him by her merest elbow in a way that would have been impossible had she not been eager too. He never expected to see her after tonight.

"Mae." His whisper was urgent. Mae's eyes came nearer, grew larger, dissolved against his face, like eyes on a screen. Her frail body breathed imperceptibly in his arms.

A dance stopped. There was clapping for an encore. Then clapping for another encore with what had seemed only a poor bar of music in between. There was another dance, scarcely longer than a kiss. They were heavily endowed for love, these two, and both of them had played with it before.

Down below, Al Fitzpatrick's awareness of time and space had reached a pitch that would have been invaluable to an investigator of the new mathematics. Bit by bit the boat presented itself to him as it really was, a wooden hulk garish with forty-watt bulbs, peopled by the commonplace young people of a commonplace town. The river was water, the moon was a flat meaningless symbol in the sky. He was in agony – which is to speak tritely. Rather, he was in deadly fear; his throat was dry, his mouth drooped into a hurt half-moon as he tried to talk to some of the other boys – shy unhappy boys, who loitered around the stern.

Al was older than the rest – he was twenty-two, and out in the world for seven years. He worked in the Hammacker Mills and attended special high-school classes at night. Another year might see him assistant manager of the shops, and Mae Purley, with about as much eagerness as was to be expected in a girl who was having everything her own way, had half promised to marry him when she was eighteen. His wasn't a temperament to go to pieces. When he had brooded up to the limit of his nature he felt a necessity for action. Miserably and desperately he climbed up to the top deck to make trouble.

Bill and Mae were standing close together by the lifeboat, quiet, absorbed and happy. They moved a little apart as he came near. "Is that you, Mae?" called Al in a hard voice. "Aren't you going to come down and dance?"

"We were just coming."

They walked towards him in a trance.

"What's the idea?" Al said hoarsely. "You've been up here over two hours."

At their indifference he felt pain swelling and spreading inside him, constricting his breath.

"Have you met Mr Frothington?" She laughed shyly at the unfamiliar name.

"Yeah," said Al rudely. "I don't see the idea of his keeping you up here."

"I'm sorry," said Bill. "We didn't realize."

"Oh, you didn't? Well, I did." His jealousy cut through their absorption. They acknowledged it by an effort to hurry, to be impersonal, to defer to his wishes. Ungraciously he followed and the three of them came in a twinkling upon a scene that had suddenly materialized on the deck below.

Ellsworth Ames, smiling, but a little flushed, was leaning against the rail while Ham Abbot attempted to argue with a distraught young husky who kept trying to brush past him and get at Ames. Near them stood an indignant girl with another girl's soothing arm around her waist.

"What is it?" demanded Bill quickly.

The distraught young man glared at him. "Just a couple of snobs that come here and try to spoil everybody else's good time!" he cried wildly.

"He doesn't like me," said Ellsworth lightly. "I invited his girl to dance."

"She didn't want to dance with you!" shouted the other. "You think you're so damn smart – ask her if she wanted to dance with you."

The girl murmured indistinguishable words and disclaimed all responsibility by beginning to cry.

"You're too fresh, that's the trouble!" continued her defender. "I know what you said to her when you danced with her before. What do you think these girls are? They're just as good as anybody, see?"

Al Fitzpatrick moved in closer.

"Let's put 'em all off the boat," he suggested, stubborn and ashamed. "They haven't got any business butting in here."

A mild protest went up from the crowd, especially from the girls, and Abbot put his hand conciliatingly on the husky's shoulder. But it was too late.

"You'll put me off?" Ellsworth was saying coldly. "If you try to lay your hands on me I'll rearrange your whole face."

"Shut up, Ellie!" snapped Bill. "No use getting disagreeable. They don't want us; we'd better go." He stepped close to Mae, and whispered, "Goodnight. Don't forget what I said. I'll drive over and see you Sunday afternoon."

As he pressed her hand quickly and turned away he saw the argumentative boy swing suddenly at Ames, who caught the blow with his left arm. In a moment they were slugging and panting, knee to knee in the small space left by the gathering crowd. Simultaneously Bill felt a hand pluck at his sleeve and he turned to face Al Fitzpatrick. Then the deck was in an uproar. Abbot's attempt to separate Ames and his antagonist was misinterpreted; instantly he was involved in a battle of his own, cannonading against the other pairs, slipping on the smooth deck, bumping against non-combatants and scurrying girls who sent up shrill cries. He saw Al Fitzpatrick slap the deck suddenly with his whole body, not to rise again. He heard calls of "Get Mr McVitty!" and then his own opponent was dropped by a blow he did not strike, and Bill's voice said: "Come onto the boat!"

The next few minutes streaked by in wild confusion. Avoiding Bill, whose hammer-like arms had felled their two champions, the high-school boys tried to pull down Ham and Ellie, and the harassed group edged and revolved towards the stem rail.

"Hidden-ball stuff!" Bill panted. "Save it for Haughton. I'm G-Gardner, you're Bradlee and Mahan* – hip!"

Mr McVitty's alarmed face appeared above the combat, and his high voice, ineffectual at first, finally pierced the heat of battle.

"Aren't you ashamed of yourselves! Bob – Cecil – George Roberg! Let go, I say!"

Abruptly the battle was over and the combatants, breathing hard, eyed one another impassively in the moonlight.

Ellie laughed and held out a pack of cigarettes. Bill untied the motor-boat and walked forward with the painter to bring it alongside.

"They claim you insulted one of the girls," said Mr McVitty uncertainly. "Now that's no way to behave after we took you aboard."

"That's nonsense," snapped Ellie, between gasps. "I only told her I'd like to bite her neck."

"Do you think that was a very gentlemanly thing to say?" demanded Mr McVitty heatedly.

"Come on, Ellie!" Bill cried. "Goodbye, everybody! Sorry there was such a row!"

They were already shadows of the past as they slipped one by one over the rail. The girls were turning cautiously back to their own men, and not one of them answered, and not one of them waved farewell.

"A bunch of meanies," remarked Ellie ironically. "I wish all you ladies had one neck so I could bite it all at once. I'm a glutton for ladies' necks."

Feeble retorts went up here and there like muffled pistol shots.
"Goodnight, ladies,"* Ham sang, as Bill shoved away from the side:

> "Goodnight, ladies,
> Goodnight, ladies,
> We're going to leave you now-ow-ow."

The boat moved up the river through the summer night, while the launch, touched by its swell, rocked to and fro gently in the wide path of the moon.

2

O N THE FOLLOWING SUNDAY afternoon Bill Frothington drove over from Truro to the isolated rural slum known as Wheatly Village. He had stolen away from a house full of guests, assembled for his sister's wedding, to pursue what his mother would have called an "unworthy affair". But behind him lay an extremely successful career at Harvard and a youth somewhat more austere than the average, and this fall he would disappear for life into the banking house of Read, Hoppe and Company in Boston. He felt that the summer was his own. And had the purity of his intentions towards Mae Purley been questioned he would have defended himself with righteous anger. He had been thinking of her for five days. She attracted him violently, and he was following the attraction with eyes that did not ask to see.

Mae lived in the less offensive quarter of town on the third floor of its only apartment house, an unsuccessful relic of those more prosperous days of New England textile weaving that ended twenty years ago. Her father was a timekeeper who had fallen out of the white-collar class; Mae's two older brothers were working at the loom, and Bill's only impression as he entered the dingy flat was one of hopeless decay. The mountainous, soiled mother, at once suspicious and deferential, and the anaemic, beaten Anglo-Saxon asleep on the couch after his Sunday dinner were no more than shadows against the poor walls. But Mae was clean and fresh. No breath of squalor touched her. The pale pure youth of her cheeks, and her thin childish body shining through a new organdie dress, measured up full to the summer day.

"Where you going to take my little girl?" Mrs Purley asked anxiously.

"I'm going to run away with her," he said, laughing.

"Not with my little girl."

"Oh, yes, I am. I don't see why she hasn't been run away with before."

"Not my little girl."

They held hands going downstairs, but not for an hour did the feeling of being intimate strangers pass. When the first promise of evening blew into the air at five o'clock and the light changed from white to yellow, their eyes met once in a certain way and Bill knew that it was time. They turned up a side road and down a wagon track, and in a moment the spell was around them again – the equal and opposite urge that drew them together. They talked about each other and then their voices grew quiet and they kissed, while chestnut blossoms slid in white diagonals through the air and fell across the car. After a long while an instinct told her that they had stayed long enough. He drove her home.

It went on like that for two months. He would come for her in the late afternoon and they would go for dinner to the shore. Afterwards they would drive around until they found the centre of the summer night and park there while the enchanted silence spread over them like leaves over the babes in the wood. Someday, naturally, they were going to marry. For the present it was impossible; he must go to work in the fall. Vaguely and with more than a touch of sadness both of them realized that this wasn't true; that if Mae had been of another class an engagement would have been arranged at once. She knew that he lived in a great country house with a park and a caretaker's lodge, that there were stables full of cars and horses, and that house parties and dances took place there all summer. Once they had driven past the gate and Mae's heart was leaden in her breast as she saw that those wide acres would lie between them all her life.

On his part Bill knew that it was impossible to marry Mae Purley. He was an only son and he wore one of those New England names that are carried with one always. Eventually he broached the subject to his mother.

"It isn't her poverty and ignorance," his mother said, among other things. "It's her lack of any standards – common women are common for life. You'd see her impressed by cheap and shallow people, by cheap and shallow things."

"But, Mother, this isn't 1850. It isn't as if she were marrying into the royal family."

"If it were, it wouldn't matter. But you have a name that for many generations has stood for leadership and self-control. People who have given up less and taken fewer responsibilities have had nothing to say aloud when men like your father and your Uncle George and your Great-grandfather Frothington held their heads high. Toss your pride away and see what you've left at thirty-five to take you through the rest of your life."

"But you can only live once," he protested – knowing, nevertheless, that what she said was, for him, right. His youth had been pointed to make him understand that exposition of superiority. He knew what it was to be the best, at home, at school, at Harvard. In his senior year he had known men to dodge behind a building and wait in order to walk with him across the Harvard Yard, not to be seen with him out of mere poor snobbishness, but to get something intangible, something he carried within him of the less obvious, less articulate experience of the race.

Several days later he went to see Mae and met her coming out of the flat. They sat on the stairs in the half-darkness.

"Just think of these stairs," he said huskily. "Think how many times you've kissed me on these stairs. At night when I've brought you home. On every landing. Last month when we walked up and down together five times before we could say goodnight."

"I hate these stairs. I wish I never had to go up them any more."

"Oh, Mae, what are we doing to do?"

She didn't answer for a moment. "I've been thinking a lot these last three days," she said. "I don't think it's fair to myself to go on like this – or to Al."

"To Al," he said startled. "Have you been seeing Al?"

"We had a long talk last night."

"Al!" he repeated incredulously.

"He wants to get married. He isn't mad any more."

Bill tried suddenly to face the situation he had been dodging for two months, but the situation, with practised facility, slid around the corner. He moved up a step till he was beside Mae, and put his arm around her.

"Oh, let's get married!" she cried desperately. "You can. If you want to, you can."

"I do want to."

"Then why can't we?"

"We can, but not yet."

"Oh, God, you've said that before."

For a tragic week they quarrelled and came together over the bodies of unresolved arguments and irreconcilable facts. They parted finally on a trivial question as to whether he had once kept her waiting half an hour.

Bill went to Europe on the first possible boat and enlisted in an ambulance unit. When America went into the war he transferred to the aviation and Mae's pale face and burning lips faded off, faded out, against the wild dark background of the war.

3

IN 1919 BILL FELL ROMANTICALLY IN LOVE with a girl of his own set. He met her on the Lido and wooed her on golf courses and in fashionable speakeasies and in cars parked at night, loving her much more from the first than he had ever loved Mae. She was a better person, prettier and more intelligent and with a kindlier heart. She loved him; they had much the same tastes and more than ample money.

There was a child, after a while there were four children, then only three again. Bill grew a little stout after thirty, as athletes will. He was always going to take up something strenuous and get into real condition. He worked hard and drank a little too freely every weekend. Later he inherited the country house and lived there in the summer.

When he and Stella had been married eight years they felt safe for each other, safe from the catastrophes that had overtaken the majority of their friends. To Stella this brought relief; Bill, once he had accepted the idea of their safety, was conscious of a certain discontent, a sort of chemical restlessness. With a feeling of disloyalty to Stella, he shyly sounded his friends on the subject and found that in men of his age the symptoms were almost universal. Some blamed it on the war: "There'll never be anything like the war."

It was not variety of woman that he wanted. The mere idea appalled him. There were always women around. If he took a fancy to someone Stella invited her for a weekend, and men who liked Stella fraternally, or even somewhat sentimentally, were as often in the house. But the feeling persisted and grew stronger. Sometimes it would steal over him at dinner – a vast nostalgia – and the people at table would fade out and odd memories of his youth would come back to him. Sometimes a familiar taste or a smell would give him this sensation. Chiefly it had to do with the summer night.

One evening, walking down the lawn with Stella after dinner, the feeling seemed so close that he could almost grasp it. It was in the rustle of the pines, in the wind, in the gardener's radio down behind the tennis court.

"Tomorrow," Stella said, "there'll be a full moon."

She had stopped in a broad path of moonlight and was looking at him. Her hair was pale and lovely in the gentle light. She regarded him for a moment oddly, and he took a step forward as if to put his arms around her; then he stopped, unresponsive and dissatisfied. Stella's expression changed slightly and they walked on.

"That's too bad," he said suddenly. "Because tomorrow I've got to go away."

"Where?"

"To New York. Meeting of the trustees of school. Now that the kids are entered I feel I should."

"You'll be back Sunday?"

"Unless something comes up and I telephone."

"Ad Haughton's coming Sunday, and maybe the Ameses."

"I'm glad you won't be alone."

Suddenly Bill had remembered the boat floating down the river and Mae Purley on the deck under the summer moon. The image became a symbol of his youth, his introduction to life. Not only did he remember the deep excitement of that night but felt it again, her face against his, the rush of air about them as they stood by the lifeboat and the feel of its canvas cover to his hand.

When his car dropped him at Wheatly Village next afternoon he experienced a sensation of fright. Eleven years – she might be dead; quite possibly she had moved away. Any moment he might pass her on the street, a tired, already faded woman pushing a baby carriage and leading an extra child.

"I'm looking for a Miss Mae Purley," he said to a taxi driver. "It might be Fitzpatrick now."

"Fitzpatrick up at the works?"

Enquiries within the station established the fact that Mae Purley was indeed Mrs Fitzpatrick. They lived just outside of town.

Ten minutes later the taxi stopped before a white colonial house.

"They made it over from a barn," volunteered the taxi man. "There was a picture of it in one of them magazines."

Bill saw that someone was regarding him from behind the screen door. It was Mae. The door opened slowly and she stood in the hall, unchanged, slender as of old. Instinctively he raised his arms and then, as he took another step forward, instinctively he lowered them.

"Mae."

"Bill."

She was there. For a moment he possessed her, her frailty, her thin smouldering beauty; then he had lost her again. He could no more have embraced her than he could have embraced a stranger.

On the sun porch they stared at each other. "You haven't changed," they said together.

It was gone from her. Words, casual, trivial and insincere, poured from her mouth as if to fill the sudden vacancy in his heart:

"Imagine seeing you – know you anywhere – thought you'd forgotten me – talking about you only the other night."

Suddenly he was without any inspiration. His mind became an utter blank, and try as he might, he could summon up no attitude to fill it.

"It's a nice place you have here," he said stupidly.

"We like it. You'd never guess it, but we made it out of an old barn."

"The taxi driver told me."

"...stood here for a hundred years empty – got it for almost nothing – pictures of it before and after in *Home and Country Side*."

Without warning his mind went blank again. What was the matter? Was he sick? He had even forgotten why he was here.

He knew only that he was smiling benevolently and that he must hang on to that smile, for if it passed he could never recreate it. What did it mean when one's mind went blank? He must see a doctor tomorrow.

"…since Al's done so well. Of course Mr Kohlsatt leans on him, so he don't get away much. I get away to New York sometimes. Sometimes we both get away together."

"Well, you certainly have a nice place here," he said desperately. He must see a doctor in the morning. Dr Flynn or Dr Keyes or Dr Given who was at Harvard with him. Or perhaps that specialist who was recommended to him by that woman at the Ameses'; or Dr Gross or Dr Studeford or Dr de Martel…

"…I never touch it, but Al always keeps something in the house. Al's gone to Boston, but I think I can find the key."

…or Dr Ramsay or old Dr Ogden, who had brought him into the world. He hadn't realized that he knew so many doctors. He must make a list.

"…you're just exactly the same."

Suddenly Bill put both hands on his stomach, gave a short coarse laugh and said, "Not here." His own act startled and surprised him, but it dissipated the blankness for a moment and he began to gather up the pieces of his afternoon. From her chatter he discovered her to be under the impression that in some vague and sentimental past she had thrown him over. Perhaps she was right. Who was she anyhow – this hard, commonplace article wearing Mae's body for a mask of life? Defiance rose in him.

"Mae, I've been thinking about that boat," he said desperately.

"What boat?"

"The steamboat on the Thames, Mae. I don't think we should let ourselves get old. Get your hat, Mae. Let's go for a boat ride tonight."

"But I don't see the point," she protested. "Do you think just riding on a boat keeps people young? Maybe if it was salt water—"

"Don't you remember that night on the boat?" he said, as if he were talking to a child. "That's how we met. Two months later you threw me over and married Al Fitzpatrick."

"But I didn't marry Al then," she said. "It wasn't till two years later when he got a job as superintendent. There was a Harvard man I used to go around with that I almost married. He knew you. His name was Abbot – Ham Abbot."

"Ham Abbot – you saw him again?"

"We went around for almost a year. I remember Al was wild. He said if I had any more Harvard men around he'd shoot them. But there wasn't anything wrong with it. Ham was just cuckoo about me and I used to let him rave."

Bill had read somewhere that every seven years a change is completed in the individual that makes him different from his self of seven years ago. He clung to the idea desperately. Dimly he saw this person pouring him an enormous glass of applejack, dimly he gulped it down and, through a description of the house, fought his way to the front door.

"Notice the original beams. The beams were what we liked best…" She broke off suddenly. "I remember now about the boat. You were in a launch and you got on board with Ham Abbot that night."

The applejack was strong. Evidently it was fragrant also, for as they started off, the taxi driver volunteered to show him where the gentleman could get some more. He would give him a personal introduction in a place down by the wharf.

Bill sat at a dingy table behind swinging doors and, while the sun went down behind the Thames, disposed of four more applejacks. Then he remembered that he was keeping the taxi waiting. Outside a boy told him that the driver had gone home to supper and would be back in half an hour.

He sauntered over to a bale of goods and sat down, watching the mild activity of the docks. It was dusk presently. Stevedores appeared momentarily against the lighted hold of a barge and jerked quickly out of sight down an invisible incline. Next to the barge lay a steamer and people were going aboard; first a few people and then an increasing crowd. There was a breeze in the air and the moon came up rosy gold with a haze around.

Someone ran into him precipitately in the darkness, tripped, swore and staggered to his feet.

"I'm sorry," said Bill cheerfully. "Hurt yourself?"

"Pardon me," stuttered the young man. "Did I hurt you?"

"Not at all. Here, have a light."

They touched cigarettes.

"Where's the boat going?"

"Just down the river. It's the high-school picnic tonight."

"What?"

"The Wheatly High School picnic. The boat goes down to Groton, then it turns around and comes back."

Bill thought quickly. "Who's the principal of the high school?"

"Mr McVitty." The young man fidgeted impatiently. "So long, bud. I got to go aboard."

"Me too," whispered Bill to himself. "Me too."

Still he sat there lazily for a moment, listening to the sounds clear and distinct now from the open deck: the high echolalia of the girls, the boys calling significant but obscure jokes to one another across the night. He was feeling fine. The air seemed to have distributed the applejack to all the rusty and unused corners of his body. He bought another pint, stowed it in his hip pocket and walked on board with all the satisfaction, the insouciance of a transatlantic traveller.

A girl standing in a group near the gangplank raised her eyes to him as he went past. She was slight and fair. Her mouth curved down and then broke upward as she smiled, half at him, half at the man beside her. Someone made a remark and the group laughed. Once again her glance slipped sideways and met his for an instant as he passed by.

Mr McVitty was on the top deck with half a dozen other teachers, who moved aside at Bill's breezy approach.

"Good evening, Mr McVitty. You don't remember me."

"I'm afraid I don't, sir." The Principal regarded him with tentative noncommittal eyes.

"Yet I took a trip with you on this same boat, exactly eleven years ago tonight."

"This boat, sir, was only built last year."

"Well, a boat like it," said Bill. "I wouldn't have known the difference myself."

Mr McVitty made no reply. After a moment Bill continued confidently, "We found that night that we were both sons of John Harvard."

"Yes?"

"In fact on that very day I had been pulling an oar against what I might refer to as dear old Yale."

Mr McVitty's eyes narrowed. He came closer to Bill and his nose wrinkled slightly.

"Old Eli," said Bill, "in fact, Eli Yale."

"I see," said Mr McVitty dryly. "And what can I do for you tonight?"

Someone came up with a question and in the enforced silence it occurred to Bill that he was present on the slightest of all pretexts – a previous and unacknowledged acquaintance. He was relieved when a dull rumble and a quiver of the deck indicated that they had left the shore.

Mr McVitty, disengaged, turned towards him with a slight frown. "I seem to remember you now," he said. "We took three of you aboard from a motorboat and we let you dance. Unfortunately the evening ended in a fight."

Bill hesitated. In eleven years his relation to Mr McVitty had somehow changed. He recalled Mr McVitty as a more negligible, more easily dealt-with person. There had been no such painful difficulties before.

"Perhaps you wonder how I happen to be here?" he suggested mildly.

"To be frank, I do, Mr…"

"Frothington," supplied Bill, and he added brazenly, "It's rather a sentimental excursion for me. My greatest romance began on the evening you speak of. That was when I first met – my wife."

Mr McVitty's attention was caught at last. "You married one of our girls?"

Bill nodded. "That's why I wanted to take this trip tonight."

"Your wife's with you?"

"No."

"I don't understand…" He broke off, and suggested gently, "Or maybe I do. Your wife is dead?"

After a moment Bill nodded. Somewhat to his surprise two great tears rolled suddenly down his face.

Mr McVitty put his hand on Bill's shoulder. "I'm sorry," he said. "I understand your feeling, Mr Frothington, and I respect it. Please make yourself at home."

After a nibble at his bottle Bill stood in the door of the salon watching the dance. It might have been eleven years ago. There were the high-school characters that he and Ham and Ellie had laughed at afterwards – the fat boy who surely played centre on the football team and the adolescent hero with the pompadour and the blatant good manners, president of his class. The pretty girl who had looked at him by the gangplank danced past him, and with a quick lift of his heart he placed her, too; her confidence and the wide but careful distribution of her favours – she was the popular girl, as Mae had been eleven years before.

Next time she went past he touched the shoulder of the boy she was dancing with. "May I have some of this?" he said.

"What?" her partner gasped.

"May I have some of this dance?"

The boy stared at him without relinquishing his hold.

"Oh, it's all right, Red," she said impatiently. "That's the way they do now."

Red stepped sulkily aside. Bill bent his arm as nearly as he could into the tortuous clasp that they were all using, and started.

"I saw you talking to Mr McVitty," said the girl, looking up into his face with a bright smile. "I don't know you, but I guess it's all right."

"I saw you before that."

"When?"

"Getting on the boat."

"I don't remember."

"What's your name?" he asked.

"May Schaffer. What's the matter?"

"Do you spell it with an *e*?"

"No; why?"

A quartet of boys had edged towards them. One of its members suddenly shot out as if propelled from inside the group and bumped awkwardly against Bill.

"Can I have part of this dance?" asked the boy with a sort of giggle.

Without enthusiasm Bill let go. When the next dance began he cut in again. She was lovely. Her happiness in herself, in the evening, would have transfigured a less pretty girl. He wanted to talk to her alone and was about to suggest that they go outside when there was a repetition of what had happened before – a young man was apparently shot by force from a group to Bill's side.

"Can I have part of this dance?"

Bill joined Mr McVitty by the rail. "Pleasant evening," he remarked. "Don't you dance?"

"I enjoy dancing," said Mr McVitty; and he added pointedly, "In my position it doesn't seem quite the thing to dance with young girls."

"That's nonsense," said Bill pleasantly. "Have a drink?"

Mr McVitty walked suddenly away.

When he danced with May again he was cut in on almost immediately. People were cutting in all over the floor now – evidently he had started something. He cut back, and again he started to suggest that they go outside, but he saw that her attention was held by some horseplay going on across the room.

"I got a swell love nest up in the Bronx," somebody was saying.

"Won't you come outside?" said Bill. "There's the most wonderful moon."

"I'd rather dance."

"We could dance out there."

She leant away from him and looked up with innocent scorn into his eyes.

"Where'd you get it?" she said.

"Get what?"

"All the happiness."

Before he could answer, someone cut in. For a moment he imagined that the boy had said, "Part of this dance, Daddy?" but his annoyance at May's indifference drove the idea from his mind. Next time he went to the point at once.

"I live near here," he said. "I'd be awfully pleased if I could call and drive you over for a weekend sometime."

"What?" she asked vaguely. Again she was listening to a miniature farce being staged in the corner.

"My wife would like so much to have you," went on Bill. Great dreams of what he could do for this girl for old times' sake rose in his mind.

Her head swung towards him curiously. "Why, Mr McVitty told somebody your wife was dead."

"She isn't," said Bill.

Out of the corner of his eye he saw the inevitable catapult coming and danced quickly away from it.

A voice rang out: "Just look at old daddy step."

"Ask him if I can have some of this dance."

Afterwards Bill only remembered the evening up to that point. A crowd swirled around him and someone kept demanding persistently who was a young boiler maker.

He decided, naturally enough, to teach them a lesson, as he had done before, and he told them so. Then there was a long discussion as to whether he could swim. After that the confusion deepened; there were blows and a short sharp struggle. He picked up the story himself in what must have been several minutes later, when his head emerged from the cool waters of the Thames River.

The river was white with the moon, which had changed from rosy gold to a wafer of shining cheese on high. It was some time before he could locate the direction of the shore, but he moved around unworried in the water. The boat was a mere speck now, far down the river, and he laughed to think how little it all mattered, how little anything mattered. Then, feeling sure that he had his wind and wondering if the taxi was still waiting at Wheatly Village, he struck out for the dark shore.

4

H E WAS WORRIED AS HE DREW near home next afternoon, pos- sessed of a dark, unfounded fear. It was based, of course, on his own silly transgression. Stella would somehow hear of it. In his reaction from the debonair confidence of last night, it seemed inevitable that Stella would hear of it.

"Who's here?" he asked the butler immediately.

"No one, sir. The Ameses came about an hour ago, but there was no word, so they went on. They said—"

"Isn't my wife here?"

"Mrs Frothington left yesterday just after you."

The whips of panic descended upon him.

"How long after me?"

"Almost immediately, sir. The telephone rang and she answered it, and almost immediately she had her bag packed and left the house."

"Mr Ad Haughton didn't come?"

"I haven't seen Mr Haughton."

It had happened. The spirit of adventure had seized Stella too. He knew that her life had been not without a certain pressure from sentimental men, but that she would ever go anywhere without telling him...

He threw himself face downward on a couch. What had happened? He had never meant things to happen. Was that what she had meant when she had looked at him in that peculiar way the other night?

He went upstairs. Almost as soon as he entered the big bedroom he saw the note, written on blue stationery lest he miss it against the white pillow. In his misery an old counsel of his mother's came back to him: "The more terrible things seem the more you've got to keep yourself in shape."

Trembling, he divested himself of his clothes, turned on a bath and lathered his face. Then he poured himself a drink and shaved. It was like a dream, this change in his life. She was no longer his; even if she came back she was no longer his. Everything was different – this room, himself, everything that had existed yesterday. Suddenly he wanted it back. He got out of the bathtub and knelt down on the bath mat beside it and prayed. He prayed for Stella and himself and Ad Haughton; he prayed crazily for the restoration of his life – the life that he had just as crazily cut in two. When he came out of the bathroom with a towel around him, Ad Haughton was sitting on the bed.

"Hello, Bill. Where's your wife?"

"Just a minute," Bill answered. He went back into the bathroom and swallowed a draught of rubbing alcohol guaranteed to produce violent gastric disturbances. Then he stuck his head out of the door casually.

"Mouthful of gargle," he explained. "How are you, Ad? Open that envelope on the pillow and we'll see where she is."

"She's gone to Europe with a dentist. Or rather her dentist is going to Europe, so she had to dash to New York…"

He hardly heard. His mind, released from worry, had drifted off again. There would be a full moon tonight, or almost a full moon. Something had happened under a full moon once. What it was he was unable for the moment to remember.

His long, lanky body, his little lost soul in the universe, sat there on the bathroom window seat.

"I'm probably the world's worst guy," he said, shaking his head at himself in the mirror – "probably the world's worst guy. But I can't help it. At my age you can't fight against what you know you are."

Trying his best to be better, he sat there faithfully for an hour. Then it was twilight and there were voices downstairs, and suddenly there it was, in the sky over his lawn, all the restless longing after fleeing youth in all the world – the bright uncapturable moon.

Note on the Texts

The text of 'The Smilers' is based on the version published in *Smart Set* (June 1929). The text of 'Myra Meets His Family' is based on the version published in the *Saturday Evening Post* (20th March 1920). The text of 'Two for a Cent' is based on the version published in *Metropolitan* (April 1922). The text of 'Dice, Brassknuckles and Guitar' is based on the version published in *Hearst's International* (May 1923). The text of 'Diamond Dick and the First Law of Woman' is based on the version published in *Hearst's International* (April 1924). The text of 'The Third Casket' is based on the version published in the *Saturday Evening Post* (31st May 1924). The text of 'The Unspeakable Egg' is based on the version published in the *Saturday Evening Post* (12th July 1924). The text of 'John Jackson's Arcady' is based on the version published in the *Saturday Evening Post* (26th July 1924). The text of 'The Pusher-in-the-Face' is based on the version published in *Woman's Home Companion* (February 1925). The text of 'One of My Oldest Friends' is based on the version published in *Woman's Home Companion* (September 1925). The text of 'Not in the Guidebook' is based on the version published in *Woman's Home Companion* (November 1925). The text of 'Presumption' is based on the version published in the *Saturday Evening Post* (9th January 1926). The text of 'The Adolescent Marriage' is based on the version published in the *Saturday Evening Post* (6th March 1926). The text of 'Your Way and Mine' is based on the version published in *Woman's Home Companion* (May 1927). The text of 'The Love Boat' is based on the version published in the *Saturday Evening Post* (8th October 1927). The spelling and punctuation have been Anglicized, standardized, modernized and made consistent throughout.

Notes

p. 6, *'Smile, Smile, Smile' or 'The Smiles That You Gave to Me'*: 'Smile, Smile, Smile' probably refers to the First World War marching song 'Pack Up Your Troubles in Your Old Kit Bag, and Smile,

Smile, Smile', originally by Welsh songwriters George Henry Powell (1880–1951) and Felix Powell (1878–1942), which featured in the Broadway show *Her Soldier Boy* (1916). 'The Smiles That You Gave to Me' refers to the song 'Smiles' by Lee S. Roberts (1884–1949), with lyrics by J. Will Callahan (1874–1946), which originally featured as part of the Broadway musical revue *The Passing Show of 1918*.

p. 6, *four bits*: A bit is one-eighth of a dollar. Four bits is therefore fifty cents.

p. 12, *the Biltmore lobby*: The Biltmore was a luxury hotel in New York City.

p. 13, *Kelly Field*: A US airbase in San Antonio, Texas.

p. 17, *flivver*: A cheap car.

p. 22, *tonneau*: The rear part of an open motor car.

p. 30, *supes*: Supernumeraries; theatrical extras.

p. 41, *'Dixie'*: A marching song sung by Confederate soldiers during the American Civil War.

p. 42, *jelly beans*: "Jelly bean" was a slang term for an idler.

p. 49, *surrey*: A four-wheeled carriage with two seats.

p. 52, *Mrs Humphry Ward*: Mary Augusta Ward (1851–1920), who wrote under the name Mrs Humphry Ward, was a British novelist who enjoyed great success with novels like *Robert Elsmere* (1888), which engaged with contemporary debates within the Anglican Church and advocated social activism and support for the poor.

p. 53, *motometer*: An instrument counting an engine's revolutions.

p. 53, *Tarleton, Ga.*: Fitzgerald wrote three stories set in the Georgian town of Tarleton: 'The Ice Palace' (1920), 'The Jelly Bean' (1920), which, like this story, features a character called Jim Powell, and 'The Last of the Belles' (1929).

p. 55, *the Adirondacks, the Thousand Islands, Newport*: The Adirondacks are a mountain range in Upstate New York. The Thousand Islands are an archipelago of around 1,500 islands in the St Lawrence River between the Canadian province of Ontario and the US state of New York. Newport is a city on Aquidneck Island in the north-eastern state of Rhode Island.

p. 65, *sub-deb dance*: That is, a dance for sub-debutantes, teenage girls not yet old enough to be formally presented to fashionable society.

p. 73, *porte-cochère*: A gateway for carriages.

p. 77, *Diamond Dick!*: The cowboy hero of a large number of serialized stories and dime novels set in the American West published from 1878 onwards. The earliest stories were by William B. Schwartz.

p. 78, *an apache slouch*: An "apache" was a Parisian street ruffian.

p. 79, *'Beale Street Blues'*: A 1916 song by the US musician William Christopher Handy (1873–1958), who is considered the "father of the blues".

p. 83, *the Sound*: Long Island Sound, an estuary of the Atlantic lying between the coast of New York State and Connecticut to the north and Long Island to the south. Associated with wealth, the Sound includes a number of highly exclusive neighbourhoods.

p. 88, *A blackamoor was two-timing the lady... the colour of pale cinnamon*: Presumably a song by the ragtime and early jazz composer Ferdinand Joseph LaMothe (1890–1941), better known by his professional name Jelly Roll Morton ("jelly roll" being vulgar slang for the female genitalia), whose lyrics were often self-referential.

p. 97, *Telamonian Ajax*: In Greek mythology, Ajax, hero of the Trojan War, was the son of Telamon.

p. 111, *could introduce Mr Trotsky to Mr Rockefeller and there wouldn't be a single blow*: The point being that the former, the Russian revolutionary Leon Trotsky (1879–1940), and the latter, the US industrialist John D. Rockefeller (1839–1937), represent opposing ideologies (Marxism and capitalism respectively).

p. 121, *The Sheik*: A novel by the British author Edith Maud Hull (1880–1947), published in 1921, about a young, upper-class woman who is abducted and then repeatedly raped by an Arab sheikh, with whom she nevertheless falls in love.

p. 121, *Little Lord Fauntleroy*: A children's novel by the British-born US author Frances Hodgson Burnett (1849–1924), published in 1885–86, about a poor New York boy who unexpectedly becomes the heir to a British earldom.

p. 156, *the Island*: Rikers Island, New York City's main prison, located in the East River between the Bronx and Queens.

p. 178, *a man named Gerbert... the whole of European civilization*: A reference to Gerbert of Aurillac (*c*.945–1003), who became Pope Sylvester II (999–1003) and was renowned for his scholarship.

p. 181, *Lafayette-love-Washington*: A reference to the close friendship between George Washington (1732–99), commander-in-chief of the Continental Army during the War of American Independence in 1775–83 (who would go on to be the first president of the United States), and the French statesman Gilbert du Motier, Marquis de Lafayette (1757–1834), who fought with the colonists during the conflict. Lafayette claimed that Washington was the father he had never known.

p. 188, *Voleurs!*: "Thieves!" (French).

p. 189, *the Tuileries*: A public garden in Paris.

p. 190, *rubberneck wagon*: A sightseeing bus.

p. 190, *Mr Carnegie*: The Scottish-born US steel magnate and philanthropist Andrew Carnegie (1835–1919).

p. 190, *Landru, the Bluebeard of France, had murdered his fourteen wives*: The French serial killer Henri Désiré Landru (1869–1922) murdered ten women over a period of five years, after seducing them and embezzling their financial assets.

p. 190, *Louie's girl and Louie's wife*: Respectively, Jeanne Bécu, comtesse du Barry (1743–93), chief mistress of Louis XV (1710–74), and Marie Leszczyńska (1703–68), who was married to King Louis in 1725.

p. 193, *kale*: A US slang term for money.

p. 194, *bijoutier*: "Jeweller" (French).

p. 195, *the little village of Château-Thierry... five years before*: The Battle of Château-Thierry, a commune in the Aisne *département* of the Picardy region of northern France, was fought on 18th July 1918. It was one of the first battles in the First World War to involve the American forces, who had entered the conflict in 1917.

p. 200, *the Battle of San Juan Hill*: Fought on 1st July 1898 near the city of Santiago de Cuba, Cuba. It was part of the Spanish-American War (1898), which occurred following the US intervention in the Cuban

War of Independence (1895–98), and resulted in a US and Cuban victory over the Spanish.

p. 200, *Kenesaw Mountain Landis*: The US federal judge Kenesaw Mountain Landis (1866–1944) was named after the Battle of Kenesaw Mountain of 27th June 1864, during the American Civil War, at which his father had fought on the side of the Union.

p. 202, *DKE*: Delta Kappa Epsilon, a college fraternity founded at Yale in 1844.

p. 209, *Akron*: The "small Ohio city" referred to earlier.

p. 222, *Back Bay*: An exclusive residential neighbourhood of Boston.

p. 223, *bien soignée*: "Well turned out" (French).

p. 238, *Rudolf Rassendyll*: The hero of the swashbuckling adventure novel *The Prisoner of Zenda* (1894) by the English author Anthony Hope (1863–1933).

p. 260, *beat her with a riding crop like the heroes of Ethel M. Dell*: The melodramatic romance novels of the British writer Ethel M. Dell (1881–1939) were peopled by stock characters including overbearing, macho heroes and shy, submissive women.

p. 266, *'Babes in the Woods'… 'Moonlight Bay'*: 'Babes in the Wood' (1915) is a song with music by Jerome Kern (1885–1945) and lyrics by Schuyler Greene, originally included in the Broadway musical *Very Good Eddie* (1915). 'Moonlight Bay' (1912) is a song with music by Percy Wenrich (1887–1952) and lyrics by Edward Madden (1878–1952).

p. 268, *the race*: The Harvard-Yale Regatta, an annual rowing race between the two universities, which began in 1852. Since 1878 the race has taken place on the Thames River, near New London, Connecticut.

p. 272, *Save it for Haughton. I'm G-Gardner, you're Bradlee and Mahan*: Percy Duncan Haughton (1876–1924) was head football coach at Harvard from 1908 and 1916. Henry Burchell Gardner, Frederick Bradlee (1892–1970) and Eddie Mahan (1892–1975) all played in the Harvard team during this period.

p. 273, *Goodnight, ladies*: A folk song attributed to the US composer Edwin Pearce Christy (1815–62) and originally sung as part of a minstrel show.

Extra Material

on

F. Scott Fitzgerald's

*The Love Boat
and
Other Stories*

F. Scott Fitzgerald's Life

Francis Scott Key Fitzgerald was born on 24th September 1896 at 481 Laurel Avenue in St Paul, Minnesota. Fitzgerald, who would always be known as "Scott", was named after Francis Scott Key, the author of 'The Star-Spangled Banner' and his father's second cousin three times removed. His mother, Mary "Mollie" McQuillan, was born in 1860 in one of St Paul's wealthier streets, and would come into a modest inheritance at the death of her father in 1877. His father, Edward Fitzgerald, was born in 1853 near Rockville, Maryland. A wicker-furniture manufacturer at the time of Fitzgerald's birth, his business would collapse in 1898 and he would then take to the road as a wholesale grocery salesman for Procter & Gamble. This change of job necessitated various moves of home and the family initially shifted east to Buffalo, New York, in 1898, and then on to Syracuse, New York, in 1901. By 1903 they were back in Buffalo and in March 1908 they were in St Paul again after Edward lost his job at Procter & Gamble. The *déclassé* Fitzgeralds would initially live with the McQuillans and then moved into a series of rented houses, settling down at 599 Summit Avenue.

Early Life

This itinerancy would disrupt Fitzgerald's early schooling, isolating him and making it difficult to make many friends at his various schools in Buffalo, Syracuse and St Paul. The first one at which Fitzgerald would settle for a prolonged period was the St Paul Academy, which he entered in September 1908. It was here that Fitzgerald would achieve his first appearance in print, 'The Mystery of the Raymond Mortgage', which appeared in the St Paul Academy school magazine *Now and Then* in October 1909. 'Reade, Substitute Right Half' and 'A Debt of Honor' would follow in the February and March 1910 numbers, and 'The Room with the Green Blinds' in the June 1911 number. His reading at this time was dominated by adventure stories and the other typical literary interests of a turn-of-the-century American teen, with the novels of G.A. Henty, Walter Scott's *Ivanhoe* and Jane Porter's *The Scottish Chiefs* among his favourites; their influence was apparent in the floridly melodramatic tone of his early pieces, though themes that would recur throughout Fitzgerald's mature fiction, such as the social difficulties of the outsider, would be

Schooling and Early Writings

introduced in these stories. An interest in the theatre also surfaced at this time, with Fitzgerald writing and taking the lead role in *The Girl from Lazy J*, a play that would be performed with a local amateur-dramatic group, the Elizabethan Drama Club, in August 1911. The group would also produce *The Captured Shadow* in 1912, *The Coward* in 1913 and *Assorted Spirits* in 1914.

At the end of the summer of 1911, Fitzgerald was once again uprooted (in response to poor academic achievements) and moved to the Newman School, a private Catholic school in Hackensack, New Jersey. He was singularly unpopular with the other boys, who considered him aloof and overbearing. This period as a social pariah at Newman was a defining time for Fitzgerald, one that would be echoed repeatedly in his fiction, most straightforwardly in the "Basil" stories, the most famous of which, 'The Freshest Boy', would appear in *The Saturday Evening Post* in July 1928 and is clearly autobiographical in its depiction of a boastful schoolboy's social exclusion.

Hackensack had, however, the advantage of proximity to New York City, and Fitzgerald began to get to know Manhattan, visiting a series of shows, including *The Quaker Girl* and *Little Boy Blue*. His first publication in Newman's school magazine, *The Newman News*, was 'Football', a poem written in an attempt to appease his peers following a traumatic incident on the football field that led to widespread accusation of cowardice, compounding the young writer's isolation. In his last year at Newman he would publish three stories in *The Newman News*.

Father Fay and the Catholic Influence

Also in that last academic year Fitzgerald would encounter the prominent Catholic priest Father Cyril Sigourney Webster Fay, a lasting and formative connection that would influence the author's character, oeuvre and career. Father Fay introduced Fitzgerald to such figures as Henry Adams and encouraged the young writer towards the aesthetic and moral understanding that underpins all of his work. In spite of the licence and debauchery for which Fitzgerald's life and work are often read, a strong moral sense informs all of his fiction – a sense that can be readily traced to Fay and the author's Catholic schooling at Newman. Fay would later appear in thinly disguised form as Amory Blaine's spiritual mentor, and man of the world, Monsignor Darcy, in *This Side of Paradise*.

Princeton

Fitzgerald's academic performance was little improved at Newman, and he would fail four courses in his two years there. In spite of this, in May 1913 Fitzgerald took the entrance exams for Princeton, the preferred destination for Catholic undergraduates in New Jersey. He would go up in September 1913, his fees paid for through a legacy left by his grandmother Louisa McQuillan, who had died in August.

At Princeton Fitzgerald would begin to work in earnest on the process of turning himself into an author: in his first year he met confrères and future collaborators John Peale Bishop and Edmund Wilson. During his freshman year Fitzgerald won a competition to write the book and lyrics for the 1914–15 Triangle Club (the Princeton dramatic society) production *Fie! Fie! Fi-Fi!* He would also co-author, with Wilson, the 1915–16 production, *The Evil Eye*, and the lyrics for *Safety First*, the 1916–17 offering. He also quickly began to contribute to the Princeton humour magazine *The Princeton Tiger*, while his reading tastes had moved on to the social concerns of George Bernard Shaw, Compton Mackenzie and H.G. Wells. His social progress at Princeton also seemed assured as Fitzgerald was approached by the Cottage Club (one of Princeton's exclusive eating clubs) and prominence in the Triangle Club seemed inevitable.

September 1914 and the beginning of Fitzgerald's sophomore year would mark the great calamity of his Princeton education, causing a trauma that Fitzgerald would approach variously in his writing (notably in *This Side of Paradise* and Gatsby's abortive "Oxford" career in *The Great Gatsby*). Poor academic performance meant that Fitzgerald was barred from extra-curricular activities; he was therefore unable to perform in *Fie! Fie! Fi-Fi!*, and took to the road with the production in an attendant capacity. Fitzgerald's progress at the Triangle and Cottage clubs stagnated (he made Secretary at Triangle nonetheless, but did not reach the heights he had imagined for himself), and his hopes of social dominance on campus were dashed.

Ginevra King and Ill Health

The second half of the 1914–15 academic year saw a brief improvement and subsequent slipping of Fitzgerald's performance in classes, perhaps in response to a budding romance with Ginevra King, a sixteen-year-old socialite from Lake Forest, Illinois. Their courtship would continue until January 1917. King would become the model for a series of Fitzgerald's characters, including Judy Jones in the 1922 short story 'Winter Dreams', Isabelle Borgé in *This Side of Paradise* and, most famously, Daisy Buchanan in *The Great Gatsby*. In November 1915 Fitzgerald's academic career was once again held up when he was diagnosed with malaria (though it is likely that this was in fact the first appearance of the tuberculosis that would sporadically disrupt his health for the rest of his life) and left Princeton for the rest of the semester to recuperate. At the same time as all of this disruption, however, Fitzgerald was building a head of steam in terms of his literary production. Publications during this period included stories, reviews and poems for Princeton's *Nassau Literary Magazine*.

Army Commission

The USA entered the Great War in May 1917 and a week later Fitzgerald joined up, at least partly motivated by the fact that his uncompleted courses at Princeton would automatically receive credits as he signed up. Three weeks of intensive training and the infantry commission exam soon followed, though a commission itself did not immediately materialize. Through the summer he stayed in St Paul, undertaking important readings in William James, Henri Bergson and others, and in the autumn he returned to Princeton (though not to study) and took lodgings with John Biggs Jr, the editor of the *Tiger*. More contributions appeared in both the *Nassau Literary Magazine* and the *Tiger*, but the commission finally came and in November Fitzgerald was off to Fort Leavenworth, Kansas, where he was to report as a second lieutenant in the infantry. Convinced that he would die in the war, Fitzgerald began intense work on his first novel, *The Romantic Egoist*, the first draft of which would be finished while on leave from Kansas in February 1918. The publishing house Charles Scribner's Sons, despite offering an encouraging appreciation of the novel, rejected successive drafts in August and October 1918.

Zelda Sayre   As his military training progressed and the army readied Fitzgerald and his men for the fighting in Europe, he was relocated, first to Camp Gordon in Georgia, and then on to Camp Sheridan, near Montgomery, Alabama. There, at a dance at the Montgomery Country Club in July, he met Zelda Sayre, a beautiful eighteen-year-old socialite and daughter of a justice of the Alabama Supreme Court. An intense courtship began and Fitzgerald soon proposed marriage, though Zelda was nervous about marrying a man with so few apparent prospects.

As the armistice that ended the Great War was signed on 11th November 1918, Fitzgerald was waiting to embark for Europe, and had already been issued with his overseas uniform. The closeness by which he avoided action in the Great War stayed with Fitzgerald, and gave him another trope for his fiction, with many of his characters, Amory Blaine from *This Side of Paradise* and Jay Gatsby among them, attributed with abortive or ambiguous military careers. Father Fay, who had been involved, and had tried to involve Fitzgerald, in a series of mysterious intelligence operations during the war, died in January 1919, leaving Fitzgerald without a moral guide just as he entered the world free from the restrictions of Princeton and the army. Fay would be the dedicatee of *This Side of Paradise*.

Literary   Fitzgerald's first move after the war was to secure gainful
Endeavours   employment at Barron Collier, an advertising agency, producing copy for trolley-car advertisements. At night he continued to work hard at his fiction, collecting 112 rejection slips over this period. Relief was close at hand, however, with *The Smart Set* printing a revised version of 'Babes in the Wood' (a short story that had previous appeared in *Nassau Literary Magazine* and

that would soon be cannibalized for *This Side of Paradise*) in their September 1919 issue. *The Smart Set*, edited by this time by H.L. Mencken and George Jean Nathan, who would both become firm supporters of Fitzgerald's talent, was a respected literary magazine, but not a high payer; Fitzgerald received $30 for this first appearance. Buoyed by this, and frustrated by his job, Fitzgerald elected to leave work and New York and return to his parents' house in St Paul, where he would make a concerted effort to finish his novel. As none of the early drafts of *The Romantic Egoist* survive, it is impossible to say with complete certainty how much of that project was preserved in the draft of *This Side of Paradise* that emerged at St Paul. It was, at any rate, more attractive to Scribner in its new form, and the editor Maxwell Perkins, who would come to act as both editor and personal banker for Fitzgerald, wrote on 16th September to say that the novel had been accepted. Soon after he would hire Harold Ober to act as his agent, an arrangement that would continue throughout the greatest years of Fitzgerald's output and that would benefit the author greatly, despite sometimes causing Ober a great deal of difficulty and anxiety. Though Fitzgerald would consider his novels the artistically important part of his work, it would be his short stories, administered by Ober, which would provide the bulk of his income. Throughout his career a regular supply of short stories appeared between his novels, a supply that became more essential and more difficult to maintain as the author grew older.

Newly confident after the acceptance of *This Side of Paradise*, Fitzgerald set about revising a series of his previous stories, securing another four publications in *The Smart Set*, one in *Scribner's Magazine* and one in *The Saturday Evening Post*, an organ that would prove to be one of the author's most dependable sources of income for many years to come. By the end of 1919 Fitzgerald had made $879 from writing: not yet a living, but a start. His receipts would quickly increase. Thanks to Ober's skilful assistance *The Saturday Evening Post* had taken another six stories by February 1920, at $400 each. In March *This Side of Paradise* was published and proved to be a surprising success, selling 3,000 in its first three days and making instant celebrities of Fitzgerald and Zelda, who would marry the author on 3rd April, her earlier concerns about her suitor's solvency apparently eased by his sudden literary success. During the whirl of 1920, the couple's *annus mirabilis*, other miraculous portents of a future of plenty included the sale of a story, 'Head and Shoulders', to Metro Films for $2,500, the sale of four stories to *Metropolitan Magazine* for $900 each and the rapid appearance of *Flappers and Philosophers*, a volume of stories, published by Scribner in September. By the end of the year Fitzgerald, still in

Success

his mid-twenties, had moved into an apartment on New York's West 59th Street and was hard at work on his second novel.

Zelda discovered she was pregnant in February 1921, and in May the couple headed to Europe where they visited various heroes and attractions, including John Galsworthy. They returned in July to St Paul, where a daughter, Scottie, was born on 26th October. Fitzgerald was working consistently and well at this time, producing a prodigious amount of high-quality material. *The Beautiful and Damned*, his second novel, was soon ready and began to appear as a serialization in *Metropolitan Magazine* from September. Its publication in book form would have to wait until March 1922, at which point it received mixed reviews, though Scribner managed to sell 40,000 copies of it in its first year of publication. Once again it would be followed within a few months by a short-story collection, *Tales of the Jazz Age*, which contained such classics of twentieth-century American literature as 'May Day', 'The Diamond as Big as the Ritz' and 'The Curious Case of Benjamin Button'.

1923 saw continued successes and a first failure. Receipts were growing rapidly: the Hearst organization bought first option in Fitzgerald's stories for $1,500, he sold the film rights for *This Side of Paradise* for $10,000 and he began selling stories to *The Saturday Evening Post* for $1,250 each. *The Vegetable*, on the other hand, a play that he had been working on for some time, opened in Atlantic City and closed almost immediately following poor reviews, losing Fitzgerald money. By the end of the year his income had shot up to $28,759.78, but he had spent more than that on the play and fast living, and found himself in debt as a result.

The Fitzgeralds' high living was coming at an even higher price. In an attempt to finish his new project Fitzgerald set out for Europe with Zelda and landed up on the French Riviera, a situation that provided the author with the space and time to make some real progress on his novel. While there, however, Zelda met Édouard Jozan, a French pilot, and began a romantic entanglement that put a heavy strain on her marriage. This scenario has been read by some as influencing the final drafting of *The Great Gatsby*, notably Gatsby's disillusionment with Daisy. It would also provide one of the central threads of *Tender Is the Night*, while Gerald and Sara Murphy, two friends they made on the Riviera, would be models for that novel's central characters. Throughout 1924 their relations became more difficult, their volatility was expressed through increasingly erratic behaviour and by the end of the year Fitzgerald's drinking was developing into alcoholism.

Some progress was made on the novel, however, and a draft was sent to Scribner in October. A period of extensive and crucial revisions followed through January and February 1925, with the novel already at the galley-proof stage. After extensive negotiations with Max Perkins, the new novel also received its final title at about this time. Previous titles had included *Trimalchio* and *Trimalchio in West Egg*, both of which Scribner found too obscure for a mass readership, despite Fitzgerald's preference for them, while *Gold-Hatted Gatsby*, *On the Road to West Egg*, *The High-Bouncing Lover* and *Among Ash Heaps and Millionaires* were also suggestions. Shortly before the novel was due to be published, Fitzgerald telegrammed Scribner with the possible title *Under the Red, White and Blue*, but it was too late, and the work was published as *The Great Gatsby* on 10th April. The reception for the new work was impressive, and it quickly garnered some of Fitzgerald's most enthusiastic reviews, but its sales did not reach the best-seller levels the author and Scribner had hoped for.

Fitzgerald was keen to get on with his work and, rather misguidedly, set off to Paris with Zelda to begin his next novel. Paris at the heart of the Roaring Twenties was not a locale conducive to careful concentration, and little progress was made on the new project. There was much socializing, however, and Fitzgerald invested quite a lot of his time in cementing his reputation as one of the more prominent drunks of American letters. The couple's time was spent mostly with the American expatriate community, and among those he got to know there were Edith Wharton, Gertrude Stein, Robert McAlmon and Sylvia Beach of Shakespeare & Company. Perhaps the most significant relationship with another writer from this period was with Ernest Hemingway, with whom Fitzgerald spent much time (sparking jealousy in Zelda), and for whom he would become an important early supporter, helping to encourage Scribner to publish *The Torrents of Spring* and *The Sun Also Rises*, for which he also gave extensive editorial advice. The summer of 1925 was again spent on the Riviera, but this time with a rowdier crowd (which included John Dos Passos, Archibald MacLeish and Rudolph Valentino) and little progress was made on the new book. February 1926 saw publication of the inevitable follow-up short-story collection, this time *All the Sad Young Men*, of which the most significant pieces were 'The Rich Boy', 'Winter Dreams' and 'Absolution'. All three are closely associated with *The Great Gatsby*, and can be read as alternative routes into the Gatsby story.

With the new novel still effectively stalled, Fitzgerald decamped to Hollywood at the beginning of 1927, where he was engaged by United Artists to write a flapper comedy that was never produced in the end. These false starts were not, however, adversely affecting Fitzgerald's earnings, and 1927 would represent the highest annual earnings the author had achieved so far: $29,757.87, largely from

Paris

Hollywood

short-story sales. While in California Fitzgerald began a dalliance with Lois Moran, a seventeen-year-old aspiring actress – putting further strain on his relationship with Zelda. After the couple moved back east (to Delaware) Zelda began taking ballet lessons in an attempt to carve a niche for herself that might offer her a role beyond that of the wife of a famous author. She would also make various attempts to become an author in her own right. The lessons would continue under the tutelage of Lubov Egorova when the Fitzgeralds moved to Paris in the summer of 1928, with Zelda's obsessive commitment to dance practice worrying those around her and offering the signs of the mental illness that was soon to envelop her.

Looking for a steady income stream (in spite of very high earnings expenditure was still outstripping them), Fitzgerald set to work on the "Basil" stories in 1928, earning $31,500 for nine that appeared in *The Saturday Evening Post*, forcing novel-writing into the background. The next year his *Post* fee would rise to $4,000 a story. Throughout the next few years he would move between the USA and Europe, desperate to resuscitate that project, but make little inroads.

Zelda's Mental Illness

By 1930 Zelda's behaviour was becoming more and more erratic, and on 23rd April she was checked into the Malmaison clinic near Paris for rest and assistance with her mental problems. Deeply obsessed with her dancing lessons, and infatuated with Egorova, she discharged herself from the clinic on 11th May and attempted suicide a few days later. After this she was admitted to the care of Dr Oscar Forel in Switzerland, who diagnosed her as schizophrenic. Such care was expensive and placed a new financial strain on Fitzgerald, who responded by selling another series of stories to the *Post* and earning $32,000 for the year. The most significant story of this period was 'Babylon Revisited'. Zelda improved and moved back to Montgomery, Alabama, and the care of the Sayre family in September 1931. That autumn Fitzgerald would make another abortive attempt to break into Hollywood screenwriting.

At the beginning of 1932 Zelda suffered a relapse during a trip to Florida and was admitted to the Henry Phipps Psychiatric Clinic in Baltimore. While there she would finish work on a novel, *Save Me the Waltz*, that covered some of the same material her husband was using in his novel about the Riviera. Upon completion she sent the manuscript to Perkins at Scribner, without passing it to her husband, which caused much distress. Fitzgerald helped her to edit the book nonetheless, removing much of the material he intended to use, and Scribner accepted it and published it on 7th October. It received poor reviews and did not sell. Finally accepting that she had missed her chance to become a professional dancer, Zelda now poured her energies into painting. Fitzgerald would organize a show of these in New York in 1934, and a play, *Scandalabra*, that would be performed by the Junior Vagabonds, an amateur Baltimore drama group, in the spring of 1933.

His own health now beginning to fail, Fitzgerald returned to his own novel and rewrote extensively through 1933, finally submitting it in October. *Tender Is the Night* would appear in serialized form in *Scribner's Magazine* from January to April 1934 and would then be published, in amended form, on 12th April. It was generally received positively and sold well, though again not to the blockbusting extent that Fitzgerald had hoped for. This would be Fitzgerald's final completed novel. He was thirty-seven.

Final Novel

With the receipts for *Tender Is the Night* lower than had been hoped for and Zelda still erratic and requiring expensive medical supervision, Fitzgerald's finances were tight. From this point on he found it increasingly difficult to produce the kind of high-quality, extended pieces that could earn thousands of dollars in glossies like *The Saturday Evening Post*. From 1934 many of his stories were shorter and brought less money, while some of them were simply sub-standard. Of the outlets for this new kind of work, *Esquire* proved the most reliable, though it only paid $250 a piece, a large drop from his salad days at the *Post*.

Financial Problems and Artistic Decline

March 1935 saw the publication of *Taps at Reveille*, another collection of short stories from Scribner. It was a patchy collection, but included the important 'Babylon Revisited', while 'Crazy Sunday' saw his first sustained attempt at writing about Hollywood, a prediction of the tendency of much of his work to come. His next significant writing came, however, with three articles that appeared in the February, March and April 1936 numbers of *Esquire*: 'The Crack-up', 'Pasting It Together' and 'Handle with Care'. These essays were brutally confessional, and irritated many of those around Fitzgerald, who felt that he was airing his dirty laundry in public. His agent Harold Ober was concerned that by publicizing his own battles with depression and alcoholism he would give the high-paying glossies the impression that he was unreliable, making future magazine work harder to come by. The pieces have, however, come to be regarded as Fitzgerald's greatest non-fiction work and are an essential document in both the construction of his own legend and in the mythologizing of the Jazz Age.

Later in 1936, on the author's fortieth birthday in September, he gave an interview in *The New York Post* to Michael Mok. The article was a sensationalist hatchet job entitled 'Scott Fitzgerald, 40, Engulfed in Despair' and showed him as a

Suicide Attempt and Worsening Health

depressed dipsomaniac. The publication of the article wounded Fitzgerald further and he tried to take his own life through an overdose of morphine. After this his health continued to deteriorate and various spates in institutions followed, for influenza, for tuberculosis and, repeatedly, in attempts to treat his alcoholism.

His inability to rely on his own physical and literary powers meant a significant drop in his earning capabilities; by 1937 his debts exceeded $40,000, much of which was owed to his agent Ober and his editor Perkins, while Fitzgerald still had to pay Zelda's medical fees and support his daughter and himself. A solution to this desperate situation appeared in July: MGM would hire him as a screenwriter at $1,000 a week for six months. He went west, hired an apartment and set about his work. He contributed to various films, usually in collaboration with other writers, a system that irked him. Among these were *A Yank at Oxford* and various stillborn projects, including *Infidelity*, which was to have starred Joan Crawford, and an adaptation of 'Babylon Revisited'. He only received one screen credit from this time, for an adaptation of Erich Maria Remarque's novel *Three Comrades*, produced by Joseph Mankiewicz. His work on this picture led to a renewal of his contract, but no more credits followed.

Sheila Graham   While in Hollywood Fitzgerald met Sheila Graham, a twenty-eight-year-old English gossip columnist, with whom he began an affair. Graham, who initially attracted Fitzgerald because of her physical similarity to the youthful Zelda, became Fitzgerald's partner during the last years of his life, cohabiting with the author quite openly in Los Angeles. It seems unlikely that Zelda, still in medical care, ever knew about her. Graham had risen up from a rather murky background in England and Fitzgerald set about improving her with his "College of One", aiming to introduce her to his favoured writers and thinkers. She would be the model for Kathleen Moore in *The Last Tycoon*.

Among the film projects he worked on at this time were *Madame Curie* and *Gone with the Wind*, neither of which earned him a credit. The contract with MGM was terminated in 1939 and Fitzgerald became a freelance screenwriter. While engaged on the screenplay for *Winter Carnival* for United Artists, Fitzgerald went on a drinking spree at Dartmouth College, resulting in his getting fired. A final period of alcoholic excess followed, marring a trip to Cuba with Zelda in April and worsening his financial straits. At this time Ober finally pulled the plug and refused to lend Fitzgerald any more money, though he would continue to support Scottie, Fitzgerald's daughter, whom the Obers had effectively brought up. The writer, now his own agent, began working on a Hollywood novel based on the life of the famous Hollywood producer Irving Thalberg.

Hollywood would also be the theme of the last fiction Fitzgerald would see published; the Pat Hobby stories. These appeared in *Esquire* beginning in January 1940 and continued till after the author's death, ending in July 1941 and appearing in each monthly number between those dates.

In November 1940 Fitzgerald suffered a heart attack and was told to rest, which he did at Graham's apartment. On 21st December he had another heart attack and died, aged just forty-four. Permission was refused to bury him in St Mary's Church in Rockville, Maryland, where his father had been buried, because Fitzgerald was not a practising Catholic. Instead he was buried at Rockville Union Cemetery on 27th December 1940. In 1975 Scottie Fitzgerald would successfully petition to have her mother and father moved to the family plot at St Mary's.

Death

Following Fitzgerald's death his old college friend Edmund Wilson would edit Fitzgerald's incomplete final novel, shaping his drafts and notes into *The Last Tycoon*, which was published in 1941 by Scribner. Wilson also collected Fitzgerald's confessional *Esquire* pieces and published them with a selection of related short stories and essays as *The Crack-up and Other Pieces and Stories* in 1945.

Zelda lived on until 1948, in and out of mental hospitals. After reading *The Last Tycoon* she began work on *Caesar's Things*, a novel that was not finished when the Highland hospital caught fire and she died, locked in her room in preparation for electro-shock therapy.

F. Scott Fitzgerald's Works

Fitzgerald's first novel, *This Side of Paradise*, set the tone for his later classic works. The novel was published in 1920 and was a remarkable success, impressing critics and readers alike. Amory Blaine, the directionless and guilelessly dissolute protagonist, is an artistically semi-engaged innocent, and perilously, though charmingly unconsciously, déclassé. His long drift towards destruction (and implicit reincarnation as Fitzgerald himself) sees Blaine's various arrogances challenged one by one as he moves from a well-heeled life in the Midwest through private school and middling social successes at Princeton towards a life of vague and unrewarding artistic involvement. Beneath Fitzgerald's precise observations of American high society in the late 1910s can be witnessed the creation of a wholly new American type, and Blaine would become a somewhat seedy role model for his generation. Fast-living and nihilist tendencies would become the character traits of Fitzgerald's set and the

This Side of Paradise

Lost Generation more generally. Indeed, by the novel's end, it has become clear that Blaine's experiences of lost love, a hostile society and the deaths of his mother and friends have imparted important life lessons upon him. Blaine, having returned to a Princeton that he has outgrown and poised before an unknowable future, ends the novel with his Jazz Age *cogito*: "'I know myself,' he cried, 'but that is all.'"

Flappers and Philosophers

Fitzgerald's next publication would continue this disquisition on his era and peers: *Flappers and Philosophers* (1920) is a collection of short stories, including such famous pieces as 'Bernice Bobs Her Hair' and 'The Ice Palace'. The first of these tells the tale of Bernice, who visits her cousin Marjorie only to find herself rejected for being a stop on Marjorie's social activities. Realizing that she can't rid herself of Bernice, Marjorie decides to coach her to become a young femme fatale like herself – and Bernice is quickly a hit with the town boys. Too much of a hit though, and Marjorie takes her revenge by persuading Bernice that it would be to her social advantage to bob her hair. It turns out not to be and Bernice leaves the town embarrassed, but not before cutting off Marjorie's pigtails in her sleep and taking them with her to the station.

The Beautiful and Damned

The Beautiful and Damned (1922) would follow, another novel that featured a thinly disguised portrait of Fitzgerald in the figure of the main character, Anthony Patch. He was joined by a fictionalized version of Fitzgerald's new wife Zelda, whom the author married as *This Side of Paradise* went to press. The couple are here depicted on a rapidly downward course that both mirrored and predicted the Fitzgeralds' own trajectory. Patch is the heir apparent of his reforming grandfather's sizable fortune but lives a life of dissolution in the city, promising that he'll find gainful employment. He marries Gloria Gilbert, a great but turbulent beauty, and they gradually descend into alcoholism, wasting what little capital Anthony has on high living and escapades. When his grandfather walks in on a scene of debauchery, Anthony is disinherited and the Patches' decline quickens. When the grandfather dies, Anthony embarks on a legal case to reclaim the money from the good causes to which it has been donated and wins their case, although not before Anthony has lost his mind and Gloria her beauty.

Tales of the Jazz Age

Another volume of short stories, *Tales of the Jazz Age*, was published later in the same year, in accordance with Scribner's policy of quickly following successful novels with moneymaking collections of short stories. Throughout this period Fitzgerald was gaining for himself a reputation as America's premier short-story writer, producing fiction for a selection of high-profile "glossy" magazines and earning unparalleled fees for his efforts. The opportunities and the pressures of this commercial work, coupled with Fitzgerald's continued profligacy, led to a certain unevenness in his short fiction. This unevenness is clearly present in *Tales of the Jazz Age*, with some of Fitzgerald's very best work appearing beside some fairly average pieces. Among the great works were 'The Diamond as Big as the Ritz' and the novella 'May Day'. The first of these tells the story of the Washingtons, a family that live in seclusion in the wilds of Montana on top of a mountain made of solid diamond. The necessity of keeping the source of their wealth hidden from all makes the Washingtons' lives a singular mixture of great privilege and isolation; friends that visit the children are briefly treated to luxury beyond their imagining and are then executed to secure the secrecy of the Washington diamond. When young Percy's friend John T. Unger makes a visit during the summer vacation their unusual lifestyle and their diamond are lost for ever. The novella 'May Day' is very different in style and execution, but deals with some of the same issues, in particular the exigencies of American capitalism in the aftermath of the Great War. It offers a panorama of Manhattan's post-war social order as the anti-communist May Day Riots of 1919 unfold. A group of privileged Yale alumni enjoy the May Day ball and bicker about their love interests, while ex-soldiers drift around the edges of their world.

In spite of the apparent success that Fitzgerald was experiencing by this time, his next novel came with greater difficulty than his first four volumes. *The Great Gatsby* is the story of Jay Gatsby, born poor as James Gatz, an *arriviste* of mysterious origins who sets himself up in high style on Long Island's north shore only to find disappointment and his demise there. Like Fitzgerald, and some of his other characters, including Anthony Patch, Gatsby falls in love during the war, this time with Daisy Fay. Following Gatsby's departure, however, Daisy marries the greatly wealthy Tom Buchanan, which convinces Gatsby that he lost her only because of his penuriousness. Following this, Gatsby builds himself a fortune comparable to Buchanan's through mysterious and proscribed means and, five years after Daisy broke off their relations, uses his new-found wealth to throw a series of parties from an enormous house across the water from Buchanan's Long Island pile. His intention is to impress his near neighbour Daisy with the lavishness of his entertainments, but he miscalculates and the "old money" Buchanans stay away, not attracted by Gatsby's *parvenu* antics. Instead Gatsby approaches Nick Carraway, the novel's narrator (who took that role in one of the masterstrokes of the late stages of the novel's revision), Daisy's cousin and

The Great Gatsby

Gatsby's neighbour. Daisy is initially affected by Gatsby's devotion, to the extent that she agrees to leave Buchanan, but once Buchanan reveals Gatsby's criminal source of income she has second thoughts. Daisy, shocked by this revelation, accidentally kills Buchanan's mistress Myrtle in a hit-and-run accident with Gatsby in the car and returns to Buchanan, leaving Gatsby waiting for her answer. Buchanan then lets Myrtle's husband believe that Gatsby was driving the car and the husband shoots him, leaving him floating in the unused swimming pool of his great estate.

All the Sad Young Men

Of *All the Sad Young Men* (1926) the most well-known pieces are 'The Rich Boy', 'Winter Dreams' and 'Absolution'. All three have much in common with *The Great Gatsby*, in terms of the themes dealt with and the characters developed. 'The Rich Boy' centres on the rich young bachelor Anson Hunter, who has romantic dalliances with women, but never marries and grows increasingly lonely. 'Winter Dreams' tells the tale of Dexter Green and Judy Jones, similar characters to Jay Gatsby and Daisy Buchanan. Much like Gatsby, Green raises himself from nothing with the intention of winning Jones's affections. And, like Gatsby, he finds the past lost. 'Absolution' is a rejected false start on *The Great Gatsby* and deals with a young boy's difficulties around the confessional and an encounter with a deranged priest.

'Babylon Revisited' is probably the greatest and most read story of the apparently fallow period between *The Great Gatsby* and *Tender Is the Night*. It deals with Charlie Wales, an American businessman who enacts some of Fitzgerald's guilt for his apparent abandonment of his daughter Scottie and wife Zelda. Wales returns to a Paris unknown to him since he gave up drinking. There he fights his dead wife's family for custody of his daughter, only to find that friends from his past undo his careful efforts.

Basil and Josephine

Between April 1928 and April 1929, Fitzgerald published eight stories in the *Saturday Evening Post* centring on Basil Duke Lee, an adolescent coming of age in the Midwest, loosely based on the author's own teenage years. A ninth story, 'That Kind of Party', which fits chronologically at the beginning of the Basil cycle, was rejected by the *Saturday Evening Post* because of its description of children's kissing games, and was only published posthumously in 1951. These stories were much admired by both Fitzgerald's editor and agent, who encouraged him to compile them in a book with some additional stories. Fitzgerald did not act on this advice, but between April 1930 and August 1931 he published, again in the *Saturday Evening Post*, five stories focusing on the development of Josephine Perry, a kind of female counterpart to Basil Duke Lee. In 1934 Fitzgerald then considered collecting the Basil and Josephine stories in a single volume and adding a final one in which the two would meet and which would transform the whole into a kind of novel, but he shelved the idea, as he had doubts about the overall quality of the outcome and its possible reception. He was still favourable to having them packaged as a straightforward short-story collection, but this would only happen in 1973, when Scribner published *The Basil and Josephine Stories*.

The next, and last completed, novel came even harder, and it would not be until 1934 that *Tender Is the Night* would appear. This novel was met by mixed reviews and low, but not disastrous sales. It has remained controversial among readers of Fitzgerald and is hailed by some as his masterpiece and others as an aesthetic failure. The plotting is less finely wrought than the far leaner *The Great Gatsby*, and apparent chronological inconsistencies and longueurs have put off some readers. The unremitting detail of Dick Diver's descent, however, is unmatched in Fitzgerald's oeuvre.

Tender Is the Night

It begins with an impressive set-piece description of life on the Riviera during the summer of 1925. There Rosemary Hoyt, modelled on the real-life actress Lois Moran, meets Dick and Nicole Driver, and becomes infatuated with Dick. It is then revealed that Dick had been a successful psychiatrist and had met Nicole when she was his patient, being treated in the aftermath of being raped by her father. Now Dick is finding it difficult to maintain his research interests in the social whirl that Nicole's money has thrust him into. Dick is forced out of a Swiss clinic for his unreliability and incipient alcoholism. Later Dick consummates his relationship with Rosemary on a trip to Rome, and gets beaten by police after drunkenly involving himself in a fight. When the Divers return to the Riviera Dick drinks more and Nicole leaves him for Tommy Barban, a French-American mercenary soldier (based on Zelda's Riviera beau Édouard Jozan). Dick returns to America, where he becomes a provincial doctor and disappears.

The "Pat Hobby" stories are the most remarkable product of Fitzgerald's time in Hollywood to see publication during the author's lifetime. Seventeen stories appeared in all, in consecutive issues of *Esquire* through 1940 and 1941. Hobby is a squalid Hollywood hack fallen upon hard times and with the days of his great success, measured by on-screen credits, some years behind him. He is a generally unsympathetic character and most of the stories depict him in unflattering situations, saving his own skin at the expense of those around him. It speaks to the hardiness of Fitzgerald's talent that even at this late stage he was able to make a character as amoral as Hobby vivid and engaging on the page. The Hobby stories are all short, evidencing Fitzgerald's skill in his later career at compressing storylines that would previously have been extrapolated far further.

Pat Hobby Stories

The Last Tycoon   Fitzgerald's final project was *The Last Tycoon*, a work which, in the partial and provisional version that was published after the author's death, has all the hallmarks of a quite remarkable work. The written portion of the novel, which it seems likely would have been rewritten extensively before publication (in accordance with Fitzgerald's previous practice), is a classic conjuring of the golden age of Hollywood through an ambiguous and suspenseful story of love and money. The notes that follow the completed portion of *The Last Tycoon* suggest that the story would have developed in a much more melodramatic direction, with Stahr embarking on transcontinental business trips, losing his edge, ordering a series of murders and dying in an aeroplane crash. If the rewrites around *Tender Is the Night* are anything to go by, it seems likely that Fitzgerald would have toned down Stahr's adventures before finishing the story: in the earlier novel stories of matricide and other violent moments had survived a number of early drafts, only to be cut before the book took its final form.

– Richard Parker

Select Bibliography

Biographies:
Bruccoli, Matthew J., *Some Sort of Epic Grandeur: The Life of F. Scott Fitzgerald*, 2nd edn. (Columbia, SC: University of South Carolina Press, 2002)
Mizener, Arthur, *The Far Side of Paradise: A Biography of F. Scott Fitzgerald*, (Boston, MS: Houghton Mifflin, 1951)
Turnbull, Andrew, *Scott Fitzgerald* (Harmondsworth: Penguin, 1970)

Additional Recommended Background Material:
Curnutt, Kirk, ed., *A Historical Guide to F. Scott Fitzgerald* (Oxford: Oxford University Press, 2004)
Prigozy, Ruth, ed., *The Cambridge Companion to F. Scott Fitzgerald* (Cambridge: Cambridge University Press, 2002)

EVERGREENS SERIES

Beautifully produced classics, affordably priced

Alma Classics is committed to making available a wide range of literature from around the globe. Most of the titles are enriched by an extensive critical apparatus, notes and extra reading material, as well as a selection of photographs. The texts are based on the most authoritative editions and edited using a fresh, accessible editorial approach. With an emphasis on production, editorial and typographical values, Alma Classics aspires to revitalize the whole experience of reading classics.

For our complete list and latest offers

visit

almabooks.com/evergreens